THE

DISOBEDIENT

WIFE

ANNIKA MILISIC-STANLEY

INDEPENDENT · INNOVATIVE · INTERNATIONAL

Published by Cinnamon Press
Meirion House
Tanygrisiau
Blaenau Ffestiniog
Gwynedd LL41 3SU
www.cinnamonpress.com

The right of Annika Milisic-Stanley to be identified as author of
this work has been asserted by her in accordance with the
Copyright, Designs and Patent Act, 1988. © 2015 Annika Milisic-
Stanley.
ISBN 978-1-909077-82-9
British Library Cataloguing in Publication Data. A CIP record for
this book can be obtained from the British Library.

Designed and typeset in Garamond by Cinnamon Press. Cover
design by Adam Craig © Adam Craig.
Cinnamon Press is represented by Inpress and by the Welsh Books
Council in Wales.
Printed in Poland

Acknowledgements

I would like to thank Zlatan Milišić, Louise Grogan, Nicola
Alton, Susan Armstrong, Fiona Mills, Naomi Murphy,
Rebecca, Ron and especially Lil Stanley, for their extensive
reading, help and encouragement. Thanks to Katherine Arms
for the title. Finally, my thanks go to novelist Stephen May
and Dr Jan Fortune for awarding this book the 2015
Cinnamon Press Novel of the Year.

Author's Note

In 2008, there were a series of small explosions in Dushanbe. No one claimed responsibility. There are ten banned opposition parties in Tajikistan. Many of them are multi-national and would like to see Central Asia become an Islamic superstate. Religious minorities are not allowed to register new places of worship and all mosques and churches are required to be registered. Proselytising and missionary activity was officially banned in 2008.

This novel is a work of fiction. Any references to real people, events, establishments, organisations or locales are intended only to give the fiction a sense of reality and authenticity. Other names, characters, places and incidents portrayed therein are either the product of the author's imagination or are used fictionally.

To the Women of Tajikistan

and to another unsung heroine, my Mother

THE DISOBEDIENT WIFE

PROLOGUE

October 31st, 2008, England

Tajikistan, you come to me at dawn, when I am most vulnerable. I wake to a new day and reach for an outstretched arm, listen for a sigh. Then I remember; my world has gone crazy. I think of you as a sweet nightmare lived in a harsh land of frozen deserts and steel-grey mountains, a place that hardly a soul has heard of, nor can find on a map. The friends I clung to will scatter like starlings across the globe. Nargis, Ivan and the others will forget, moving on to work for new masters.

The life I constructed dissolved like the mirage of my marriage even as I packed my suitcases to board the air ambulance out of Dushanbe. It is painful to think that my home was let to a new tenant within weeks, my garden, so briefly nurtured, now lies abandoned, dying of thirst in the unrelenting Tajik sun. All traces will be erased until the Dutch tulips I laid last September rise above the earth to bloom in April and pronounce that I really was there. The language, learned and badly spoken, is already fading from my dreams. I catch sight of Cyrillic script on my old papers and mourn.

Tajikistan: A few cheap souvenirs, fading photographs in albums and my memories are all I have left of you. I brush these thoughts away by day, busy in the business of constructing a new existence.

1

December 4th, 2007

In the early hours snow fell, covering grey high rises, broken pavements and potholed roads, transforming the city into a winter fairyland. Trees lining the once majestic Soviet-era boulevards became white turrets, their icy tentacles bending down to caress walkers on their way to work. White-bearded city gardeners in velvet robes and embroidered pillar box hats stroked branches with long wooden poles, urging them to release their burdens to the pavement below.

In the hushed winter quiet, Dushanbe, a bustling centre of the Occidental world, seemed temporarily frozen in time. To the West lay the ancient cities of Samarkand and Bukhara, among the original agricultural settler sites of ancient Persia. Circling kestrels had come in from the East, their golden eyes tired of scouring the frozen wastelands of Gorno Badahkshan on the Chinese border. The icy steppes of Kazakhstan and tundra hinterlands of Siberia lay thousands of miles to the north, while southerly roads led to impenetrable Afghan mountain ranges and endless war.

In a small mahalla hamlet on the city outskirts, Nargis stirred and opened her eyes. She lay for a few moments beside sticky-faced children and a golden-toothed crone on layers of velveteen quilts. Her breath rose through the frozen air in blue tendrils to the ceiling. The roof creaked uncomfortably under the weight of snow. She gathered herself and leapt up from the makeshift bed, glancing at the time on her mobile phone. Dressing quickly, she covered darned underclothes with a long shapeless kurta, of synthetic velvet. Nargis kissed her son awake. Over frozen, stockinged feet, she donned thick beige thermal leggings and brightly patterned socks from the Pamirs. Hodoiiman,. it's freezing, she thought, rubbing callused hands together, blowing on stubby fingertips to bring them back to life. Gulya her mother, grunted from the pile of quilts and wiped cataract eyes.

'Extra cold this morning isn't it shireen? I will make tea.'

It had been the harshest winter for decades. The traditional haveli was woefully inadequate to handle temperatures so far below freezing, with cracked windowpanes, a leaking door and mud brick walls which allowed the moisture to seep through and turn to frost. Six people lived, ate and slept in this small room divided by a ragged net curtain. Political disputes with Central Asian neighbours meant that the electricity was frequently cut off by the Uzbeks and Kyrgyz. Nargis pulled on a pair of rubber-soled slippers.

'The workers freeze to death while the President and his daughters sleep in gleaming new palaces fit for kings,' her mother muttered.

Outside, the snow had temporarily covered the muddy yard, turning it into a pristine carpet in the morning sunlight. The snow-covered mountains were clearly visible, rising above the valley, tinged orange by the sunrise. Nargis emerged from the house. She had a round, sallow face, thin lips, blue with cold, a long Persian nose and large black eyes surrounded by crow's feet. Her black hair was tied back in a single, thick plait. Nargis frowned. The jerry can in the house was empty, her son-of-a-donkey brother having neglected his duties as usual. Her body aching from a night on a frozen floor, she teetered across crackling ice to the outside tap and found it lifeless. Swearing under her breath, she kicked the unforgiving pipe.

'Which idiot turned the water off?' she screeched. The yard remained silent, the ice mocking her. She was loathe to face the patronising smirk of the sow next door but it was even more demeaning to show up at work reeking like a farm dog. She had long since run out of the cheap Chinese perfume she wore when married. A few moments later she staggered back on the slippery snow carrying icy water and set it down in the dank, wooden wash house. Bracing herself, she lifted her dress and rubbed her arm pits with an icy cloth and a dab of grey glycerine. Thick, black hairs on her arms stood up in the cold. With no lover and no money to pay for fripperies, she had given up her weekly ritual at the local beauty parlour. A long, jagged scar on her back throbbed in the cold air.

Said was still asleep. Her mother allowed him to doze all morning like a lazy alley cat. He liked to stay in bed during winter and watch black and white television, complaining that there was little to get up for, having lost his job at the cement factory.

'Said,' she shouted hoarsely. 'Water's in the wash house. Wake up, you lazy ass.' Hussein, her eldest son, appeared at the door grinning.

'I would tell you what Said said, but I can't, because you'll slap me,' he said with a giggle. He wore an old duffle coat over his school uniform, a blue polyester suit with an orange, white and green cravat, the colours of the Tajik flag, tied around his neck. His black hair was coarsely brushed, his cheeks rosy in the biting air.

Nargis slid over to him, as graceless as a puppy on ice, and planted a kiss on his cheek, straightening his cravat. She clasped his cheeks with tender fingers and spoke sternly. 'Learn well and work hard.'

'I will, Mum. Hey Guys, wait.' Several boys passed the house and Hussein shot out of the gate to catch them. In his hand, he held breakfast and lunch, a half-moon of naan bread. He stopped and turned to wave, his school satchel bobbing on his back. She watched him as he disappeared from view, shading her eyes against the snow-white brightness. Seven years old, he had a serious, quiet nature and deep, all-knowing eyes. Hussein had not forgotten the past, his hidden fears breaking though his calm demeanour with nightmares that afflicted him night after night. Nargis tried to shield him, knowing that his father's death had robbed him of his childhood.

She entered the house, now full of wood smoke. Gulya, her skinny mother, was preparing a pot of sweet black tea on an ancient stove, using fresh snow scooped from the yard. Above, a rickety metal chimney pipe sucked the smoke out into the open air and a pile of dried sheep dung hung in a sack. Grey tendrils escaped from Gulya's faded Russian headscarf, her hands clad in fingerless gloves. She was a village girl, brought up to survive. She gestured for Nargis to sit, a frown rippling the wrinkles in an ash-smeared face.

'Here shireen, drink.' Nargis took the bowl of steaming, sugary tea and clutched it to her chest, warming blue hands. She yawned. Her phone had rung in the middle of the night, waking them all up. An unknown number. She had answered, only to hear the sound of vomiting, followed by a click. It happened once in a while, leaving her with a sense of disquiet.

She took a small piece of naan from a cloth in the corner and sat down on an ancient quilt. In the room next door, Said stood up and stretched his teenage limbs, grumbling under this breath. Nargis smiled at him.

'Don't fall in the latrine.'

He grunted, slamming the door on his way out. Gulya tittered into the flour sack.

'Mother, how long do you think this winter is going to last? It is early in December for snow.' She dipped the stale naan into her tea to soften it. 'Life is hard enough without nature conspiring against us.'

Gulya squatted, kneading rolls of dough with vigour. Her arms and hands were those of a much younger woman, the stress of civil war and poverty having aged her. Wires sparked in the wall and a bare light bulb came on, signalling a return of electricity to the mahalla.

11

'I don't know, shireen. I just hope that we can survive to spring.' She surreptitiously stroked the white talisman she wore around her neck to ward off the evil eye.

'Of course we'll survive, we always do,' Nargis said. 'Just in what state, I don't know.'

Nargis's father, Abdul, grunted in his sleep beyond the curtain. There was a possibility of work that morning in the nearby quarry. A day's work cutting rock with a pick axe could earn Abdul and Said ten somoni, just over three dollars each. This would buy food for four days; a kilo each of onions, potatoes and carrots, a few eggs for the children, fifty grams of tea leaves, a small bag of sugar, salt and a little cotton oil. Gulya took him tea in a cracked bowl and he struggled into an old overcoat and hat. Grey bearded and blue lipped from a heart condition, he had deep wrinkles in his sun battered face. His ruddy skin and thin, stooping gait gave away an insatiable need for vodka, a vice left from Soviet days that sat unhappily with his desire to be a good Muslim. Awake now, he looked at Gulya with bleary eyes and accepted the proffered bread and tea. She squatted, servile like a pet monkey, her eyes downcast until he was finished, then whisked away his tea bowl. Her eyes flicked to the gaudy Chinese clock hanging on the mottled, bare wall.

'Nargis, is it not time for you to go? You always say these foreigners are very particular about punctuality.'

They needed her income, the principle reason her parents took her in. Assisted by missionaries, Nargis had managed to learn rudimentary English while working as a housemaid for a group of American students. Now she worked as a maid and nanny for a foreign family, four days a week on good wages. Nargis sighed. She felt a heavy weight of responsibility on her shoulders. It frustrated her that of four adults, she was the only one making any regular income.

My useless family. Today is the day I change my life.

She glanced upwards to the place in the roof cavity where her savings lay hidden in a tea tin and stared at her parents in irritation.

'I know I'm running late, but surely they can wait for a woman to finish her tea,' she said, swallowing her bread. Her phone rang. She frowned when she saw the number. 'Alo?' she answered gruffly. 'Yes, I sorry, I little late, I be there soon.' There was a pause and her face fell. Her tone changed, like a mother soothing an angry child. 'Bus, you know, they not come because of snow. Wait, I see bus coming, they almost here,' she gasped, panting a little for good measure. Her mother sniggered into her dough and Abdul shook his head, his battered chusti skullcap shaking from side to side. 'I be there soon, I promise.'

Nargis rang off and looked at Gulya with an expression of distaste. 'That silly ewe is already moaning and I'm only a few minutes late. You have no idea what it's like.'

Gulya clicked her tongue. Nargis slipped the phone into her coat pocket and stroked the plaited rat's tails on her sleeping daughter's head, feeling a familiar guilt. Little Bunavsha had no school to go. No uniform, no satchel, no school fees. She would have to stay home and help her grandmother bake naan bread to sell on the street from a creaky pram.

She's here though, not like my poor baby Faisullo, all alone in an apartment with the grey in-laws.

Struggling to her feet, Nargis donned tatty, embroidered irinka slippers, a rough headscarf and left the house.

2

By the time she arrived at the heavy wooden door Nargis was almost an hour late. The gate guard was shovelling snow from the driveway, his metal spade screaming in protest against icy concrete. She entered quietly and removed her slippers in the small vestibule, glancing at herself in the hallway mirror. Hodoiiman, I look horrible in Said's coat, she thought. Look at my hair, so dirty. She shrugged. No one sane washes their hair in wintertime. She tied a handkerchief over her offending plait and glanced at her hands, they looked clean enough. She ascended mahogany stairs and tapped at an ornately carved door.

'Yes?'

'It's Nargis, Madam.'

'About time. Come in.'

Nargis entered. Mrs Harriet Simenon, the Memsahib, and British lady of leisure, sat in her king size bed wearing a silk negligee, her pedicured toes poking from under the end of the goose feather duvet. The bed looked soft and warm and the oil heaters crackled and cranked. A tower of tomes lay on the floor by the bed. A television was on, tuned to a low chatter. Leo, fourteen months old and shunted from the crook of Harriet's bony arm, sat up in his baby-grow looking at Nargis with a sweet, confused expression. Harriet threw her mobile telephone onto her bedside table with a loud clatter. She scowled. The dark circles under her hazel eyes were puffy and her cheeks were pale. Her hair was scrumpled, tied in a bun with stray strands falling around her face.

'You are very late.'

'I'm sorry Mrs Harriet,' Nargis said, looking at the floor. 'We had water problem, our outside pipe hard and no bus because of snow.'

Harriet rolled her eyes. Nargis reached out to pick up a dirty coffee cup.

14

'Leave it,' Harriet snapped. 'Just take Leo away.'

Nargis recoiled from the cup and picked up the baby. He gave her a hug in welcome, his chubby arms encircling her neck. His nappy smelled of pungent sweetcorn. She loved him, such a comfort. It was two weeks since she had seen her own baby boy. Nargis gently carried him to the bathroom to wash and change. Harriet followed.

'Leo ended up in my bed yet again. He's teething like hell and I feel half dead.'

Nargis made sympathetic noises and tickled Leo under his chin, smiling to make him laugh. With a dramatic sigh of irritation, Harriet pulled a towel off the rail and went to have a hot shower.

As soon as Mrs Harriet was gone, Nargis put the baby down on the fluffy mat and hiked up her dress to dangle awkwardly over the icy toilet seat. She would be damned if she was going to use the servants privy in these temperatures. Leo crawled over to the toilet brush, his favourite illicit toy. With a sharp exclamation, Nargis picked it up in its pool of bleach and wedged it onto a windowsill. The other maid always forgot to put it high up out of reach, the stupid ewe. Nargis returned to the bedroom with him and drew back the burgundy brocade curtains with a theatrical flourish. Bright morning light flooded in through shining wood framed windows, their sills piled with a foot of new snow.

Mrs Harriet returned, wrapped in a bathrobe, her hair hanging in long damp strands. She removed her robe and stood in her underwear, peering at her stretch marks in the mirror, lifting flaccid skin with a sigh.

Nargis glanced at her as she straightened the counterpane. Doe-like eyes, a childish, up-turned nose, rose-bud mouth. She had the figure of a young teenager. Her bejewelled hands gave her away, criss-crossed with blue veins, tipped with red talons. She spent the next ten minutes at her dressing table, drying, drawing, stroking and

15

brushing herself into perfection. Nargis wandered about the room picking up strewn pieces of clothing, a soiled nappy from the night. She made the bed, plumping cushions and smoothing sheets. Harriet sprayed her hair liberally and glanced at Nargis in the mirror. Her expression hardened.

'Nargis, I know I was sharp with you before but I needed you this morning.' Her voice rose. 'If you are late again, I might have to find another nanny who can be on time.'

Nargis took a small intake of breath and stood still before Harriet, staring at a stain on the carpet. The colour drained from her face. *We will starve.*

'Yes Ma'am. It won't happen again, Ma'am. I am very sorry, Ma'am,' she whispered in a monotone.

Harriet's features relaxed. She glanced at her reflection and picked up some eyebrow tweezers. 'Alright then. Apology accepted. Now go and get Alexandra's breakfast.'

Nargis let out a sigh and flushed, the heat of the room suddenly overwhelming her. She crept to the study downstairs on trembling legs. Outside, dripping icicles reflected the light like crystal as winter rays streamed in to light up dancing particles of dust. A bony girl of four years sat on an expensive silk sofa in stripy pyjamas, transfixed as usual by the television. Her father sat hunched over his desk tapping at his computer with long tapered fingers. Mr Simenon was an important man with an important job, Mrs Harriet had explained. He didn't like to be disturbed. Nargis hesitated at the doorway. An aromatic, Italian espresso smouldered on the desk next to him.

'Good morning, Mister Simenon,'

The man turned from his desk with an angry glare. Nargis took an involuntary step backwards.

'Morning Nargis.'

He frowned at his computer screen and slid fingers through his salt-and-pepper hair. Nargis could smell the musk of his aftershave. He did not look up again.

'I come take Alexandra for breakfast.'

At the sound of her voice, the little girl leapt from the sofa and ran to take her hand.

'I've been waiting for you, Gissie. I'm hungry.'

On Saturday mornings, Nargis cooked for the children, the cook having insisted on weekends off.

'I make England blini,' she called wearily, opening fridges and laying the table. Alexandra jumped up and down in excitement, her slippers flashing with tiny pink fairy lights. She was recovering from another violent stomach virus and needed fattening up.

'Is it Saturday, Nargis?' she asked, hauling herself up onto a chair. 'We always have blini on Saturday.'

'That's right. Clever girl.'

Mrs Harriet entered and took some flour from the cupboard. She opened the packet, shrieked and threw it into the dustbin.

'Damn it. It's crawling with weevils,' she shouted.

Nargis shrugged. Silly woman, that's imported, much better than the stuff I buy. I will sneak it home later for Mother's naan. Flour dust wafted up from the dustbin and a large cockroach ambled back into the pipework below the sink. Harriet screeched and ran from the room. Nargis could hear her shouting at her husband and smirked.

Later, Nargis made a café latte with the gleaming, stainless steel machine and carried it to a covered veranda on a silver tray. Harriet lay sprawled on sumptuous quilts on a traditional Persian tea platform, reading an old British newspaper. The diamonds at her ears, neck and fingers sent rainbow refractions to the ceiling. A diary lay next to her, covered in childish purple scribbles. She sighed and turned a yellowed page.

'I shouldn't read this paper, Nargis. It makes me homesick for the grey drizzle and narrow pavements of England. How nice it would be to go to a country pub for roast beef and Yorkshire pudding in front of a roaring fire.' She sighed again.

Nargis half hovered in the doorway, wanting to go back to Leo. He might choke on the blini, she thought, stepping from one foot to another. Mrs Harriet often babbled at her and Nargis guessed there was no one else for her to talk to.

'We are going for dinner with the Greens at the Beirut Bistro at seven. Did you remember that I need you to babysit?'

Nargis nodded. She was already looking forward to putting her feet up with a Russian soap opera. Nargis jumped as her phone rang once and stopped. An unknown number. Harriet pursed her lips. Nargis wasn't allowed to take calls when she was working.

'Henri's driver will take you home.'

'Yes Ma'am.' She was glad to work whenever she could.

'Mr Simenon likes time alone with me without the brats to distract. Never mind that we know all the menus in Dushanbe off by heart.'

'Is good. You like eat nice food, yes?'

Nargis never went out at night in winter. The city died as darkness fell and became a windy, spooky place. Most of the street lights had not worked since the war. Workers would scatter like a dropped jar of beads, memories of lawlessness and anarchy, fresh in their heads. Only a few restaurants stayed open to entertain a smattering of Chinese salesmen in cheap suits or groups of arrogant, blue-eyed off-duty Russian army officers with platinum-blonde wives. There was a creaking discotheque popular with the French Legionnaires and a pub called O'Donnell's with shamrock-green awnings. Tajik and Russian divorcees risked rape and reputation to meet lonely international men there. Nargis had heard this at missionary meetings when she had been at her lowest ebb, but unlike her, they could be saved.

She had worked for The Simenon family from Saturday to Tuesday, four days a week since February, nearly ten months. Another maid worked the other days.

'But Mr Simenon, sir, I would like work more days for you,' she had protested.

He had frowned, steely eyed. 'No. It is four days or none at all. That way we will always have someone in the house to look after things. If you don't like it, there's the door.'

Mrs Harriet had sat hunched up, silent. She seemed mute when he was around.

During her first month in Tajikistan, other than delivering and picking up her daughter from the American school, Mrs Harriet had stayed in her bedroom, occasionally venturing into the garden with Leo. She seemed sad and spoke on the phone for hours with friends in England. She would spend all day in her pyjamas watching television, only dressing a few minutes before her 'Henri' came in from work. They were tense around each other and each morning, Nargis would find empty wine glasses strewn around the house.

She remembered the first week when Mr Simenon asked her to accompany Mrs Harriet and the driver, Ivan, on a tour of the city. Nargis sat in the white four-by-four, pointing out various places: Peikar, the upper class supermarket popular with foreigners, Green Market for fresh vegetables and fruit, Nova Clinic, an international surgery with a foreign doctor and imported medicines.

'I can't read the Cyrillic on the street signs. Is there a decent gym with an indoor pool where I can go to swim and work out?' Harriet asked Ivan.

He shook his head. 'No Madam. We don't have in Dushanbe. Not since Soviet times. There is place for summer, Lake Varzob, but water is dirty. Sometime rich people have personal sauna for winter.'

It was late February, a grey, cloudy winter's day that made the skin of passers-by seem sallow, their eyes dull. A melancholy light fell across the decrepit buildings and Soviet high rises in the distance. The mountain peaks were covered in thick fog, levelling the landscape and making the city into a flat wasteland. Harriet gazed out of the window.

'How will I survive in this hell hole?' she muttered holding little Leo on her lap. She turned with fake cheer to Nargis. 'It's all so grey and tired looking.'

Nargis agreed. Shop signs were old, broken and hanging off buildings. Pavements were cracked and the wide streets were potholed and strewn with piles of rubbish. The old Soviet city parks were decrepit; sorry remnants of playgrounds and park benches rusty and splintered by the harsh Tajik seasons. Packs of feral dogs roamed the city in the gloom. A brave new world of the Mafia's making; forever locked into the hardship of civil war without actual fighting.

Mrs Harriet blew her nose with a cotton handkerchief. Her hands shook. 'I feel as though I have dived headlong into a black and white film.'

Nargis had to admit it was depressing. The city of her childhood, once a prosperous, state-subsidised Soviet outpost, had become grey and empty since the Soviets left. Sad-looking people wandered in woollen and leather shrouds of black and brown and stooped miserably against the steppes winds at broken-seated trolleybus stops.

She tried to be positive. 'Dushanbe always look worse in winter. You no need go out, Ma'am.'

Most afternoons she accompanied Mrs Harriet on brief forays into town, pushing Leo in the pram through all sorts of weather. Mrs Harriet insisted Leo needed air and was oblivious to the shocked disapproval of the wiry Babushkas on the street.

'She's a foreigner, they like to take their babies outside,' Nargis shrugged, complying as ordered.

The Simenon house was located just off the main boulevard, Rudaki Avenue. Running from North to South, many expatriates referred to the city as 'Dushanbe Street'. All side streets led to rural Tajikistan, small gated compounds housing modest farms, households that kept lowing cows, chirping poultry and raucous roosters, cherry and apple trees and small plots of potato, parsley and carrot. Harriet's kitchen teemed with bluebottles in the summer, attracted by ditches of raw sewage that lined local lanes. On Rudaki Avenue, small, badly-lit shops with dusty window frontages jostled alongside mobile phone providers and drab, dirty grocery stores selling tinned vegetables, bread and vodka. Many shops were empty, beyond the means of most local salaries. Like a country in a cave, the ruling powers did not allow the light of globalisation to pierce the old Soviet darkness. Tajikistan remained resolutely un-Anglophone, traditional yet secular, tightly controlled. There was nowhere to buy an international novel, newspaper or magazine. Media was restricted, the prisons filled with local journalists, intellectuals and members of Islamic opposition parties. Mrs Harriet constantly bemoaned the lack of BBC radio; suspended the year before their arrival for licensing anomalies.

Nargis would wait, shivering on the pavement with the pram, while Harriet entered small shops and glanced around. Occasionally, naive returnees from Russia came back to open small, short-lived businesses only to be extorted or else closed down on a triviality to be taken over by one of the President's ubiquitous daughters as soon as they managed to turn a profit. A large store in the town centre, 'Central Universal Department Store' consisted of small stalls awash with poor quality Iranian plastic, kitsch Turkish chinaware and cheap Chinese electrical goods. Harriet would wander from stall to stall, fingering items and yawning. Passing through ancient Soviet entrance ways, she searched the dim gloom of the stalls for something, anything, to buy. Usually, she emerged empty-handed while Nargis waited, her nose full of the fatty smells of the Chinese dumpling stall.

On Sundays, Mr. Simenon sometimes left his precious computer for an hour to join them for a stroll with the children. One day, they passed a luxury sports store with its glistening counters, racks of skimpy sportswear and luminous football boots. It was empty, the price of a pair of shorts far beyond the monthly salary of most Tajiks.

'Henri, how can they remain open?' Harriet asked. 'They can't be making any money. There's never a soul in there.'

Her husband chuckled and glanced at Nargis, who stood behind, holding Alexandra's gloved hand in her own.

'*Cherie*, this is clearly a money-laundering enterprise for the elite who, in any case, prefer to shop in Moscow,' he whispered. 'Drug Money.'

Harriet stared at the made-up, skinny shop assistants giggling with leather-jacketed security guards.

'Do they know?' she asked.

Mr Simenon turned to Nargis with a wink. She shrugged and turned away. What could she say? Her own father had suffered at the hands of the Tajik gangs.

After a few months, Harriet adapted her expectations. She would be happy with the most trivial of things: finding a new plant for the garden or a friend for her daughter, the acquisition of a much craved foodstuff or a new place to eat lunch with friends.

Nargis swept the kitchen, cleaned the bathrooms and went to fetch Leo, who had woken from his nap. As the electricity failed in the house, the deep baritone rumble of the generator could be heard from the garden. Lifting the baby from his cot, she gazed absent-mindedly out of the bedroom window. She could hear Harriet talking to her mother on the phone. She always talked in that cheery, bright way to her.

'It's going to snow again later. It would be amazing to have a white Christmas, seeing as we won't make it back this year. It will look pretty in the garden with my outdoor fairy lights.'

Nargis grimaced. Most Tajiks felt the snow as a terrible curse. The recent electricity cuts had caused deaths on the hospital operating table and people lost limbs from frostbite for lack of heating. Hussein had missed a week of school, with wooden desks frozen closed, the children were sent home after an hour. No refunds were given for the wasted school fees. She sighed. Lucky Mrs Harriet. Wilfully ignorant of hardship and poverty, the world began and ended at her door. Nargis almost admired the way that she seemed to care for no one except her children, her husband and, of course, herself.

'There's no point getting too attached,' Nargis heard her say one day. 'As soon as we arrived, the two-year timer was set. Thank God.'

December 4th, 2007, Tajikistan Countdown: 13 months, 22 days

I had to go to Henri's workplace yesterday. A newly built mansion downtown, painted pastel pink with Persian carpets, green tinted glass windows, Greek pillars and an imposing mahogany staircase. It looks more like a kitsch Tajik Palazzo than an office. It was crawling with the some of the prettiest local talent I've seen in Dushanbe. Was Henri in charge of hiring? Ambitious girls, all looking for a foreigner to deliver them from this place. No wonder Henri likes his work, they must fawn over him. Bimbos hired to window dress, serve coffee and type, just like I was. Henri says I'm paranoid. Has he forgotten? I was a sassy twenty-two year old, new in London and determined to get myself a good looking, rich man to keep me in style. I had no qualms whatsoever about leading Henri astray. It was every woman for herself, as I saw it, but now I shiver when I think of it, her defeated face peering from the shadows, the expression in her eyes as he lifted his suitcases into my car. Over the past eight years, I have changed, so much that sometimes even I struggle to remember who I once was. Of course I should worry. Like Mother says, 'Complacency has no place in a good marriage'. All those perfect, inviting bodies ready to lie down for him, untarnished by childbirth and sleepless nights.

Well, those bitches stared at me, judged me, whispering to each other. I ascended the staircase to his office with envious eyes stabbing the back of my head. Of course, just my luck, he was out; a meeting at some embassy. I dropped his lunch with the supercilious Rottweiler guarding his office and ran. I don't belong there, or anywhere. Wherever I go, I'm the outsider. They talked about me after I left, my ears were tingling. Henri says I'm stupid, he says they all like me. Sure. The funny thing is, I'm envious of those girls. I miss office life. The extended meetings to gossip at the photocopier, arranging our girls nights out. I miss being part of a team. I miss being useful, needed. I miss being good at something aside from cooking and adorning my husband's arm.

I long to go home for Christmas but Henri won't let me. He says I won't be able to handle the long stopover in Istanbul, that I'll lose Alex or Leo in the airport. Apparently Turkey is full of child snatchers who will sell them for sex. I know he is probably right, but I can't help feeling sad. I wish I could go alone. I love my children, I love Henri, but God, there are days when I'd give anything to be back in England in my old life.

3

On Sunday afternoon a peaceful silence descended on the house. Outside, it was snowing and Nargis struggled to stay awake, fuelling herself with sugary tea breaks shared with the weekend gate guard. Alexandra ignored her, deep in her world of growling animals and chuffing trains. Nargis did not clean as Mr Henri didn't like the disruption of the hoover, nor the smell of wood polish and bleach. She sat cross-legged on a Tajik quilt swallowing her yawns, her velveteen dress splayed out like a bridal train. English children's books transported her to a different planet, to a place where everyone lived in brick houses with inside bathrooms and drove cars, where people had pet dogs called Spot. We live like animals when people in other countries have everything, she thought. In her bag, Nargis had her son's latest schoolbook. She took it out and and smoothed the cover, her lips curling. It was adorned with Tajikistan's President, 'farzandi azizam', the father advising his children.

Nargis stared out at the falling flakes. On crisp winter days when the freeze thawed, they would play hide and seek behind the cracked greenhouse with its rows of herbs poking out through the snow, the trenches of manured soil primed for spring. They would crouch in the sleeping rose garden and creep under green tarpaulins covering the old stables. Last weekend, she had helped Alexandra ride her tricycle on the cleared driveway, pink and shiny with ribbons on the handlebars. Baby Leo toddled about in a snow suit, gurgling at the breeze blowing through the bare branches of the apple trees. In October they had collected the walnuts that plummeted like small bombs to crack open on the cement beneath, digging them out from the lily beds for bread and desserts. They picked quince from the trees for jam. In November, the red, rusty leaves fell and the last, tired roses bloomed. Harriet never joined them.

Nargis was not allowed to disturb her master for anything other than emergencies. Alexandra was only supposed to leave her side to go to the toilet; on her uncooperative days Nargis was reduced to bribery with enticements from the kitchen. When they were not dining out, Mrs Harriet sat with Mr Simenon in the cosy study decorated with African artefacts. A large living room hung with heavy brocaded curtains and gilded mirrors sat empty, only used for parties. So many rooms, thought Nargis, comparing the airy spaciousness of their mansion with her one-roomed haveli.

Mr Simenon worked all day, taking important phone calls, pacing up and down, issuing orders. She would hear loud snores reverberating from the bedroom as Mr Henri took a siesta after lunch. They nearly always ate alone on Sundays. Harriet explained that Mr Henri did not like the children to interrupt his appreciation of a fine wine or ruin his thought processes when conversing on important topics. A red-headed Russian in spandex and large hooped earrings sometimes arrived to perform massage. Nargis would hear groans of agony emanating from Harriet's bedroom and wondered why she paid good money for such a painful experience. Occasionally, Nargis heard other sounds. Muffled moans and gasps of the sexual pleasure she had once known and now tried to forget. Envious with longing, red faced with embarrassment and desperate to stem the bitter-sweet pain between her legs, she would whisk the children out for a bracing walk.

Sitting in the luxurious surroundings of Mrs Harriet's world, with its flowery wallpaper, wooden floors, Afghani silk carpets and plaster cornicing, she felt she inhabited two Tajikistans. The first was cold, harsh and cruel, a never ending struggle with the elements that conspired to hold her underwater. The other was lavish, foreign and warm and when she was in it, anything seemed possible and all was light, her woes temporarily forgotten. On her evening return to family, she was as Persephone, forced from summer on Earth to the chill of the Underworld.

She did not resent Harriet, believing her blessed with divine luck. She knew there was no point in aspiring to have her life. Harriet Simenon was a foreigner, a Westerner from the world beyond the grip of the Soviet past; comfortable in the world of global travel, luxury items and glossy magazines. All Nargis desired was to find a measure of security, fix her modest family haveli, educate and feed her children. If she could only achieve those things she would get Faisullo, her baby boy, back from the grip of her bastard ex-husband and her conniving mother-in-law.

Most grand money-making schemes soon fell by the wayside, but six months before she had hit on a plan. Nargis chewed a fingernail and stared out at the snowy, ice blue garden beyond the veranda. A man in the mahalla had moved to Khujand, a city in Northern Tajikistan. He was looking for a quick sale for his shop, cash only. She bargained hard and as the months passed without a buyer the price had dropped. She had been offered a final selling price; two thousand somoni. In addition, Nargis knew there was a further hundred somoni to pay to get a stamp on the papers, just in case his relatives contended the sale later. Nargis had been saving ever since, a hundred somoni secreted into the money tin every month. She had received a call that morning on her way to work.

'It's a good shop and I want to give you the chance to buy it first, but I have another buyer, so you need to move fast.'

She had three days.

Nargis couldn't resist telling the guard about it on her lunch break. A happily married man, Nargis trusted Musso enough to sit on his camp bed and drink his sweet green tea. They huddled around the oil heater rubbing fingerless-gloved hands and chatted above the crackle of the transistor radio.

'Once I have my shop I'll go to my in-law's home dressed in a shiny new kurta and Russian furs.'

The guard grinned, his wrinkles cracking tanned skin like a hide of leather.

'My nails will be manicured blood red and my face will be painted with the black kohl and rouge of a beautiful Tajik bride, dripping with Arabian gold necklaces from Dubai.'

'Is that right? Indian gold?'

'That's right, only the best.' Nargis paused. 'Faced with my strident businesswoman's confidence, the hateful in-laws's resolve will crumble to dust. My child will run into my arms and I'll carry him from the apartment on my shoulders to the cheers of the neighbourhood.'

Nargis sat quietly for a moment. Her earlier spark was gone, her expression sombre. Baby Faisullo, what are you doing now? Where are you? Who are you with? Do you miss me? Nargis glanced at the clock on the wall and resolved to visit her in-laws later the next evening. Musso, a devoted father of five, shifted in his wooden chair and passed her the cracked teapot.

At the age of twenty-eight, widowed and separated from her second husband, Nargis supplemented her living as a nanny by selling paintings to foreigners. Her artist was in his fifties, marooned by Mother Russia. He lived with his mother in a ramshackle Russian summerhouse in the mahalla. Dushanbe's bohemian community had leaked out in the 1980s; the Jews to Israel, the Russians to relatives in the Motherland and the Germans who had been relocated by Stalin from the East to Tajikistan; back to Germany. Those that stayed after the collapse of the Soviet Union were freed from the rigours of Communist social realism only to become trapped once again, painting for the tourist tastes of foreigners.

Nargis had knocked on the artist's door one day, offering to sell his pieces on commission. She took his canvases and went to seek out the rich and the bored; international consultants in their grey suits and woollen coats, French Legionnaires in uniform and idle embassy wives. Sometimes she would wait by diplomatic number-plated vehicles parked outside shops frequented by strangers, or else, stand on the pavement outside popular restaurants at lunch time, hailing the passing clientele to stop and admire her wares. She hated selling on the street; her embarrassment mirrored in their light eyes and awkward stammers; the restaurant managers moving her on with painful prods and harsh curses. The responsibility of friendship weighed heavily on her now, knowing the artist and his mother waited for good news in an empty, unheated home in a state of semi-starvation.

Just two days before, on one of her days off, Nargis had been to the gallery café to collect the fee for a sold painting. One of the few eateries for Western style cakes and sandwiches in Tajikistan, 'The Shepherds Crook' was run by missionaries who offered employment, training and Bible study to vulnerable Tajik women. Like most of the other foreigners in Dushanbe, Mrs Harriet considered it an oasis of homely comfort, especially in winter. She went there several times a week for home cooked food and a friendly smile. Decorated with colourful local art and handicrafts for sale, the café offered wireless internet to those with their own laptops and was a popular lunch place for expatriate housewives, bureaucrats and American language students living with local families.

'I cannot fathom their motivation. There's no point in even trying to have a conversation with them,' Harriet had once whispered to her. Nargis agreed. She had worked for four language students as a maid before coming to the Simenon House. It was there, working for them, that she noticed their propensity for folkloric Tajik art. They usually spoke Farsi, Dari or Russian, an odd choice of languages to want to learn, or so it seemed to her. Do they want to sit in these armpit-of-the-earth places for the rest of their working lives? she wondered. Nargis dreamed of life in America or Britain, lands of opportunity. They seemed homesick and slightly out of place despite their efforts to fit in, and therefore enjoyed the All-American menu and welcoming atmosphere, so different to the apathetic service and unpredictable food in the other cafés in Dushanbe.

She alighted from the mashutka at the bottom of a steep hill, walking half a mile up to the café through the sharp light of morning. The snow had turned to sludge, leaking through her velvet slippers into her stockings, making her feet freeze. Finally, she reached the café. A bell tinkled and a few icicles fell into the thawing ditch as she slammed the door. Saodat, the café manageress, greeted her on her way to the kitchen. She was a born again Christian who felt it her life's work to try to convert as many godless Tajiks as possible. Vulnerable divorcees, unmarried girls with babies, women with disabled children and other social outcasts were attracted to the café in their droves for what it could offer, provided that they consider Christian conversion. They had found her penniless and desperate. Stitching her wounds, they comforted her children and helped her off the street when her parents refused to take her in. Nargis had resisted baptism, although she secretly attended church a few times a year and held on to a Bible, hidden in a quilt in her house. In return, they sold some of her paintings, using their whitewashed walls as an eclectic gallery. She wanted to believe what they told her; that if she read the Bible, came to church and prayed to their Jesus God, all would be transformed in her life and things would get better. The problem was that. she could not accept that she needed to be cleansed of sin. I have done nothing wrong, she thought. My husband, Poulod; he is the one who has sinned, not I.

'Assalom Nargis, how are you?' greeted a skinny, jeans-clad girl from behind the coffee bar. Her hair was cropped short like a boy's and she was drying coffee cups, lining them up along the counter with quick, nervous movements. 'How are your children, your family?'

'We are all fine, thank you. I just came to collect two hundred dollars for a painting that sold last week, thanks be to God.' Nargis clasped frozen, red hands together and tried to look pious. 'Saodat is expecting me.'

The girl's lips rose to a smile. 'Well, that's great. Praise the Lord. One moment.'

Nargis sat on a metal chair in the corner to wait. In the cafe beyond, she noticed the golden-hair of Mrs. Harriet, who was chatting animatedly with friends, her manicured nails giving colour and force to her hand gestures. Her back was to the door. Saodat, the café manageress, appeared from the kitchen with a plate of steaming chilli bean soup for a customer. She smiled at Nargis.

'Praise God, we're busy today, but I'll be with you soon shireen,' she called. Nargis grinned. On a nearby table, a woman with curly hair in a red tracksuit sat with a freckly boy. 'Eat your carrot sticks, honey, they'll make you see in the dark.'

'I don't need to see in the dark, Mom, I've got my head lamp.'

Nargis's slippers left puddles on the floor as the snow melted into them. Her feet ached as they returned to body temperature and the feeling returned to icy toes. She rubbed them surreptitiously. Suddenly, the electricity failed, lights went out, heaters stopped burning and the wireless internet disconnected. Customers sat dismayed in the grey gloom, grimacing into coffee cups, closing their laptops with angry clicks. The place felt colder in the blue-tinged, wintery light. A few moments later, there was a strong smell of fuel as the waitresses switched on kerosene heaters and the cook moved cakes into ovens running on dirty city gas.

Mrs. Harriet stood up, frowning, already wrapped in a fur-trimmed coat. Nargis watched as she swaddled her slim neck in a dark pink pashmina and sheathed elegant hands in purple suede gloves. She brought her half-eaten lunch to the counter to be wrapped to take home. If she saw Nargis, she did not acknowledge her. She stood with her back to Nargis and drummed fingers on the countertop. Nargis cowered in the corner until Harriet left, leather boots crunching in the slush, an icy draught blowing in through the door as she air-kissed her friends goodbye.

Nargis glanced towards the canvases leaning against the grubby wall of the guard house. She had carried two unframed acrylic paintings with her to deliver to the café after work. One depicted buzkashi, the Mongol precursor to polo, an ancient game played on horseback across Central Asia. Infamous among Tajiks and across the border in Afghanistan, burly men rode half-wild Arabian horses up and down a loosely marked pitch, often breaking through the borders, scattering spectators, chasing a goat's carcass for grand prizes. A recent presidential decree had banned the sport. Other decrees outlawed large weddings, funerals and high school graduation parties. The government did not want large numbers of people to gather together, perhaps fearing that drunken merrymakers would cause revolution or mayhem. Yet still, Tajiks still came together every weekend from January to March for colourful displays of macho bravery.

She got up and held the painting to the light, surveying it with a critical eye. It was nearly buzkashi season. The painting was a vivid rendition that would make a good souvenir. She was glad to note that her friend had followed orders. On a recent visit to his studio Nargis was annoyed to see that he had painted tortured abstracts of grey and black, speckled with blood-red droplets.

'Hodooiman, Dimitri, what is this? You have to stick to making the souvenirs. This will never sell,' she scolded. He had turned to her with glistening eyes.

'And what of me? My soul is dying day by day,' he whispered, reaching for a bottle of homemade vodka with shaking hands. Nargis gritted her teeth.

'Choose. Your soul or your stomach.'

The second painting was a garish mountain landscape complete with purple glacial river, distant villages painted in rusty reds and craggy hilltops of light green. They sold well to newcomers enchanted with the beauty of the barren Tajik landscape and not yet bored by the endless panoramas for sale in Dushanbe.

Musso nodded towards the paintings as he stacked their tea bowls on a tray.

'Very nice.'

Nargis smiled. 'Let's hope the foreigners agree.'

Nargis had learned to swallow her pride when hustling paintings and ask foreigners or, more rarely, rich Tajiks, for donations in old clothes and food. She knew how to prick a conscience, her pale brow glistening with sweat from wandering the streets carrying heavy canvases. Necessity did not honour false conceit, even though this went against Tajik tradition. She cited her early widowhood, the little ragged children waiting at home without any food and her elderly parents. She found it easy to summon tears. They probably did not always realise that her tears were genuine, drawn from the grief she still felt for her first husband and the lost baby. Old clothes now warmed her and her family through the winter. At other times though, people banished her empty-handed, their anger at her audacity covering their guilt.

'She had the gall to ask me for food scraps and old clothes. Can you imagine? Solicited for charity in my own house. What a cheek,' they would cry, outraged. Their firm hands on her back as they pushed her from their compounds burned through the material of her dress, branding her with shame.

At diplomatic parties, standing in Western-style fitted kitchens with harassed foreign hostesses and platefuls of meat, cheese, canapés and strange foreign foods she had never seen before, she had a curious feeling of invisibility. Like a ghost, she hovered in the background, picking up snippets of conversation on the latest policy shift, the recent energy crisis or the cotton debt problem. Most foreigners were supposed to be in Tajikistan to assist the poor, people like her, but they stayed safely in the confines of glittering receptions and conferences, rarely stepping beyond the comfort zones of the office; content to read about Tajik reality in the latest survey report or to discuss it at the next meeting. They seemed to live only to socialise.

Nargis was tired of begging at the gates of the rich or else watching as others moved forward. Yes, she had taken the leftovers from birthday parties, the half-drunk bottles of R.C Cola and abandoned pink cupcakes that made her children smile. Second-hand clothes and children's toys, broken and salvaged from the dustbin, were hidden in a sack, taken home and were mended with glue or darned as new. She had never, however, dared ask any of them for outright help until that day, five months before, when she asked Mrs. Harriet for a cash loan to buy the shop.

'Absolutely out of the question,' Mrs Harriet had cried. Her heart-shaped chin jutted upwards and she frowned at Nargis as though suspecting her of a crime. 'You've only worked for us for a few months and are still on probation.'

For days afterwards, Nargis felt the suspicious eyes of her mistress on her, no doubt assessing whether to leave her handbag unattended, her jewellery box unlocked.

Nargis took a scrap of paper and did some sums with a lidless pink felt-tip abandoned on Alexandra's desk.

Later that evening, Nargis hesitated at the door to Mrs Harriet's bedroom. Her heart was pounding. She was in heavy debt, had a creditor to avoid on every corner.

Later, berating herself, she walked the snow-sided roads to home, the question unspoken on her lips.

The next day, Nargis and Leo were in the kitchen. Mrs Harriet flitted in and out restlessly. Earlier, Nargis had overheard her on the telephone.

'They want me to come into school. An emergency meeting. Yes, today. Surely it's obvious, she's moved around so much, she's totally confused.' Harriet's voice rose to a screech. 'No, I am not blaming you. Yes, it's true. We do pay them a fortune... Yes, I agree, they should sort it out themselves... But Henri, she's your daughter too.' A sound like a sigh. 'Yes, I know you are busy. I'll go on my own.'

Leo closed his mouth against another spoon of imported Kazakh fruit yoghurt. Nargis tried to make him laugh, pulling funny faces.

'Here comes the train. *Choff-choff-choff*.'

He turned his head away and stared out of the window. Then he shifted in his highchair and opened his mouth to whine. Nargis, seeing an opportunity, slipped a spoon of yoghurt in. Leo spat it out and pouted. It dribbled down his chin onto his bib. She sighed and wiped his face. 'Come on, shireen, you must eat.'

Before him lay a plate of cheese and tomato sandwich squares. Sensing that his mother would soon leave without him, he was being difficult, refusing to eat despite Nargis's exasperated entreaties. The sight of yoghurt and cheese, two foods that her own children did not eat more than a few times a year, emboldened Nargis to speak up. Her stomach growled and she thought of the naan and fried egg waiting for her in the guard house. Harriet entered the kitchen and sat down in her sheepskin to wait for the driver. She opened a magazine, flicking unseeingly through the pages.

Nargis inhaled. 'Mrs. Harriet, I need talk to you about problem.'

Harriet glanced at her with cold eyes.

'Yes. What now?' she snapped.

Nargis squirmed, wracking her brain for the correct English words. 'My village has shop I want buy. I got savings and little money from selling paintings, but I need ask you credit so I can buy and also buy thing…things for sell.'

Nargis held her breath. Beads of sweat grew on her upper lip and forehead and she wiped them away with a dirty sleeve. Harriet shut the magazine and scowled.

'As I recall, we've been through this already. Why on the earth don't you go to a bank?'

Nargis cleared her throat. 'Bank want papers and I don't have,' she said. Her voice shook and she held her hands tightly to stop their trembling. *Please, please God.*

Harriet yawned, tapping little-girl pink, manicured nails on the table. 'Where the hell has the driver got to? I don't want to be late.' She pulled out her phone and checked the time.

'Ma'am?'

Suddenly, Leo threw his drink on the ground with force. The bottle burst open, milk spreading across the tiles in white rivulets. Harriet grimaced.

'Leo! Naughty boy,' she scolded. Nargis sprang from her chair to fetch a mop. Harriet shuddered as Leo started to bawl louder and watched as Nargis cleaned up and took Leo from the highchair, balancing him on one hip. Harriet's expression changed and she sighed.

'Hmm. I suppose we could lend you some money. You can pay off the debt by babysitting, for nothing, obviously. Then you will be able to keep all your profits without having to keep them aside for me. It will be easier for you, I'm sure.'

Colour flooded Nargis's face. 'I need three hundred fifty dollars, one thousand somoni, please ma'am.'

There was a pause. Harriet frowned. 'That's six weeks wages. That's a lot of money you know.'

Nargis waited, still. Leo wriggled in her arms. *Please.*

'I'll lend you two hundred and ten dollars, your wages for December, no more than that. That's a long time to work without wages though, are you sure you'll manage?'

Nargis let out a nervous giggle that she quelled, not wanting to appear impertinent. Just a little short, she would have to beg for time with the owner to pay the rest later. She felt sure he would agree. She felt a surge of elation. She kissed Leo on each cheek.

'Yes Ma'am. Thank you, rahmat.'

Harriet waved away the thanks. She reached into her handbag and casually pulled out a clipped wad of hundred dollar bills, counting off the cash into eager fingers.

December 6th, 2007, Tajikistan Countdown: 13 months, 20 days

I lent Nargis money for a new business venture. I rejected her once before, back in late summer, yet she dared ask me a second time. I guess she must be desperate. She does a good job with the children and I can't bear to lose her, it's such a bloody nightmare, training new nannies. Alex and Leo adore her, their 'Gissie', they'd be heartbroken if she left now. I won't tell Henri, as he'll be furious, worrying that she's a drug addict or a gambler and that we will wake up one day to find our valuables gone. For him, maids are no more than human tools, domestic robots on the outermost edge of his consciousness. It felt odd to be useful and it lightened my mood for a while. Good luck to her, I admire her spirit.

The meeting at the kindergarten was terrible, two teachers assembled themselves before me, Good Cop and Bad Cop. Bloody Henri, he should have been there, I was outnumbered. Alex lashes out, refuses to obey simple orders and spends hours in 'time out' at various 'naughty' steps, benches and corners. She's only four. I think they should give her a little leeway. I said as much to the strict one, only to note the exchange of supercilious looks passing between the two women, the patronising tone of voice from Good Cop; Bad Cop turning shrill when I brought up the astronomical school fees. Apparently Alex hasn't any friends because she's so often moody and refuses to share. Well, I know how she feels. Bad Cop postulated that she has 'no moral compass' and that she does not know the difference between right and wrong. That's a lie. Good Cop suggested that she's angry and confused by the changes that happen in her life without warning and beyond her control. I shrugged my shoulders and tried not to smirk. 'Isn't that just a facet of everyday expatriate life that we all face?' I asked. We are all floating aimlessly in the same boat, where ever the wind takes us. I swallowed the frustration and promised to talk to her, but in the end, I can only sympathise. Bad Cop warned me that she needs to improve, that there have been complaints from other parents about her biting and pinching the other children, she has drawn blood. Later, Henri tried to calm me down with a Gaelic shrug. 'Ce n'est pas grave, ma chou. Alexandra is a special, gifted child and requires a more sophisticated approach than these 'crude' Americans are capable of.' Still, I worry.

Tomorrow is Tuesday, a dull mid-week day in winter, the kind of day I have come to dread. I might try to make walnut ice cream if I can find Russian UHT cream anywhere. There's no fruit in the market in winter and chocolate is expensive, whereas we have sacks of our own walnuts sitting in the attic.

Nothing else planned all week except lunch with Patty and Veronica. Henri says Patty is a racist bigot and that Veronica should try getting out of her tracksuit for a change. He hates women who wear sportswear outside the gym, especially when they're fat. Veronica has been very low since she found out that their posting in Dushanbe might be extended for an extra year. Lately, she bakes or buys enormous racks of pastries, brownies and cookies every day, ostensibly for the twins. I know though that she polishes off whatever they don't want and wakes in the night to eat downstairs, alone in the dark. She's gaining a kilo a month but we don't like to mention it. Her husband tells her off constantly and jokes about the great looks she had when they met; how she was his blue-eyed betthäschen (I looked it up: 'Bed Bunny' in German). When I asked him what this meant, he just winked. It's as if he thinks she tricked him into marriage by being thin. If her husband made her happier though, perhaps she wouldn't eat so much. As for Patty, well she is tactless at times, but it's unintentional. I refuse to stop seeing my friends, no matter what Henri says. It's bad enough that he has banned our weekend get-togethers. 'They bore me,' he said and that was that. If I defy him, he'll just be embarrassing and walk out mid-sentence, like the last time. Going for a nap halfway through our BBQ. I could have fallen through the floor.

Lunch at The Shepherd's Crook, again, is not particularly exciting but it's better than staying at home, staring at the floral wallpaper. It gives me a reason to get up in the morning, or rather, not to return to my bed after the school run. There is no worse feeling than someone cleaning your bedroom when you are lying in it. There are only so many beauty treatments I can do in a week and there's nowhere to go in the snow. I'm nearly paralysed by boredom. It is bleak, overcast and the sky, a single tone of grey that blankets us down in fog, is sucking the life out of me. Then there is the mud. Granite coloured sludge that oozes in putrid ditches of more grey. If only there was a proper gym or somewhere to do a course, learn a new skill. I'm not talented or creative and I don't believe I can save the world like most of the other foreigners I meet. I'm too self-conscious to go jogging. Ladies don't do sport in Tajikistan, not since Soviet times, it is considered shameful to perspire in public. I stopped calling the Tajik teacher. The barrier has come down, I will get no further than school-girl patter. Arabic, Kiswahili, they were the same. Why spend two years learning a language only to leave and never hear it again? I see no point to it. Besides, Henri is disparaging. He says it is better I don't speak at all than that I 'desecrate' a language. He urges me to find more interesting, 'cultured' friends, throwing me scrawled names and numbers on bits of paper, the educated, accomplished wives of colleagues; women charity directors who teach English as a Foreign Language and learn Tajik folk instruments in their spare time. He doesn't understand that those sorts of people don't want to waste their time with me, that their eyes glaze over when I tell them I am a Stay At Home Mother. Most of them passionately hate little children and they're either divorced, gay or resolute spinsters. They wear horrible clothes and sensible shoes. And they all work. The irony is not lost on me that Henri wants me to be friends with the very women he would never have picked for himself.

No, in Tajikistan, you can no more choose your friends than you can choose your family. When I meet someone who understands, we cling to each other like twins in the womb. We have the same problems to deal with, day in, day out. All of us have husbands that accuse us of moaning. They don't appreciate the effort it takes to fill our days, walking the grey streets, until we know every pot hole, every crack, aimlessly searching for something that we never seem to find, because it isn't here. Veronica calls it 'sehnsucht'. It's German for 'the inconsolable longing of the human heart for something otherworldly and undefined'. That woman is not as stupid as she looks. I wonder if we are looking for our past selves, looking for the effortless fun we once had, when we knew who, and where, and what, we were.

I once inhabited a dynamic, glistening world of computers and shag pile. I reigned as Queen of my kingdom, exercising control over appointment diaries and the minutes of board room meetings of powerful men. Even the strip lights, grey winter rain and bottom pinching in the lift did not dampen my spirits, I strode to the tube in trainers and navy pinstripe and met girlfriends in Soho bars twelve hours later for flirtatious encounters with sexy, rugby-playing bankers from Harrow and Eton. I would wake up satiated, a little hung over, in their beds with views overlooking Canary Wharf, leaving a few moments later, warm with the knowledge that I would have a date that night if I wanted one. Often, I didn't. I needed no one. Stopping for a bacon butty on the way back to my flat, buying the morning paper, reading the Sunday supplements in bed. It was not a very worthy life, but I had a niche and knew my way around it.

As it is now, I fill in time and count days. My friends here in Tajikistan understand how an article in a magazine, a song or a sudden craving for an unavailable food can make me weep. They share *the frustration of being a trailing wife trapped in a luxurious prison, the loneliness of the forsaken career, no one to converse with all day long but a silent journal or a sulky maid.*

To outside eyes I know we look spoilt. The endless purchase of new curtains. The continuous packing and unwrapping, a mountain of cardboard boxes and enough brown tape for ten lifetimes, the paper cuts and a river of tears for broken heirlooms. The ceaseless newness of the expat wife's curse; a life lived on the move. The upheaval of an existence in constant flux, uprooted every two to three years.

Henri says I chose this when I married him. 'Stop complaining, you are better off than ninety-nine percent of Tajiks,' he tells me. That may be true. Yet, when we met I had only ever been to Ibiza and the Costa Brava. I thought diplomatic life sounded glamorous. What a joke.

4

The next day, Mrs Harriet decided that they should walk to the café for lunch. She emerged from the house in huge sunglasses and a faux-fur coat.

'A bit of fresh air does the baby good,' she said as they left the compound, poking at a snow drift with a walking stick. Nargis squinted in the glare and tried to see where she was going, nearly pushing Leo into the snowy verge. It was sunny and crisp, the searing whiteness all but snow-blinding her. The path ahead was covered in the vivid yellow of solidified dog urine, hopping bird tracks and black footprints. The road along the ridge had collapsed in the night, leaving a gaping gash in the hillside. Once a huge pothole, it had ripped apart to expose the rocks and earth beneath. Snowmelt had begun to stream into the hole, carrying away debris. An old man stood stooped, with his bare hands in the half-frozen dirt, trying in vain to repair it with mud and stones.

'Henri will be very cross when he sees this,' Harriet murmured. They gingerly lifted Leo in his pram across the rubble. Nargis slipped and slid in the slush in her thin-soled slippers. 'This was his short cut to the office.'

A cloud the colour of steel descended, cloaking the sun. Nargis looked up to the sky and grimaced. Just as they reached the café it started to sleet.

The trainee behind the counter greeted them in stilted English as they entered, brushing wet boots on the mat, assailed by the sweet smell of fresh cinnamon buns. Nargis sat down with Leo in a little children's area adorned with toys. On another table Saodat sat hunched over a large ledger doing the weekly book-keeping. She smiled a greeting at Nargis, her fingers tapping calculator keys. A pasty looking American girl in shapeless men's jeans and an oversized varsity college sweatshirt sat in a corner typing on a laptop.

'Assalom.' She smiled at Nargis, confident of her perfect Tajik. 'I'm emailing friends in Wisconsin. He is so cute, do you mind if I take a picture of you two for my blog?'

Another couple, a blonde language student and a dashing young Tajik language teacher, judging by her animated hand gestures and his jovial miscomprehension, sat a little too close together laughing and whispering with heads bent.

Mrs Harriet's friend, Patty, entered the café, shutting the door with a loud slam and shook sleet-drops off her woollen hat, fluffing up her auburn hair into a bouffant. As she struggled out of her jacket, her fingers glittered with diamond and sapphire.

'Hey, Harriat darlin'. Can you believe this goddamn weather? My husband insisted on leavin' Texas, "to Give Somethin' Back" for goodness sakes. I should have done my research because as far as I'm concerned it is my life I'm givin'.'

Patty wore a permanent sneer of dissatisfaction. She pulled up a chair to the table and sat, scraping the tiled floor. 'Honestly, Dushanbe is gettin' me all worked up. The darn win'er's too cold, the water's too dirty and there's nothin' to buy. I'm wore out the way no one speaks any darn English and I spend all day tryin' to train the maid to do what I want. I'll swear she's worse than a Maria back home. My Pa used to say, "like a one-legged man at a butt kickin' contest", it's makin' me crazy.' Patty stared at the student-teacher couple. 'Doesn't she know she's just his ticket outta this dump?' She opened the menu, grimaced and snapped it shut. A young Tajik waitress hovered nervously with a notepad.

'I don't know why I bother lookin', I know exactly what I'm havin'. Bean salad. They're tinned so I won't get sick.'

Harriet ordered herself a quiche and a toasted sandwich for Leo.

'Do you want something Nargis?' she called.

'Just green tea.' In truth, Nargis was starving, but she felt embarrassed that she couldn't read the menu very well and didn't know what food to order.

Harriet rolled her eyes and gestured towards Nargis. 'Get her a cupcake.'

Veronica came in and sat down. She over-ordered as usual. An embassy wife from Hamburg, she was lost in Tajikistan's disorganisation.

'I think I will buy that carrot cake for the twins play-date later. Only sixty somoni, eighteen dollars? Ya. I take it,' she shouted.

Nargis looked up at the commotion. She found the way Veronica yelled all the time shocking. Mr Simenon couldn't bear her bossiness and had banned her from their dinner parties. Nargis heard that she had fired seven different maids for no greater sin than forgetting to change a toilet roll. Tajik maids talked about her with horror.

'What's up, Ronnie? You look as nervous as a long tail' cat in a room full o' rockin' chairs.'

'Christian has the meeting today with Finance Minister. They start the vodka sessions in sleazy city bars at one in the morning so I know he'll be home at three in the morning with lipstick on his face.' There was an uneasy silence. 'He says it is just part of his job. Ha! I told him, Christian, *mein schatz*, I am sick of you cavorting in the kitchen with the nanny. He says he is only practising his Russian, but I see the way she looks at him. He thinks I am having the paranoia. Do you think I'm paranoid?'

Veronica frowned and picked at the tablecloth. The other women were silent. She looked very small and vulnerable, like a child sitting all alone in a busy school playground. Harriet touched Veronica's arm but Patty kept her eyes down, rummaging in her handbag for hand sanitiser. Harriet's eyes settled on Nargis.

'My nanny is buying a shop, aren't you Nargis?' Nargis grinned and shifted in her chair. Saodat looked up again from her book-keeping and winked at Nargis. 'I've lent her the money and now she's going to be a successful businesswoman.'

Patty looked doubtful and wrinkled her nose. 'That was awful nice o' you, sugar. I never encourage that sort of thin' with my staff though, you never know where it'll end.'

Does she think I am deaf or just too stupid to understand? Nargis thought.

'I mean, just this mornin' a crowd of peasants from the neighbourhood came to my front door asking to take water from the pipe out back. It hasn't frozen because we've been keepin' it runnin' for the dogs. Course, I told the guards to tell them to get lost, we can't have these sorry-assed people tramplin' all over the yard.'

Harriet's face betrayed a flicker of shock. Nargis felt a flash of anger. Veronica swiped her blonde bob out of her eyes and delved in her handbag for her ringing phone.

'Patty, you are so right. It's a security issue.' Her eyes darted doubtfully to the Tajik language teacher seated nearby and she lowered her voice to a guarded whisper. 'You don't want to encourage these people.'

Patty's bean salad arrived. She unwrapped a fork from its serviette, rubbed it for invisible dirt and frowned at the back of the departing waitress.

'I should uh ordered the chilli. And who's to say she won't use up the money and then come cryin' for more in a few weeks?'

Nargis wanted to melt into the floor. Saodat looked over at Nargis. She blushed and jiggled Leo on her knee. He got down and started crawling about. Harriet rolled her eyes.

'And just wait, you will see, others will find out and then they'll all be queuing up for the loans too,' said Veronica, staring at her phone. Harriet coughed and pointed. Too late, the two women glanced over at Nargis. Her back was stiff as a plank. They could not see her expression. Veronica's barbecue beef sandwiches arrived at the table, oozing extra sauce with a big hunk of warm American apple pie slathered in homemade vanilla ice cream.

'I think you should fire your nanny, Ron,' said Harriet, deliberately changing the subject.

'Harriet dear, I tried but Christian won't let me. Absolutely out of the question, he says. He says the kids like her and it's not her fault I'm having jealous feelings. She's impossible, taking naps on the sofa and serving herself cokes from my fridge. The other cleaner says she even saw her trying on my jewellery when I was out. Now that other cleaner; she, I can trust.'

'Get rid of her,' said Harriet shortly.

Veronica sighed. 'Ya. I fire her later.'

But it's not her fault, Nargis thought. She had experienced that man's wandering hands herself not long ago at a barbecue. He had crept up behind her in the garden and stroked her bottom, laughing at her reaction. Nargis knew their nanny, a pretty, slightly built, happily married woman with three small children. I'm sure that daughter-of-a-donkey maid is lying.

Nargis got up. 'It time for Leo go nap,' she said. 'Cold rain stop. I make him go sleep in pram.'

Harriet shrugged but didn't look up.

'Sure. You'll have to walk the long way home via Rudaki. That shortcut is dangerous and could landslide again with all this sleet. I'll get a lift back with Veronica.'

Nargis was dismissed as a group of scruffy foreigners entered. Clearly Westerners, the women were dressed in Tajik velveteen kurtas with cotton ezore trousers underneath and long shawls on their hair to keep the snow off. The men looked like lumberjacks, sporting large unkempt beards, dirty fingernails and hiking boots.

'Look out,' whispered Patty. 'It's the weirdo brigade.'

Harriet sniggered into her latte.

'What on earth do they think they look like?' whispered Veronica.

Harriet shrugged and dug a fork into her quiche.

'They must be in Dushanbe for the weekend, perhaps from another town like Turzon Zoda, Khujand or Qurghon Teppa.'

Christian foreign aid workers lived in the hinterland towns working in local clinics and schools, paid for by American fundamentalist organisations and churches. Many had lived in Tajikistan for years, some since the civil war and the collapse of the Soviet Union. They had learned the local language, adapted to local customs and dress. They even lived in traditional housing and ate national dishes. Yet for all that, they were treated with suspicion by the government and with cheery bemusement by most locals. Nargis smiled and they greeted her in polite, perfect Tajik. She could not understand why anyone would want a life like hers by choice but she admired them for their zeal. Why swap the advantages of being born in a wealthy country for all the disadvantages of Tajik life? Why walk about scruffy, when you could afford to dress well? Certainly, the Russians in Dushanbe could not understand such aspirations. They laughed at foreigners who bothered to learn Tajik, which they saw as a useless, inferior language, little better than a Persian dialect by comparison with their sophisticated Russian. Of course, Patty had a theory.

'You wanna know what I think? They're just plain old white trailer trash from the Bible Belt. Instead of turnin' to hillbilly life, they've tuned into mid-Western evangelicalism, going overseas to hold prayer meetin's and preach at the unsuspecting natives. I guess by comparison with the violence and immorality of trailer towns in North Dakota, Tajikistan is gonna' look like the Promised Land.'

Well, I prefer those Americans to you, Nargis thought. She donned her brother's oversized coat, strapped Leo into the pram and wheeled him out into oozing grey slush.

It's started to snow again outside, thick flakes drifting down like wet feathers as though the clouds were having a pillow fight above us. Luckily, it is not settling, too warm for drifts. It lands on the puddles and mud and dissolves to nothingness. The sky is pale grey and hangs low over the treetops, pressing down on us like a vice.

After that conversation in the café I felt stupid about lending Nargis money. It's too late now though, she came to me all excited and happy to say that the owner called and has agreed to the sale. I couldn't bring myself to tell her that I had changed my mind. She just better not ask me for anything else. I have to keep my eyes open. Remember that old maid in Algiers, (what was her name? Aida), stealing all the discs from my CD cases and making off with food in her handbag. And that driver in Cairo, Mohamed, who took my money and used it to fund his 'brown sugar' dope habit. How was I to know? He was so friendly, so helpful. He listened to the azan call to prayer on the radio every morning with bloodshot eyes from sitting up half the night with sleepless, colicky babies, so he said. Little did I know, he wasn't even married. Instead, he spent his nights wandering the ancient tombs of the City of the Dead, where shadowy people gathered to smoke drugs. I lent him money for his ailing mother's medical care. I later found out that his mother was in perfect health. Two months later he crashed our car while stoned and Henri fired him. He was furious with me when he found out we had run up debts with half of Zamalek, the backlash of my lazy habit of sending Mohamed with cash to pay our bills and do my shopping for me at the souk. I had to go shop by shop, paying angry men off for two months worth of carpentry (new shelving), plumbing (pipes for the new dishwasher), electrics (the satellite dish). I even owed that toothless Alexandrian with his box of iced seafood, fillet knife and butchers block, who stood at the corner every morning in puddles of fresh fish guts. His expression when I came to order. I thought he would fillet me in his bloodstained galibaya and white turban.

Henri called this morning to ask me to pack his suitcase, a bottle of French brandy and a case of his best Vin Rouge de Bordeaux and jars of pickles, tinned olives and snacks. I sigh inwardly but I perform the tasks he asks of me like a good wife. He needs time away from us, I can understand that. He was already quite old for a young family when we met and it is hard on him. He's taken four days off work to go skiing with some of the younger, intrepid Francophone crowd, Swiss and French singletons.

In Tajikistan, skiing was once popular amongst the urban elite but like so much else, the glory days of 'Tajik-Ski' are long in the past. A crumbling, 1970's ski resort named Takob still opens, but the four-hour journey on the old mountain road is usually impassable and the hotel sounds like a location for a horror film. A five-storey cement building, dark, dirty and cold with cell-like rooms teeming with nocturnal insects and an ancient, smoke-stained restaurant serving tepid soup and stale bread on chipped crockery. No wonder he needs liquid fortification. Henri told me enough to put me off going for life, yet he wants to go again. I guess bringing a wife and two snivelling kids along would not suit his image. We would spoil the party atmosphere. Besides, I am a terrible skier. None of the creaking chair lifts work, necessitating a long, sweaty walk to the top of the ski slope carrying skis and poles for a 500m descent through pristine powder and burning sunlight. Henri is welcome to it, though I can't help feeling a little resentful. When have I ever been away without the children?

I'll stay here alone, with Nargis to help me, as usual. The wind is whipping up, blowing the snow in a semi-horizontal direction so that it taps against the window panes, a cacophony of wet fingerprints. Trapped in the house, I'll clock-watch, bake bread, read, play a little with Alex; games of Ludo and Disney puzzles, dot-to-dot and colouring books. I'll sit on the sofa, watching Nargis hoover and dust. She won't speak unless spoken to. She'll negotiate her way around me with the vacuum as though I were a stone statue or a side table she has seen many times before, just another piece of the Simenon household. I have a sudden vision of her dusting me, spraying my cheeks with wood polish and rubbing it in with a duster to make them gleam. I'll indulge myself with wine at lunchtime, sleep through the afternoons and wake up feeling sick.

Alex looked at me with narrowed eyes after her father's phone call and climbed into my lap. 'What's wrong, Mummy?' she said. Her eyes were sad, too sad for a four-year old. 'Nothing Alex, I just have a piece of dust in my eye'. I blinked away the tears, screwed my face into a distorted smile and stood up, holding her close. Lately I am always cold, my bones like ice, no matter how many layers I wear. 'Let's have some of Mummy's special chocolate and feel better.' Alex brightened then. She knows I keep bars of Cadbury's dairy milk in my bedroom for emergencies. Nargis averted her eyes, an unwilling witness to my cracking. I am sure she finds me as pathetic as I find myself, an overgrown princess, crying great tears of self-pity from her gilded tower. Still, how I wish unmarried, young people would call me with a joke; invite me dancing or skiing; infect me with their hope and laughter.

After Henri left, I went to Veronica's for a coffee. Patty came over too, slurring, I could have sworn she was drunk. She needs to cut down. We sat chain smoking in her kitchen, complaining about Tajikistan for over two hours, a litany of woes. By the time I left, I felt as though someone had secreted heavy weights into the soles of my shoes and sewn pebbles into the hems of my clothing.

5

Nargis finished sweeping the shop with a small broom of twigs and stood back proudly. It was not much, but it was hers. She had never owned anything of significance and felt the same nervous joy as when she had held her new born babies for the first time. She was warm from her exertions, her breath made small clouds in the frosty air. That morning she had enquired about a shop sign with her maiden name inscribed: 'Maroza Nuizaniev Nargis', though she dropped the idea when she heard the price. The sign painter saw her hesitation and raised a bushy eyebrow.

'Maybe in a few months?'

About the same size as their family haveli, it had a porch, painted blue bay windows that faced the small street and Varzob River beyond and large, double fronted wooden doors. On one door hung a sprig of thorns to ward off the evil eye, a gift from her mother. Glass-fronted cabinet counters adorned each side of the shop with ancient metal scales screwed into the counter on one side. In one half of the shop the shelves stood empty. On the other, Nargis had set out the foodstuffs she had managed to buy that morning at the market with her father: transparent bags of macaroni, recycled mineral water, bottles of brown cotton oil for cooking, a small sack of flour, white onions and red potatoes. She had also bought exercise books, pens and sweets as a small school was situated nearby and she hoped to attract children with their meagre pocket money. Nargis glanced at the empty shelves critically. No, they would not do. Food was so expensive these days, it had cost her everything she had just to buy the pitiful amount before her.

That afternoon, a lady had come to the shop accompanied by her husband, Mullah Azikav, with a business proposal. Nargis knew her by sight but they weren't friends. She was a foreigner from the south. A pretty young woman, she had a naïve face and an appealing smile. Nargis felt a pang of pity for her when she saw her husband, almost old enough to be her grandfather, one of her father's backgammon peers. He hovered by the door looking uncomfortable, as though the shop was a private boudoir for women.

'I'd like to know if you could rent me half the shop,' the woman said, her Tajik accented with the dialect of the Khatlon. 'I'm tired of sitting on the street to sell my little things, the snow makes my feet numb and my teeth chatter too hard to speak to customers.' She giggled, a nervy, sound that set Nargis's teeth on edge. Her husband, standing behind her, grinned, his mouth a cave dotted with golden stalactites. Her name, Savsang, Tajik for the Iris flower, suited her. She had a graceful figure, long brown hair tied in plaits and large, liquid eyes. She wore a glittering kurta embroidered with sequins and a matching headscarf on her head. Savsang had been dispatched from her village in conservative Southern Tajikistan when she was barely twelve to marry her paternal cousin, the mahalla mullah. Despite attracting interest, the men stayed away from her out of respect for her husband. As mullah, Azikav held religious and moral authority in the mahalla, sought out to mediate in disputes and recite prayers in memoriam, officiate at marriages and funerals.

Nargis conceded that allowing Savsang to rent half her shop would fill the bare shelves, attracting more customers as well as bringing in cash. Already this morning, her mother had complained that little Bunavsha needed a new dress and winter shoes. Slightly built with fragile health, she had another throat infection. Gulya flew into a rage, ranting all morning and accusing her of caring more about business than her children.

Nargis sighed, thinking of her lazy, able-bodied brother and father lying at home. Her brother had lost his job at the nearby cement factory when the owner was unable to pay the electricity bill. He had to close for the winter and the workers had no choice but to return to their villages with two months wages owed. The mahalla was full of unemployed, angry men. They sat in groups of frustrated idleness, waiting for work on makeshift wooden benches. Then evening fell and they went home to interfere in domestic decisions, drinking the naan money and hitting their wives in impotent fury. She could not understand why her brother did not make more of an effort to find a job. She supposed it was because he had no children to feed. He was only eighteen, with no passport or identity papers, so he was not able to travel to Russia. He was still a spoilt, lazy teenager, expecting her to provide everything. Were it not for her memories of her darling Ahmed, Nargis would have dismissed all Tajik men. Well, she thought, my lazy brother can work in here, my good-for-nothing Father too, when I go to work for Mrs Harriet.

Her phone rang, but stopped as she reached for it. It rang again. She reached for it once more and it stopped. An unknown number. Nargis added it to her list of barred numbers. Poulod, her husband. It had to be him, tormenting her from some industrial town in Russia. The scar on her back throbbed. The shop felt lonely, the darkness outside drawing in, thick mist rising from the river beyond. A memory came to her of his mottled skin, the tufts of coarse hair on his back, his breasts wobbling like white jellies as he thrusted and panted on top of her. His fat hands tightening around her neck as he climaxed. She bit her lip and stared out at the encroaching blackness. Poulod must never find out about this shop. She stowed her broom, closed the double-fronted doors with two huge padlocks and strode home.

The freeze thawed once more and Dushanbe's streets became brown lakes. Gutters roared and concrete ditches ran with refuse, sewage and food scraps that rushed out from under the metal doors of residential compounds. Sophisticated young women in black leather coats and high-heeled boots picked their way through the dirt to study or work as shop girls, alongside older women in head scarves and thick cardigans. School children in smart navy suits balanced precariously on muddy half thawed verges like meerkats, the passing drivers oblivious of their spray.

Once prosperous, the upper-class area of Dushanbe housed the Museum of Antiquities with its reclining Buddha, an Opera House and leafy boulevards with apartments decorated with motifs from the Samarkand Islamic period. This was where rich folk dressed in Russian furs went to shop for groceries.

Harriet scratched her head and wandered around the Peikar supermarket grumbling. Nargis followed behind, pushing a small trolley.

'There are tins and tins of other types of fish, but no tuna again.'

Food shortages were common and unpredictable. Last month, imported long life milk had returned to the shelves after six weeks of absence. Nargis had been dispatched with Ivan to scour the smaller grocery shops and kiosks in the city for dusty, long forgotten packages of milk from back shelves. The children were accustomed to drinking at least half a pack per day but local milk was often curdled and smelled strongly of the farmyard. Harriet began to stockpile food, storing tall tinned towers and boxes of milk in the attic. The month before, the city lacked tin foil and dark chocolate. Nargis pointed at Russian red caviar on offer, but Harriet dismissed it as out of date, toxic. Labels had to be read carefully in Tajikistan but it was suspected that supermarkets stuck new ones on when they ran out of date. There was no fresh meat this morning and the cheese was uninspiring, large rectangular lumps of processed 'Gouda' and 'Edam' imported from former Soviet republics. Harriet opened a big freezer and pulled out a small Brazilian frozen chicken covered in ice crystals.

'Nargis, do you think this has already defrosted in a power cut?'

'I think, maybe.'

This morning, the power came and went in sudden surges of light, low then radiant, then dark again as though a mischievous child were playing with the city dimmer switch. It made Nargis nauseous. She worried about fire, thinking of the bare wires that hung from the wall in her shack. Several weeks before, Harriet's house had filled with the smell of burning plastic as a socket caught alight, the orange flames attracting Leo who crawled towards it. Harriet replaced the chicken with a sigh. Her phone rang. She talked for a few seconds and whoever it was hung up. Harriet scowled.

'Henri has invited people from the US Embassy for dinner on Saturday night. Whoopee. Only nine days to Christmas and he wants me to make a four course meal for six, served with a smile and fresh flower pieces while wearing my best designer heels. "Nothing fancy", he said, ha ha.'

Nargis understood that this was what Henri expected when he said Harriet should "do her bit". She looked around.

'What will you cook?'

Harriet picked up a dusty tin of Russian pickles and scrutinised the label.

'No idea. I am tempted to hire catering from the French restaurant, but Henri would kill me, they charge twenty-five dollars a head for a three-course menu.'

A few days before, Mr Simenon had come home from his ski trip and fired the cook. A stocky figure in a brown leather coat and black headscarf, she left without a fight, with a hastily typed reference and a generous final wage packet in her hand. It made Nargis twitchy. Her employers had argued, their raised voices resonating around the house as Nargis tried to pretend all was normal with the children.

'How could you do this without even consulting me first?' Harriet had screamed.

'Harriet, may I remind you of the words of Moliere, "*manger bien et juste*". When you make the money, you can make the decisions. I want you to cook for me the way you used to before, beautiful meals served by candlelight in the dining room instead of having to eat the cook's greasy, bland slops under kitchen strip lights with toddlers for company. *Faire votre part.*'

There was a sound of glass smashing and the study door slammed. More shouts, inaudible. Nargis winced. Mrs Harriet appeared in the kitchen with glittering eyes and the jagged edges of a broken whisky tumbler, blood spurting from a small cut on her hand. Nargis scanned her face, no obvious bruises, no sign of a struggle. She sprang forward to take the glass with eyes downcast. She felt a jolt of sympathy when she saw Mrs Harriet's lips quivering, her face twitching wildly to stop the tears.

She was muttering to herself. 'Fuck you Henri, you had children, now live with them.'

Mrs Harriet filled the trolley with packets of fruit juice and milk from Russia, biscuits for the children and a few boxes of Finnish porridge oats.

'I can't bring myself to buy any of this,' she said, gesturing towards the dusty jars of stewed fruit and tins of pickled vegetables. People crowding past them did not seem to agree. Rich migrant workers back from Russia for New Year, they would be in Dushanbe until the spring. Nargis eyed them. Wearing smart, sexy clothes, with well cut, coloured hair, they did not look like locals any more. Image was everything in Tajikistan and as the new bourgeoisie they were expected to show off and share their prosperity with family, friends and neighbours during the festive season. They piled their trolleys high with cream cakes covered in chopped peanuts, Korean pickled mushroom and Kim-chi cabbage in chilli and garlic, Russian smoked sausage, vodka, RC cola and beer. Nargis had a sense of being watched. I wonder if some of these people know him? He might be on his way home too. She shuddered.

Mrs Harriet paid the bill, which came to over fifty dollars.

'Prices have gone up again,' she observed. 'Of course, I know this shop is expensive compared to what you would pay.'

Nargis grunted. She was aware of the price rises, depressed at how little stock she had managed to buy for the shop for New Year. She did not dare ask for an increase in wages. Mr Simenon was already quibbling over the necessity of Harriet's employees. They wandered out past the outstretched, liver-spotted hands of a grey haired beggar into the sharp winter sun, a shop boy carrying bulging orange carrier bags.

Sitting at the endless traffic lights on Rudaki Avenue, there were more luxury cars than usual. A creamy Porsche Carrera SUV drove up alongside with green tinted windows. Mrs Harriet's driver, Ivan, held back to let him cut into the queue.

'Do you think that's a drug baron, Ivan?' Harriet teased. 'Henri says that at least hundred tonnes of pure grade heroin processed in Afghanistan passes into Tajikistan every year. It's worth a billion dollars!'

Ivan's ice-blue eyes found hers in the driving mirror. He chuckled with forced jocularity and tapped leather gloves on the steering wheel.

'Well, Madam Harriet, I wouldn't mind some of that,' he said.

Harriet frowned as car doors all around them opened at the red light.

'Ugh! Look at all these disgusting men spitting yellow phlegm on the street. It's no wonder there's a Tuberculosis epidemic in Tajikistan.'

Dotted in twos and threes along Rudaki Avenue, stood the grey-uniformed traffic police with their orange batons and piercing tin whistles. Harriet's car had diplomatic licence plates so they were not subjected to the daily stops and harassment for papers with the inevitable five to fifty somoni "administration" fee. Of course, drivers of luxury vehicles were never stopped, no matter how fast they drove through town.

Green Bazaar was packed. A small covered market with peeling gates topped by an antique Soviet sign in Cyrillic, it was the only place with local colour in the Dushanbe winter. Vibrantly attired Uzbek and Tajik traders with red noses and white hands clamoured for Harriet's attention, yelling 'Dotchka, Lady' as she wandered past. They ignored Nargis. Others sat semi-hidden like blue-lipped statues behind stalls piled high with naan bread, carts of semi-defrosted bits of chicken and turkey next to dirty buckets of grey, slimy water containing writhing river fish. They wore fingerless gloves and heavy jackets to do battle with the icy shade but they were freezing on their perches. In the dead of winter they did not have much to sell other than herbs, onion, carrot and cabbage; much of already half rotten. Nargis thought anxiously of her little stock of onions. How long I spent sifting through sacks to find ones that were not spoilt. I hope people are buying them.

Malnourished school-age boys offered to carry their bags by hand and short, black-eyed porters beckoned towards their blue wooden hand carts, some daring to grasp at Mrs Harriet's sleeve as she passed by. Nargis wondered if her stupid brother was keeping an eye on the school children, making sure they did not steal extra pens or sweets. Was he flirting with local girls, or worse, sleeping with the door locked? Mrs Harriet lifted her chin high, stared straight ahead while Nargis smiled apologetically at everyone as she passed.

'When I focus on my tasks, the people disappear and become nothing more than challenges to overcome,' Mrs Harriet once explained. Clutching her designer handbag to her chest she picked her way past open ditches and frozen Korean ladies in pom-pom hats, trading pickled delicacies with wooden chopsticks.

Plastic kiosks purveying cassette tapes on one side of the market blared out Afghani wedding tunes, deafening passers-by. There was a woefully inadequate hardware section, selling poor quality tools and tins of Iranian paint. It peeled off the walls after one month and the colours had to be mixed to the right shade by hand using red, yellow and blue tubes of pigment. Inside a cavernous warehouse, traders sold homemade curd, cheeses, honey, sweets and nuts. Russian women huddled in a far corner, selling rough cuts of pork to the dwindling Christian Orthodox population, the meat sliced with machetes from a stinking pink corpse.

Mrs Harriet bought fat beetroot and a kilo of half frozen, muddy carrots, a hard clove of garlic and a bag of frozen onions. Nargis smiled. Mine are much better, she thought. She stopped to buy a piece of fairly fresh looking mutton hanging off a meat hook in a butchery kiosk. She prodded and poked it for a while and asked Nargis to request the price of the whole leg. In the summer meat dangled in forty degree heat and developed a hard yellow crust on the fat, but it was fresher in winter.

'If I marinade it from now to Saturday afternoon it will be tender enough to fall off the bone,' said Mrs Harriet. Nargis shrugged. She would have boiled it a long time then refried it in dark cotton oil and salt but she knew foreigners didn't like the taste of cotton oil. Her mouth watered. When did I last eat meat? The butcher deftly removed the mutton from its hook and started hacking at it with a blunt looking axe.

'I'm so homesick for the packaged cuts of meat in Britain. What I wouldn't give for a branch of Marks and Spencer,' she said with false jollity.

'Marki Spener?'

She shook her head and waved Nargis away. 'Never mind.'

December 12th, 2007, Tajikistan Countdown: 13 Months, 12 days

I impressed myself with my cooking last night. Even Henri seemed pleased. I am only sad that those Americans probably had no idea of the effort it took to find, cook and serve a three course menu in the Tajik winter. It was nothing short of a miracle.

A room full of people, talking, laughing, eating. They are strangers, the perfect guests. I observe as they chew my mutton dressed as lamb, the meal I spent three days preparing. I pour wine but never fill my glass. I am suspended like a perfect piece of art on invisible wires. I have left my body far behind, my pert behind perched at one end of the table. I watch myself smile and serve, I am elegant and gracious and distanced. I read his signals as he trained me to do, a hand gesture for the next course, a raised eyebrow if too familiar, too human, too much Me. I perform, I flirt. I do 'my bit'.

7

Nargis arrived at Harriet's house at nine in the morning. The guard reluctantly left his black and white television to let her into the compound and she climbed the marble steps, knocking on the front door. After five minutes she let herself in. Harriet had a towel wrapped around her head and was still in a state of semi-undress, over-plucking her eyebrows into long, thin arches in the hallway mirror, a piano concerto by Rachmaninov pounding away on the stereo. Shrieks of pleasure could be heard from the study where little Alexandra was building tower blocks to demolish with her father. Barely acknowledging her arrival, Harriet handed over fitful Leo, his cheeks flushed and swollen with teething and went to her bedroom to lie down.

'I'm exhausted, the dinner party went on and on.'

As Nargis had left her house that morning, winter sunshine had flooded the muddy yard, yet in the space of half an hour the snow had once again started to fall. Her pitiful slippers were once again drenched with melted slush. Her nose had started to run and she blew it on an old grey hanky that had belonged to her father and stuffed it back up her sleeve. Harriet returned to the hall to fetch her phone and saw her footwear, removed by the front door. She stopped, pursing her lips.

'Why do you Tajiks wear house slippers in the snow Nargis?' she asked.

Nargis flushed. She looked at her slippers making a puddle on the parquet. The feet of her stockings were wet through and she had left large foot prints on the varnish.

'I sorry Madam. I clean floor,' she said, blushing.

Harriet's expression softened for a moment. 'Yes, please clean up that puddle or it will leave a stain on the wood. But Nargis, that was not why I asked. Why on the earth do you wear house slippers out in the snow instead of boots. Is it traditional Tajik dress? Don't your feet get cold?'

Nargis squirmed. Wearing slippers has become Tajik tradition because no one has money for anything else, she thought. On the way to work that morning she had had to spend precious shop profits on urgent medicine for Bunavsha, using up the money for Hussein's school fees that week. She would have to knock at the headmaster's house later and beg him for mercy, citing her miserable background and Hussein's good marks. Her eyes stung and her head started to ache.

'I not have anything else to wear. In Tajikistan there is no shoes for good price and Chinese cheap shoe leak.'

Nargis wiped her eyes which had started to tear up. She bit her lip. Don't cry, don't cry, she told herself furiously.

Harriet did not speak. They stood in the doorway while Harriet scrutinised her for what felt like an age. Nargis was aware of what she looked like, she could see herself in the mirror. Her worn apparel, the threadbare elbows of her old pink kurta and the darned, faded Pamiri socks on her feet. Her hair was frizzy with damp, drawn back into a greasy plait. Her long, noble nose was swollen and red and a drip of snot hung there, unwiped. Harriet turned away with an unreadable expression. Nargis guessed that it had not occurred to her that she would be unable to afford a simple pair of winter boots. What does she think I spend my money on? She had told Harriet about her children and that she was a widow.

That afternoon, Harriet came into the playroom carrying an old pair of elegant leather winter boots.

Nargis blushed a deep red.

'Mrs Harriet, I can't.'

'Nargis, I want you to have them. I don't need them anymore.'

Harriet had a strange expression on her face as she watched her put them on. Nargis felt she had committed a violation, an intrusion, even though Harriet had initiated it. Like seeing your dead husband's suit on another man,

Nargis thought, cringing. The boots were long with a high heel and Nargis walked awkwardly in them. She looked even more bizarre with long black boots, brown headscarf, pink dress and a man's coat, but she did not care, her feet dry in sheepskin and leather. Mr Simenon noticed. His eyes narrowed and he beckoned Harriet into his study.

December 13th, 2007   Tajikistan Countdown: 13 months, 11 days

Henri is very annoyed. He says I will spoil the servants with my sentimentality, that they will take advantage. I can't see what the big fuss is about as I have mountains of shoes. I'm sick of seeing her walk around in the snow in thin house mules. Her toes will drop off with frostbite or she will catch pneumonia. Then what would I do? Henri wouldn't care, off to work as usual, but I really need her.

'I don't like it,' he said, 'you are setting yourself up for problems in the future'.

I'm raising her expectations, he says. You can't be friends with les domestiques. Yet, I spend all my time with her, so why not? What is this, this colonial neurosis? Like Kipling's Adela in A Passage to India, *Henri imagines dark deeds, future misdemeanours against us that have no grounding in reality. Why can't we be friends? I trust her with my children. She knows many of my most intimate secrets; when I bleed, when I'm ill, when I am sad. She knows what I drink, what I eat. She probably guesses when we have made love, when our sheets are soiled. She washes my underwear, cleans my toilets and scrubs my dishes. She wipes my children's bottoms and soothes their cuts. Yes, she is paid to do all of these things but she does them well, with care, with kindness. I've spent months watching her and I see that she has grown fond of the children, especially Leo, almost as though he were hers. It does not make sense that we cannot be friendly to one another when she is as close to the children as an aunt. I am tired of playing the role of ice queen, keeping her at arm's length with English reserve.*

63

Who invented the rules of servant/mistress propriety? I disagree with Henri, with Patty and Veronica. We should look after her. We should help her because she helps us. Of course, I will not tell any of this to him, there's no point.

Later I had lunch with Patty and Veronica at the Beirut Bistro. Veronica was elated, bubbling over with happiness. She looked different too, dressed in silk and stockings, her hair styled and set, she greeted us with glasses of one hundred and fifty dollar French Champagne. It turns out that Christian has been offered a new posting in Bangkok. She waited to tell us the good news in person. What a bitch! She has already decided where they will live (Bangkapi suburb; green, wonderful, garden, penthouse), which school to send her children to (The Swiss School, marvellous teaching standards, world class orchestra, olympic swimming pool) and what she will do for a living. Yes, Veronica is going to go back to work as a concierge with one of the large hotels, perhaps the Bangkok Hilton; she has an old contact there who will recommend her. She has gone on an diet, all the better to squeeze back into her old work suits and instead of ordering her usual shish kebabs and mezze for two, she picked at a bowl of fattoush salad and laughed at all her own jokes. A waiter popped open another bottle and as I drank, I felt waves of envy with every sentence about her new, glittering life beyond Dushanbe. Like a toddler, I wanted to stamp my feet and throw my hummus across the room. I left most of my mezze, my appetite gone. Her monologue on all things Thai went on and on. The shopping. The beaches. The diamond ring that she would buy with her first pay check. In the end, I couldn't resist and asked her, 'How will you keep your daughters safe with all those paedophile sex tourists?' She probably thought I was alluding to her husband, though I didn't mean that. 'They will be perfectly fine, as will I,' she spat.

Patty was monosyllabic. She started with champagne, then ordered a few vodka tonics to wash down the bitterness. As Veronica talked, my fondness for her dissipated. She will be gone soon. What is the point of her now? We perched on embroidered Lebanese cushions trying to keep the happiness for her from leaching out of our voices.

Tomorrow we are going trekking with Russian hiking guides and a group of enthusiasts. Henri insisted that I come and try out snowshoeing. The weather forecast predicts snow tonight, sunshine tomorrow, perfect conditions for trudging through snowdrifts with tennis racquets attached to my feet. Though I'm looking forward to getting some exercise, I'm shy, nearly mute, in the company of working expatriates. Fluent in Russian and well-versed in diplomacy, these are intimidating, seasoned experts on economic policy, Geo-Soviet politics, peacekeeping and embassy spying. When I do dare voice my thoughts, I imagine how I must sound to them, tinny and shallow, nothing but a twee, middle-class secretary-turned-housewife. Some listen politely, while others don't bother to hide their disdain. Get back in the kitchen with the children where you belong. At a recent Embassy lunch, I did end up in the kitchen with a screeching Leo, seated at the wooden table among the canapés, the soup tureen and a blank-faced Mongolian butler. I mustn't humiliate myself or say the wrong thing, because it reflects badly on Henri, they'll think he married an idiot. I'll keep myself to myself on the hike and try not to embarrass him.

On Sunday evening, Nargis walked to the bus stop through wet petals of falling snow and fading light. The new snow made a crunchy, grinding noise under her heels and she revelled in it like a child popping balloons. It had been an exhausting weekend, babysitting into the early hours on Friday night, working all Saturday, back again this morning for nine hours of childcare with a teething baby and a busy four-year-old who demanded a six-foot snowman. Mrs Harriet and Mr Simenon had spent the day in Varzob Gorge, half an hour from Dushanbe. They came back flushed with their exertions and a camera full of photos that Mrs Harriet showed to the children. Nargis peered at stunning views of snowy peaks, the landscape silent under ice. Why bother going up there? Another strange foreigner's pastime. Harriet looked unusually bright and alive and the hiking seemed to have done her good, despite the sunburn streaks on her nose and cheekbones. Her photos captured rocky rivers in valleys of red rock and granite, as well as the sharp orange-white light of sun on snow. Out there, only half an hour from the capital, farmers subsisted on muddy terraces with orchards of fruit trees, local breeds of tick-covered cattle and herds of black and brown sheep and goats.

'Look Alexandra, the farmers use donkeys to carry things down from the mountains,' Mrs Harriet said.

Nargis saw two battle-scarred wolf-dogs snarling at the camera from behind a rickety fence and shuddered. 'Those bad animal, for fighting,' she said.

There were pictures of curious, dirty urchins with dreadlocked hair, dressed in tracksuit trousers and spangled dresses, holey cardigans and cheap mud-covered wellington boots. They reminded Nargis of Hussein and Bunavsha, shivering at home.

After work, she went to visit Faisullo, her beautiful baby boy. It was as hard to leave him as ever, sorrow choked her so that her throat felt sore.

Nargis's sinuses throbbed as she trudged along and she wrapped her scarf across her face. Drawing her brother's coat around her in a bear hug, she thought about the last week. Savsang had arrived at the shop, glowing with excitement, a market porter weighed down with boxes of things to sell. Biscuits and crackers, packets of butter and sausages, crisps, noodles, New Year decorations, children's clothes in plastic covers from China, cheap cosmetics, toothpaste and hair clips. She became alarmed when she saw how much her new business partner had bought. She had yet to see more than half her rent money.

'I am so happy Azikav let me rent from you, in spite of…everything.' Savsang paused, looking sheepish.

'What?'

Savang turned away and picked up some items for stacking.

'Well, you know.'

'No, I don't.'

Savsang's voice turned to a whisper and she peeped out at the street for eavesdroppers. Her eyes were wide but friendly. 'In spite of the fact you left your *second husband.* You know.'

'Ah.'

'I admire you having the courage to do it, but you know... People around here... They talk.'

Nargis sighed. She went to make them a pot of tea. Savsang was too silly to bother fighting with.

She had arrived at the mahalla a little after seven after a frustrating journey. The buses had stopped early and she had no cash for a taxi. After walking around four kilometres through falling snow, she had managed to flag down a kindly off-duty minibus driver who took pity on her. Though tired, she decided to go to the shop and count the takings, kept in a small tin under the counter.

Savsang sat inside, casting a shadow on the wall, listening to the radio in the faded glaze of a bare light bulb. She did not shut up shop until eight that night, her small children in the care of her husband's cousin. Savsang greeted Nargis went back to her programme, a dramatic soap opera about three students caught in a desperate love triangle. Nargis looked at her macaroni packets and onions. Compared with Savsang's side of the shop, her own looked drab and incomplete. Quite a large amount of her stock had sold though. She was aware she needed to pay her friends back for their loans before New Year when they would need it for festivities. While out working her brother and father had been minding the store, taking turns. Yet, the tin was not where it should have been and there was no sign of either of them. They had not told her what they had done with the takings for the previous day as they were already asleep when she got home on Saturday night. She looked askance at Savsang, sitting with her little radio. No, as dim as she was, there was no way she would steal her money.

Stumbling in her haste to reach the house, she half fell through the darkness of the narrow alley up to the creaking gate. The falling snow gave the yard a white glow, lighting up the gloomy night. Inside, the children were huddled together watching television on an old Russian black and white with their grandmother. There was no sign of Abdul or Said.

'Mother, it's only me,' she called.

Gulya stood up, wringing gnarled hands.

'Shireen, your father and brother have not come home.'

'Where are they?' Nargis asked. 'The money is not in the shop.'

Gulya sucked in her breath. She looked older in the light of the weak bulb that came and went. She shook her head. and ran from the house, down the snow covered hill towards Rahman's choi hona, the mahalla 'tea' house.

'Father,' Nargis cried.

Abdul was seated on a purple quilt with Said. He already looked inebriated and smiled at his daughter, displaying rows of yellow teeth. He had removed his traditional velvet gown and sat in a threadbare checked shirt, his hat skewed on his head.

'Dobri Vecher,' he said merrily, slurring his words and swaying his small glass in the air. Vodka spilled out and landed in his lap, causing all the men to laugh.

The men sat around a low table. A china teapot, a vodka bottle, a bowl of nuts and several shot glasses were arranged on a small cloth as a centrepiece. One man snored softly, his mouth open to reveal tobacco-stained teeth and a stream of dribble. At her father's greeting, Said looked up and grinned. Her brother seemed as unaware of her anger as her father. The two of them sat with six others, a wad of cash lying on the floor next to them. Rahman looked apologetically at her and lit a cigarette. In the next room his wife sat watching television, embroidering a dress with sequins. He nodded towards his wife as if to warn her that she may be needed. She nodded back, her thick jowls wobbling in the dim light. He was used to outraged women showing up and dragging their men off into the night. Experience had taught him that many of these situations turned violent and he did not want blood on his carpet.

'Would you like to sit down and join your kin?' he asked. Tajik women rarely drank in public unless old or rich.

'No, Rahman,' spluttered Nargis. She could barely breathe. 'What are you doing, you stupid fools?' she yelled.

The men laughed and murmured vague insults. Rahman need not have worried about a fight. They were so drunk they could barely move. Abdul frowned but did not speak. He was still swaying from side to side. She lent down, whisked away the wad of cash and yanked a square shape from her father's coat pocket. She opened it with trembling fingers. It was the tin that had contained all the takings from the last two weeks, and Savsang's rent money, almost seven hundred somoni. It was nearly empty, with only one hundred and fifty somoni left, about fifteen dollars. Nargis calculated that five hundred and fifty somoni was enough for about eighteen bottles of vodka. How long had her father been stealing her takings?

Said slumped backwards on the quilt in a drunken faint. A tell-tale stain darkened his leg as she watched, horrified. Her artist friend Dimitri, still dressed in paint-stained trousers, staggered outside. She could hear him retching in the alley. Her money, dripping into the carpet, staining the mahalla with foul vomit. The little room reeked.

Shaking with anger, Nargis stumbled home in the mud with her money tin, crying bitter tears.

8

Nargis arrived at the Simenon household after a sleepless night. White winter sun shone across the garden, searching out any specks of snow in the shadows. Harriet was in the kitchen, back from the school run.

'Morning Nargis, how are you?' she asked, bustling about. Nargis murmured a non-committal response and went to the children's room to fold and put away their clothes. She felt crushed with misery and rage, numb to her daily chores. Her mind kept returning to her shop, her debts, the promises she'd made to loyal friends to pay back their loans. The blisters on her feet from walking the streets of Dushanbe with paintings to sell. Tears came and she blotted them on her kurta. The old hag, Firuza, had called on her way to work to say that her husband would be back from Moscow for New Year. She could hear her baby Faisullo babbling in the background.

'Kelline, we hope you will come to greet our son when he arrives home,' her mother-in-law said. 'He often talks about you on the telephone and begs me to forgive you for the scandal you caused. I always told him to marry a virgin, they're less smart and more grateful.'

Nargis held her tongue. That daughter-of-a-donkey still had her little Faisullo, she had to be civil.

Firuza paused. 'I'm sure if you ask nicely he will take you back.'

Squashed in the jolting mini-bus, Nargis felt sick. Marrying that bastard Poulod and becoming your 'Kelline' was the worst mistake of my life, she thought.

'I promise you, I'll think about it.'

The scar on her back throbbed as she folded blankets and plumped pillows. She knelt down to pick up a mountain of toys scattered across the carpet. Her knees cracked and her shoulders ached. Leo crawled to her and she stopped cleaning to hold him close.

'Sweet boy. I love you, my little sausage,' she whispered.

An hour later, Harriet came to find her.

'Nargis, I've made chicken-noodle soup for lunch. You can give some to Leo at twelve o'clock.' She pulled on a stiletto-heeled boot. 'I'll be spending the morning having a facial at 'L'Expertise', then lunch with Patty. Veronica won't be here. She left for Christmas in Berlin, the lucky cow. Berlin and then Bangkok.' Harriet sighed. 'Can you set the table and buy some naan?' She threw a few coins on the kitchen table and strode out, ignoring Leo's frantic wails. Nargis waited until her footsteps had died away and then sat down in the kitchen with Leo on her lap and a bowl of green tea. She stirred in three large dollops of sugar and wiped her eyes.

It was part of Harriet's weekly routine to go to a Tajik beautician called Nigora. A plump woman in her fifties with large warm hands that pressed her skin with creams and oils. On Wednesdays she had a manicure and pedicure and, on Fridays, once a month, she dyed the roots of her hair.

Just before one, Mrs Harriet returned smelling of rosewater and cold cream. The soup was simmering on the stove and warm naan lay in a bread basket.

'I feel refreshed now,' she said.

Leo held out his arms to be cuddled. Nargis stirred the soup and the chicken-scented clouds of steam caressed her face. Her stomach growled.

'Patty come. I put her in dining room next door.'

Harriet evaded Leo, planting a kiss on his forehead.

'Serve us and then put the baby down for his nap.'

Patty sat by the window, sunglasses perched on her nose, squinting in the winter sun. Her hair flamed in the sharp light, her crepe-skin betrayed by cracked foundation a few shades too dark. The room stank of her perfume and a faint smell of stale mushrooms.

'Hi Patty, I'm sorry, my facial went over time.'

Patty had already opened a bottle of sparkling mineral water and was perusing the table with a critical eye. Nargis came in with the bread and a lump of Russian butter on a dish.

'It's nice to eat some home cookin', the restaurants here are bigger'n Dallas,' she drawled. 'That French place. I am amazed it keeps goin'. I mean, who eats there apart from foreigners?'

Nargis grinned. No one ordinary in Dushanbe eats out except for foreigners, you silly ewe, she thought. Harriet stared out of the window at the street below.

'Lonely consultants with laptops seem to like it. Apparently rich Tajiks prefer places with private rooms, a good supply of vodka, girls, and shashlik kebabs. They certainly wouldn't pay French prices.'

Nargis shrugged in agreement. Her ex-husband Poulod would fit right into that scene if he could only afford it.

'Brian told me somethin' funny last night. He's heard that some sorry foreigners move in with Russian lookers when their families leave for summer vacation. Then, come autumn they're back home, goin' to parent-teacher evenin' at school, pushin' the trolley round the market on the weekend, even attendin' church.' Patty gave a cackle.

Harriet grinned. 'I'm glad Veronica got Christian to go back to Berlin with her.'

Patty shook her head.

'I can't imagine Henri doing that. He's very rude about men who use prostitutes. He laughs at men marrying local girls, obviously only after Western passports.'

'I'm glad I'm here, keepin' my eye on Brian. You just never know when temptation's gonna' hit 'em, do you?'

Nargis returned with a tureen of hot soup and started to dole it into bowls. Patty frowned.

'I'll do m'own,' she snapped. Nargis gave her the ladle. 'Oh my Gosh, Harriet, I'm dreadin' spring. All them stomach viruses runnin' wild. It is a wonder we don't all get sick just by breathin' Dushanbe air. I'm fixin' the maid to wash her hands whenever she touches dishes or silver wear, leave alone food.'

'Well, you can rest assured I made this soup myself and Nargis always washes her hands. Would you like wine?'

'Sure. I got nowhere to go. Or maybe a vodka tonic?'

Harriet got up from the table and poured Patty a generous vodka. Patty took a slug and wiped her lips.

'That's good. Takes the edge off, you know? I haven't been right since Veronica told us her news.'

Nargis gritted her teeth. The sight of the bottle took her back to Rahman's teahouse. Another stupid alcoholic. Nargis had often observed Patty drinking an innocent looking glass of 'water' at Harriet's parties, only to see her stumbling out of the door later, drunk on the arm of her red-faced husband.

'Nargis, bring some tonic water,' Harriet called.

From the dining room window, the two women watched a Tajik woman and her young daughter wander by. The woman was wearing a thick velvet kurta patterned with sequins and her hair was covered in a red shawl. She wore ezore trousers under her kurta and slippers and pushed an old pram full of naan wrapped in plastic. Nargis glanced outside. She thought of her mother, probably out selling naan at that precise moment with Bunavsha.

'Will you look at that? Dumber than dirt,' said Patty. 'Where do they think they're goin' to sell all that bread, with a bakery on ever' corner?'

Harriet watched the couple ambling past.

'Maybe they're trying their best with the options they have available to them. I mean, it's hardly easy to get a good job in Tajikistan, is it?'

Patty and Nargis looked at Harriet in astonishment.

'Now, just you wait a minute. They deserve to be sellin' naan from a baby carriage, because they do nothin' else to better themselves.'

Harriet's eyes flickered towards Nargis, who left the room with a loud clatter.

'All I'm saying…'

'No, Harriet. Don't you dare feel badly for these people.' Nargis stood still and listened. 'They deserve what they got 'cause they're trapped by their own inertia.'

Nargis pictured her menfolk lying around at home, sick with hangovers and slammed a cupboard door in the kitchen.

'It's the same in the U.S.A. Sorry-assed freeloadin' ever'where I look. Nobody ever drowned in sweat. We tax payin' folks have to pay for these sorry sons uh bitches. It gets me real aggervated. I thank God ever'day we have George Dubya and Laura in the White House, sortin' out those durn Yankee liberals an' protectin' us from these Moslems with Homeland Security and Guantanamo.'

Patty slurped loudly on her soup. Harriet was silent. Nargis heard her change the subject after a few moments, asking her about her preparations for Christmas. In the kitchen, Nargis wiped a cloth round the counters and threw dirty dishes into the sink. She snatched the pram, bundled Leo into it and stormed out, slamming the door.

Later, Mrs Harriet came into the kitchen.

'Alexandra has a Christmas nativity play this afternoon and I'll take Leo. You can leave early seeing as you worked through your lunch hour.'

Harriet stood in the doorway, hesitating. Then she said, 'Nargis, I'm sorry about what Patty said earlier.'

Nargis turned around to respond but before she could comment, Harriet was gone.

15th December, 2007, Tajikistan Countdown: Too depressing to calculate.

Patty outdid herself today. She got really drunk, slurring her words and swaying when she stood up. She stayed over three hours, nearly finishing the bottle. I don't understand why Patty stays in Dushanbe. She could go home, they have a house there. In the end I had to kick her out so that I could go to the school nativity play.

Alexandra was a beautiful angel. It really didn't matter that she fell over in the aisle, poor thing, she cried and cried. Henri wasn't there, he had an important meeting, but I took enough photos for an album. As a special treat I let the children go to the fast food outlet on Somoni Avenue for a celebratory plate of soggy chips with ketchup, a slice of spongy 'margarita' pizza and a play in the grubby looking ball pool. There were a few other locals, dark-eyed men smoking in leather jackets with demure looking wives in glittering dresses, monobrows and kerchiefed headscarves, well wrapped babies held in bony arms. Hopefully, the children won't get ill, I picked out all the salad and sanitised their hands well before they ate.

Nargis looked strange today, even worse than usual. There was a new look in her eyes, one I haven't seen before. Yes, that is what it was, she looked defeated. I wonder if this shop is too much for her. I didn't say anything but let her go home early. The last thing she probably wanted was my sympathy, especially after Patty's tirade about Tajiks. I have to admit, Henri was right about Patty. She is too much at times, even for me, but Journal, I ask you this; who else do I have?

9

Abdul slowly became aware of his surroundings. He could hear the thump-thump of his wife kneading naan dough in the room next door and the excited sound of his grandchildren's voices as they played in the muddy yard with friends. His bones ached. He realised he was lying with his face pressed into the threadbare carpet, dressed in his heavy winter coat. He tried to move his head and was hit by pain behind the eyes. Had he been in a fight? Struggling to sit up, Abdul opened one eye and saw that he was covered in dried blood from a gash in his hand. Nausea washed over him and he crawled towards the open door for some bracing winter air.

'Gulya! Prepare me some tea. Assist me woman. I'm ill,' he cried as he kicked the door open.

Outside in the yard the children scattered like birds. He slowly struggled up the hill to the toilet. It was a pit latrine, dug years before and getting perilously full. It reeked of stale urine and vomit.

'Gulya,' he shouted. 'Woman, come out here and wash down this latrine, it's a fucking disgrace.' Either his wife was ignoring him or she had turned deaf in her old age.

Nargis appeared at the crooked gate, her hair unkempt.

'You ungrateful child,' Abdul hollered. 'Coming and taking money from an old man in front of the whole village. I have never been so ashamed in my life to have such a daughter. First you taint my family name with scandal and now this. All the men are laughing at me.'

Nargis clenched her fists.

'Father, I did not leave my husband so that I could have my life wasted by another man. What kind of Muslim steals the food out of the mouths of his grandchildren and the clothes off their backs for alcohol? What kind of father are you to steal from your own daughter?'

She stopped to breathe, shaking. Gulya came to the yard and laid a restraining hand on her daughter's arm.

'Shireen, hush, he is your aksakal.'

Abdul ignored Nargis and climbed the muddy steps to the latrine.

Gulya gestured towards the neighbouring garden and whispered, 'Nargees. The walls have mice and mice have ears.'

Their neighbour, Sitora, stood at her tap-stand, smirking. Nargis turned on her heel and strode towards the shop.

Savsang was inside, Russian pop music blaring. When she saw Nargis she hurriedly switched her radio off and went to sit on 'her' side.

'*Assalum Alai'kum,*' she greeted piously. 'How are you today?'

'Oh please, don't ask,' said Nargis. She sat down heavily and put her head in her hands. Savsang's eyes narrowed.

'What's wrong?'

Nargis sat up and looked around, staring at the bulging shelves of produce, the piles of butter and 'halal' chicken sausages and boxes of biscuits. She noted with irritation that Savsang had placed strands of coloured tinsel across the front windows, so that customers could no longer see inside the shop from the street and they sat in the semi-darkness. She sighed.

'It's nothing.'

She got up to make tea on a sparking hob and came back with two bowls. 'Savsang, I don't want to pry into your affairs, but I have to ask, how have you managed to buy so many things to sell?'

'If I tell you, will you promise not to tell my husband?'

Nargis was taken by surprise. 'Of course.'

Savsang shifted her graceful body in her chair and leaned forward. 'I have taken a loan with the bank,' she whispered.

Nargis was impressed and envious. 'How do you do that?' she asked.

Savsang looked warily at the door as if her husband might be hiding among the tinsel strands. 'You go to the bank, ask for the loan and give them your identification and your house ownership papers. Then they give you whatever you want.'

Nargis sat back deflated. She did not have official identification documents or house ownership papers; her stupid husband had never obtained one from the previous owner of their house before he left for Russia. Her family lived in fear, paralysed by their inability to afford new papers and terrified that the old owner's family would find out and claim the house as their own.

'If you like,' said Savsang, 'you can share some of my loan with me. I took a little bit too much.' She giggled. In answer to Nargis's questioning look, she leaned forward again and stage whispered, 'Eight hundred and fifty dollars.'

Nargis gasped. No wonder Savsang had filled the shop with goods to bursting point. Yet, when Nargis looked around, she did not think that there were nearly enough items to make up that amount of money. New Year's Eve was in two days and the tinsel hung around the shop, unbought. Children's clothes in polythene adorned the tops of the shelves, yet they had not attracted one glance from customers. What else had she done with the money? Nargis noticed she was wearing a pair of gold earrings. There was also a new purple woollen coat with a faux fur collar hanging off her chair. It looked Turkish, high quality.

'What will happen if you can't pay the money back?'

Savsang looked slightly anxious.

'Well, that won't happen, dear, but they have kept the house papers as a guarantee as well as my identification document.'

Nargis stared. 'Your house? They will take your house if you don't pay? And your husband doesn't know?'

Savsang fiddled with her bracelet. 'Well, my friend Hassan says you only have to pay the bank back with small amounts. He helped me to arrange everything.'

Nargis raised an eyebrow. 'Who's Hassan?' she asked. 'Is he your brother?'

Savsang twisted her bracelet harder. She giggled. 'No, just someone I met at the market one day.'

As Nargis was locking up later, she noticed a quilt rolled against the side of the wall, empty bottles of beer and an open packet of cigarettes. She assumed they belonged to Said or Abdul, more evidence of her takings, wasted. She picked the cigarettes up and put them in her shop to sell as singles. She had not seen Said since her confrontation at Rahman's. No doubt he was staying at a friend's house, sleeping off a miserable hangover and too frightened to face her wrath.

It had not been a good day for takings. Only a few customers had come in to buy potatoes and flour and Nargis had sat bored, staring out of the window at the slow comings and goings of people on the road outside. Several people entered and said that they would like to buy meat and vodka from her for New Year, if she would bring them to the shop. She sighed, wondering how she would find the money. Savsang had also had a dismal day, only selling one strand of tinsel and a few sausages.

Nargis looked at the decorations and wondered about the mullah's reaction if he found out that Savsang had wagered their home with the bank. She was certain he would beat her and possibly divorce her, using the Islamic law of Talok, especially since she was his second wife.

Savsang had two children, a little girl aged four and a boy of six. What would happen to them? She was running low on supplies but had little money to buy more. In the meantime, Savsang's wares were spreading themselves along the shelves into her half of the shop. She scowled at the gay tinsel and closed the door, fastening the heavy padlock.

She trudged home through potholed lanes, walking slowly in the evening cold, greeting passing villagers on their way home for the night. Old Russian country houses from more prosperous times stood along the road, alongside more recently built mud brick houses. All shared cracked windowpanes, peeling paintwork and some of the doors and windows were lined with plastic sheeting, Tajikistan's version of double glazing. Front gardens were clogged with weeds and the roadside ditch was full of stagnant sewage, algae and food waste.

The wide river bank lay beyond the houses, at a winter low. The mahalla lay north of the confluence of the Varzob and the Kofharnihon rivers. It had once filled in spring to become a roaring gush of glacial water. Nowadays it remained little more than a trickle throughout the year, the water syphoned off to a hydroelectric dam near the city for summer electricity. Dushanbe's rubbish collection trucks stood still in the evening light alongside excavator machines used to dig out river rock for construction. When the wind blew from the West, the mahalla was assailed with the smell of burning waste from the large piles of rubbish deposited on the river bank each day. Down river, the waterworks extracted the polluted, untreated river water for the city population to drink. Beyond the river, snow-covered mountains rose majestically out of the valley gorge, their tops stained orange by the winter sunset. It was beautiful if one ignored the man-made filth.

At home, Abdul was nowhere to be seen and Said was keeping out of her way. The children were seated with Gulya, eating Chinese packet noodles and naan out of a large pot. They gave her wan smiles, slurping on the noodles. 'Roatan' noodles had become a mainstay in the diet of many households in Tajikistan. Cheap and filling, they were prepared in a few minutes. They were alternated with a poor stew of stale bread mixed with oil, potato, a little onion and water. The children soon finished eating and went into the other room to lie down on quilts and sleep. Over noodles and bread, Nargis told her mother about Savsang's foolishness and about Abdul and the lost money. Gulya shook her head and sighed.

'Shireen, I don't know what to do about him. He never used to be so bad but he's getting worse as the years pass. When he has had a drink, he doesn't care about anything, even his own grandchildren. He was never like this when his mother was alive and lived with us. I tried to stop him going to Rahman's house.' She wiped her eyes with a corner of her kurta. 'Perhaps you should sell the shop. It might be impossible to keep it going with such a father and brother to rely on.'

Nargis started, almost choking on her bread.

'No,' she retorted. 'How can you suggest such a thing? I worked for months, begged friends for help and took loans for that shop. It's all I have and I'm not going to give up now. I never want to be reliant on anyone else again. I'll find someone else to help me. But I'm scared. Savsang might have let the bank think it's hers. What if they take it away? I still haven't got the paper stamped that proves it's mine.'

Gulya looked at her. 'Savsang is a strange woman. You need to be carful of her,' she said.

'What do you mean?'

'She came to the house on Saturday night when you were working late and asked for the key.'

'Why would she want the key at night?' asked Nargis. Her mind went back to the quilt, the beer bottles and cigarettes. 'Savsang is seeing another man,' she whispered to herself, horrified. 'What a fool.'

Gulya was momentarily speechless.

'No. Her husband is the mullah of our mahalla, a pure, holy man of the *Quran*,' she said, scandalised. 'We have to tell him.'

'We can't do that,' said Nargis, regretting her outburst. 'Mother, promise me you won't tell anyone. You know how news travels here.'

Gulya frowned. 'But…'

'If he finds out, he will hit her and put her in hospital. I am sure he will divorce her and then she'll lose everything, her house and her children. They are still so little. Her parents will disown her. I can't let that happen.'

Memories of her own husband's violence and jealousy flooded her. Her mother sneered, her golden teeth glinting in the flickering light.

'You are too soft, Nargis,' she said sternly. 'All husbands hit their wives, especially when they find out they are cheating on them. And they deserve it too. You know the old saying. My mother used to repeat it over and over when I came to her weeping in the early days of marriage: 'Nobody beats a good wife who is obedient.'

10

Zavon Ismailov sat idle in his thick duffle coat, waiting, munching on sunflower seeds from a triangular packet of newspaper. One by one he toothed open the small crispy kernels, spitting the shells out of a chink of open window. The radio was on, bleating out a tinny Russian pop song, drowning the din of the construction yard. The high-rise would stretch skywards on land once used for a fruit orchards, a facade of progress and prosperity to cover poverty and repression. The City Mayor continually built multi-storey monstrosities across Dushanbe, hotels for phantom tourists; they remained at least two thirds empty or half-finished, testament to the power of corruption. Not that Zavon was political, but he couldn't help but wonder what it was all for and who was paying for it. He shifted in his seat, trying to stretch his large bulk.

With curly hair turning grey at his temples, he had a pleasant, easy going nature. People felt comfortable with him, even strangers, a useful quality for a taxi driver. Driving a taxi put food on the table but he preferred to work with his hands, by himself in his garage workshop. He had survived the civil war by fixing cars, home appliances and electronic equipment. A woman got into the car in front and it sped away. She reminded him of his wife, still in Moscow. Their marriage had fizzled out.

'I see no future, either for us or for Tajikistan,' she had said one day, mixing herself a vodka cocktail. 'Russia is my country now.'

Her hair, once long and black like raven's feathers was dyed mahogany and she wore a tight miniskirt. She yawned and took a drag from her cigarette. 'I am going out tonight with my girlfriends. I hope you'll be gone when I get back.'

For five long years Zavon and his wife had joined the million or more Tajik immigrants to Russia, moving from city to city, job to job, sending money home. They started off in makeshift accommodation in garages and eventually wound up in a vast dormitory under the immense Cherkikovskii market in Moscow, where his wife worked as a vendor. Eventually, they obtained residency papers but he had hated immigrant life. He longed for Tajikistan's kinder winter and the dry heat of the summer and missed the easy familiarity of his city. He hated being treated like a second class citizen by the brash Russians and found the size of Moscow intimidating. He and other Tajiks worked on construction sites in southern Moscow by day, travelling home in groups to protect one another from the skinhead groups, from ultra-nationalists who would beat them to death for fun if they could catch a 'black face' alone. They faced constant harassment from law enforcement, running from the frequent purges that targeted immigrant communities. He grew tired of paying bribes, of thanking the police for allowing him the 'pleasure' of working. Humiliated and alone, he returned home when his mother died, leaving an infirm husband and no other children, relieved to have an honourable excuse.

Their child, Dilya, lived with his mother-in-law in a Soviet era apartment in the twenty-third micro-district of Dushanbe. Visits took place in a stuffy apartment chaperoned by a shrewish grandmother in near silence, while an old clock ticked the minutes like a metronome and he desperately searched for something to say. Dilya was a pretty wisp of a thing, like her mother, but in character she resembled Zavon and was withdrawn. They had left when she was two years old. Zavon's wife promised to bring her to Russia later, but never did. Zavon had never visited her school, nor met her friends. He had no idea of her likes and dislikes. He had barely ever seen her cry, nor laugh. He found their meetings deeply embarrassing and sad and he burned with regret.

Zavon lived with his ailing father in an apartment block near Sultoni Kobir Bazaar, a huge market for hardware and machinery. Their seclusion was companionable. Zavon tinkered on car and motorbike parts at a rickety kitchen table, listening to an old wireless each evening. His father read the daily newspaper Zavon brought for him and sat out on the balcony in his wheelchair, where he fed birds and watched the activity on the streets below. An old bat from a village on the outskirts of town came once a week to do the washing and scrub the floors.

Zavon often longed for the touch of a woman, lying alone in his bed at night. He considered marrying again but had not met a girl he liked. He pondered whether to go to a local bar with friends. They met divorcees, women who were more liberal than traditional Tajik ladies. For fifty somoni or about fifteen dollars he could spend the night with one. But he couldn't bring himself to do it, partly out of honour to his mother's memory and partly because he thought of Dilya and how he would kill any man who used her in that way.

He had been surprised at the rush of feelings when his old school friend's widow jumped into his taxi one day. It was October and the nights had started to darken earlier, although it was still warm during the day. He was hungry, tired and looking forward to getting home for a cold wash. He was about to unscrew his yellow TAXI sign for the night, when a poorly dressed, straggly woman opened the door carrying half a sack of flour and slid into the backseat.

'Hofiz Sherozi Avenue please, the mahalla just below the cement factory,' she said. Her voice was distinctive and firm. 'Four somoni, okay?'

An outstretched, girl-like hand with bitten fingernails holding four coins reached towards his ear.

He looked in his mirror, about to argue and saw to his surprise that it was Ahmed's widow.

'Nargis! Assalom,' he greeted, turning to give her a shy smile. She slowly smiled back in recognition, her eyes creasing at the corners.

'Zavon! It's been a long time,' she said. Beads of sweat laced her forehead and she wiped her face with a sleeve. He felt a pang of pity for her frayed, faded cuffs, greasy plait and the callused hand, hastily withdrawn into her pocket.

'I will take you home, or wherever you want to go, for free.'

'Rahmat,' she murmured.

During the ride to her mahalla, they talked about the old days. Zavon had been best friends with her first husband, Ahmed. He had watched jealously as Ahmed fell in love, wishing he could find someone as pretty and devoted as Nargis. Only fifteen when they met, they were married on her sixteenth birthday. Zavon had attended his burial six years later with other men from their community. He recalled seeing her at the funeral Hodoii prayers.

'How have you been? You know, since Ahmed passed...' he asked, looking at her in his mirror. He noted that she had lost weight and aged a little, but that her kurta still covered a pleasing figure. Her black eyes, once so spirited, were somber and surrounded by crows feet. Her hair had unwound from its plait and fell around her face in a stringy mess. All the same, he thought, you could still see that she had once been a lovely girl.

She frowned. 'Life has had its ups and downs.' She caught his eyes in the mirror. 'I married again, a second time, but I left him last year. You might have heard?'

He shook his head. 'No. I don't know anyone from school anymore. After all, almost everyone is in Russia these days.'

Nargis sighed. 'Yes, that's true.'

'And do you have children?'

'Yes, three. And you? How's your wife?'

Nargis vaguely remembered him taking up with a pretty, delicate looking city girl several years after her own marriage. It was Zavon's turn to grimace.

'My wife's in Russia, Moscow. We have a daughter, Dilya, who lives here with her grandmother.'

'Were you in Russia a long time?'

'Five years. But I missed Tajikistan and when my mother died, I returned home to care for my father.'

Nargis commiserated politely.

The taxi pulled off the main road and ambled slowly into the mahalla.

'So this is where you live now, eh?' Zavon asked, looking around.

'Yes. My parents had to move during the war.'

She blushed and shifted forward to put her hand on the door handle. 'Please can you stop here on the main street?'

'Of course. It would be nice to see you again,' said Zavon, a little awkwardly. 'I miss my old friend Ahmed and hardly ever see anyone from school around here anymore. I'd like to see someone else from old times.'

She gave him a searching look. He looked away, unable to hold her stare. The old attraction he had for her persisted, he was sure she could feel it. It embarrassed him, she was a widow, for God's sake, and he was no teenager. He shifted in his seat uncomfortably.

'Maybe, if I can find the time, we could meet for samosa at Green Bazaar one of these days.'

They swapped phone numbers, Zavon assuring her that whenever she needed a taxi he would come without hesitation and for free.

'Please send my best regards to your parents.' He shook her small hand as formally as he could.

The sun was setting behind the hills that rose sharply from beyond the river bank. Orange and red skies tinted the mahalla with pretty colours, making the scruffy road and ramshackle houses appear rustic, almost pretty. In the distance the mountains appeared to shine in the soft evening light. A group of grubby children played in the street, pushing old bicycle wheels with hooks on wooden poles, an ancient game brought back to life by poverty. A small child, perhaps two years old, stood staring at him as he drove past. He wore an orange woollen hat on his head and Tajik rubber pointed shoes. His babysitter, a girl of perhaps four years of age, pulled on his hand as a car swung around the corner towards the little group. He glanced in the back mirror, at Nargis, stumbling along, struggling with her heavy sack. He had no idea why she hadn't wanted him to drive her all the way to her doorstep. Perhaps she is scared of what her mother will say, he thought. Zavon remembered his old friend Ahmed as clearly as if he had seen him the day before.

11

Nargis came to Harriet's imposing metal gate and rang the doorbell. Borun, a thin, stooped guard opened the gate with a gruff greeting, superciliously letting her pass. They did not like each other since she had rebuked him for being too forward in the guardhouse one lunch time.

'Married twice and now divorced? You must like it, eh?'

He had pinned her to the wall and only let her go after he had had a good feel of her breasts with an oily hand. Furious, Nargis threatened to tell Mr Simenon if he so much as looked at her again. Ever since, he had treated her like an insect. Resolutely patronising, he was wearing an ostentatious black Russian fur hat and a traditional jomas, a long velveteen gown bordered with silk thread. He shut the gate behind her with a penetrating clang. Unlike with the other guard, Musso, Nargis refused to lunch with Borun in the guard house. He talked as he ate, spraying spittle around the small room. Small and spindled, aged about sixty, he had a trimmed black moustache and dyed black hair covered in hair oil. Married, with a grown up son in St Petersburg, he kept a succession of cheaply made-up, ancient mistresses who reeked of musky perfume. When the foreigners were away Nargis had heard them giggling in the sagging guardroom bed. The perfect sycophant in the Simenons' presence, he would stop on his way home to bemoan his low wages and poor working conditions to anyone who would listen.

'Does he have to spit that green tobacco into the flower beds all the time?' Mrs Harriet asked. He constantly complained about Musso to Mr Simenon, who barely tolerated his presence. Alexandra did not like him, always evading his attempts to plant a sloppy kiss on her forehead or throw her into the air.

Nargis entered the house. Almost as soon as she hung up her coat, Mrs Harriet appeared in the hall. She looked excited. It was a shock, so different from her usual expression. Nargis stood in the hall, uncertain.

'Come into the kitchen for a chat, Nargis, have some tea.'

Nargis forced a smile.

'Yes, Mrs Harriet.'

They sat down at the kitchen table, Nargis stifling a yawn. Leo toddled in and climbed up into her lap. Her black hair was plaited, the top of her head hidden under a blue floral headscarf and she wore cheap dangling earrings that immediately captivated the child.

'You look quite romantic today, like a Romanian gypsy.'

Harriet laughed, a forced sound and Nargis looked blankly at her.

'Mr. Henri is going to Almaty tomorrow for five days on business, so I'll be alone here until the night before Christmas Eve. I'll need you to work longer hours than usual and stay to help me put the children to bed.'

'Yes Ma'am, but Mrs. Harriet, I will need taxi if it is dark, no bus after seven.' Nargis knew that Mrs Harriet could not call Ivan, an office driver, for personal favours when Mr Simenon was out of town. Harriet frowned.

'Alright, provided it is not too expensive.'

The microwave pinged and Harriet jumped up to take out a steaming mug of hot milk to which she added an espresso and some sugar, stirring it in with a silver teaspoon. Her movements were clumsy. Nargis guessed she had forgotten all about the promised tea. Mrs Harriet sat back down and leaned forward.

'So tell me Nargis, how's your new shop going?'

Nargis felt surprised and slightly affronted. Lends me money and now it is her business, she thought.

'Shop is open and lady I rented to there today. She selling my things too.'

Harriet's mouth fell open. 'You rented it out? But I thought you were going to run it yourself?'

'It still mine. She pay to rent and took loan for things to sell.'

Harriet was shocked when she told her about Savsang's house deeds and her husband's ignorance.

'What a fool to risk her home like that.'

'It worse,' said Nargis with a dramatic sigh. 'She has lover.'

'She has another man?' Mrs Harriet chuckled in wry amusement. 'You Tajiks never fail to do the exact opposite of what one would expect.'

She took a sip of her espreso.

Nargis felt a flicker of annoyance. I am nothing like Savsang, she thought.

'And your part of the shop? Is that going well?'

Nargis sighed inwardly. She debated whether or not to tell her the truth. 'No, it is not good. My father, he has vodka problem and took almost all money for drink.'

Harriet started to tap her fingernails on the table, her earlier gaiety gone.

'He took everything?'

Nargis picked at a splinter sticking out of the table and kept her eyes down. Her cheeks burned.

'Yes. All money from shop, seven hundred somoni. One hundred and fifty somoni left. He buy vodka and drink with my brother and friends.' Nargis felt frustration rising up to choke her. She took a ragged breath. 'I will sell food left and look for way to make more money in meantime.'

Harriet sat back and looked at her. 'Why did you leave your dad in charge of the money if you knew he had such a serious addiction?'

Nargis was discomfited by the scrutiny and stared at the floor. 'I didn't know he was that bad,' she cried.

There was a pause. Harriet leaned forward and lowered her voice.

'I'm sorry Nargis. I know what it's like. My mother has been an alcoholic for years, ever since my father left her, but she hides it well.'

Nargis's eyes widened. She looked up to find Harriet's eyes full of sympathy and felt a jolt of surprise.

December 18th, 2007. Tajikistan Countdown: 13 Months, 12 days

The chair is hard, straight backed but I daren't move a muscle. Blue-eyed Sofija, the best manicurist in Dushanbe, sits opposite me and concentrates, deftly painting each of my toenails with a perfect white curve. A stooped, brown-skinned cleaner in a blue coat limps by sweeping up hair clippings and wiping low mirrors with a chamois. I smell hairspray and dust. Heavily made-up hairdressers with purple rouge and blue eye shadow sit chatting in Russian. I feel their envy and resentment. No one talks to me, no one can. It's lonely but at least I had somewhere to go today. I brought my journal so that I have something to do other than staring hopelessly at Sofija. A purpose. A structure to my day as I count down the minutes of two years.

My pedicure will cost ten dollars, a pit stop at Shepherd's Crook Café for a cappuccino and a slice of carrot cake, another ten. The normal expenditures of the bored, cosseted, foreign homemaker. It's nothing to me, everything to her. I should help her again, but what if this is an elaborate scam? I know what Henri would say; 'Quand le vin est tiré, il faut le boire.' Once you start, there's no going back. Why do I hesitate? Nowadays, after years of living as a vulnerable expatriate, lost at sea, a 'stupid' foreigner, I trust no one, least of all myself. I'm like one of them now, these expatriate housewives I surround myself with, flailing about helplessly, the little power I have to effect change, wasted. I'm pathetic.

12

That afternoon Harriet drove Nargis home early, taking the children with her.

'Henri refuses to stay alone with them for more than a few minutes while he packs for his trip to Almaty, but I suspect it's because the Australian Tennis Open is on.'

The sleet had stopped and the sun had come out. Employer and employee sat in uneasy silence while Harriet drove north on Rudaki Avenue, out of the town centre, past Varzob Bazaar, the cement factory and down to the riverside. Nargis was too astonished to talk. As she turned into the hamlet, Harriet tried to start a conversation.

'Well, this is very picturesque,' she said brightly. 'Very nice indeed.'

Nargis grinned. She had been nearly struck dumb at Harriet's insistence that she see the shop that afternoon. At least she had managed to sneak off to ring ahead and warn her mother. As they drove slowly along the river road she fervently hoped Gulya had folded away their bedclothes and swept the house. Mrs Harriet will see how poor we are, but it can't be helped, she thought. Perhaps it is a good thing.

There were a few people milling about, women walking with small children and elderly women chatting on a bench at the corner. Nargis nodded at her father soberly as they drove past a clutch of old men playing backgammon. She did not point him out. He watched them pass. Her children appeared at the car in tatty woollens and black pointed rubber boots. They were accompanied by Gulya. She wore her usual black velveteen kurta dress, fingerless gloves, a faded grey cardigan and a black embroidered headscarf. The children's faces were streaked with mud from the yard.

'Mrs Harriet, this is my mother, Gulya, and my children, Hussein and Bunavsha,' said Nargis hurriedly. They got out of the car. 'Mother, why didn't you wash them?' she hissed. 'They look like they've been rolling in a pig sty.'

Gulya smiled. 'A good mother is never ashamed of her children. I've prepared the house for guests, that's all I had time for.'

Nargis turned to Harriet.

'My mother says you should come in house for tea before I take you to shop.'

'Oh... pleased to meet you,' said Harriet. She looked uncertainly around her, aware that the sun would soon set. 'Why don't we just go to the shop straight away. There isn't time...'

Nargis stared at her beseechingly.

'Please come in, just for one cup of tea. If you don't, my mother will be insulted.'

Harriet hesitated, then shrugged her shoulders and followed. A little hand reached up to find hers. Alexandra looked anxious.

'Mummy, why does that old woman have golden teeth?' Alexandra asked. 'She looks like the witch in the gingerbread house.'

Nargis shook her head with a smile.

'Children, so funny things they say.'

'People made golden false teeth before, when the people called Soviets were here,' Harriet murmured. 'But it is not nice to call a nice old grandma a witch.'

They picked their way through the sludge and up a small alley to the house, entering the yard through a makeshift metal gate made of old pipes. Harriet's stiletto-heeled boots sank into the muddy ooze. She walked unsteadily, carrying a wriggling, protesting Leo. All the way to the house Nargis's mother chatted in Tajik, smiled at the children and made welcoming gestures. Nargis saw Harriet looking around her as they entered their yard. She was embarrassed to note the dirty dishes that sat congealing next to a bar of grey soap by the tap stand. Assorted junk collected from dumps by her brother leant against a fence. It looked ugly and unkempt, as usual. Removing their shoes, they entered the house.

'Is this your house or does it continue...' Harriet said, tailing off as she realised that what she saw was all there was. An old carpet covered one wall and their ancient television sat in the corner. There were no knick-knacks, no pictures or photographs on the walls. Nargis saw it afresh through Harriet's eyes, the chipped, ill fitting door, the cracked windowpanes stuffed with plastic bags.

Nargis pointed at the quilt rolled out on the floor and gestured for her to sit down. She watched Harriet's face change as she realised that the 'wall' dividing the rooms was only made of material. Her mouth was open. Suddenly the wires for their old bread oven sparked in the socket, making them jump. The flickering light bulb only served to highlight the grubby paintwork, cracks and mould marks on the damp walls. Harriet looked around her, clearly uncomfortable. Gulya went outside with an old kettle to fill it for tea.

Alexandra entered gravely. With characteristic aplomb she stated, 'This is very a small house, Mummy.'

Harriet sat down awkwardly next to a pile of quilts stacked on top of a traditional metallic decorated chest, a *sanduk,* beside an old wardrobe. Nargis was struck by how odd it was that Mrs. Harriet, with her glossy blonde hair and perfect French manicure, was sitting in her shack. Alexandra sat down next to her mother, looking a little fearful. Nargis knew when she went to other people's houses, there were playrooms full of plastic colours and drawing tables, light, warmth and comfortable sofas.

Alexandra frowned and piped up, 'Mummy, where are all the toys?'

Harriet laughed uncertainly.

'There aren't any toys, I am afraid.' Nargis said. 'My children don't have any.'

Alexandra was aghast. 'Weren't your children good for Father Christmas last year, Gissie?' she asked.

Nargis was confused. 'Father Christmas?'

Harriet cleared her throat and pushed her daughter towards the doorway where Hussein stood shyly watching.

'Yes. He is coming soon so maybe your children will get toys, if they have been good.'

'Don't be silly, darling.' Harriet laughed self-consciously. 'You can play without toys you know. Use your imagination,' she said with exaggerated cheerfulness.

Bunavsha, five years old, entered and went to Alexandra holding out a dirty grey rag doll. She was very thin, with olive skin and knobbly wrists and ankles, her dark brown hair in a ponytail. She wore a kurta of the same material and shapeless style as her grandmother's under a faded pink cardigan. They had used leftover pieces of material for the child's dress. Alexandra was wearing a pretty outfit, a pink embroidered woollen sweater and matching purple velvet trousers with delicate flower motifs. She had a pink ribbon in her thin strawberry blonde hair. Bunavsha pointed and babbled excitedly.

'There, you can play with the dolly,' said Harriet to her daughter, relieved.

'My daughter likes Alexandra's shoes,' said Nargis. 'They are the same colour as her namesake flower.'

'Bunavsha means purple?' said Harriet, confused.

'No, the purple flower. The one in window in kitchen.' said Nargis.

'Oh...Violet. I bought those African Violets from an old Russian lady on the street,' said Harriet awkwardly.

'Many Tajik women are named after flower. I am Nargis, after yellow spring flower.'

'Narcissus? Like the daffodil?'

'Yes. My mother, Gulya, is after name for flower, Gul. My sister, who die eight year before, was named Lola, tulip.' Gulya looked downcast as she said the name. Alexandra got up and scampered into the room next door with Bunavsha while Gulya squatted and poured water into a teapot. She took a small tin from the wardrobe and took out a pinch of black tea leaves, throwing them in with a flourish. Reaching up into the dark recesses of the wardrobe, she brought down a cloth bundle and unfolded it to reveal some pieces of stale naan bread.

'We eat here, like picnic,' said Nargis. She saw Harriet hesitate, then pick up a piece of bread. She held it gingerly between two fingers. Alexandra came back into the room whining.

'I'm hungry, Mummy.'

Usually on visits to other people's houses, there was juice and cookies or bananas for the children. Alexandra looked around but didn't see any. Perplexed, she pressed past Nargis to sit down next to her mother. Bunavsha and Hussein were on their best behaviour. They may be dirty and poor but they have good manners, Nargis thought. She shot Hussein a proud smile. Gulya watched Alexandra, her lips pursed in disapproval. Harriet blushed and grabbed her roughly by the arm.

'Shhh…,' she hissed. 'You had lunch an hour ago.'

'But I want something to eat, Mummy,' she cried again and picked up a piece of the bread, stuffing it into her mouth. She scowled.

'Yuk! I don't like this, Mummy. It's too dry,' she moaned, throwing the piece back onto the cloth with the rest in disgust.

'Alexandra, behave,' ordered Harriet, picking out the piece.

Harriet would not hesitate to throw such old bread out, Nargis realised.

'I want a drink, Mummy,' Alexandra moaned, grabbing Harriet's tea bowl and making it slosh over the side. 'Isn't there any juice?'

Nargis looked embarrassed and dispatched her son to buy biscuits; 'Picheen', a Russian word Harriet recognised.

'Please don't buy biscuits for us, you know she just ate lunch,' Harriet begged.

Before long, little Hussein returned to the house with a type of locally processed halal sausage and some plain biscuits from Nargis's shop. As soon as Leo saw the sausage he held out his chubby hand and shrieked. Nargis laughed and fed Leo and Alexandra sausage and poured more tea for herself, while her two children watched them eating from the doorway. Leo was wolfing down the sausage, barely chewing at all and Harriet looked crestfallen.

'They don't need to eat, Nargis,' she pleaded. 'Please give some to your children.'

'They know that guests are served first.'

Her heart gave a twinge. They did look pale and pinched underneath the dirt, especially by comparison with these well-fed foreign kids. Hussein was frightened but Bunavsha was less subdued and tried to entice Alexandra to play, talking to her determinedly in Tajik. Harriet didn't eat much. Nargis guessed she found the bread too stale, sticky in her throat, as she took huge gulps of tea after each bite. She is probably wondering if she will catch diseases from the stained crockery. All the while, Gulya squatted next them on stockinged feet, pouring out tea and trying to force the food in Harriet's direction.

'I don't think she wants any more, Mother,' said Nargis.

'You must think we behave terribly at home,' said Harriet suddenly. 'The children break toys almost daily and we pour half-drunk sippy-cups of milk down the drain. I am forever chucking old food from the fridge and putting stale bread in the dustbin. You must think we are wasteful gluttons,' she said.

Nargis opened and closed her mouth.

Gulya looked from one to another. 'What did she say?' she hissed.

Harriet grinned at Nargis and Gulya relaxed.

'It's okay. There's no need to translate that.'

Nargis laughed.

'Don't worry, I won't.'

Gulya seemed to view Harriet as a fairy godmother come to save them. She embarrassed Nargis by insisting she translate her pleas for work. Nargis saw Harriet sigh and was grateful when she asked her questions about her mother's previous employment. Gulya had never had paid work, being too busy with children. She could not speak Russian or barely read or write, having never been to school. Harriet wondered how this was possible, as she had thought that in Soviet times everyone was forcibly educated, even the girls.

'Gulya's uncle, a Headmaster, paid her parents for her to work in house as maid while he marked her examinations as A,' Nargis explained.

'He stole your future from you,' Harriet said, appalled.

'Oh well. What is past, is past,' she said, waiting for Nargis to translate. 'Besides, it is not so important for girls to go to school. They just get married.'

Harriet chuckled.

'Your attitude reminds me of my own mother sitting in Dorset.'

Gulya nodded her head towards Harriet and grinned. 'Ask her for some cash,' she hissed. 'That man came again this morning for the electricity bill and I am tired of hiding in the latrine.'

Nargis winced.

'Mother, I will not.'

'Well, maybe she can find a good job for your brother. I am sure she knows people.'

Nargis sighed.

'We can't ask Mrs Harriet for the world. It's not fair,' she scolded.

Before long, Harriet decided they must move from the house and see the shop. Leo was restless and it was past four o'clock. She yawned and shifted on the uncomfortable quilt, the hard floor making her bones ache.

Extricating them from the house, Nargis led the way. Alexandra reluctantly walked with Hussein and Bunavsha. As they strolled along past gaping potholes, different villagers came to greet Nargis, taking in their little procession with curiosity. She kept up a running commentary as they passed people and houses.

'She is a nurse, lives nearby, nice lady. That old lady is Russian, she lives with her son in the house we just passed. He is an artist called Dimitri, a good friend of mine.'

Nargis frowned at the memory of that night at Rahman's Teahouse. Dimitri had come by the next day with sorry stammers and downcast eyes to apologise for his part in the debacle.

'I sell his paintings at The Shepherds Crook Café.'

She knew everyone and they all greeted her respectfully, eyeing her elegant companion. They reached a small building with blue peeling window frames, a front porch and a huge, ancient metal set of scales outside for weighing grain. The shop was locked.

'Where is that silly woman now?' Nargis muttered to herself crossly, kicking a stone into the concrete ditch. The children sat despondently on the front stoop.

'Does she often leave so early without telling you?' asked Harriet. 'It's only half past four. Surely this is the best time to sell food to people going home from work?'

Nargis nodded, looking grim. As they stood there, several people came by and peered through the window wanting to buy things for dinner. She asked some little boys whether they had seen Savsang.

'Oh yes,' said a plucky little fellow aged about seven. 'She left in a taxi, about half an hour ago. We watched her lock the door and leave. She wouldn't give us any sweets.'

Nargis's face was dark and fierce. Harriet looked disappointed. peering through the front window.

'It looks rather like the old haberdasheries and department stores of England until the 1970's.'

Nargis looked inside. The floor was swept. At least Savsang was keeping the place clean and orderly. Nargis called her mobile telephone but there was no answer.

'How much do you want to bet she is with her boyfriend?' said Harriet wryly, wandering over to look at another shop window. Nargis felt affronted.

'She can't be,' she said, dialling again. After a brief conversation Nargis closed her phone. 'This making me crazy,' she said, horrified. 'A man answered and told me Savsang is 'busy' and can't talk.'

Harriet shrugged, raising her eyebrows. 'I am sure she *is* 'busy', Nargis.'

19th December, 2007, Tajikistan Countdown: 14 months, 11 days

I am still reeling. I can't believe that someone I employ to work in my house lives in such conditions. It was like the African poverty one sees on the television, but worse in a sense, because it was so cold and dank. The mud, ankle deep in her yard, reminded me of a Dorset dairy farm. No wonder she looks so terrible sometimes; her greasy hair under her kerchief, her pallor, the stains on her coat. Now, I understand what she is up against. When I saw her pit latrine, the wooden washhouse on the hill, the way they all have to sleep and eat in that tiny shack, I felt tearful. How could I not have known? I assumed she lived in an old Soviet high-rise block made of brick and plaster like our other employees, not a shed of mud, wood and polythene. Her children were so sweet, so polite. So pinched and skinny underneath the dirt.

Her shop looked great. I felt ashamed when I saw it, my earlier suspicions were utterly unfounded. All the effort she makes to try to rise up and better herself, then her useless father takes her money, pisses it away on vodka. It really is too tragic. I am going to help her if she asks again. I will lend her whatever money she needs to stay afloat.

Henri was angry and confronted me when we returned, when I admitted to him where we'd been. 'I thought I told you to distance yourself from that woman,' he yelled. 'Why are you going against my wishes? She will take advantage of you and then your "friendship" or whatever you think you have with her, will be over.'

I was defiant. I didn't like his tone. I told him, 'I think we should give her a pay rise actually, just a few more dollars per month because of the rise in food prices.' Henri's lip curled. 'You see, it's already happening. Il faut réfléchir avant d'agir'. *First the boots, now a pay rise. Next, it will be taxi fare and 'Nargis, ma cherie, you look tired put your feet up while I do-the hoovering for you,' (When Henri is angry he speaks in staccato, his Bruxelles accent thickening.) 'She has set out to make you feel guilty and* voila: *You are going to act exactly as she hopes, spoiling her for all future employers. What will come next, eh? Eh?'*

I left the room in a hurry then, thinking about the loan, hoping he would not read the truth in my eyes. Thank God he doesn't know about that. I must admit, he has a point. I do feel guilty, but not in the way he thinks. I must try not to complain so much around her.

13

A rich family in the mahalla were having a large celebration for New Year and tradition dictated that as wealthy Tajiks, they must host family and friends in flamboyant style. Osh or pilov in Russian, a traditional Central Asian dish, would be cooked with rice, onion, chickpeas, chopped carrots and fried lamb, swimming in brown cotton oil and black onion seeds in a huge cast iron deg over a roaring fire; doled out to all. The mistress of the house, a plump, haughty lady with a long Russian leather coat covering her ornately embroidered kurta dress entered the shop, looking around in thinly disguised disdain.

'We will pay you eight somoni per kilo if you can deliver 50 kilos of rice to our home by New Year. I'm asking you, as a favour to your family.' Nargis made a quick calculation in her head. She stood to make about one hundred somoni or just around 30 dollars, a nice profit, provided she could find transport to Ghissor Market, a small town around forty-five minutes from Dushanbe, and a loan for the rice. Rice was cheap there, only six somoni a kilo.

'Of course I will. Thank you for coming to me.' Nargis smiled at her with a confidence she did not feel. With her shop supplies growing thin, Nargis was desperate to restart her ailing business. I have to accept, she thought. If I turn her down she will never ask me again. If I can get the money for the rice I'll be able to buy the vodka and the meat that others have asked for. I will be able to recover.

The deal had played on her mind the whole day. As Harriet sat drinking tea in Gulya's house, Nargis wondered how to broach the subject. How will Mrs Harriet react? Will she be angry? Worse, will she fire me? It was a risk she had no choice but to take.

The following day, whilst feeding the children their pancakes for breakfast, Nargis mentioned a 'favour'. Harriet's elegant shoulders slumped. Nargis knew that she would be thinking of the warnings given to her by her friends that day at the café.

'What? What is it?'

Nargis took a deep breath and tried not to stammer.

'I need borrow two hundred somoni, sixty dollar. Please. I will buy rice for rich family early tomorrow and make good profit to replace money gone by Father. I give you whole money back in two days.'

Harriet looked sternly at her.

'Is this why you asked me in for tea yesterday?' she said. 'Are you playing me for a fool?'

Nargis reddened.

'No, Mrs Harriet. Tajiki people always invite guest for tea, is tradition. There nobody else I can ask, except you.'

She held her breath. Harriet took a sip of coffee and stared at her. Then the corners of her mouth turned up and she raised her hands in mock surrender.

'I already decided that if you needed more, I would lend you more, one more time.' Harriet waggled a finger at her. 'One more chance, to replace the one you lost. I want to have faith in you Nargis.'

Nargis was flooded with gratitude. She grabbed Harriet's hand and shook it formally, her left hand on her heart.

'Rahmat, Mrs Harriet.'

Harriet smiled. Their hands dropped back to their sides.

'Do you promise to return the money to me, in full, in two days?'

Nargis nodded wordlessly.

'Okay then. Keep your money safe this time. I really do wish you the best of luck.'

Nargis struggled with herself for a night before calling Zavon. They had not spoken since meeting in September. She had been too cautious to call, knowing that a friendship would set tongues wagging in the mahalla. If I don't ask, I will have to waste money on bus tickets and a market porter. I know he will take me for free. She held her breath and dialled his number.

'Da?' answered a gruff masculine voice.

'Assalom,' said Nargis, faltering. 'This is Nargis.'

'Nargis, how are you these days?'

'I am fine. I've opened a small shop. How are your family?'

Conversational preamble over, Nargis gathered her courage.

'I wonder… I wonder if I might ask you for a favour.'

'Ask. Anything.'

'I wonder if you might be able to take me to Ghissor Market tomorrow. I need to buy forty kilos of osh berinj and it would be very helpful if…'

'What time?'

'About six if possible,' she said. 'Before you go to work.'

'Oof, so early in the morning.'

Nargis smiled girlishly into the phone.

'Yes, I must go early, in order to buy the cheap rice before it is sold out. I would be so grateful. For the sake of our old friendship, won't you come?'

'Sure. I'll be there at half past five. I told you that you can rely on me for help any time and I meant it.'

The next morning, Nargis shivered in the darkness on the street below her house. The wintry dawn had not yet begun to break. She fervently hoped that no one would see her. There would be awkward questions or curious stares from the neighbours to endure. She had decided to stop flirting. It was not fair on the poor man, when she really only wanted him for his car. Zavon's taxi moved into view. Too late, Nargis spotted Sitora, the most vociferous gossip in the mahalla, leaving her compound and coming down the alley towards the street. What is she doing up at this hour? Cornered, Nargis responded to her greeting. Zavon got out and courteously opened the back door and Nargis was forced to make introductions.

'Sitora, this is Zavon, an old friend of my first husband. He's helping me bring osh berinj from Ghissor Market,' she said, trying to look nonchalant.

Sitora peered inquisitively into the vehicle. What is she looking for in there? Nargis thought in irritation. She nodded in Zavon's direction.

'Assalom Alai'kum, I greet you with God,' she whispered devoutly, with a sarcastic grin.

Nargis gritted her teeth and got inside the vehicle, slamming the door. Well, it couldn't be helped. No doubt by noon that day the whole mahalla would be buzzing with the news. A divorced widow getting into a strange man's car at dawn could only mean one thing.

The trip was quick without many cars on the road. Nargis gazed at fields of barren cotton plantations, the small farm shacks at the side of the road.

'I only have to remember the cotton farmers to know I am not the worst off in Tajikistan,' she said.

Zavon clicked his tongue.

'I heard the authorities are forcing them to grow it again this year instead of food, even though cotton prices are low. They have no choice though, they are all indebted to the government for the cost of seed. They will probably have to remove students from schools again to pick it.'

Billboards came into view every few kilometres, depicting the President as a wholesome farmer in a field of wheat, a kindly teacher to all school children, a progressive engineer in the factories. Flapping Tajik flags lined the highway. Past Ghissor lay the border with Uzbekistan, a land of plenty from whence the rice came.

The market was already alive with busy bargain hunters. Nargis pinpointed a stall and haggled hard. After ten minutes, they agreed on a good price and shook hands, six somoni a kilo. She could barely contain her elation. After a quick tea break, Zavon lifted the heavy sacks into the boot and drove her back to her shop in comfortable silence. As they came to the small building, he looked impressed.

'This looks like a good little business.'

Nargis smiled.

'Insh'allah, it could be.'

He brought the car to a halt and turned to Nargis where she sat in the back seat.

'It has been nice to see you again.'

Nargis smiled at him despite herself.

'You are too kind. Thank you so much for your help. When I have more money I will pay you back for this journey today.'

'No need,' said Zavon indignantly. 'I am happy to help any time I can, I told you.' He shifted slightly in his seat. 'I know that it has not been easy for you since Ahmed died.'

Nargis stared out of the window.

'It is so long ago, eleven years since we were married but still my memories of Ahmed are sharp,' she said.

'I can imagine. You were a great love match.'

Ahmed had been a tall young man with deep brown, trusting eyes and beautiful olive skin. She had loved stroking his chest under her fingertips as they lay together after their marriage and had never been so happy or in love as during those days. They lived with his parents and sister in a small room in their two room apartment, a room that became their private paradise on sunlit afternoons when the in-laws were at work. The civil war had just ended and Dushanbe was rife with criminals, guns and food shortages, but inside their room, held by Ahmed, Nargis felt safe. She decorated it with small bunches of narcissus, her namesake flowers, or sweet smelling roses stolen from the neglected flower beds outside abandoned Soviet municipal buildings.

Even though she was so young she had agreed to the marriage readily. She knew Ahmed loved her. He treated her like a queen, saving six months for the dowry. On her sixteenth birthday she left her home for his. She basked in his adoration, a welcome change from the treatment she received at home, ignored by her parents in favour of her brother. He worked night shifts as a security guard at one of the foreign organisations in town, faithfully bringing his wages home. He did not drink or play with desperate war widows. After the wedding, a small affair typical of wartime, Nargis still had a term of school left. Each morning they met for a few moments as she left for school. She returned to him each afternoon and lay next to him for a few hours.

After a year, Hussein was born. He slept with them in their little room. Later, Bunavsha was born and made their family complete. Nargis was so happy, she failed to notice that Ahmed had grown pale and thin. While the rest of his body grew skinny, a lump on his throat started to grow. He refused to visit a doctor, saying that they needed the money for the children. By the time the cancer was diagnosed it was terminal. After only three months, he died, aged 27, leaving them devastated, her parents pushing her straight into the arms of Poulod. Nargis stirred herself from her memories to see Zavon looking at her with concern. Her eyes were wet. She wiped them with her sleeve. A high proportion of young Tajiks got unexplained tumours. There were sinister rumours that the Soviets had used Tajikistan as a dumping ground for radioactive waste, hidden in long forgotten, unmarked caches to degrade for a thousand years, leaching into the water-table and the soil, destroying lives.

'You were very far away just then,' Zavon said. Nargis shifted towards to door of the car. It was useless to imagine ever having another man in her life. She was still not over Ahmed's death and did not believe she ever would be. She had made the mistake once before, trying to marry a second time, even after acknowledging that she would never love anyone else. She had no picture of Ahmed, Poulod having destroyed the one photo she had, but she didn't need one. She had memories of him in her head. She felt guilty for leading Zavon on. Any contentment to be found with Zavon will never be felt as deeply as the loss of Ahmed, she thought. It was time to stop taking advantage.

'Zavon, I don't want to hurt your feelings. You've been so kind. I have to tell you, though, that I will never be able to have another husband.'

Zavon glanced away and his ears turned red. After a moment he spoke.

'I understand, though I don't know why you would feel you need to tell me that.'

Nargis felt stupid. I must have misread the signals, she thought, berating herself. Of course he's not interested in me in that way, he's still married. Keeping eyes averted, Zavon helped her with her sacks of rice. He drove away slowly with a small wave. Nargis sighed heavily, swore under her breath and went to work.

14

A day later, Nargis went to work to find Harriet tapping away on her laptop in the study, Leo on one knee. Nargis picked up a coffee cup and straightened a cushion. Then she went to Harriet with her hand outstretched.

'Mrs Harriet, here is all your money.'

Nargis thrust a wad of somoni notes into her hands. Harriet's face lit up. Her eyes shone.

'Nargis, I can't tell you how delighted I am. So you managed to get the rice yesterday morning?'

Nargis nodded.

'Yes, I…'

'That's great.' Harriet gestured to the computer screen with a flourish. 'Nargis, I think I can get you some more work with foreigners. You need the income to really get things going.' She gestured at her laptop. 'I'm writing a free advert in our English newsletter for expats in Tajikistan. I'm sure I'll find you another job for those days when you are not with us. We don't have to tell Mr Henri about it.'

Nargis did not know how to react.

'I don't… thanks.'

'I said you speak English, have experience with children and that I can provide a good reference. Look.'

Nargis peered at the screen. All she could see was a small white box with unintelligible writing.

'Thank you,' Nargis murmured.

She left the study to make the beds and change Leo, who had a sagging nappy. Why the sudden interest in my affairs? She wondered. Nargis almost preferred Mrs Harriet as she was before; superior and indifferent. This new version was like an overeager puppy. Nargis yawned, climbing the stairs with heavy legs as Leo tried to struggle from her grasp. Doesn't she realise I have been up since before dawn lugging sacks of rice around the mahalla with

Said? How does she think I have the energy for more hard work with foreigners?

That evening, the children bathed and clothed in pyjamas, Nargis got ready to go home. It was dark outside and bitterly cold with a chill wind blowing icy gusts into the window panes, making them rattle. She wondered if Harriet had called a taxi and waited anxiously at the door. Half an hour passed and she decided to go to her.

Nargis found Harriet laughing uproariously on her internet phone with girlfriends overseas. A large glass of red wine sat on the table, half the bottle gone. She caught sight of Nargis hovering by the study entrance and groaned.

'Hold on a minute,' she said. 'Nargis, why are you still here?' she asked coldly. Nargis looked at the floor.

Because you want me to stay late, you silly ewe.

'I was waiting to ask if you call me taxi.'

Harriet pretended to hit herself on the head.

'Silly me,' she said, trying to laugh it off. 'I completely forgot. You'll have to walk down to the hotel on the corner and pick one up there. Borun can accompany you.'

Nargis frowned. She was not going anywhere in the dark with that pervert. Damn her, she thought.

'I have number of friend with taxi,' she said quickly.

'I can see you aren't keen on going with Borun,' Harriet chuckled. 'I can't say I blame you. He gives me the creeps too with his slimy, wet lips, tobacco stained teeth and oiled-back comb-over.' She giggled into her headphones. 'No Sarah, I'm not talking about Henri. That sod's living it up in Kazakhstan tonight while I have to sit here in dull old Dushanbe.' She turned back to Nargis. 'Pass me the number.'

Nargis was full of gratitude when Zavon's car pulled into the driveway. Said's coat was woefully inadequate against the harsh wind and the snow had begun to fall once more. This time I must pay the fare, she thought.

'I can't thank you enough for coming to get me in this miserable weather,' she said, full of remorse for the way she treated him the day before. His crows feet creased around his eyes.

'Don't mention it. It is not often I have such a sweet meeting with a customer, even one who is just a lovely friend,' he said, winking with exaggerated significance. Nargis laughed, taken aback. She relaxed.

'Well, I like to have the chance to see friends too, it can't always be work, work, work you know.'

'You know our great poet Rudaki said:

> There is no happiness in this world,
> better than meeting a friend,
> there is no bitterness more bitter to the heart,
> than separation from a friend.

Nargis grinned. She looked at his strong, reassuring hands on the steering wheel and snuggled into the warmth of the blanket in the back seat. She suddenly had an overwhelming urge to stroke the soft hairs on the nape of his neck. What a shame he's married. She blushed at the unbidden thought and pushed it firmly back into her subconscious.

Date: 23rd December 2007, Tajikistan Countdown: 13 months, 7 days

Henri will be back from Kazakhstan later. I shall cook something lovely for us and open some good wine. This week has dragged on and on with no one to talk to. I regret the silly argument we had on his last night here. He's been unusually quiet, only calling once to see how we were. I miss him.

I feel increasingly lost, adrift. It is slowly dawning on me that nothing I do has any meaning whatsoever. Nargis paid me back as promised, but it was a short-lived triumph. Any sense of purpose I felt in trying to help evaporated when I saw her lack of enthusiasm for my efforts. She probably thinks I'm nothing but an interfering busybody, fiddling in her private affairs. Nargis: A project, something to do to pass the time. Who would want to be reduced so? Now, I wonder if Henri was right after all. Perhaps my behaviour will do nothing but make things uncomfortable for both of us; the barriers are simply too insurmountable to bring down. I was angry with myself and short with her later, I couldn't help it. I knew she was waiting for a taxi but I ignored her there in the hall, a pathetic sort of revenge for my own shortcomings. I got drunk and can hardly remember how I got to bed. I have no idea if Leo woke in the night. If he did, I didn't hear him cry.

15

On her next day off, Nargis was at the shop. She had already swept the dust onto the street and was wiping neglected counters when her phone rang. She glanced at the number. It was not one she recognised. Zavon?

'Alo' she answered breathlessly.

'Good afternoon, dear wife,' said a voice.

Poulod. She nearly dropped the phone. Her stomach turned over and she felt a tingling sensation on her skin. His hand strangling her as he ripped her underwear. The thrusting pain. She reached for her stool and sat down.

'What do you want?' she said with false bravado.

'I'm back from Russia for New Year. I was calling to see what you are doing, where you are and whether you would like to see our son later,' he said. His voice was as cloying as syrup. 'I would love to see you again, shireen.'

Nargis grimaced. Now that he was back in town, it would be difficult to visit Faisullo. It had already been almost two weeks since she had last seen him and every extra day felt like a year. Poulod did not have a job to go to, nor many friends left in Dushanbe, so he would be hanging around like a bad smell. Most men were economic migrants these days. She had no idea how long he would stay in Tajikistan or even if he had a job to return to in Russia. Possibly he had a new family there, a new wife and child to hit.

Nargis wished he would divorce her and leave her in peace. He would idle in his parent's apartment, watching old films on television all day while his mother waited on him with tea and plates of his favourite foods. Despite the forcefulness with which he had held on to his son when she left him, he had never shown interest in Faisullo. He was now two and a half years old and could be difficult, though he was shy of his father, not really knowing who he was. Nargis worried that the first time Faisullo behaved like a normal toddler- throwing a tantrum, refusing to obey or destroying something precious- Poulod would react in the same way he had with Hussein and Bunavsha, by using his fists. She made up her mind.

'I'll come to your apartment this afternoon with my brother. Let your mother know we're coming.'

The visit was difficult. Faisullo was overjoyed to see them, hugging his mother and refusing to leave her side. Said, embarrassed, stood awkwardly in the doorway. Bringing him as chaperone was necessary in case Poulod asked her mother-in-law to leave on some pretext. She was terrified to be alone with him. The year before, when visiting her son, he had tried to rape her in daylight, pinning her to the ground, his vodka breath nauseating her. Only the early entrance of her father-in-law had stopped him. He had reluctantly let her go, breathing heavily, while she, sobbing, pulled up her underwear, rearranged her dress over bruised thighs and fled. With Said standing guard, she knew he would restrain himself. She asked Firuza, flitting in and out of the living room like an agitated bee, for permission to take Faisullo for a walk to get some sweets. Poulod refused.

'The child stays here,' he growled. He sat immobile on a chair before them like a fat, malignant tumour, staring at her with an expression designed to intimidate, his thick legs splayed to accommodate his huge, saggy testicles, his large feet in stained, fetid socks. His face reminded her of a fleshy, overripe apricot and his full, wet lips and sunken dark eyes repulsed her. With swarthy skin, his excessive drinking in Russia had already stained his face with the tell-tale signs of vodka addiction. His fists hung from thuggish muscular arms. His neck was thick, shoulders broadened from many hours lugging heavy machinery on construction sites.

For all his work abroad, it did not seem that Faisullo had been bought any new clothes, nappies or toys. Nargis hated

Poulod, an emotion so strong it made her breathless. She tried not to let her emotions show, knowing that he would make her life more difficult if he knew the extent to which she wished him out of her life. It amused him, she knew, to taunt her with his presence. He would enjoy provoking a limping, injured animal, bullying a crippled child at school or teasing a blind beggar with bits of paper instead of real money. He did not speak, did not take his eyes off her. Nargis ignored him and concentrated her attention on playing with Faisullo, seated on the floor with a small toy boat.

When she finally got up to leave, Faisullo panicked, his little face pale, his eyes dark and filling with tears. He toddled after her into the hall.

'Mamma, no go,' he wailed. His crying turned to sorrowful sobs. 'No leave me, Mamma,' he begged, clinging to her legs with all his strength. 'Take me, Mamma,' he cried. 'I want see 'Navsha and 'Sein. Why me no come?' he screamed. She extricated herself from his grip and gave his struggling little body to his grandmother. Trying to block out the sound of his wailing, she walked quickly down the stairs from the apartment. Her heart felt as though it were being pierced. She found it hard to breathe and felt dizzy, grabbing Said's arm for support. Poulod came to the top of the dank stairwell.

'Hey, bitch,' he yelled, all semblance of self-control gone. 'I'll be seeing you soon, cunt!' He spat a globule of phlegm on the ground. The door slammed. Nargis and Said walked faster, not knowing if he had decided to follow them out onto the street. Her legs trembled and her heart did not slow its beating until she was safely on the bus.

Christmas Day, 2007, Tajikistan Countdown: 13 Months, 5 days

I got up early to try to make it feel authentic for the children. I'm drowning in homesickness, worse than ever. As luck would have it, there was no snow today, only sleet and fog. It was an overcast, ordinary day, the yellowing slush scraped into messy piles in the garden, the surrounding mountains hidden under a dense metal-grey bucket of cloud, the lawn a morass of mud. The fairy lights displayed nothing but orange Persimmon fruit rotting on wet branches. I dressed grumpy children in woollen hats and went to an American nativity service with guitars and tambourines at the Russian Baptist church. I sang and smiled and cringed, missing the purity of Anglican carols sung by candlelight. Henri, staunchly atheist, refused to join us, even though I begged him to come.

The turkey was stringy and dry, a deep-frozen lump from far flung Brazil. I made a Christmas pudding with only half the ingredients needed and without suet. It was the wrong colour, alarmingly beige. We ate it with homemade frozen vanilla yoghurt, there being nowhere to buy fresh cream or custard powder. No party crackers of course. The table felt too small, too silent. I missed my mother's drunken frivolity, my uncle's coarse jokes, the yearly debate about whether or not to watch the Queen's Speech. Alexandra groaned and pushed the food around her plate. Henri dutifully masticated the rubbery turkey, washing it down with red wine.

The Chinese Christmas tree is flashing, blue and red lights that give me a headache. We can't leave it on for too long without a faint smell of burning plastic. The children like it though, so it will do. The house is strewn with garish pink and orange tinsel. This morning, I filled handmade Pamiri stockings with sweets, oranges and bad quality Chinese toys that fell apart after five minutes of play.

Henri promised me he wouldn't work, yet I saw him twitching, one eye on his Blackberry, even as we unwrapped presents. What can possibly be so important? He has done nothing to contribute to the day except show up, having been away in Almaty until the 23rd. I sense his absence, how he is going through the motions for what he believes is appropriate 'family man' behaviour. After dinner, I called my mother

117

and we waved into the webcam, smiling in Santa hats until our faces ached. I imagined the easy familiarity of cousins, aunts and uncles around her table. Her special port jelly and a roaring fire in the hearth, her homemade pudding drenched in rum and lit with blue, dancing flames. I briefly spoke to Grandmother. Her cracked, powdery face was fuzzy and the sound broke but I could still hear the sadness in her voice. She is ninety-one, nearly deaf, out from the nursing home for the day. 'Stay healthy, Granny,' I shouted. 'We will be with you next year.' I blinked away the tears and reached for the wine.

For the fortnight leading up to New Year, city children were treated to gifts from Bo Boy Barfi, the Tajik version of Father Christmas and his sidekick, Barfak, the snow girl. Pantomimes played in the Mayakovski Theatre, filling the stalls with sweet-sucking, crisp-crunching, over-excited youngsters. Nargis sat in the theatre trying in vain to translate, wishing her children were there too. Harriet got tickets for the City Circus, a huge concrete arena where they sat crammed together in draughty wooden seats to watch gymnasts, acrobats and snake charmers, a relic from Soviet times. There was a special party at Alexandra's school and different Embassy events. Beautiful songs were sung about the Jesus-God and Mrs Harriet listened with red eyes, knocking back hot brandy and spiced wine, choking on mince pies. Nargis chewed her lip and watched; she was like a woman drowning. Mr Simenon seemed not to notice, immersed as usual in his laptop. How terribly Mrs Harriet misses her England home, Nargis thought. She made extra efforts to be cheerful with the children.

All Dushanbe celebrated the main holiday of the winter, New Year's Eve, holding parties and open air concerts in city squares. Fireworks began at nightfall and continued in flashing bursts to midnight. Children set off bangers in the street, frightening old ladies and sending the stray dogs into a frenzy of barking. A huge, gaily decorated 'New Year Tree' was erected before the brassy arches of Somoni

Statue and local singers came to regale audiences with traditional songs on rickety wooden stages.

'I have no desire to go out into the cold and watch fireworks,' said Harriet. 'The Christmas season is finally over and I've no more energy. Henri will open his 1997 Chateau Neuf Du Pape and lie on the sofa watching the celebrations in real time long after I go to bed. What will you do, Nargis? Will you go out somewhere to hear a band? The Botanical Gardens, perhaps? Patty called to say that they've put up a stage for live music opposite her house. She is very cross about it.'

Nargis shook her head. The once majestic Botanical Gardens depressed her, the lower branches of trees hacked off by thieves in winter for firewood, the serene lily pond clogged with weeds and algae and the old, magnificent hothouse cracked and rusted with neglect. She shrugged.

'I think I will work in shop.'

Nargis felt a mixture of sadness and hope for what the New Year might bring. Her family had been invited to a party, so at least on that night, they would eat well. As she left that evening, Mrs Harriet stopped her on the street outside the compound.

'Hey, Nargis, wait a moment.'

Harriet rushed to catch up with her. She was blushing and flushed in her sheepskin coat and her hair was in disarray, a hat hurriedly clamped down on her head. A flurry of snow blew up into their faces, light flakes falling from a dark grey sky. From her pocket she surreptitiously produced two little presents wrapped in glittering paper and ribbons. As she spoke, little clouds of vapour made smoke-like funnels in the frozen air.

'I… I know you don't celebrate Christmas in your home, but I thought for New Year, your children would like a toy. I… It's not much, just a little something.'

The shop was dark and chilly when Nargis arrived to set up for the night. Savsang arrived and they switched on the radio, made steaming bowls of sweet tea and waited for customers. Jolly, carefree teenagers came in to buy small presents and bottles of Pepsi from Savsang. They served to remind Nargis that she had aged before her time. She longed to go out and enjoy the night like she used to, but her girlfriends from school were long married with husbands and mother-in-laws who disapproved of any association with a woman like her. I am little more than a prostitute in their eyes, she thought. While the husbands wondered, the mother-in-laws whispered and watched and cursed. Instead of joining the rest of the nation in celebration, she sat in the semi-darkness serving customers, carefully printing the detail of each sale in her small exercise book, filled with a grim sense of purpose.

Savsang sold a few more strands of tinsel but her artificial New Year trees sat untouched in the corner. She sighed over them and lamented her stupidity at having bought ten so close to New Year. Nargis made sympathetic noises and wondered how she would ever pay off her debt to the bank. A few days later she came into the shop shrouded in a headscarf. When she removed it, Nargis could see that her upper lip was bruised and cut and her jaw was mottled with a purple stain. Nargis's face fell. Savsang shrugged. Her eyes were dark.

'Hassan. I lent him some of the bank loan to thank him for his kindness in arranging everything for me. He hit me when I asked for my money back. I told my husband I fell.'

Nargis guessed the loan would be long term, their relationship short.

'Did he say...?'

'He's spent all the money. He still loves me though, I know it. After he hit me, he begged me to run away with him to Russia but I refused. It was the hardest decision of my life but I can't abandon my children.'

Nargis nodded in sympathy.

'No one could do that.'

'One of my earliest memories is the day I was told I was to be betrothed to Mullah Azikav. He is a respected member of our clan. I was about four years old. I was brought up to respect tradition, duty and never question my parent's wishes. I honestly never expected to fall in love, to become as weak and helpless as a fish on a hook. I've never experienced the kind of passion I had with Hassan before.' Her voice was full of longing.

Nargis smiled. 'I had that with my first husband, Ahmed.'

Savsang blushed and hung her head. Tears glittered on her eyelashes. 'I've stained the white cloth that symbolises my female purity. Now, all I can do is try to live piously for the rest of my life.'She touched her split lip tentatively and winced. 'When Hassan refused to give me anything to pay the bank this month, I threatened to tell his wife. That was when he hit me and said he would tell my husband I'm a whore.'

'Donkey!'

Savsang shook her head. 'No. He's just disappointed that I love my children more than I can love him.' She blew her nose. 'I'll pay January's rent when I can.'

Nargis pitied her too much to insist. To Gulya, she said, 'I cannot throw her out of my shop. She will lose everything, the stupid ewe.'

Nargis was astute enough to know that Savsang did not stand a chance of making back the money she had lost. Even if she sold her New Year decorations at discount price she would not make enough to pay the bank off and still bring home a wage to her expectant husband. It was just a matter of time before he found out. Nargis noticed her gold earrings had disappeared. Taken back to the jewellers to pay December's interest to the bank.

16

Rudaki Avenue was calm, warm in the afternoon sunshine. Harriet put on a sheepskin hat and joined Nargis and Leo as they were leaving, saying she needed a little air. A wedding procession drove past, horns blowing and ribbons flying. They waved at a painted, mono-browed bride smiling proudly in a sateen white meringue.

'Nargis, it's New Year, 2008. It's time for new beginnings, don't you think?'

Nargis thought of her shop, her children and her unresolved relationship with Poulod.

'Yes, I hope. But Nav Ruz in springtime is when we Tajiks celebrate new start.'

'I need to work in an office again. I have asked Patty's husband to help find me something.'

'You, Mrs Harriet? Work?'

Nargis's mouth fell open. Work? She lives the life of a queen, eating in the best places, spending hours in fancy salons, no scrubbing or worrying about paying for food, electricity, or water. Nargis shook her head and chuckled. Harriet smiled wanly.

'I knew you wouldn't understand. Henri won't either. I guess I want to be needed. I am so useless here in Tajikistan and Leo will start school soon. Then, what will I do with myself? My life has no meaning at all.'

Nargis considered this.

'I think I see. Owning shop make me feel good. Better than sitting in husband apartment as the Kelline, being watched all time by mother-in-law. Earn money is good too.'

Harriet looked down and they walked on, in an awkward silence.

'Anyway… Let's stop for tea,' Harriet said.

They passed the rustic city mosque with its blue minaret, an ugly, newly built bank with blue glass and yellow plastic tiling that belonged to the President's son-in-law. The sun shone, casting orange rays across the buildings, a moment of colour in all the grey. Leo fell asleep in the heat, his head lolling forward in his stroller. They stopped at the grandiose, white marble Rohat Tea House, an enormous, popular Tajik café infamous for its ability to give people stomach viruses. Harriet's phone rang. She answered, gesturing to Nargis to take a seat, order the tea. In some agitation, she paced back and forth in front of steep steps, her phone glued to her ear. Nargis heard her laugh hollowly.

'Never mind. I just thought I would try, thank you for your help.'

She rang off and looked down, swallowing her disappointment. Nargis felt a pang of sympathy for her, despite herself. Harriet rubbed at her eyes angrily and came to the table.

'It seems it's not enough to *want* to work,' she said. 'You have to have something specific to offer. Of course, I don't, other than secretarial skills and then, only in English. Hopeless really.'

She sighed and stirred her tea. For a moment it seemed to Nargis that Mrs Harriet was trapped, a caged nightingale. They sat in silence under the beautiful, hand-painted ceilings of the tea house. A rare example of Central Asian art in Tajikistan, they were painted in blue, red and green with flowery motifs echoed in the bright head scarves of the waitresses. Nargis loved these ceilings. They reminded her of better times. She had been maybe seven or eight years old when she sat here with her little sister Lola and drunk tea out of delicate bowls, utterly awestruck. Her father had smiled a lot as a young man.

A pot of green tea and a few meat samosas arrived. Indian pop music blasted Bhangra on a fuzzy, mounted television. Two men on another table were smoking over tea cups, azure-suited and dark eyed with green velvet, square-shaped hats on their heads. They glanced over briefly, flashed glinting teeth and went back to their card game. Harriet stirred sugar into her tea and gazed out onto the street. Her eyes did not register the shops opposite, full of hand-painted crockery and tapestries from Uzbekistan.

Earlier that day, Harriet had hosted several newly arrived couples at her house. She made a huge effort over the food, preparing everything to perfection, yet during the lunch she seemed detached, adrift, joining Nargis in the kitchen on unnecessary pretexts almost as though she preferred her company to theirs. Leo sat on the floor under the dining table with a sing-song toy, playing the same tune over and over until Henri ordered Harriet to take him away.

'Those women will be working here in Dushanbe,' she had said wistfully. 'Rita has an important job in a charity and the other one is writing her PhD on the Soviet collapse.'

Nargis peeped from the kitchen and saw two serious looking women sitting in stony silence. One glanced at her watch. They didn't look like much fun.

'Maybe you should have call Veronica and Patty as well?' said Nargis.

Harriet winced. 'I don't think so. I'd feel even worse.'

Over the last few months, Harriet had started drinking at lunchtime alone, a few glasses of white wine. As the afternoon passed, the bottle emptied and joined a growing pile for the maid to carry out to the municipal rubbish skip on the street. The day before, Nargis walked into the kitchen at 11am to find Harriet staring at her manicured, red painted hands holding a bottle and a corkscrew.

'These are my mother's hands,' she said shakily. Nargis understood. She put the bottle back in the fridge, yet the wine was back at Harriet's side by lunchtime.

They finished their tea and paid the bill. Harriet looked at her watch.

'It's getting cold. If you take Leo home, I'll go and collect Alexandra by foot. It's the only thing I had to do this afternoon so I'd better not be late.'

She turned to Nargis, stopping the pram with her hands.

'Nargis, thanks for listening. Mr Henri will be home tonight from his business trip. I feel so lost when he's away so much.'

'It nothing. Mrs Harriet, you will find job, no give up.'

'You're sweet, but I don't think I will. No one wants me, not even for free.'

Wandering slowly down ancient, sycamore tree-lined boulevards, Nargis lifted the stroller over cement ditches and deep potholes. She thought about her employer. All that easy money, shining beauty, that nice house and two lovely, healthy children, yet she still wasn't happy. What makes a person happy? she wondered. I am happy when I am in my shop, serving customers; making enough money for clothes, medicines and food for the children and knowing I am the one who keeps them out of the gutter; the sound of their laughter; the precious moments I spend with my little Faisullo… Mrs Harriet has got it wrong.

The sunlight was fading and it was growing cold and blue, the sunset casting long, freezing shadows across the street and onto the buildings. It would snow soon, the air smelled clean, changing from a wet leaf, papery smell in the sunshine to pure ice, the kind of cold that made the nose ache and reddened cheeks. The puddles had already started to crackle underfoot. She shivered and buttoned her brother's coat, pulling on gloves and her headscarf and checking the blankets were secure around Leo. He had woken up, but sat patiently in his all-in-one winter coat like a beetle lava, blue eyes peeping out from his woollen balaclava. A proud threesome of prosperous, unobtainable teenage virgins with relatives in Russia paraded past in daringly tight jeans, glittery spangled T-shirts and stilettos. They grinned at Leo in their make-up masks, wrapping

Turkish wool around lithe bodies. A lone woman sat at the trolley-bus stop in a holey cardigan, waiting patiently with a pinched face for a sparking, Soviet relic to transport her east across the river to the high-rises. At the junction with the Presidential Palace, they watched as the trolleybus was carefully re-hooked back up to the electricity line by a pole bearer.

January 14th, 2008, Tajikistan Countdown: 12 months, 16 days

I'm convinced that the only way I can be happy again is if I find a job. I daren't tell Henri, but I've asked all my friends to find me work. I'll do anything in an office, even volunteering. To be honest, this will probably come to nothing in any case. Already, friends are calling to tell me they have failed to find me anything. Patty rang and said that her husband says that with no degree and without fluent Russian or Tajik it's useless. Dushanbe is full of local girls looking for secretarial positions, girls who are probably more intelligent, younger and prettier than me and willing to do anything for their bosses, including those 'special' tasks not in the Terms of Reference.

So I ask you Journal, is this my life? You answer me coldly: Yes, and you'd had better accept it or go mad. To move from post to post as Henri's 'dependent', unanchored to anything aside from marriage and children. It's not enough, but it should be. I know I sound like a spoilt princess. But I'm scared I'm going to become like them, those expatriate women with no home of their own, no roots and nothing to do but snarl at the poor maids. Shall I wait eagerly for monthly PTA meetings to pester beleaguered school teachers or live from one glittering charity gala to the next? Shall I give in and join a golf club? Will I greet middle age with an ever enlarging arse and an undiagnosed drink problem? Soon I will be un-needed and unappreciated because the way things are now, I'm little more than a pretty appendage. So, I ask you Journal, what are my options? Divorce and life as a single mother in England? An affair? With whom? This is such a small place, everyone knows everyone and I'd be found out in a second.

17

Mrs Harriet was up early and bright the next day, already arranging the chairs around the edge of the imposing living room when Nargis came in to work.

'We're in here,' she called. 'It's the International Women's Club meeting, so I need some help getting everything organised.'

'You again, Mrs Harriet?' Nargis felt a flash of resentment. It was a terrible waste of money, in her view, hosting thirty fussy foreigners, not to mention the time it took to clean up afterwards.

'Yes, I offered. I thought, why not? I have both the time and space. Besides, I enjoy having something to do.' Harriet smiled, handed over Leo and rushed out for fresh cupcakes and scones at The Shepherds Crook Café.

Nargis stacked teacups and saucers on the bureau and filled the milk jug, wondering who would come. She was fascinated by the women from India who wore orange silk saris with red spots on their faces and hennaed hands. A shy Japanese woman had bowed at Nargis when she entered, perching on the sofa to eat a biscuit delicately with tiny, papery hands. For a few hours the house was filled with magical language and colour. Nargis helped serve and greet, listening to snippets of conversation. Tajiks came too sometimes but did not tend to return, intimidated by people like Patty who were openly rude about the facilities and standard of living in Dushanbe. Some came in smart suits, direct from the office. Grandmothers, students, breastfeeding mothers and even the women accompanying contractor husbands working on roads and bridges outside Dushanbe came. Childless and curiously peripheral, they lived outside the city for much of the year in workers camps with Chinese labourers. Christian missionaries in Tajik dress with plaited hair and a clear-skinned glow came with zealous entreaties to attend events. Then there were the ones like Harriet, living in lonely luxury, almost completely removed from Tajik reality.

The gate bell rang.

'Hi yer, anyone in?' a cheery voice called from the hall. Nargis hurried to see who it was and found the gate guard with Mrs Emma, the IWC Chairwoman.

'Hi, Nargis, how are yer I'm come early to help set things up. It's dead ace of Harriet to host so much.'

Emma was dressed brightly as usual with untamed, frizzy red hair coming loose from a bandana and a pair of blue framed glasses perched on her nose. She removed her coat with little hands dwarfed by big silver Indian rings and kicked off sheepskin boots. The guard, Musso, had insisted on carrying her large plastic folder from the gate. He passed it to her and smiled, closing the door behind him. Everyone liked Mrs Emma; she was ceaselessly kind. She spoke English with a funny accent from Northern England. Nargis gestured towards the kitchen.

'Please come in, you like tea?'

'Aye, ta love, I'll aver tea and a long sit down.' She sat down at the kitchen table and pointed at her folder. 'This is my little presentation for the meetin today.'

Her enormous dangling earrings jangled and swung as she talked. Usually she sat breastfeeding in meetings, her large white breasts with light pink nipples on display, but today the baby had been left behind.

'Me fella's got the day off so I left him with a bottle of me expressed cow-juice and Thomas the Tank Engine,' she said with a smile. She opened the folder and took out some pamphlets. 'Want one?'

Nargis looked at the pamphlet for clues. 'Women's Refuge', written in Tajik. She grew serious and contemplative.

'Very good thing,' she said. 'For woman who have bad husband? Thank you for paper.'

Harriet entered, her cheeks flushed with cold and eyes unusually bright. Emma got up and hugged her. Nargis put the kettle on and started washing up.

'Look at you, all done up. I've got me stuff here, look, me bag's chocka. Have a gander at this.' Emma passed a pamphlet to Harriet. 'This is what I want the club to get behind. Reminds me a' the family centre in Merseyside whur I used to work. Wife battering's terrible in Tajikistan, so I think we should help raise money for the women's refuge.'

'Is this a pamphlet for Tajik women?' Harriet asked. 'Why is it such a problem?'

Emma dug in her folder.

'I'll read you a bit of my prezzy that the refuge gave me, hang on a tick.' Emma cleared her throat and began to read in a stilted staccato. '"Civil war, economic collapse and the resurgence of culturally traditional Tajik values after the Soviets left have all combined to lower women's status in society". Basically, wife battering's one of dem outcomes of social breakdown.' She turned to Nargis. 'It's pretty normal here in Tajikistan, isn't it?'

Nargis was silent at the sink.

Harriet snorted. 'Well, if Henri dared hit me I would leave him straight away,' she said. 'I would go home to England with the kids and get divorced.'

Nargis frowned and scrubbed the pot harder. Some do, she thought.

Emma shook her head. 'Aye but they can't just leg it. A woman who tries to get divorced will be disowned or laughed outta court unless she's got a nice, rich old man. It's a total scandal to get divorced here, it's 'haram', you know, shameful. Women without men to protect them get treated like whores because so many end up on the street. It's hard to remarry and they lose their children to their fella's family.'

Nargis nodded vigorously and forgetting herself, perched on a chair. 'Is true.'

'They lose their children?' repeated Harriet. She looked astonished. Emma smiled sadly.

'Straight up, love. It gets worse.' Emma read again from her presentation. '"Some women, usually second wives, are only married with the Nikoh, an Islamic marriage ceremony performed by a mullah. They're supposed to register the marriage officially, but they often don't bother".'

'But why do these women agree to become concubines?' asked Harriet, perplexed.

Emma shrugged. 'Dunno. Loadsa reasons. Some are dozey but others are just out on their arses, sorry, I mean "poor". They got no choice. Parents get a nice dowry for a virgin. Others are older, by that I mean older than twenty-five and scared of being bin-bagged, chucked out on their todd. Second wives have no legal rights whatsoever. If their fellas meet someone else though, it's a doddle.' She read out loud: '"There are many stories of men calling wives from Russia to tell them Talok three times over the phone. Afterwards, these men believe they are divorced under Islam, even though Islamic scholars have publicly spoken out against it".'

'Can you imagine, Nargis?' Harriet blurted.

'Yes. Is real. You foreigners don't know...' Nargis reddened and sprang from the chair trembling. Her scar ached now.

Emma's eyes narrowed. 'What's up Nargis, love? I hope I haven't offended you like?'

'I had bad second husband. Parents made me marry him after Ahmed, my first husband die.' Nargis recalled the intense pressure she had felt not to be a burden. Gulya had been particularly vociferous: "An only son with a nice home and good prospects, yet he is willing to marry a widow with two children. He could have anyone, but he wants you, you lucky girl. You won't get better than that," she had whispered insistently. Numb with grief and unable to think straight, she had eventually succumbed. Tears came to Nargis's eyes, dismissed in a blink.

'Did he deck yer?' Emma put a fist to her own face.

Nargis nodded. 'Yes, he beat me and little boy and took baby, only nine week old. I had to live on street until parents forgive me.'

Harriet gasped. 'My God.'

Emma touched her arm.

Nargis's cheeks burned. 'But I was never prostitute. Caravan of Faith, Americans people, help me with cleaning job to please their Jesus. Eventually milk for baby dry and husband went in Russia. Baby stays with Bibi... Grandmother.'

'Nargis, I honestly had no idea.' said Harriet. She was peering at her with an almost perverse curiosity, as though she had come to work naked. Nargis frowned, embarrassed at her outburst. She had revealed too much and she hated herself for the pity in Harriet's voice. She shook off Emma's hand and backed out of the room.

'Sorry. Please forget what I say...'

'Nargis sweetheart, please don't be embarrassed,' said Emma. 'What you've been through is nothing to be ashamed of. In the U.K we'd call you a "Survivor".'

Nargis baulked. Her eyes flashed.

'I have no shame. I proud.'

January 16th, 2008, Tajikistan Countdown: 12 Months, 14 days

I can't get her story out of my head. I lie awake at night thinking about her. That husband. I shudder to think what he did to her. Now I know why she grows pale and subdued whenever Henri's in a foul mood. Does she really fear he will hit me? Or worse, the children?

I dream of working, though nothing has come of my efforts so far. My friends in England don't understand, they say they'd love to have a maid to do everything and no mortgage to pay. They think I have a sophisticated, jet-setting lifestyle. I hate to shatter their fantasies.

I'm a terrible mother. When Leo cries for me in the night I feel suffocated, trapped. He still wakes up four times a night, only happy when he is in my bed, clinging to me like a limpet. Sometimes when I am walking him up and down the hallway I cry too, from pure exhaustion. I'm wishing his babyhood away. I'm so relieved I had a boy after Alexandra, this tedious stage of nappies and sleeplessness will soon be over forever. Not that I ever admit that to anyone.

Henri is away again, another business trip to Kazakhstan. He seems to love the place. He barely bothered to say goodbye and the children hardly notice his absence. I can't remember the last time he visited Alex's school, he has been there perhaps twice in the last year. He mentioned to me in passing that he has put their names down at his old boarding school in Brussels but I don't think I will be able to let Alex go in three years, she's so little and she has problems fitting in wherever she goes. I thought expatriate children were all supposed to be adaptable, so-called 'third culture kids' that can slot in anywhere. Henri says they should have a good Belgian education. What do I know? I guess he doesn't want Alex to end up like me, I know I don't.

18

Henri Simenon returned home that night at eleven o'clock. It had started to snow once more, soft flakes falling silently. Their home was cloaked in fresh white powder so that it resembled a Christmas gingerbread house. As he entered, he stowed his suitcase, hung up his wool coat and removed snow-covered leather boots. His Blackberry bleated. He checked his messages and deleted some. He found Harriet watching the TV in the darkness of the study.

'*Bon soir, ma Cherie.* You didn't need to wait up.' He gave her a cursory kiss on the cheek and turned on his computer. He liked to check the markets last thing at night, an avid player on the stocks. He ran his fingers through his shoulder length hair, flicked it back off his face and poured himself a scotch. He was filled with a sense of wellbeing. It had been another fantastic trip, good to get away. Tajikistan could be a real drag.

'Have you worked hard? Was the flight alright?'

'Actually no, I didn't work hard. As luck would have it, the meetings were blissfully short and sweet and several were cancelled at short notice.' Leaving me plenty of time to take advantage of the five star hotel facilities, he thought. 'I just stayed in my room and worked,' he lied. Better not upset the *fifille* by mentioning the fine dining or the company. Not for Kazakhstan the food shortages. He checked his email anxiously. *Rien.*

Harriet was flicking through TV channels aimlessly. A litany of canned laughter, news, canned laughter, Russian pop, Bollywood whine, a dubbed Charlie Chan, Afghan wedding music, American weather girl, repeated over and over. He could feel her eyes on him as he typed in the flickering light. He knew she would be frowning.

'You are so vain, Henri,' she muttered. 'You pretend you work hard for humanitarian, political causes, but really it is all about your self-image. Without your work, you would be as lost at sea as I am.'

Henri took a deep breath. He didn't feel like indulging her in an argument tonight, nor the messy, conciliatory love-making that would follow. He turned to her enquiringly. Instead of the critical glare he was expecting, she seemed crestfallen. Maybe she just missed me?

'Would you like a drink? *Un liqueur peut-etre?*'

'Sure,' said Harriet unenthusiastically, picking off a piece of lint from a cushion.

Henri came over to her with a small glass of Baileys and sat down. He turned off the television and put his hand on her arm, stroking her soft downy skin.

'What's the matter, *Amour?*'

'I'm just feeling a little low tonight,' she whispered.

Henri rubbed red rimmed eyes. They itched from long hours staring at the computer. After four days of coasting, the final day had been hard, with one frustrating meeting after another, followed by a long flight with poor service and tight, uncomfortable seats. He fervently hoped that Harriet was not about to start another one of her depressing conversations about Tajikistan. They had discussed it umpteen times, whenever Harriet got itchy feet, complaining about the lack of facilities and her fears for the children's health and education. In truth, Henri hated moving, with the stress of finding a new home, meeting new colleagues and having to prove himself in a completely new team. Tajikistan suited him… so long as there were business trips. A big fish in a small pond, as the English would say.

'So?' said Henri, caressing her neck.

'I feel so useless.'

'What do you mean?'

'I have nothing to do,' she said. Suddenly Henri understood. Of course, that was it. He turned to her and embraced her, stroking her empty belly. Well, I can change that.

'Is it time for another one?' he said. *'Bénie soit-elle.'*

She looked confused. 'No, I haven't finished yet,' she said, cradling her drink.

Henri laughed. 'I was not referring to that,' he said, his voice ripe with meaning.

She flicked her eyes from the television to him. 'Henri, please tell me what you're talking about.'

'You said you feel useless. Well, I hold the key to that,' he said.

Harriet stared at him. 'You do?'

He chuckled happily. Sometimes, he thought fondly, he understood her better than she did herself.

'Another baby? That is what you were talking about wasn't it, *ma mignonne*?' he said, giving her a warm embrace. He leaned in to kiss her but Harriet pulled away and stood up.

'Fuck you Henri. I mean really, God damn you. Is that all anyone thinks I am good for?' she cried. 'You and everyone else, you all think the same. It is so demeaning. There is more to me than staying at home making babies and polishing the bloody silver.'

She strode out of the room, slamming the door. Henri was shocked. He felt his face tingling. She rarely swore and never at him. He could take passive aggressive side swipes once in a while, but this was unacceptable. Was it the time of the month? He got up, followed her out of the room to the kitchen.

'*Merde,* Harriet, what is your problem now?' he hissed. 'I am trying to understand, but you're really pushing my patience with your hysterical outbursts.'

He stood in the doorway, hands on his hips. She rubbed her eyes. She looked terrible under the strip lights, as if she had not slept the whole week. Henri felt a sudden pang of guilt, quickly quelled. Harriet flicked the switch on the kettle.

'Is there any point in trying to explain, again? You are so obviously unable to understand anything about me, Henri. You have University degrees and purpose to your life beyond family relationships. I have none, only a few GCSEs and a secretarial course. Your job gives you status. I have none, except as your wife. You know who you are and what you are capable of. I don't have a clue. And I never will, living this life, moving all the time.'

Henri kept his eyes expressionless, a practised poker face he used in work meetings with emotional colleagues. Harriet paced the floor.

'My life: What does it mean? What am I doing with it? I am not talking about my roles as a wife to you or mother to the children. I am talking about being an individual, a person who used to use her brain.'

Henri swallowed a yawn. God, she could be dull. The downside of marrying a woman so much younger than him, he supposed. What does she know about life? She'd be in her prime at forty-five. Would she be a red Côte d'Or Burgundy or a Grand Cru Chablis? He was interrupted by the vibration of his Blackberry. As she turned to reach for the tea caddy, he glanced at it and quickly texted back. *Mon Dieu*, Harriet was still droning on, oblivious.

'I admit, I blame myself for being lazy and complacent. I feel as if my relationship with Nargis switched on something in my head and made me realise how empty I am. How trivial and insignificant my life is.'

Henri ran his fingers through his hair, momentarily confused. Nargis? Ah, the maid. His eyes narrowed. The bloody maid? What did she have to do with this?

'I am not sure I follow.'

'I have completely lost myself with three moves in eight years, especially since we came here to this godforsaken shit hole.'

Henri's shoulders slumped. Oh, here we go again. It gets so tedious. Harriet poured hot water into a mug and opened the fridge.

'And by the way, I don't want any more children.'

'Hmm.'

Henri digested this last part. He tried not to feel disappointed or hurt, though it seemed she was dismissing motherhood for the sake of some selfish dig at him. They had nannies and other servants, he could not see what she was making such a fuss about. All she has to do is get pregnant and give birth, I handle everything else, he thought indignantly.

'I want to work and use my skills.'

Henri guffawed sarcastically.

'Skills? What skills? Are you going to blow dry hair or give people a manicure?'

Harriet gasped. 'Now you're just being unkind.'

He glanced at her. Her eyes were huge, sparkling with tears. She would have enjoyed the spa and the eating out in Almaty. Perhaps she needs a holiday, he wondered, dismissing the idea immediately. There was no way she could go anywhere without him. Especially not with *les enfants*. He knew full well she might decide not to return. He tried to reassure her, reaching for her hand.

'Come on, Harriet, everyone knows you have many talents. You are my beautiful girl, *ma fifille*. I love you. The children love you. You are a great wife and mother. I will always take care of you and give you whatever you need. What more do you want? You knew the nature of my work when you married me. Do you really want to live alone in Europe and do your own cleaning? How would you cope? You need me, *Cherie*.'

Harriet got up from the table, hunched like an old woman. Henri suppressed a snort. Did she have to be so dramatic? She wrapped her nightgown around her slight frame and picked up her tea. She was red-faced, as though trying not to cry. He shrugged his shoulders.

'I just don't know what else to say to you,' he said.

She tried to smile. 'No, you're right. It's not your fault, I have no one to blame but myself. I'm sorry,' she said. 'I am going to bed.'

19

It was seven o'clock in the evening. Poulod dressed in a clean shirt, a black leather jacket and pointed leather shoes and left the stuffy atmosphere of his parent's apartment. It was good to get away from the disapproving gaze of his old man for the evening. Turning left down the familiar street, he walked along the broken pavement past tenement buildings. The orange reflection of the sunset on the windows hurt his eyes. He felt muggy from inactivity, stiff from sitting in a chair all day watching rotten Tajik TV. He flexed his fists. Dushanbe was damn boring after Moscow. Nothing to do except sit in the company of a two year old all day, give me a fucking break. He had asked his mother to take the kid out of the room, as he couldn't stand his ceaseless chirping. The kid was puny and frankly, disappointing. He still shat himself and couldn't speak more than a few words. He had hardly grown since last year, but chatted all the time, never shutting his mouth. He called his mother to remove him from his sight, couldn't she understand, he needed to relax.

He checked his watch: February 1st. He shuddered. Only one precious month left before he would have to return to his job at the Pokrovskaya vegetable warehouse south of Moscow. They usually closed the factory down between January and March, as it was too cold and the vegetables froze and rotted later, unacceptable to the supermarkets. He worked twelve-hour days, six days a week, for a lousy four hundred dollars a month as a vegetable packer, putting stinking carrots, radishes and sweetcorn into boxes and encasing them in polythene. In winter the warehouse was freezing, in the summer they sweltered. At noon, a bell rang and they had a half hour lunch break when they were made to queue like labour camp prisoners and given a bowl o tasteless carrot and sweetcorn sludge, of course, with dry black rye bread. And they had the gall to call it borscht.

He hated his job but it beat the hell out of the manual labouring on a construction site quarry he had put in for eight months last year. Each hour, supercilious Russian supervisors with clipboards went round the factory floor, making sure everyone was packing properly, shutting up chatting workers with threats of dismissal. They particularly delighted in taunting Tajik and Uzbek workers. They loved telling the 'Asians' to do extra tasks like cleaning the reeking factory toilets and sweeping the floors and threatened them with the police if they didn't comply. Poulod had the miserable luck to get Anatoly Viktorovy as his factory zone manager, a class-A prick, a blond, balding, blue-eyed snob who took an instant dislike to him.

'You've missed a bit,' he would say, peering into one of the boxes with a supercilious glance. 'Do it again.'

Poulod had to fish out the box and unwrap the polythene, in front of the smirks of the other workers, and repack the box, all the while controlling himself, forcing himself not to smash his fat face in. God. His fists itched to hit someone.

Poulod counted the minutes each day on a big metal clock that hung at one end of the factory warehouse. Hours slipped past with no more to entertain him than his imagination. Sometimes he envisaged how he would love to torture Anatoly, slowly, deliciously. He could see it all in front of him. He would bend him over a chair, stuff carrots in his ass, wrap polythene around his face and slowly ease off his extremities, one by one with a large pair of pliers. Otherwise he spent hours planning out his evening activities, every drink, every bar, every woman he would flirt with and which one he would pay for a fuck at the end. In his fantasies she was always a blue-eyed blonde with long legs, a Russian pedigree. He also thought about Nargis. How to get her back. That black-eyed bitch with her little bastards. She didn't deserve him, had never deserved him. Like his old mum always said, he should have taken a dumb virgin, not that clever little cunt. He took to calling her mobile in the early hours when he got into vodka-fuelled furies, knowing he would wake her, hoping it would scare her.

This evening, Poulod was heading to a local shop to buy vodka by the shot. Some of his old mates came there each evening, to pass the time in male company, argue about the state of things in Tajikistan and share information on the latest Russian job opportunities. He looked up at the apartments. Most of the windows above were cracked, some were missing. He could still remember when they were first built as monuments to progress, gleaming in the harsh Tajik sunlight. He had been about five years old when he attended the grand opening, a tremendous fanfare with an official Soviet parade, a band playing shiny instruments. Poulod had been given a flag to wave and journalists had taken pictures. Soviet officials hailed the new coming of the Union and the success of the socialist State. His retired parents were given an apartment as workers in the now struggling Dushanbe Textile Company.

Dushanbe was going to seed. The whole country was going to hell. It made him furious. No wonder the Russians treated them like garbage. The great Republic of Tajikistan had been a huge failure, you only had to leave for a while and return to realise that. Their great President, having just won a third term in November, did nothing but issue absurd decrees on beards, miniskirts and veils, build grand palaces for himself and fight the political opposition. Most of them now sat in prison for life or else simmered with intent across the Uzbek border. The rest of the world moved on while Tajikistan went backwards. Poulod kicked a clod of mud off the pavement. The grass verges had been recently hoed and dug and the smell of earth filled the air.

He still hadn't decided what to do about that snivelling wife of his. Technically they weren't officially divorced. She didn't have the money and he didn't have the inclination.

Somewhere in his head he still wanted her back. The knowledge grated at him. He thought that maybe if he offered her an interesting business proposition she might talk to him again, even come back. Right now she insisted on staying in her parent's rat hole shack with her pathetic kids from her first marriage to that wimp, Ahmed. A neighbour for several years, Poulod had long admired Nargis's sexy figure. After he heard she was widowed, he had sent his mother to make enquiries to her parents as to whether Nargis would consider remarrying. Surprisingly she agreed. She showed up willing to make the best of it, with two sad, snotty children in tow and a few possessions in an old suitcase, a faded photo of her dead husband, some old clothes. Ahmed had not left her with much.

Initially they got on okay. The slut was willing to lie back and open her legs whenever he wanted. Yet for all her physical presence in his bed, he sensed that she was still in love with her dead husband. He tried to get through to her, to no avail. Never much good at expressing himself, he did not have the words to soften her heart. Even after he tore the little ID photo to pieces in a jealous rage, she did not forget Ahmed. Instead of the happy wife he had hoped for, she became increasingly distant. She cried every time they had sex and refused to go out with him, preferring to go to the park with her children. It started to piss him off. It didn't help that as Hussein grew he increasingly resembled his father.

Poulod started to feel insane with rage whenever Nargis gave her son the love he never saw. It was as if Ahmed had reappeared from the grave. When Hussein was rude, tired or being childish, Poulod fancied it was the ghost of Ahmed doing it to make him angry. He lashed out, hitting him whenever he felt like it, especially when Nargis was not watching, threatening him with more if he told. After a while he instructed his mother not to give them any hot meals, just bread. He figured if he didn't feed those kids,

Nargis would be forced to send them off to Ahmed's family, where they belonged. After all, Poulod reasoned, she was part of a new family now, a family where interlopers were not welcome. Yet, the opposite had happened. The kids left for Grandma's house, but so too did Nargis.

Nargis had packed up her stuff into her shabby suitcase and was heading out of the door carrying their three-month baby, her two other children close behind, when he came home drunk.

'Where the fuck do you think you're going?' he had yelled. Nargis had panicked, shooing the children back into a bedroom, closing the door.

As brazen as a wolf in a farm, she had turned to him.

'I'm leaving you and taking the children with me.' She looked him right in the eyes and though she was trembling, he saw she meant it. Behind the door the brats were crying. His son, Faisullo started to scream in her arms. Poulod panicked and did the first thing that came into his head. He grabbed a large pair of scissors from his mother's sewing kit and stepped towards her threateningly. He only wanted to scare her.

'You're going nowhere.'

She eyed the scissors, gratifyingly terrified.

'Please, let me go.'

'Shut up, bitch.'

But instead of keeping quiet like any normal Tajik wife would do, the stupid ewe had to say those words.

'Poulod, I don't love you. I never will. Our marriage is over.'

He almost lost his balance with fury. A white light filled his eyes and he was filled with red-hot anger. She will love me, even if I have to make her. He had grabbed her by the neck, ripping her kurta down the back with the scissors. He swore that he did not mean to, but the scissors suddenly slipped and entered her flesh. Nargis screamed and dropped Faisullo on the carpet where he lay silently.

Blood poured from her wound, gushing red and warm into her dress, dripping onto the carpet. Poulod stepped backwards, momentarily shocked at the sight of his red, wet hands. From the open door on the stairwell, a neighbour appeared. Old Mr. Vladimirov, a retired Russian professor of engineering from the Technical University. Stooped, with white oiled-back hair and smartly dressed in his woollen coat and black velvet trilby, he had probably been passing by on an afternoon stroll when he heard Nargis screaming and decided to investigate. Interfering old fool.

'Hey, look here Poulod my son, give me those scissors, there's a good lad,' he had said calmly in authoritative Russian, stepping forward and grabbing the makeshift weapon. 'I am sure she deserves it, but we don't want a murder on our hands, do we?' he said, pocketing the scissors quickly. At the mention of murder, Poulod's legs gave out from under him. He sat woodenly on the sofa, his face pale, drained. How had it got to this? He loved her, couldn't she see that? She was ripping his heart out. All this fighting and blood, this was just an expression of how much he loved her. He looked at her with tears in his eyes. What a woman. Mr. Vladimirov brought an old tea towel from the kitchen and pressed it to her naked shoulder.

'Don't touch her,' Poulod shouted. 'No one touches my wife but me.'

'Okay, okay. Calm down son, okay.'

Nargis didn't look at him. She doesn't care how much she's hurt me, he thought sadly. She knelt on the floor, urgently checking Faisullo's head and body for bruises. Then she got up, bent over almost double and barely able to hold the baby, she opened the living room door. Hussein shot out of the door and down the stairs like a rat, but three-year old Bunavsha was so frightened she had wet herself, clutching her mother's legs, making it hard to move forward.

Poulod heard Nargis whispering.

144

'Bunavsha, let go. I know you are scared but let go. We have to leave, now, quickly.'

Poulod woke from his torpor.

'Wait,' he yelled hoarsely. 'If you go, you go without my kin.'

He leapt from the sofa and chased her out into the echoey stairwell. Reaching her bent figure, he grabbed the screaming baby from her grasp.

'He stays here.'

Nargis was pale, her hands clenching the banister. She looked like she would fall down the damp, slippery stairs. He was torn, tempted to push her down the stairs for hurting him, yet wanting to pull her back inside, back into his bed where she belonged. He hesitated as she hobbled an uncertain descent, weeping all the while, her two white-faced children sobbing pitifully at the bottom of the cement steps.

Nargis refused to see him after that and wouldn't answer phone calls. Even his hope that she would return for their son's sake never materialised. It was all the fault of that damn first-born son, Ahmed's ghost. How he hated him. Several months later, Poulod left for Russia. Despite the entreaties of his parents, Nargis had not been back to stay since. His mother told him that Nargis same back to visit, sometimes more than once a week, begging for Faisullo, but they refused to give him up. They feared him, he knew, as they depended on him for money, his father having retired, his mother earning a paltry pittance tailoring kurtas for local women at eighteen somoni a time, barely enough to cover the cost of cotton thread and needles.

20

At last, the long winter was over. The unusually harsh freezes had killed the fig and pomegranate trees in Harriet's garden, laying waste to forty years of jam and juice. The alternate chill of grey windy days, late snows and the long, heavy rains of February brought the transitional period between cold and warm when disease and vermin came alive alongside the shoots of plants and budding leaves. Huge winds whipped up dust storms from the stony deserts of Afghanistan and Gorno Badakhshan in February and March, turning the air in Dushanbe brown for whole weeks and making it difficult to go outside.

Poulod continued to call Nargis at all hours until early February, when suddenly, he seemed to vanish. Savsang cleared out her half of the shop at the beginning of February, her things carried away by her stern husband. After much cajoling and begging, Nargis had allowed her to leave without paying the rent for January and unbeknownst to Gulya, had lent her fifty dollars to pay off the bank. Gulya told her that Savsang had been going door to door in the mahalla, desperately trying to shift her New Year stock.

Savsang had wept bitterly as she packed her things into a box, unstringing the tinsel and folding up the children's clothes. She begged Nargis for forgiveness, terrified at the prospect of homelessness.

'I went to see the bank manager, but he refused to consider a further loan, or to freeze the interest, which is mounting by the day.'

Nargis felt stupid about her loan to Savsang, especially as she had been so busy paying off old debts that even her salary could not cover them. Her old creditors had found out about her shop. They came every day for two weeks, threatening the family with untold problems unless she paid them off. Relatives and neighbours came for favours owed that she could not refuse to honour.

In early March, an outbreak of typhoid, the result of dirty ditch water contaminating supplies after two weeks of rain, killed one hundred people only six kilometres from Dushanbe. As news filtered back to outlying mahallas of funerals and infection, Nargis grew terrified, making her children drink only freshly boiled tea and spending precious wages on soap, bleach and lime for the latrine. The Simenon' children seemed immune. They were delighted by the slight rise in temperature and played hide and seek amongst the newly flowering daffodils. Harriet put away the scarves and jackets of winter, replacing them with floral cottons and sandals almost overnight. Alexandra delighted in the warmer weather, changing in and out of three or four different summer dresses each day, much to her mother's irritation, insisting on wearing her pink Hello Kitty swimsuit and goggles at bath-time.

But one morning, Nargis saw a new pile of vomit and diarrhoea stained sheets left by the washing machine, the empty sachets of rehydration salts. Alexandra was seriously ill, scaring Mrs Harriet as they spent a days in and out of shabby, crumbling clinics consulting different physicians and holding little hands while Alex was injected with useless medicines that did not stop the vomiting, but only made her scream in pain. Spoon-feeding rehydration salts only for them to be brought back up less than half a minute later. Hours spent debating whether she was strong enough for the SOS flight, whether it should be called in, a twelve hour wait. Until it was too late.

'I did not realise how terrible the medical care is here,' Harriet cried. Sitting knees hunched on an ancient, sheet-less metal bedstead in the children's hospital. The power had gone out. An exhausted looking paediatrician had left them after a torrent of incomprehensible Russian. Alexandra had been hooked up to a drip, her swollen hands held down so that the intravenous cannula could be inserted into the vein. In the semi-dark, the nurse asked

Harriet for her half-drunk bottle of mineral water. Nargis had come along to help, Leo left behind with the other maid.

'Why does she need my water?' Harriet asked, not understanding, her mind hazy from a long night with only minutes of sleep, holding a vomiting child over buckets and changing endless sheets.

'To mix the Ciproflaxcin super-antibiotic tablet with before we insert it into the nasal tube,' answered the weary nurse. 'It is cleaner than the water available here in the hospital.'

She pointed at a basin in the corner. 'That is only municipal water.'

Harriet was appalled.

'One of the paediatricians said it was a waterborne bacteria or cholera and that it entered the Dushanbe water system via the river. We can't know for sure because there are no laboratories to do tests in this bloody backwater.' Harriet's voice rose to a screech. 'What if it's a virus? It'll get worse if you give her antibiotics. My little girl might die. And you're telling me this is the only water you have here in the hospital?' She started to laugh hysterically. 'Where the fuck is Henri? He should have left work by now.' She burst into tears. 'Alexandra has lost almost two kilos in twelve hours. Look at her. She looks like one of those children in famines on the TV, only she's white. I don't know what to do. I wish we had called the SOS air ambulance.'

'Nobody know what to do,' said Nargis. 'But to be safe...'

'Okay fine. Where the fucking hell is my husband?' Harriet snapped.

Nargis was silent. Harriet stood up. She paced the room. After a few moments she passed the nurse her water bottle.

'I apologise. Give it to her. I'll call my driver to bring a few boxes of water bottles.'

Harriet glanced out of the window and caught sight of the new Presidential Palace glittering on the horizon. Just then, vomit erupted from Alexandra, her body racked with dry retching. Frothy yellow diarrhoea seeped from her, uncontrolled, soiling the sheet from home underneath one of Leo's nappies. She started to moan softly, thrashing about in the bed. The nurse pursed her lips and checked her drip, raising the level. Harriet stopped crying and stood watching from the window, her mouth open.

'Nargis, please would you change her nappy? I don't want her to see me like this, crying. I need to go outside for a moment.'

Nargis was shocked as she changed her, her peachy bottom having turned bony and taut. She could not imagine how a child already thin and underfed would survive this disease, whatever it was. She said a quiet prayer for her children at home and Faisullo. She wanted desperately to go to see him, to check he was alright, but she did not dare. Nothing had been said about the risk of passing this infection on but Nargis knew it was dangerous for infants. She washed her hands all the time and resolved to eat only in the guard house.

Harriet returned, her eyes glistening red.

'For the first time in my life, I understand why diarrhoea is still the number one cause of death in the world for small children,' she said with a sob.

At last, Henri appeared. He crossed the ward and took Harriet's hand, wincing at the stink emanating from the bed. Alexandra lay quietly, her eyes half shut as though drugged. Henri hovered awkwardly, unsure of whether he was allowed to approach his daughter.

'My poor baby.'

Harriet embraced him. Then she stepped back, staring.

'Have you been out drinking cocktails while your daughter is at death's door?'

'A Russian Embassy reception. I left as quickly as I...' He pursed his lips and sniffed the air with narrowed eyes. 'Have you been smoking, Harriet?'

Over the next week, Alexandra was delivered to hospital for drips and nasal tubes, injections and endless abdominal prodding by doctors. She slowly started to recover as the powerful foreign antibiotics did their work. Nargis watched in admiration as valiant hospital staff worked tirelessly in dark, dirty wards with inadequate equipment and a lack of medicines. Mrs Harriet was lucky, having the means to pay for medicines from Europe. Each day, Ivan drove to the private clinic for the rich in Tajikistan to buy them. For ordinary Tajiks, it was a lottery as to whether the medicines they struggled to afford would actually work, the pharmaceutical supply chain being riddled with corruption, just like everything else. Most tablets in the local pharmacies were fake. The paediatrician, a kind, experienced, Russian grandmother that Alexandra called 'The Black Woman' on account of her black dresses, stockings and shoes, told them that one by one, the medics were leaving Tajikistan to go overseas, unable to afford life on meagre government salaries.

'Russian construction sites and domestic households are full of our medical professionals,' she sighed.

The wards in the Children's Hospital were packed with listless children and infants affected by this latest epidemic, drips attached to their arms. Their figures huddled under patterned, torn bedsheets brought from home, pale faces peeping out with dark circles under their eyes.

The spring snowmelt washed down rivers of effluent from upriver. Turn on the taps and brownish liquid poured out, smelling of stagnant pond.

Harriet spent her evenings boiling huge pots of water for Leo's bath and fretted over him, never allowing him out of her sight. Once Alexandra came home, Henri was largely absent, working. When he was home he was tense, distracted and, despite Harriet's loud protestations, he left for a work trip up-country in Khujand.

Date: February 10th, 2008 Tajikistan Countdown: As soon as possible

This weekend I drove Alexandra to the hospital for her final nasal tube. Holding her shivering, trembling body in my arms, she had a fit of hysteria when she saw the shabby hospital entrance, knowing this was the dreaded place where faceless nurses wearing green masks held her down while strange black-eyed men inserted hateful needles and tubes into her hands and down her nose. She screamed and started to fight, desperately holding onto banisters in the stairwell with skinny arms and clinging to me when I tried to put her down on the plastic covered iron bedstead. The nurses pushed me from the room, closing the door. I was too stunned to protest and stood in the corridor outside with Nargis, my daughter's terrified cries filling my ears. Anywhere else would have an antibiotic drip, but not this bloody place. I should never have brought my children here. I rushed home, a sobbing child wrapped in the back seat on Nargis's knee and confronted Henri when he got back from his mission in Khujand. 'You have to find another job, I don't care where,' I screamed at him. Yet, he wouldn't hear of it. 'My projects are at a delicate, critical stage,' he told me. 'I have just made headway at work and if I leave now, I will be passed over for promotion.'

Privately, Nargis agreed with me. 'If I could, I would go too,' she said.

Nargis has been my only ally through this crisis. Patty couldn't, or wouldn't come, she is terrified of hospitals and illness. Veronica has been told Bangkok is off. I hear she's going to be stuck here another year, so depressed now that she doesn't go out, doesn't answer her phone. Both of them, utterly useless. When I thought Alex might die, Nargis was there, reassuring me. She has been there for me every day, a solid, comforting presence. I am eternally grateful.

I read back to the entries at the beginning of the year and I cringe. Like an ostrich with my head in the sand, I completely lost sight of what really matters: My children. How can I go back to work? They need me, especially in Tajikistan. Alex is slowly recovering. She has been off school for three weeks. With her pallor, big eyes and knobbly knees she resembles a forest fawn. My former life is on hold, I have not seen anyone since the illness began. Ronnie dispatched her driver with a box of German cartoons. Patty sent a 'special' cake with 'Get Well Soon' inscribed in icing. American parents from school have sent imported ice cream, twinkies, freshly baked cupcakes and other treats from their Diplomatic Bag. The kindergarten teacher, Good Cop, called me for a health update. Everyone is so kind, the benefit of living in such a close knit community, I suppose. They are too frightened of infection to drop by and we still don't know what it was that made her so ill. I guess we never will now. I would love to take her to England to stay with her granny but Henri says the journey would be too hard on her. He says it is too expensive if we are going to take a summer holiday too and I suppose it's his money so it's his decision. I feed her big bowls of banana porridge and wholesome chicken soup with homemade walnut bread that I bake fresh every day using the sack of nuts we collected in autumn. I force her to drink probiotics disguised as fizzy orange soda. Her hands are still sore from where adult sized cannulas were forced into tiny veins and fear clouds her face whenever the 'Black Woman' visits with her leather bag of needles. She smiles bravely, sending me quick darting glances to make sure I won't leave her. It breaks my heart and strengthens my resolve. I can't put my child through this again. We have to move.

We read books and paint and bake biscuits to decorate with coloured icing in the kitchen. Somehow, she transformed from an errant toddler into this amusing little person who can tell me her view of the world yet I didn't really notice until now. We play endless puzzles and paint our toenails with different coloured polishes. When it is sunny, we venture out for little walks. She is curious about what mosque. She likes to bang loudly on the little metal door the size of a window in the wall – our local bakery – for hot naan. I have to hold her up so she can peep through to see all the little mounds of dough on trays waiting to go into the huge, ancient wood-fired tandoor oven. I fancy she looks like Alice in Wonderland, peering through a tiny door, wishing she could enter the garden beyond. The bakers give her a special smile and pat her head with floury hands. She also loves to stop at the little wooden blue kiosk on the street run by a plump Tajik lady in Russian scarves. I let her choose a chocolate bar from Iran or sweets from Russia. Groups of grubby Tajik children with shaved heads, raggedy brown trousers and pointed rubber boots try to chat to her as we pass. The daffodils are out, lining the garden path with jolly yellow bells. The grey of winter is fading to be replaced with spring green.

Henri is away all the time now, every second week. Khorogh in the Pamirs, Ghorgon Teppa in Katlon Province, Almaty, Ashkabad and Tashkent. He is very distant, always busy. Even when he is home, I barely seem to see him. He drinks heavily every night and goes to bed late. We received another shipment of French wine and he seems determined to finish it within the month. I can't stay up with him when I know Leo will wake me at 2am. Adamant that we cannot leave Dushanbe, he says I don't realise the pressure he's under at work. How can I, when he never talks about it? He obviously thinks there is no point in explaining it to me, that I won't understand. He's moved into the spare room and blames me for Leo's continuing night time fretfulness. We have not slept together in over a month but I am so angry with him that I don't care.

21

A week before Nav Ruz, Poulod had been doing what he did every night, drinking cheap vodka until he felt that familiar buzz, his limbs relaxing into the hard chair, his mind freeing itself from manly burdens. He would keep drinking until he could just about get home without crawling in the gutter. A grocery shop by day, at night the owner would bring out a few chairs and tables and the shop counter was transformed into a makeshift bar. The bar was full of mutterings. Municipal bull dozers had moved on an unofficial mosque down the street, levelling it within hours; the few who dared protest, carted off to prison.

A man he had never seen before entered. He was tall, thick set and dark, wearing a black leather jacket, black trousers and a black shirt, the funereal outfit of a typical Tajik villain. He wore his hair long in a ponytail and had pockmarked skin and a long scar on his cheek.

The room grew quiet as he asked for an expensive bottle of top quality Standard Vodka. He spoke Tajik with a southern accent originating from somewhere near Afghanistan, possibly Kulyob, the place of origin of Tajikistan's President. The other men looked at him, some in trepidation, others, with visible envy. Here was a wealthy man. As he lifted his glass to drink, a tattoo of a black spider slid from his sleeve. No one spoke and even the old bearded lunatic sitting by the door stopped mumbling.

Poulod was sitting some way from the bar with his friend Azamjon, and whispered, 'Who's the new guy?'

'He's a mafia type. Don't know his name. He comes round here sometimes with business propositions, but only if he likes you,' he said cautiously.

Poulod looked him over and went back to his drink. He had seen many men of his type in Russia, drug gang members. He avoided them, scared by the rumours of ritual initiation, intimidation, murder, torture and gang vendettas. He did not belong to the southern clans and could only watch them make their millions from the periphery. They were easy to pick out in Moscow. Along with the Russian and Kyrgyz gangs, they controlled the heroin trade, identifiable by hand tattoos and accents. Laboratories in Tajik Northern Alliance areas of Afghanistan processed opium poppy seeds into heroin before it was moved across the border under the indifferent eyes of poorly paid, under-equipped, teenage conscripts. An American-funded bridge had opened the year before, straddling the Pyanj River between Afghanistan and Tajikistan. It was now said to be even easier to bring in drugs, hidden in fragrant trucks of fresh coriander. Everyone knew that Tajik law enforcement was a joke, with top officials controlling large swathes of the border, reaping the benefits of global heroin demand.

The mysterious man swivelled and his eyes lighted on Poulod. He came over to their table and sat down.

'I'm Jamshed,' he said. He had a thin gravely voice, no doubt the result of many years hard drinking. His eyes were frightening in their blankness.

'Poulod,' he spluttered. What does he want with me? The man drank a shot of vodka and offered the bottle to the men. He filled their glasses.

'Usually work in Moscow, do you?' he asked casually.

'Yes,' said Poulod suspiciously.

'Did you lose your job?'

'No, it was just dire.'

'I have a small business here,' murmured Azamjon.

Jamshed addressed Poulod, ignoring his companion.

'I suppose you'll be going back soon?'

'Yes, soon. Can't stay here in Dushanbe forever.'

Azamjon was a family man. Dinner and his lovely wife would be waiting at home. As he left, he shook Jamshed's hand respectfully, his hand on his heart.

'See you soon,' he said heavily to Poulod.

Jamshed watched him leave with a sneer.

'That guy will never be anything more than a shopkeeper. Now he's gone, we can talk business.'

Poulod jerked his head up in surprise. Were they going to let him join their gang? His fears were forgotten. This was a *real* opportunity to forget the bloody vegetable packing plant. He could taste the money, already picture the fancy new car he would buy (a white Mercedes), the new house he would build for his parents (three or four floors, green tinted windows and ostentatious yellow Greek pillars out front). Even Nargis would be impressed, the stupid bitch. He sat forward in his seat and cleared his throat.

'B-business? You've a proposal for me?' he stammered, not wanting to appear too keen.

'Sure. If you're willing to listen, I want to talk business. Come to this address tomorrow at two, bring identification documents and your passport as per usual employment requirements.'

Jamshed passed him a card that said "Tajik Cotton Enterprises" and got up.

'Finish the bottle, my friend.'

Poulod fingered the card, putting it in his pocket. He got up and shook his hand effusively.

'Thanks. I'll be there.'

22

The next day, Poulod had dressed carefully in a new shirt crackling with starch. He polished his shoes until they shone and combed his hair with cotton oil so that it lay flat. At one o'clock he was on a bus, on his way to the address on the card, situated in an industrial area near the airport. The bus dispatched him onto a dead street. A sign reading "Tajik Cotton Enterprises" directed him down a small track. As he walked along the dusty road to warehouses in the distance, he sweated in the midday heat, the sun beating down on his back. He wished he had some water or shade. What the hell am I doing here? he thought. It was definitely time to return to Russia. He had been putting it off, reluctant to start working again. His job at the vegetable plant would be gone by now, he was already two weeks late. The thought of returning to that factory had lowered his spirits so much he could hardly get out of bed without vodka. The reeking, overcrowded men-only dormitory, lousy food and rubbish pay did nothing to lure him back. The news of recent events in Russia had percolated to Dushanbe, with stories of increasing Russian resentment towards economic immigrants, Prime Minister Putin's Youth Guard involved in rallies and demonstrations against foreign workers. Life in Dushanbe with his mother cleaning up and cooking for him was more amenable, though he was fast running out of money. He had even grown begrudgingly fond of Faisullo who was not a bad kid, even if he was too scrawny.

He thought he would try his luck at the gas plants and construction sites in eastern Siberia this time, having heard of prospects there. He already had his train ticket and would leave in a week. It was an arduous journey on shabby trains through the steppes and plains of central Asia, dodging customs officials, sitting through endless delays at border control, sometimes taking three days or more.

As he approached the fenced off, isolated industrial lot, he saw several glistening four-wheel-drive vehicles parked outside. One was a shiny new Lexus. This was the place. The warehouse was eerily quiet. Brown dust blew across the yard and a ragged guard dog on a chain barked half-heartedly from his shade next to the barbed wire. Giving the dog a wide berth, Poulod walked through the gate and over to a peeling black door to the side. He knocked smartly and entered. Behind the door was a nervous young man of about twenty holding a Kalashnikov.

'You alone?' he said, twitching.

Poulod gulped nervously, eyeing the gun and raising his hands.

'Of course.' *What the hell is this?*

Jamshed appeared.

'He's alright,' he said. The young man relaxed and lowered his gun.

'Sorry about that, but we have to take precautions,' said Jamshed silkily.

'That's quite all right,' said Poulod, grinning inanely with nerves.

'Come through, take a seat.'

Jamshed walked into the main warehouse where about twelve men sat on chairs in the cavernous space.

'This is all now,' said Jamshed to the young sentry. He nodded and went back to his post at the door.

Poulod sat down on the only empty metal chair. It scraped on the concrete floor, echoing through the empty building. He peered askance at the others. They looked like him, sweating from the walk, fearful and anticipative. Some were older and tanned with lined faces and callused hands from hours toiling in the cotton fields of the south. They looked poor, with brown-stained, broken teeth, straggly beards and wiry, strong bodies dressed in black cotton shirts, traditional pillar box hats, pointed rubber shoes and homemade jackets of buffalo hide. They sat together subserviently, gazing at Jamshed whenever he appeared. The others wore leather jackets over protruding beer guts and were clean shaven, urban and obviously economic migrants back from Russia for the winter. They looked like him, shit scared, studying fingernails in concentration, smoking or holding their gaze to an area of the ground just in front of their feet. What are we all here for?

Jamshed sat down in front of them like a lecturer in a university hall. He bared his teeth into a snarling smile, a golden flash in the darkness of the warehouse.

'I have brought you all here today to make you a business proposition. Some of you might not feel like working with us anymore. If that's the case, I suggest you leave now, before you hear something that might make you a liability.'

None of the men moved. Poulod was stuck to his seat as if held by superglue. He was hit by an almost overwhelming desire to pee.

Jamshed continued. 'I am sure you already know what we do and what our business is.' He laughed cynically and some of the men smirked. 'We are looking for loyalty. That is number one in importance. We are looking for strength, that is number two. Lastly we want intelligence, number three.'

Poulod gulped. He had never been thought of as particularly intelligent, but he could do the first two.

'Now I want half of you to go to one side and the other half to the other.'

Carefully Jamshed chose the men to move to each group. The smart men in leather jackets were more or less on one side, the farmers grouped on the other.

'Right. You men will be drivers and loaders,' he said to the farmers. 'You others, you will be smugglers, glotateli. I don't need to tell you what you're going to be moving heh.' Again he cracked a contemptuous smile. The men sniggered with him deferentially.

Poulod was in the smuggler group. He licked his lips, pleased with his luck. At last, he would get his hands on some of that easy money washing over the fortunate and connected in Dushanbe. Jamshed beckoned to Poulod's group.

'You lot, come with me.' He paused. 'I assume you have all brought your passports as requested?'

The men nodded in assent.

'The rest of you stay here. You will get orders from someone else.'

The men, six of them, left the warehouse and went outside into the glaring sun. Jamshed pulled on a pair of sunglasses. A gleaming white Mashutka mini-bus with darkened windows drove up and the driver jumped out and opened the door.

'Get in,' growled Jamshed.

The men got in and sat down like a herd of well-trained sheep. None of them dared to speak or look at each other. Jamshed slid into the front seat and the driver slid the door closed with a thump. The men could not see out through the darkened windows and there was a compartment barrier preventing them from looking out through the front. As the engine started, the air conditioning blasted freezing air down the back of his neck. I wonder where they are taking us? He felt sick in the rolling darkness. After about twenty minutes the car same to a standstill and the door opened.

'Out,' said the driver roughly.

They were in one of Dushanbe's many 1960's Soviet high rise apartment complexes, it was virtually impossible to tell which. From the mountains beyond Poulod guessed they were still in the eastern part of the city, not far from the airport. Jamshed beckoned the men towards the entrance of one of the blocks and they climbed the damp, unpainted stairwell. A thin, young girl squeezed past coming down in the other direction. She was dressed in an orange tracksuit and blue slippers and had long brown hair pulled back into a ponytail. Her eyes were unfocused, her skin pale and covered in a thick film of perspiration and she smiled at the men as they went past.

'Zdrastovitze Slatki, hi there sweetie,' she whispered in Russian, reaching up to hug Jamshed. As she did so, her forearms were exposed, baring the tell-tale signs of smack addiction, the little pin prick scars along the vein. He ignored her. On the second floor of the building he knocked three times on an ostentatious black leather-padded door. It was opened by a fat, mean looking man with a machine gun. One by the one the men entered and were shown into a small sweatshop. A noxious smell of burning plastic filled the air. Skinny Tajik women in scruffy kurta dresses and embroidered headscarves were methodically sawing small plastic syringes into small containers, then filling them with white powder, melting each end closed with a lighter. They were bleary eyed and barely looked at the men, concentrating on the task before them. Pale, with dark circles under their eyes, they also looked like addicts. It was hot in the room, but all the windows were closed. The men were invited to sit down where a tatty quilt lay. Jamshed brought a basket, filled to the brim with the prepared syringes. Poulod started to feel a little ill. Jamshed sat down facing the men. His voice was dangerously smooth, all of the earlier jokiness gone. He looked at the men, his eyes like black pinpricks.

'Listen to me carefully. You will each be paid two thousand dollars cash to complete this mission. You will now swallow forty of these specially prepared vials, about a kilo of heroin, and board a flight to Moscow leaving in hours. You will be given papers showing you have a job in Moscow. You must not eat or drink after you swallow the merchandise. If you do, you will live to regret it. Once in Domodedovo Airport you will leave the aeroplane separately and not fraternise with one another in the airport. You are strangers to each other and it is best it stays that way. You will be met on arrival by an associate called Artyom with a black Mercedes van who will assist you in regurgitating the vials at a specially designated place. On receipt of the goods you will be paid and taken to a hotel to rest. In three days you will board a flight back to Dushanbe. Are we all clear as to the mission?'

Poulod thought, 'Hodoiiman, I don't want to do this.' But meekly nodded his assent.

The other men looked as nervous as him.

'Your Passports.'

The men meekly handed them over. While Jamshed carefully checked each one, noting names and numbers in a small notebook, an older woman appeared with a large bag of vials and counted out forty for each man. She placed a small bowl of grease that looked like vegetable oil before them.

'Smother the vial in some oil and it will be easier to swallow,' she said.

Poulod reached out his chubby hand for a vial. He was not good at fiddly work and he struggled with the small vials, especially when they were greasy. He tried to swallow one and gagged. The others were having trouble too. Come on, come on, he thought, in a panic. If only they could have some water, but that of course was impossible. After about ten minutes of trying, he swallowed one, retching and gasping as it went down. It was extremely painful as it made slow process down into his gut and he felt every centimetre of its progress until it reached his oesophagus, but he was elated. I did it. Thirty-nine of these little buggers to go, he thought jubilantly.

Their easy progress through Dushanbe Airport surprised Poulod. Not for them the endless queues or difficult questions at customs. Jamshed left them in the VIP area of the airport, where they joined swarthy, fat business men and heavily made up women in stilettos and furs

162

sitting on sagging beige leather sofas full of stub holes. Poulod looked enviously at their vodka, pots of green tea and chocolate bars. What he wouldn't give for a drink to calm his nerves. He tried to look confident like any other business traveller on his way to Moscow.

A harassed looking Tajik Air official processed their passports and papers while they stood around smoking. The air was thick and blue in the lounge. A group of suited foreigners entered carrying laptops, scowling and waving their arms exaggeratedly in the smoky air while a bored looking waitress took their orders for coffee and cokes. Soon they were asked to board the VIP bus. Nodded through by airport officials, they boarded the plane.

Poulod tried not to think about the vials in his stomach and ignored the stewardess with her trolley. To distract himself he watched an Indian film with Tajik subtitles and looked at the clouds. His stomach ached, cramping in protest and he worried constantly that a vial would break open. They landed at seven o'clock local time at Domodedovo Airport. He proceeded through to arrivals without delay, careful to keep a wide berth from the others. He had been given a small, black, hand luggage suitcase by Jamshed on departure in which there was a cheap red shirt, a bar of soap, a toothbrush and a tube of toothpaste. He kept his head down and walked briskly through brightly lit walkways, anxious not to look suspicious.

Outside, it was cold and getting dark. A wintery Moscow sunset reflected on the glassy exterior of the airport, bathing everything in orange light. Poulod was chilly in his thin leather jacket and shirt. A black van pulled up to the arrivals area and a man wound down the window.

'Artyom?'

'Get in.'

All six men entered the van. One staggered into his seat. He was pale and sweating profusely, his hands shaking.

'Quickly, I need to get this shit out of me,' he gasped in pain. The driver turned to look at him and shrugged his shoulders.

'Did he eat on the flight?' he asked.

They all shook their heads dumbly, staring at him in unease. The man groaned and started to cry loudly.

'Hodoiiman, please help me,' he begged. 'I'm dying.'

'He needs a doctor,' said one of the men.

The driver ignored him. As they drove through the gathering dark along eight lane highways the man lost consciousness and collapsed, his head knocking against the window. White foamy spittle dribbled from his open mouth. The driver glanced at him in the back and sighed in disgust, shaking his head.

'Fucking Tajiks.'

'He needs a hospital,' said another of the men tentatively.

'Shut up. No hospitals. We will deal with him ourselves,' growled the driver.

Before long they arrived at a decrepit high rise apartment building. It was already dark, but Poulod could see they were in a downtrodden part of Moscow, somewhere on the periphery of the city. The men were ordered to get out of the van and climb up the three storeys to apartment number fifteen. As they entered the building, the van pulled away. The man who had collapsed remained in the vehicle.

In a non-descript apartment, sparsely furnished, a wrinkled, platinum blonde woman in her fifties, wearing heavy make-up and ostentatious jewellery gave each man a bottle. She lit up a cigarette, inhaling.

'Drink that. The faster, the better,' said the woman.

An open door led to a dirty, stained bathroom, where there were several plastic buckets. The woman told them to go and vomit into these when they needed to, thus: 'Regurgitating the merchandise.'

They put it so prettily, thought Poulod in disgust, as he watched one man after the other run to the bathroom and hurl up the little vials.

Before long, Poulod also felt intensely nauseous. He had never felt so ill. Focus on the money, the new house, the look on Nargis's face when she sees my success. Focus on the future, that's why you are here. Staggering to the bathroom, he retched and vomited orange bile and several of the vials. It was even more painful when they came up from his stomach. Gasping, his throat burning, he saw he had only managed to bring up about four. Thirty-six to go. After around an hour and two bottles of the vile liquid, Poulod vomited all forty vials. His stomach ached from the violent cramping of his gut, his eyes watered and his face was bloodshot with effort. Never again, never again, he thought, moaning in pain, praying it would soon be over.

The woman was oblivious to the men's suffering. She chain smoked, yawned and checked her watch, sipping from a can of Pepsi, watching a soap opera on a small colour TV in the corner. Poulod staggered into the living room. From the window, he saw that the building was next door to a twenty-four-hour landfill site. Security floodlights beamed yellow into the room and an aroma of rotting cabbage and sulphur drifted upwards, making him feel even worse. The black Mercedes van was parked next to an area reserved for scrap metal.

An ashtray, a caricature of President Putin's face, was filled with cigarette stubs. He sat heavily on the faded orange carpet, where another man was already seated, leaning against the wall. His face was wet with effort, and he was doubled up with stomach cramps.

'I'm finished,' he gasped, handing her the bucket.

The woman peered inside and counted out the vials. She took out a hot pink mobile phone covered in crystal zirconia from a patent leather handbag and called someone up to the apartment.

'Two are finished.'

She turned to the men.

'Well done, you did good,' she said, almost kindly.

The driver of the van appeared, holding a Nike gym bag. He was short, blond, with bad acne and stubby little fingers. His hand also sported a black spider tattoo. He had multiple piercings in each of his ears, into which he had inserted small golden Christian Orthodox crucifixes that caught the light like disco balls and sent crosses spraying across the faded wallpaper.

'Here. Payment, arseholes,' he said, passing Poulod a small wad of hundred dollar bills from the bag. He put the vials of powder carefully into a plastic bag and set them into the gym holdall. Poulod noticed another bag already inside, but the vials were covered in blood. Poulod shuddered. He did not want to know. He averted his eyes.

After half an hour all the men had finished. Pale and shaky, doubled in pain, they made the laborious trip back down the stairs and into the van. After a short, agonisingly bumpy drive they came to a small guest house that looked to be in the middle of nowhere.

'Your home for the next three days,' said the taciturn Russian. 'I'll pick you up at six on Thursday morning. Don't be late, wear the new shirts packed in your suitcases and look smart.'

23

It was a relief when temperatures rose, the dry heat seemed to scorch away the epidemics and gradually the water to the house became clearer as the dirt, mud and mess of winter passed through the pipes to be replaced with purer glacial river water. The city bazaars were suddenly full of berries, raspberries and strawberries, early sour cherries and mulberries brought in from the Southern plains near Uzbekistan.

By late March it almost felt like summer. The main Tajik holiday of the year, Nav Ruz, was celebrated. This year Tajiks welcomed the festival with more enthusiasm than usual, having had such a harsh winter. Nav Ruz was rooted in Zoastrianism, the ancient religion once practiced across the region that pre-dated Islam. It banished the cold and dark of winter and ushered in the warmth and rejuvenation of spring. Representing life, health, and prosperity, it was rebirth and renewal, a celebration of continuity and tradition, a bridge between the old and new years. Farmers planted seeds on this special day and women spring-cleaned their houses, banishing winter mould and welcoming in summer smells and colours. Nargis's family made a traditional soup, sumalak, made from the kernels of new wheat shoots sold in the bazaars. Nargis put flowers in Bunavsha's hair and took her children to see the courting couples wandering through the city park in their shiny dresses and smartest suits, regaled by Tajik singers and traditional bands.

At Harriet's house, the climbing roses that covered the garden tapshan, the traditional Tajik tea house of ancient Persia, were in bud, about to bloom into a wonderful array of red, pink and white flowers. Harriet decorated it with sumptuous purple and red velvet quilts and cushions, a small coffee table covered in a red and gold threaded tablecloth for her Kashmiri tea set and a vase of fragrant flowers set in the middle of the carpeted, wooden platform floor. She spent many hours reading novels and jostling with Leo on the tapshan quilts, Alexandra, still thin, colouring her books beside her, enjoying the spring weather and the warm afternoons. Harriet cut back her kindergarten hours and kept her home.

'In England she would still be at pre-school, so I don't think it really matters.'

In mid-March, Henri came home one night to announce they might be leaving in August, six months early.

'Nothing is confirmed and we may not go at all, but I thought I should let you know. I have put in for a transfer and the feedback seems to be positive.'

Harriet's eyes filled with tears and she came forward to hug him. 'Thank you Henri. You do care after all.'

Harriet was overcome with gratitude, kissing his bristled cheeks over and over again in relief. His sudden decision to try to leave Dushanbe after the summer calmed her, letting her dream of her next perfect posting. Nargis overheard her chatting about it to Veronica one afternoon.

'It was a bolt from the blue when Henri changed his mind so suddenly about leaving, but I am certainly not complaining.'

'I would seize the chance and question nothing, I contemplate Germany now, my mother's place might be okay for me and the twins for a year. Christian will run wild but...' Veronica shrugged.

'True, I should seize the chance. Still, it was strange. He was so set on staying and now it is almost as though he is running away as fast as he can. When I begged him to leave for Alexandra's sake he wouldn't hear of it, yet that was only a month ago. I wonder if something happened, if there is something he is not telling me. Perhaps all his hard work is finally paying off. He has applied for a post in Nairobi, fast tracking his application through headquarters. Until now, I didn't even know that was possible.'

'Nairobi eh? You can go on the safari and see the wild animals with the children. How wonderful.'

Harriet sighed. They were sitting out on the tapshan and the scent of roses filled the air. She stared out at her green lawns, tulips waving in the breeze.

'To be honest, I don't like the idea of Nairobi, all that pollution and chaos and those famously dreadful slums right on our doorstep. I'm told there is a suburb full of expats called Muthaiga which looks nice, one can almost pretend one isn't in Nairobi at all, so I've read. It's green and leafy, with a few schools and some nice shops and restaurants. We'll join the country club, learn golf and get a villa with a pool in the garden. I don't speak any Kiswahili, but I am sure they'll speak English.'

Sitting below the tapshan on a blanket with Leo, it sounded like utopia to Nargis. She chewed a fingernail. What will I do when she goes? Harriet spent hours writing out application forms for the international schools, speaking with Kenyan estate agents and doctors and scouring maps for landmarks on the computer.

'I need to get everything prepared, just in case,' she explained. To Nargis, it was as if part of Harriet had already left, her soul flown ahead to new lands, blown overseas by the strength of her hope. Yet the lilac trees were in full bloom and the heady scent of the purple flowers filled the garden air. The red and pink tulips Harriet had brought from England were just finishing their annual display and the reticulated irises that covered one bank in the garden were out, their stunning purple and peach flowers filling Nargis with joy. The previous year, Nav Ruz had been the signal to scatter seeds of lettuce, purple basil and chive in the greenhouse and plant starter plants of tomato and pepper. This year, Harriet took no notice, barely registering her achievements in the beauty of the garden she had worked so hard to grow. The gardener took out the mower and cut the Dutch grass, so lovingly planted the year before, wandering back and forth across the sweet smelling lawn while Harriet sat indoors emailing Kenya.

Nargis's shop sat empty for almost six weeks, through most of February and half of March. Her demanding working week, Alexandra's illness and the extra hours it presented, prevented her from making any headway. No one else could go to the bazaars to buy cheap goods for sale. The cement factory started up again and Said returned to work, the village emptying of angry young men overnight. She refused to ask Abdul for help, having vowed to never again entrust her father with money. The daughter of a neighbour, a giggling virgin of eighteen, agreed to run the shop when she was working, for one hundred somoni a month. Nargis calculated that she could still make a small profit. Then, just before Nav Ruz, Savsang came to see her with one hundred and fifty somoni.

'This is part of the money I have made selling the remainder of my things to a shopkeeper in town,' she said. 'I have no idea when I will get you the rest of the rent. I'm really sorry.'

She looked terrible, with dark shadows under her eyes and enormous weight loss. Her hair was lank, her once smooth skin, covered in acne. She had tried again, without success, to persuade her old lover to return the money he owed her.

'Why don't you threaten to tell your husband?'

'I did. I caught Hassan on the street last night. He told me I was a silly ewe not to run away with him, the money is all gone now. He begged me to leave him alone so that he can mend his broken heart,' said Savsang. She wrapped her arms around herself and swayed back and forth. 'I'm in despair. Hassan knows that the only person who can help me in this is the mullah, my husband and of course, I can't tell him. I wouldn't anyway. I still love Hassan, despite what he's done.'

Nargis touched her arm. 'What are you going to do?'

'I don't know. The bank is threatening to send a bailiff to our house to value the property. If they do that, Azikav will find out. He already asks me difficult questions about why I was not successful in selling my goods and what I have done with the money. Yesterday, he hit me when I wouldn't answer.'

She lifted her hair to show a purple bruise on her lower jaw. It matched her eyes, indigo in the fading light.

'He's old but he's strong.'

Nargis offered her a seat and a bowl of green tea. Savsang gratefully accepted, her hands shaking.

Nargis had not seen her since. Later that week, the mahalla was abuzz with the news that an official looking black mercedes from the Somon Bank had come to Mullah Azikav's dwelling. Two smart, mean looking men in black leather jackets had entered his home and he had been seen shortly afterwards shouting and cursing, throwing rocks at the car and causing a great scandal. One of the men almost exchanged fisticuffs with him but neighbours held them back. Abdul had witnessed the whole debacle from his backgammon match at the street corner bench.

'It was such a shock to see our wise and holy mullah behaving like a common alley cat, fighting on the street.'

Gulya tutted, glancing at Nargis. 'I told you she would drive him mad,' she whispered.

Nargis shivered, anxious for the welfare of her friend now that the mullah knew about the loan. Savsang disappeared, taking her children with her. Nargis assumed she had left for Tosh Teppa in Southern Tajikistan where she still had a sister. It was a conservative part of the country, just twenty-five miles from the border with Afghanistan, where their village mullah would not take kindly to Savsang leaving her husband if he found out. Nargis wondered how her brother-in-law would view her arrival with three more mouths to feed. The southern areas were even more difficult than Dushanbe, with almost all the able-bodied men away for most of the year in Russia. Her brother-in-law might be home for winter. Nargis fervently hoped she had other siblings. She prayed that Savsang would not be stupid enough to come back. Her husband was a hard looking man with a long beard specked with grey and shrewd, unkind eyes. He had hit her often in the past and Nargis knew his fists would be itching to beat her half to death now that she had left him bankrupt.

When Nargis got home from work that evening, Gulya sent her back out to the shop for roatan noodles. It was already dark, the mahalla almost pitch black in the latest electricity cut. Small lights shone under door cracks, as people tried to cook their evening meal on kerosene or coal stoves, lit by oil lamps. She hated to dip into her pitiful shop stock, but it was cheaper than going to the other shop in the village. Unlocking the front door, she slipped inside, grabbing noodles and a packet of sugar. Carefully she noted it in her ledger, 'three packs of roatan, two somoni ten dirams, one kilo bag of sugar, five somoni', she wrote. From somewhere on the crowded shelves she heard the tell-tale scratching of mice, feasting on odd pieces of dried food. She heard a creaking sound from the front porch and swung round to see who it was. A dark figure stood at the door.

'Who is it?' she asked into the shadows, her voice shaking. The figure stood motionless.

'We are closed. Please announce yourself now before I call my brother,' she said boldly. Could it be Poulod? Had he followed her home? Quickly, she looked around for something to defend herself with. There was nothing to hand except the wooden broom, leaning against the counter in a small pile of dust. She grabbed it and held it tightly in front of her, ready to swing hard if he came closer. The figure came forward slowly.

'It is Mullah Azikav,' said a deep, accented voice. 'You must tell me where she is, or I warn you, I will not be responsible for my actions.'His body was supported by a wooden cane. He seemed to have aged ten years in the last week. In the faded light Nargis could make out his glinting eyes and long beard. His face was grim and he held out a one hundred somoni note.

'Here, Nargis. This is for you. If I give you a little reminder, no, a present, perhaps you will remember where she is, eh?' he said, grinning wryly. His voice rose. 'I know you women. Always something else you need to buy, hey? Nothing is ever enough for you, eh?'

All the fight seemed to leave him. He sighed and fell forward, collapsing on the ground at her feet, sobbing miserably into his hands. His wooden cane fell to the ground with a clatter. 'She has ruined me,' he cried, his muffled sobs growing louder. 'Please have pity on an old man, in the name of Allah the merciful. An old, disappointed, heartbroken man.'

Nargis gasped. She did not know how to respond, what to do. Kneeling down she offered her arm.

'Please get up, Mullah, the floor is dirty.'

Just then, Gulya entered. She had come to see what was taking Nargis so long. Silently, she surveyed the scene before her. The mullah was a respected gentleman in the mahalla and a friend of Abdul's who had grown up in a neighbouring village in the same district.

'Mullah Azikav,' she cried. 'What has happened? Dear man, how can we help you?' she asked, her thin hands grasping at his. To Nargis she hissed, 'Fetch a chair from the back room, you stupid child. You see, I told you that woman would be nothing but trouble.'

Nargis reluctantly left to fetch a chair. She could hear her mother whispering comforting words to the old man, all the while helping him up from the dirt. The mullah looked at Gulya, his wrinkled eyes gentler, imploring.

'I have come here, broken, in despair, to ask your daughter to help me, in the name of Allah, our merciful and all powerful God, to help me find my wife. I just want to talk to her. She has left me with nothing. She has ruined me. She has taken my children. I am nothing, nothing, nothing.'

As he spoke his anger and despair seemed to grip him again, leaving him fighting for breath. His face was pale, his lips blue. Gulya pursed her lips and looked at Nargis. She noticed the one hundred somoni note in his hand. Her eyes narrowed.

'My daughter will certainly tell you where she is,' she said sternly, turning to stare at Nargis. 'If she knows what is right and what is wrong, as we taught her and if she knows what is good for her.'

Nargis wrung her hands. Did she mean to throw her out over this? It was not her fault. She panicked.

'I am not sure where Savsang is,' she said hesitatingly. 'That is… she did not mention anything to me.'

The two old people looked at her, waiting for more.

'He has a right to know and he is your aksakal,' said Gulya quietly.

'Yes… well, maybe she went to a relative or a girlfriend,' said Nargis brightly. The mullah screwed up his face in consternation.

'Tosh Teppa? Would she go all that way to avoid me?'

'She was very frightened. Very stressed about the bank loan,' she said. 'She thought you might not forgive her, or that you would try to take away the children.'

The mullah wiped the sweat and dirt from his face with a handkerchief.

'But what happened to all that money?' he cried wearily, half wailing. 'She can't have spent that much in a few months. I don't understand it. I went with her to the bazaar to buy the stuff for her business. She spent about one thousand somoni there, I saw it with my own eyes. I thought that money came from the savings from her little business. She did not buy anything else. We transported it here together by bus. I helped her stack the shelves. I truly wanted her to succeed, my sweet little Savsang flower.'

Gulya looked at him. She leant down to his ear.

'Aziz, she was not faithful to you,' she whispered. 'She was seeing another man and gave him the money. I'm sorry I did not tell you before. My stupid daughter made me promise.'

The mullah sat silently on the chair for a few minutes. Then he started crying again and almost collapsed once more, gripping the counter for balance.

'It is not possible,' he yelled, tears running down his face. 'She gave away my house to borrow money for some bastard lover. She will pay for this with blood,' he said, spitting in rage. His eyes were red rimmed and full of hatred. 'This is your doing Nargis, she's been tainted by your company, your bad example to her,' he cried.

Nargis gasped.

'No, Mullah Azikav, I promise…'

'That bitch!'

Laying down the money on the counter, he stumbled out of the building and staggered off in the direction of his home.

'Please, Mullah, come back,' Gulya cried. 'We don't want your money.'

He was gone. The shop was once more silent. Nargis stood still, her eyes wide. Hodoiiman, what have I done? Why didn't I stay quiet?

'What if he kills her mother?' said Nargis shakily. 'Her blood will be on my conscience forever.'

Gulya shrugged her shoulders.

'Oh well, he got what he wanted and now he won't be back,' she said pragmatically, slipping the money into her pocket. She cackled gleefully. 'Gone to get the first bus out to Tosh Teppa I shouldn't wonder and I would love to see the look on her face when he comes knocking at the door.' Her laughter echoed through the darkness. 'Cheer up. You did the right thing telling him her whereabouts. After all, we have to live in this mahalla too you know. Anyway, you know what they say: "Even the doorstep laughs at the quarrel between husband and wife".'

Nargis picked up the broom wearily. Gulya rubbed her hands together.

'I will leave you to lock up Shireen, as there are hungry grandchildren waiting at home,' she said. Picking up the bag of noodles, Gulya hobbled off into the dark.

March 24th, 2008, Tajikistan Countdown: 4 months, 14 days

I'm sorry to say that even though we may leave in a few months, Henri works harder than ever. Another trip to Kazakhstan this week. This time he stayed the weekend too, claiming he had meetings on Saturday. I am starting to wonder. He asked me to pack a large suitcase this time with casual clothes (woollen sweaters, jeans and skiwear), hiking boots and even a few bottles of his favourite wine. I saw him throw in his swimming trunks so that he could use this sauna where the Kazakhs go to discuss business over a massage and a few shots of vodka. It seems he has made friends with some locals who take him to ski in a place called Chimbelek and to an ice skating stadium called Medeo in the mountains above Almaty. It all sounds rather nice, far better than here. I asked him, 'When are you going to take me along?' and he was evasive. I wouldn't mind seeing Kazahkstan, especially as we are leaving central Asia soon. 'How could you leave the children behind with that Tajik peasant?' he asked me, as if horrified. I thought that was strange, after all, Nargis always stays with them when we go out together and he never seems to care. 'It would just be for a few days,' I said, 'or we could take them along too. Perhaps Nargis would like to see Almaty, we can help her get a passport.' He just shook his head. 'Absolutely out of the question,' he said. And that was that.

I ask him every week if he has heard anything about our transfer. 'Non, nothing,' he tells me, always the same answer. I know I need to be patient, but I'm tired of living in limbo. I dread the prospect of another winter in Tajikistan. After a month of frantic preparations, I now feel deflated, anti-climactic. The only way to live now is to put Kenya out of my head. After all, we may not go, like poor Veronica and then where will I be?

24

It was early April. On Rudaki Avenue, the tall trees were resplendent in green foliage, providing some much needed shade. Harriet and Nargis were in the garden with Leo. Harriet chose to spend more and more time with Nargis, talking to her more like a friend than a servant. She cut beautiful pink and burgundy roses with a pair of green rose pruners from the trailing bushes that covered the tapshan and Nargis sat on the front stoop jiggling Leo on her knee. Harriet's head bent to sniff the flowers.

'Mmm. Their scent reminds me of my mother's garden in England,' she said.

'You know, rose, Sad Barg, come from Tajikistan?'

'Somewhere in central Asia, you mean?'

'No, Tajikistan. We are all named for flowers.' Nargis looked pensive. 'I still hear nothing of Savsang, Iris flower. Nearly one month since she go and the mullah gone from our mahalla.' Her voice quavered.

Harriet's eyes narrowed. 'It's not your fault, Nargis.' Harriet touched her arm. 'Really, I am sure she is alright.'

It was thirty-five degrees in the sunshine and they sheltered in the shade of the grapevines. They both wore bright cotton Salwar Kameez. Harriet did not wear shorts out of respect for the guards and had recently visited a tailor with Nargis. She wore the cheap Tajik clothes around the house, not wanting to admit to the expatriate community at large that she was "turning native" but local clothing was so much cooler, the thin folds of material allowing her skin to breathe. The tailor, Hikoyat, was a fat Uzbek woman with alarming gold teeth and five dark, lumpen step-daughters. She worked from a little house in a mahalla leading off the northern part of Rudaki Avenue, her stern looking, ancient mother-in-law reclining on a tapshan in the yard. She quickly knocked up five cotton tunic and drawstring trouser suits out of the least garish material Harriet could find in the market on an enormous, working on an ancient sewing machine with huge pedals like a church organ. Nargis made two for herself that Harriet insisted on paying for.

'A present for you, for all your help when Alex was so ill,' she said. 'We can use the remnants to make a few outfits for Bunavsha too.'

Harriet battled with the tailor to make hers a little shaped, tighter across the breasts and shorter than usual. 'After all, I can't let go of all my Western ideals. We can call it "Tajik fusion".'

When the guard Musso saw them both in their new outfits he roared with laughter.

'Much better, cooler eh?' he said, smiling.

Nargis was relieved to get out of her pink velveteen kurta. It had been years since she had had bright new clothes to wear. When Henri first saw Harriet he raised an eyebrow and beckoned her to his study for a little chat. Harriet was crestfallen afterwards.

'He hates these ethnic clothes, the loud colours. He agreed that I shouldn't wear shorts in front of Musso and Boron, but he's asked me to always wear normal attire with other foreigners.'

Harriet still met with Patty and Veronica sometimes, though less often than before. Veronica had had more trouble with the servants, this time enduring a robbery by yet another short-lived nanny in her employ.

'The agency, a proper nanny agency, sent me a heroin addict, can you imagine?' she told an astonished Harriet. 'When I told the police that she had stolen my gold rings, the twins's iPod and some other items they said she was on the records as a junkie. She has been in the prison. And she was taking care of my children. Honestly Harriet, Tajikistan is enough to drive anyone crazy.'

Today, they were both coming for lunch. As they entered the compound, the old sang-froid between Harriet and Nargis returned, the mistress-servant barrier wordlessly re-erected. Nargis got down from the tapshan and went to sit with Leo on the lawn. Patty came bustling in through the gate, her thin frame wrapped in a revealing turquoise cotton T-shirt and a short skirt that showed off brown, wrinkly knees. She was energetically fanning her flushed face with an oriental paper fan and breathed a large sigh of relief at the sight of Harriet's shaded tapshan. Then she caught sight of Harriet.

'Good Lord an' heavens above,' Patty exclaimed, looking astonished. 'What are you wearin'?'

'Do you like it? These are some clothes I had made by the tailor,' said Harriet, smiling faintly, enjoying Patty's horrified expression. Nargis hid a grin.

'You look very interestin' I suppose,' said Patty, trying to be polite, and hiding her expression with difficulty. 'Like one uh' them hippies from San Diego.'

Veronica arrived next in her land cruiser, sweating, her blonde bob wet at the temples, holding chubby, lolly-popped twins by reluctant, sticky hands. She was wearing black shorts and a tight black vest top that made her look even fatter than usual. Her thighs bulged and her bulbous arms wobbled as she stepped down from the car. The guard Borun and the gardener did not know where to look as she undulated past, nearly naked to their eyes.

'Think she has a husband?' Borun sniggered.

'Who knows? He shouldn't let her leave the house,' said the gardener. Nargis gasped and covered her smirk once more, burying her face in Leo's toy box. The men fell about laughing.

'*Ach du leibe Gott,*' Veronica exclaimed. 'Harriet, have you turned mad?'

'Why do ya' wanna bow to their Muslim ways?' said Patty. 'As a feminist, I object. We aren't Moslems, we don' have to cover up. We're Western Women, we can do whatever we want. Besides honey, how'll you get a tan?'

'I don't want a tan,' said Harriet. 'This has nothing to do with wanting to bow to Muslim ways. I get cheaper prices in the market dressed this way because the traders assume I'm married to a Tajik or living here in a local way. I don't get hassled by the street boys either, even though, to traditional Tajiks, these clothes are a little risqué.'

'Risqué? What do you mean?' spluttered Veronica, looking down at her mottled thighs splayed across the tapshan quilt. She frowned and pushed blonde tendrils off her sweating brow, eyeing Nargis on the lawn with Leo. 'I suppose this was *Her* idea?'

'Nargis did come with me to the tailor, so yes, I suppose it was her idea.'

Patty and Veronica exchanged a look. Harriet blushed. There was a pause.

At length, Patty spoke. 'Well, I am not givin' up my clothes, or dressin' like them. It's a matter uh principle. I'm sick enough of havin' to change so many thin's in my lifestyle to live here, without that too.'

Harriet shrugged. 'Fair enough.'

April 10ᵗʰ, 2008, Tajikistan Countdown: 3 Months, 15 days

Henri has been back a week. He is snappy and seems to be avoiding me, citing work meetings and receptions, no partner invited. I feel sorry for him, he is working so hard. I feel guilty about it too, it's all because I'm making him leave Tajikistan early. He's home late each night and grabs takeaways from Delhi Darbar and the Turkish restaurant, Merve, which he eats at the office. I don't really mind, it saves me having to cook fancy dinners for him in the heat. He's been working weekends here as well, leaving Nargis and I to entertain the children with walks to the park and trips to Varzob Gorge to sit on canopied tapshans high above the white-water river, eating juicy shashlik beef kebabs, naan and tea. I pack ketchup and juice and slather the children in suntan lotion. Nargis seems to enjoy our day

181

trips. She has not been to Varzob for a shashlik since she was a child. The other Tajik families we see on the river shore look comparatively well off. I asked her, 'Is it because you and your friends find it too expensive to come these days?' She shook her head. 'No,' she said, 'all my friends are married now. Their families don't approve of me, a woman that dared to leave her husband. They think I will be a bad influence on them because I am no better than a prostitute.' Nargis looked sad as she spoke. For the first time, I realised what her actions did to her, how her reputation was ruined, how brave she is. 'Don't you have any girlfriends left?' I asked, thinking of all mine, back in England. She grinned at me conspiratorially. 'Only in secret.'

The river water was freezing, too cold for swimming, but the children had fun running about in a small clearing nearby. Next door to our tapshan there were two black-eyed, fat men in designer T-shirts and jeans with bottle-blonde, giggling Russian girls. They were drunk, their table crowded with empty beer bottles and half eaten shashlik. They brought a radio with them and played Russian pop. The blondes danced wildly for their boyfriends and fell about laughing on the riverbank. I found them amusing but Nargis seemed nervous and wanted to leave.

I wish my old Henri was back, the one I fell in love with. The one I gave up my whole life for. I miss the romantic attentiveness of being the object of his love. He never compliments me anymore, it's as though I were invisible. I could walk into his study naked and he wouldn't notice. The other night I initiated sex for the first time in weeks. It was awkward, we were both fumbling. As soon as it was over Henri kissed me on my cheek like he would Alex or Leo. Then he washed himself off, put his cotton pyjamas back on and went to lie down in 'his' bedroom. It felt like he was doing me a favour, servicing his wife's needs out of some sense of duty.

I asked him why he doesn't work from home anymore. He just glanced at that damn Blackberry, tool of the Devil and said, 'It is too distracting'. He says he has to work harder if he's to have any chance of leaving Tajikistan by end of the summer. He looked at me and shrugged sadly. 'Il faut casser le noyau pour avoir l'amande.' I felt guilty for complaining then and he left without another word.

Weekends, especially Sundays, are 'family time' and my friends are busy with their husbands. They would be disapproving if they knew how Nargis and I go to Varzob and chat about our lives, exchanging confidences on the riverbank. Worse, I am bringing her children with us next week. It's just as well the kids and I have her though. Without her, we would be utterly alone.

25

Towards the end of April, Harriet and the children were invited to a little party for Hussein's Birthday. Henri had an unexpected day off. When Harriet told him where she was going, he sat sulking in front of the news, his face dark, his eyes narrow. He ran his fingers through his hair and spoke quietly.

'After all your comments when I have to work weekends I think you are a hypocrite. What am I meant to do here on my own? Cancel. Say you're ill. In four months you will probably leave Tajikistan and never see them again anyway.'

Harriet winced. His words smarted with the cruel truth. She went to him with outstretched arms.

'Please Henri. Try to understand. I'm sorry, but I have to go, they are all expecting us now.'

Henri pushed her hands away and got up, grabbing his mobile phone.

'Just remember that the next time you complain to me about working too much. I think I will go out for lunch with Nick. There's also a new friend in town, someone I met in Kazahkstan.'

Harriet frowned, uneasy. Nick was a seasoned journalist working with local reporters to build a free press, but like so many expat workers faced with impossible, idealistic goals, he had resorted to alcohol. Outside, she could hear the children shrieking on the lawn happily. Peering out of the window she saw Nargis sitting on the tree swing with Leo on her lap, the guard kicking a ball to Alexandra.

'Nick is an alcoholic womaniser. You should stay here and work like you would do anyway, not go out and get drunk with local tarts.'

Henri sniggered and put his face close to hers. She could smell the coffee on his breath. It made her gag.

'Nick and I have also have some things to discuss you know, work related stuff. I think we will go to La Luna.'

La Luna was known for vodka, business men and girls, relatively high class Russian blondes and brunettes in tight plastic miniskirts with wandering hands and red painted mouths.

Harriet shrugged. 'Enjoy yourself.'

What a difference the summer made. The muddy bog in Nargis's yard was now a flat, hard floor swept daily to keep the dust at bay, the land above and around the smelly latrine teeming with vegetables and herbs, grown by Abdul in terraced beds. Chirping birds pecked the ground for crumbs and the surrounding mountains were green and soft in the afternoon light. Gulya's naan oven had been dragged outdoors and she cooked on a small fire in one corner, squatting down to her cheap metal deg to stir a Tajik pasta; long, thick, filling strands in a sauce with onion, potato, tomatoes and garlic.

It was a lovely party, full of laughter. Harriet brought a Spider Man birthday cake and presents, secreted out of the house under Henri's nose. Hussein's face lit up, though he stayed close to Gulya, who encased his small shoulders with her body like a mother crow would her chick. The women and children sat on quilts on one side of the yard, the men on the other as tradition dictated, drinking local cola and tea. Harriet took pictures of the shy birthday boy and formal group photos of the grown ups. Henri's words came back to her like an echo. '…Leave in four months and never see them again.' She felt something approaching sorrow and it was suddenly difficult to swallow. Nargis sat on a quilt hugging her knees. She looked unusually youthful in her salwar khameez, eyes dancing at one of Said's jokes. She caught Harriet's glance and gave her a frank, open smile.

When they returned, Harriet found Henri sitting on the patio in the ebbing sunset with Nick and a tall, brassy woman painted in blood red lipstick and thick black

185

eyeliner. The table was crowded with empty Baltika 7 lager tins and tumblers used for Henri's eighteen-year old Scotch malt. The hi-fi was blasting Led Zeppelin into the neighbourhood. Alexandra skipped indoors to watch TV.

'Here's *ma fille*, Harietta.' shouted Henri jubilantly.

He was smashed, no doubt drinking solidly since lunchtime. Harriet's stomach clenched and she started to perspire. The redhead was staring at her Tajik attire with a bemused expression on her face.

'Sit down, *Cherie*, have a drink,' said Henri jovially.

She sighed inwardly.

'Hi, Nick.'

Nick lifted his bulk to envelope her in a smoky, sticky bear hug. She recoiled as his damp paunch pressed against her abdomen. Droplets of sweat were gathered like soap bubbles on his forehead. He passed her a glass, holding out the scotch bottle but she waved it away.

'I'll bring some iced water.'

Harriet looked expectantly at the other guest. She was watching Nick with a lazy smirk on her face. Slowly she extended a slim, tanned hand.

'Sill-wanna Vuković. Pleased to meet you,' she drawled, her accent exotic after Nick's West London brogue. Harriet gave Henri an acidic look. Is this one of Nick's girls from La Luna? Trust Henri to let him bring her to our house. Harriet shook her hand gingerly.

'Pleased to meet you too,' she said with a forced smile.

'Silvana works for the UN. She's from Bosnia and has come here from Almaty. You'll be staying a while, won't you Silvie? It's up to me and Nick here, to show 'er a good time.'

Silvie?

Silvana lit a thin menthol cigarette, languidly blowing the smoke up into the evening sky.

'For my sins, yes, I'm going to be stuck here for few months. Would have preferred New York or Geneva, but hey, someone obviously doesn't like me in headquarters,' she sniggered again.

'What do you do for the UN?' asked Harriet politely.

'I'm Administrator. Sorting out mess that local staff have made of the books over last year.' She sighed and stubbed out a cigarette, crossing tanned legs in high, patent leather wedges.

'She is putting herself down. Her job is crucial to the UN's survival.'

Nick laughed a little loudly and squeezed Silvana's thigh affectionately under the table. Henri looked momentarily irritated and then forced a chuckle.

'I say, hands off, *mon brave*. She's a married woman.'

Harriet sent Henri an appraising glance. He feels left out, I suppose, she thought. She was rendered invisible, overshadowed by Silvana's artificial looks. Bold and sassy with flamboyant jewellery and big blue eyes, she was in her forties and smoked heavily, judging by the overflowing ashtray. She seemed to be drinking the men under the table, yet seemed sober by comparison with their antics. Harriet was almost certain she didn't have any children.

'How long have you been married?' she asked politely.

'This time, two years. But he's third husband,' she said. To the astonished roars of laughter from the men, she grinned. 'Right now I am married to Pierre. We met on flight from Africa, over Champagne in business class and two weeks later he proposed. I thought, why not? Paris sounded good. I spent two years trying to be good vife for him, but frankly, he lives in shitty industrial town outside Paris and housevife life was not for me. My daughter likes him though, so she's still there, going to school.'

Harriet blanched. A daughter?

'Pierre worshipped me and soon I got French passport. My daughter is fourteen, she does what she vants, there's nothing I can say to her, she has her own mind, boyfriend.'

She dismissed her personal life with a swish of a jewelled hand, inhaling deeply on a new cigarette.

'What about the other husbands?' asked Nick. Harriet glanced at him. He was like a little boy drooling over a candy floss stall.

'My first husband vas mistake, sexy student from Beograd, nothing but trouble. We married so I could get out of my parents place, they were serious drag. A baby came in year. I didn't make that mistake again. We stayed together for five years. Then war started and I vas refugee in my own country, watching my fellow citizens shelling my city on TV. My second husband came along pretty soon. He was Egyptian peacekeeper, we met in bar in Republika Serbska. I liked him, he vas sweet guy. When my divorce came through, we got married and went to Cairo with my daughter. But soon I realised I didn't like it there. Too damn crowded with no freedom for liberated woman, bloody mother-in-law sticking her nose in my business all the time, criticising everything from the clothes I wore to the way I made the bloody baba ganoush. I stayed four years in Cairo and then moved to Sharm El Sheik to work in a hotel as assistant manager. I need freedom, like flower needs water and sun. After few years, I left Egypt with my daughter and eventually got job for UN in New York City.'

Everyone was silent for a moment, digesting her story. Silvana downed her scotch in one go.

'Wow,' said Nick. 'What an interesting life you've led.'

'It is pure inspiration, survival, the stuff of a great novel by Emile Zola,' gushed Henri admiringly, pouring them all another liberal scotch.

It must be the drink talking, Harriet thought. Sighing, she stood up. 'I have to get dinner ready for the kids, you lot carry on.'

She hoped this would be a signal for them to leave. Obviously it was too subtle.

'Shall I order us a few pizzas?' said Nick. 'So you don't have to cook,' he added helpfully.

'No Nick, I'm sure Harriet can rustle us up something delectable,' said Henri, looking at her in expectation. 'How's about it, *Ma Chou*? Some olives and cheese, a bit of bread and ham will do, won't it?'

Silvana nodded and Nick shook his head up and down enthusiastically. Henri had brought back some smoked beef from his last trip to Tashkent. The children loved it and there was not much left. She would have to send a guard for fresh naan. She hated it when Henri got drunk. He was a lousy host, always expecting her to do everything. She didn't have the energy for another fight.

'Sure. It will be a few minutes,' said Harriet with a sigh.

26

The next evening, at six o'clock, Nargis left the Simenon's compound and trudged to the bus stop to wait for her mini-bus. It had been a long day and she was tired. Her salwar khameez clung to her body and she reeked. Wiping a wet brow, she boarded the minibus and squeezed into a small space in the back, suffocating in the stuffy atmosphere. The mini-bus took her down past The Shepherds Crook café, along the dry riverbed, past piles of rotting waste and industrial debris. The valley looked less ugly in the evening light with the mountains clearly visible in the distance.

'Here, here, stop please,' she called to the driver and alighted, paying the eighty dirams. As she walked home she wondered about Savsang. Nothing had been seen of Mullah Azikav since that night in her shop. It was rumoured he had left Dushanbe, but no one knew where he had gone except, of course, Nargis and Gulya. As she walked home, she wandered up an alley in between the houses and peered through a crack in the wall to look at the mullah's dwelling. She was surprised to see evidence of habitation. A few dirty dishes were sitting outside by the sink, the tap was running a trickle and the clay tandoor oven smoked, its gritty embers visible in the evening light. Was Savsang home? Nargis did not dare to enter. She hurried home.

'Mother? Are you there?' she called, coming through the gate. Gulya emerged from the house with matches. She was in the middle of lighting the fire for vegetable stew. They had managed to grow some spring onions, parsley, carrots and new potatoes on the narrow terraced plot above the latrine and while Gulya lamented having to pick them so young, they didn't have anything else to use that day. It was close to the end of April and all their spare money had gone on a sack of flour the week before and Bunavsha's new school uniform, shoes and fees. She squatted by the embers, trying to coax life into the kindling.

'Yes, Nargis, what?' she asked.

'I think Savsang is back.'

Gulya stopped her work on the fire and looked up.

'Really? How do you know that?'

'Their house seems to have a woman in it again. The tandoor was working and someone had been cooking there. Do you think she's alright?'

Gulya grunted. 'Probably not.'

Nargis paced their compound wringing her hands.

'Mother, we should go over there and check to see if she's still breathing.'

'Don't be silly. It is not for us to interfere in the business between husband and wife. You will not go there and further embarrass this family. You did enough.'

'But…'

'No, Nargis. Promise me you will not go.'

Gulya started to poke about in the ashes again. Suddenly, curiosity seemed to get the better of her.

'In a few days, I'll send Abdul on a friendly visit to see his old comrade. He can tell us what's going on.'

'Alright.'

Two days passed, with Nargis peeping through the wall as she went to and from from work. She never caught a glimpse of either Savsang or the mullah, though their children were back at school, pale, withdrawn and refusing to respond to their teachers' inquisitive enquiries about their absence. Others in the mahalla started to wonder and before long the streets were alive with gossip.

Their neighbour Sitora was full of the latest intrigue. She had beaten them to it, dispatching a reluctant husband to the mullah's house with some chewing tobacco and a request for an Islamic ceremony to be performed that autumn. Now she stood across the fence, telling Gulya and her other neighbours all about it.

'The mullah went to his wife's relatives in Tosh Teppa and more or less dragged her home by her hair,' she said excitedly. 'Once the village realised that she was there against her husbands' will they refused to help, barring her from her sister's house, him being a holy man and all. Now he's keeping her hostage at home, not letting her leave to go anywhere and not leaving himself. Apparently he sits all day in the house watching her, hardly speaking and not taking his eyes off her. My husband said she was covered in bruises, with lashes on her arms as though she had been whipped and that she was limping.'

Nargis who stood listening by the fire, winced. I knew it, she thought, horrified.

'Mother, we have to help her,' said Nargis quietly, when Sitora was gone.

'Why should we?' said Gulya. 'She has been a terrible wife, behaving like a whore. She deserves what she gets.'

'I have to help her.'

'You've done enough.'

Later the family were seated outside on quilts, enjoying some rest in the cool evening temperatures when there was a tapping at the gate. Nargis called to her son to go and see who it was. Hussein came back to the family, his eyes wide.

'Grandfather, it's for you,' he said. 'It's Mullah Azikav.'

Abdul shifted himself from the quilt and went to the door. After a few moments he called Said to join him and they left together.

'Where are they all going at this time of night?' said Gulya irritably.

Nargis sat up. 'Mother, if the mullah has left with Father then Savsang is at home on her own.' Quickly she stood up and pulled on her slippers. 'I'm going. You can come if you want, or not. It's up to you.'

Gulya lifted her head from the quilt.

'Very well then, go. I have no further interest in that stupid woman. Make sure no one sees you enter and don't stay too long,' she said, lying back down. The grandchildren huddled around her bony frame.

Nargis crept into Mullah Azikav's compound. Quietly she stepped to the door of the house and whispered, 'Savsang, assalom.'

There was rustling from within and the door opened a crack and then closed.

'Go away. Leave me alone,' said a tearful voice.

'Savsang, please let me come in.'

The door opened again, only a few centimetres.

'Oh Nargis. Aziz has gone to Hassan's house to retrieve the money he owes me. For a week he's been torturing me, trying to force me to admit to my affair and tell him where he lives. In the end I had to, what could I do?' She opened the door fully and Nargis gasped. Savsang was unrecognisable. Her face was distended, covered in large blue and yellow bruises and she had a large infected gash on one cheek. One of her eyes was swollen shut and her lips were puffy and cut. Tears ran down her face as she allowed Nargis to embrace her thin frame. Nargis could feel her shaking uncontrollably through her kurta,

'Savsang. Oh, shireen.'

'He's gone there now, he says he will get the money back or kill him, he doesn't care. He told me he will take his wife's jewellery if necessary. Mine, he already sold to pay off some of the loan. With interest it was more than one thousand dollars by the time Aziz found out. Luckily the other mullahs are helping him to pay it off and save his house.'

Savsang sat down roughly on the quilt in their living area. The children were in another room. Nargis could hear them nervously whispering to each other. Nargis understood why Abdul had left with her father and brother in such a hurry. They were to be extra manpower for the mission. The mullah was too old to face a younger rival alone, but he would be a formidable opponent with her father and brother beside him.

'Don't worry about Hassan. He has brought this on himself by taking your money in the first place,' said Nargis. 'He will suffer the consequences of what he did to you.'

'But I don't want that, I don't want anyone to suffer,' she wailed. 'I never wanted anyone to know about Hassan, least of all my husband. Now Aziz knows, he will never let me live in peace. He hates me and he has repeated over and over again that he will divorce me with Se Taloq as soon as he gets all the money back. You know we were only married with Nikoh, so he can divorce me quick as that.' She flicked her fingers.

'He tells me that he beats me to destroy my looks so that no man will ever look at me again. I know he is planning to throw me out and keep the children. I suppose the only good thing is that if he pays my debts my soul will be able to rest in peace. I see no point in going on, my life is finished.'

Weeping uncontrollably, Savsang could not continue.

'Please Savsang, look at me. I am divorced and widowed, but my life is not finished.'

Savsang sobbed, wiping her sore eyes with a bloody handkerchief.

'I am not you, Nargis. You are stronger than me and your parents sometimes give you a hard time but in the end they stood by you. My parents are dead and my relatives are southerners, traditional people. As soon as my sister realised that I was staying with her against the wishes of Aziz she threw me out, fearing a scandal. He came to Tosh Teppa and I was already leaving. He caught me at the bus station trying to get on a bus back to Dushanbe. It was terrible, the sight of him, the look on his face. I knew he had found out about the money.'

Nargis swallowed her guilt. That wasn't all he found out about, she thought to herself, inwardly cursing her earlier weakness.

'You have to leave him Savsang, he is hitting you too much. It doesn't matter what you did, this is not right. You should see a doctor.'

Savsang laughed brokenly.

'What doctor? He won't let me leave the house. And who will pay the medical bills? Aziz? And where will I go, tell me?' she cried. 'No one will take me in. No one can afford to feed an extra three people and I have no relatives here. There is nothing I can do.'

'Savsang, he's a mullah, even though he is also a jealous husband. Surely he should show you more compassion?'

'He has told me that the *Quran* Verse 34 of *an-Nisa* gives permission to men to beat their wives if they fear rebellion, '*nushûz*'. There is no greater rebellion than having sexual relations with another, it is true. No one would take my side if they knew and he'll poison everyone against me. But I refuse to live on the street like a beggar.' From outside there was a sudden noise. Savsang started in fright, pushing Nargis towards the door in panic.

'God, all I need is for him to know I have been talking to you about it. Go, quickly and please don't tell anyone you've seen me.'

Nargis held her hand briefly.

'Try to stay strong and hopeful. Your life is not over. I will come again, when I can.'

Savsang, nodded and slammed the door, leaving Nargis standing in the darkness. When she got home, she told her mother what she had seen. Gulya was unsurprised and did not comment. Later, Abdul returned with her brother. Looking serious, they entered the yard and sat down on the quilts in the darkness with the women.

'A terrible business,' said Abdul soberly, shaking his head. 'She humiliated him beyond what is normal in a marriage.'

'You know what your old mother, may God bless her soul, used to say: "A wife can make a good man or a bad man out of her husband," said Gulya obliquely.

'Did the mullah get his money back?' asked Nargis.

Abdul nodded.

'When the young man saw who and worse, what his rival lover was, he did not hesitate to pay him in gold and cash. He was terribly ashamed and prostrated himself before us begging forgiveness in the name of Allah. Besides, Aziz threatened to go to his mahalla mullah to complain if he refused. The young man was frightened of the scandal that would befall him and his household if he refused. It turns out he still lives with his parents.'

'I am so glad,' said Nargis, relieved. 'Perhaps, if the debt is paid, the mullah will find it in his heart to forgive his wife.'

Nargis handed her father a bowl of tea. And maybe she will forgive herself, she thought.

A few days later the village was abuzz with the terrible news. The young, beautiful wife of Mullah Azikav had been found by neighbours in the yard. Her body charred and smoking, she had burned to death by accident refilling her kerosene lamps while the children were at school. The mullah was not there at the time, having gone to the bank. Nargis heard the news from a customer in her shop. Her legs gave out from under her and she had to sit down on a wooden stool. She killed herself, but she died in protest, she thought, tears springing to her eyes. Poor, poor Savsang, I should have helped her to leave, given her a bed in our house, anything. Nargis gazed sadly at a few strands of tinsel softly waving in the summer breeze. The customer told her that out of respect to the mullah the villagers were bringing condolences and small offerings to the house and speaking of the death as an "accident", when really, no one knew what had happened.

'Of course, everyone is thinking the same thing, although it doesn't make sense, a nice young woman like that with a mullah as a husband, a comfortable home and two sweet children,' she said, looking meaningfully at Nargis.

'What did the police say?' she asked faintly.

The customer shook her head mockingly, guessing her thoughts.

'They recorded a verdict of "accidental death" and put the body in the house to be dry washed with soil using the sand of Tayammum, you know, because she was so burned. Their neighbour Shabnam is preparing her body for burial. Of course there will be no autopsy as the mullah has forbidden it in accordance with Islam. Apparently the evidence suggested that she was refilling the kerosene lamps with fuel near the tandoor when one caught alight. Her kurta was drenched in kerosene so they decided that one of the lamps, once alight must have spilled onto her dress.'

Nargis winced and a tear rolled down her cheek. The customer continued, eager to impart all her information before leaving.

'There, there, don't cry. I suppose you were friends? I mean her things were here in the shop weren't they? The burial will be held tomorrow at noon. I am sure the whole village will come and the mullah will hold a proper religious burial followed by a funeral fotihah-honi with osh pilov in three and seven days. I hear that the neighbours are already helping to prepare it.'

Nargis covered her face with her hands.

'I don't know what to say,' Nargis said and wept.

May 27th, 2008, Tajikistan Countdown: 2 months, 11 days

So, she killed herself. Savsang, the lady with a lover. Burned to death in a glittering, synthetic ball of flame in her own back yard. Poor Nargis was devastated, she rang sobbing, to tell me the news. I told her, 'Now Nargis, this is not your fault, you must not blame yourself.' She rang off, unable to speak. Tajikistan is a cruel place for a young woman who marries the wrong man. I was going to offer a donation for the funeral but later I felt it cheapened their friendship to bring everything down to cash. Especially since that was what she died for.

27

For a week, Nargis was too upset to leave the house. Harriet had been sympathetic, telling her to take all the time she needed, they would manage. Nargis watched with bowed head, as the burial procession passed her house, the menfolk from the mahalla carrying Savsang's white-clothed body inside a cheap wooden box. Her father, Abdul, walked behind, having first attended the recitation of the Salat-al-Janazah prayers held at the site of her death. She prayed for Savsang's soul as the somber group marched past. Tears streamed down her face when she saw their six-year old son, white-faced and solemn, marching quickly to keep up.

Mullah Azikav headed the procession, resplendent in a traditional black velvet gown and black hat, the chapan and torqi, his black beard shiny and eyes downcast. Far from the stooped, despairing figure of a few weeks ago, he now looked reborn, proud, walking with broad shoulders thrust out. Nargis knew what would happen next. At the cemetery her body would be taken from the box and placed in the ground facing Mecca. One by one, the men would take turns to pour three handfuls of soil into the grave reciting the incantation: "We created you from it and return you into it and from it we will raise you a second time."

Gulya and Abdul attended the fotiha-honi prayer ceremony for Savsang held three days after her death, joining the separate banquets for men and women from the mahalla. Her mother went to help prepare osh pilov with the other women from the mahalla, but Nargis could not face it. Calling off sick, she lay in the cool darkness of the house and wept. It was as though all the sadness of the past few years was draining from her. She was convinced it was suicide by immolation, the purest form of protest left to Tajik women. Were she not so weak, Mullah Azikav would never have gone to Tosh Teppa and driven Savsang over the edge. Gulya tried to rally her spirits, making endless bowls of tea and shooing the children outside.

'You are being silly shireen, he would have worked it out on his own in the end. She only had two sisters, both living in the south, ten miles from one another. Savsang was a weak woman who did not have the courage to face her husband's punishment, so she chose death, or so you would have us believe. At least she didn't kill her children too.'

Nargis disagreed. Suicide took courage. Even if the mullah had thought to go to Tosh Teppa on his own, she might have had time to escape, had Nargis not disclosed her whereabouts. Lying in the darkness, she reflected on Faisullo growing up with those grey, tired people, alone in the stuffy air of that hated apartment. How will he understand my abandonment when he grows up? She thought of Ahmed, gone these last four years. Why didn't I insist he went to a doctor earlier? She pondered on the damage done to Hussein who had never recovered after living with Poulod, frightened to speak up, preferring to blend into the crowd, suffering terrible nightmares from which he woke pale and trembling.

She had asked him about his dreams and he always said, 'Poulod kills you with the scissors and you are lying in a pool of blood.'

She was to blame for all of it. How stupidly she had lived her life.

After seven days she got up. Gulya forced her out of her depression, saying that she needed to go and earn, they had nearly finished their sack of flour.

'Harriet promised to pay me for this week as I am in mourning,' Nargis murmured from her quilt.

'Well, a week for Savsang is long enough. Time to get up. .If you work, you'll find pleasure,' Gulya said, recalling a Tajik proverb.

Immersing herself in mundane tasks at the shop, counting out kilos of sugar, flour, potatoes and macaroni, she gradually felt herself growing numb to the sadness. It felt good to return to Harriet's house, cuddle little Leo and play games with Alex. She lost herself in her work. Smaller hodoii banquets were to be held with prayers on the twentieth and fortieth days after the burial. Bizarrely, she had benefitted from Savsang's death, the mullah dispatching his relatives to her shop to buy foodstuffs for every ceremony. She turned them away guiltily, but they returned, claiming the mullah had insisted they buy it from her. Does he believe I meant to help him at her cost? she wondered. Nargis decided to attend the twentieth day prayers at Mullah Azikav's house.

As she entered the compound, her eyes glistened. She had been here only twenty-two days before, trying to persuade Savsang to stay strong. She now saw that her words had only served to strengthen Savsang's resolve to end it all. A white piece of material was strewn across the yard, behind which neighbours and relatives were busy cooking osh rice, shorba, a soup of potatoes, mutton and carrot, pots of tea, baking naan in the tandoor and discreetly washing the dirty dishes of the endless stream of well-wishers. Savsang's four-year old daughter, Zebo, was inside the house, sitting listlessly on the quilt next to their neighbour Shabnam's children, her thin little arms clutching a new doll. She still seemed in shock, not speaking to anyone except to answer 'yes' and 'no' to kindly questions.

Around the room, quilts and tablecloths had been placed on the floor. As women entered the house, many were tearful and cried into handkerchiefs, consoling each other as well as Savsang's sisters, newly arrived from Tosh Teppa. All wore white lace-edged funeral cloths on their heads. The men's party was held separately in an adjoining room and only Savsang's sisters were permitted to enter to serve them. Once the guests were assembled on the quilts a small prayer was said. The women held hands up to their faces and when the prayer finished, they drew their hands to their foreheads and down to their chins to bless Savsang's soul. Bowls of fruit, sweets and biscuits sat on the cloth as well as piles of naan. After the women finished the shorba, plates of osh pilov were served. From her seat, Nargis could hear the men toasting Savsang's happy life with Mullah Azikav and making speeches. Vodka was not permitted, this being the house of a holy man, but they toasted anyway, out of tradition.

The women were far less gregarious. Sitora was whispering to the women next to her, doubtless telling them about the events in the weeks leading up to the death. They were friends from other suburbs of Dushanbe who would not have heard the gossip. Nargis wished she would cease her poisonous rumour-mongering and let Savsang's soul rest in peace. No one from the mahalla dared to say anything, knowing that Sitora had information on every single villager present. Eventually it was time to go home. Nargis breathed a sigh of relief. She just taking her leave when the mullah drew her to one side.

'I am sorry for Savsang's passing,' she murmured, keeping her eyes downcast.

'Yes, well. It is has been difficult for the children, as you can imagine,' he growled. 'Their wellbeing and reputation are my main concern now. With that in mind, I would like you to keep what happened to yourself.'

'I will never speak of it, I promise,' said Nargis hastily, edging towards the door. She allowed herself a quick glance at his face. He looked relieved, letting out a large sigh. Stroking his black beard, shiny with hair oil, he returned to his guests.

Nargis pulled on her slippers. As she walked home, her phone rang. It was Poulod's home number. Nargis debated whether or not to answer, but decided that it could be an emergency concerning Faisullo. She had not seen him for two weeks.

'Alo?'

'Assalom ailikom.'

Nargis scowled. This greeting was blasphemy from a man like him.

'Yes, Poulod, what is it? Is Faisullo alright?'

'He is fine. I want to see you about him and talk about his future. When can we meet?'

'What is it you want to discuss?'

'I will tell you that when we meet. So, when and where?'

Nargis panicked.

'You can come to the shop, it's on the main street near the bus stops and has a large set of scales out front. It is better we meet there than at my parents' house. My family don't want to see you, especially the children.'

'A shop, eh? Fine, have it your own way. I will be there at half past five tomorrow evening.'

He hung up. Nargis was perplexed, flustered and full of questions. It was typical of him to torture her in this way, she thought. Could it be possible he was finally going to let her have Faisullo? Was he arranging a divorce at long last? Perhaps he had another woman in Russia he wanted to marry. She was suddenly full of fear. Perhaps he wants to take Faisullo to Russia with him. I will not let him. I will have to. What will I do? Rushing home, she could not sleep that night for worrying.

June 5th, 2008, Tajikistan Countdown: 2 months, 9 days

That man, her husband Poulod, is back in her life. Nargis was as jumpy as a grasshopper today. She told me about his phone call. I offered to help, but really, what can I do? Henri wants nothing to do with the personal lives of 'les domestiques' and would never obstruct a husband from meeting with his wife. He wants nothing to do with local intrigue and avoids political discussion. I told her to be careful, to make sure she has help nearby. She just laughed.

The house hunt in Nairobi continues. So much for the Colonial stuccoed villa in the mango trees, the romantic 'Out of Africa' lifestyle that I dreamed of. Modern Nairobi seems to be a hotbed of crime and, according to Henri, only the crazy, white Kenyans with guns and Rottveilers keep remote villas these days. I am told I will need to put the children into a school up in the coffee plantations in a place called Peponi and we will hire a burly local driver to take them back and forth as it is not safe to drive alone. Car jackings are common and violent burglaries too. We will rent an apartment in a modern condominium, for better security. I am less and less enamoured with the idea of Nairobi but what can I do? I am the one who tore us away from here prematurely, it's my fault. I daren't voice my feelings to Henri, but I'm hoping now that the whole thing will fall through.

28

Nargis walked nervously to the shop from the bus stop with the other workers. The heat rose from the street, bouncing off the melted tarmac, sliding up sticky legs. Her feet were swollen and hurt in her cheap plastic Chinese sandals. Mr Simenon and Harriet had left for lunch at a new hotel to celebrate a friend's birthday. Alexandra, angry to be left at home by her parents, had spent the afternoon teasing Leo and making a huge mess with felt tips, glue and glitter all over the veranda. Nargis entered the shop, pleased to see that quite a few new entries were in the ledger. She congratulated her young neighbour on the days' work.

'Many people have been in today, eh? Well done, shireen.'

She let her go for the evening and set a pot of water on the kerosene burner in the back room. In half an hour Poulod was due to arrive. Drinking green tea, she felt the stresses of the day wash away. She put a sharp knife to hand behind the counter. She'd given the children strict instructions to go straight home from school and not leave the house. She did not want Hussein to see Poulod in the mahalla, knowing it would terrify him. Her chest felt tight as she peered out at the street.

I wonder what he wants? Why hasn't he done us all a favour and gone back to Russia? The last time Nargis had been to see Faisullo, two weeks before, Poulod had been away "on business". Nargis had assumed he had gone. It was a relief to visit without her husband's overbearing presence. Can't he find himself some stupid Russian ewe to marry? She sat for a while, nibbling on her thumbnail. Then she fiddled with the shop stock, re-stacking a shelf of tinned peas and pickles. A customer entered and deliberated for long minutes over whether to buy one kilo of potatoes or two. Nargis served her brusquely, one eye on the door.

At quarter to seven, an old silver Mercedes drew up to the shop. Tajik music blared out a corny love song. Nargis leaned over the counter to get a better look. Whoever it was had very bad taste in music, perhaps a man of her father's generation. To her surprise, Poulod emerged from the car. Had he brought a friend? He spent a few minutes examining the paintwork, rubbing at imaginary spots on the bonnet. Uneasy now, she waited for him to enter. She decided to stay behind the counter, clutching her knife. He came in through the double doors stalked by a trail of cheap aftershave. His huge bulk filled the shop, making her claustrophobic. Wearing a new shirt and a grey shiny suit, he had grown his hair in the back and wore a minuscule ponytail. It looked absurd. He also seemed to have started a small moustache. One of her mother's favourite proverbs came to her mind: "Even though a donkey goes to Mecca, still it is but a donkey".

Nargis felt revolted at the sight of him, though she was curious about the car.

'Assalom Alaikum,' he breathed, taking a seat on a small stool. It creaked in complaint. His thick legs bulged in his shiny suit trousers. He eyed her tea bowl.

'Aren't you going to offer me a little tea?' he asked graciously. Damn. I should have brought the teapot and another bowl in here, she thought. With great reluctance Nargis moved from her place behind the counter and went to the back room to pour him a bowl. As she brushed past him he grabbed her hand.

'It is good to see you, Nargis, I've missed you,' he said, displaying a mouth of stained teeth. Nargis retrieved her hand from his sweaty clasp and darted behind the counter.

'Why are you here, Poulod?'

'I've come to make you a business proposition. I see you have a business now, but the few somoni you make selling macaroni and flour is nothing compared with what I have to offer.'

'Alright. Tell me about it.' I would rather have a fat, red cockroach as a business partner than this idiot.

'In the last month alone, I have been to Moscow five times and made ten thousand dollars,' he said proudly. 'You see that car? It's mine.'

Nargis sucked her teeth. Ten thousand dollars in one month? Who does he think I am?

'Sure. Ten thousand dollars. What were you doing there Poulod? Selling your beautiful body?'

His eyes narrowed.

'Don't mock me, woman, I'm telling you the truth.'

'I'm sorry.' She did not want a fight tonight. She forced an expression of polite interest onto her face. 'How did you do it?'

Poulod leaned back on the stool, looking pleased with himself.

'I'm a smuggler.'

'What do you smuggle?'

'That would be telling.'

He looked at her in excitement. 'Have a guess.'

'I don't know.'

Nargis was frightened. Had he joined the mafia? Never religious nor moral, she wouldn't put it past him. He could be smuggling guns, people or worse, narcotics. She would have to be more careful not to make him angry.

'That sounds dangerous. Manly,' she said, flattering him a little.

He smiled arrogantly. 'It is dangerous but easy money.' He paused for dramatic effect, smoothing his oiled hair with a small tortoise shell comb from his pocket. Nargis no longer wanted to know what he was up to, but did not know how to stop him telling her without making him angry. She hesitated, uncertain.

'Alright, I can see you really want to know,' he said fatuously. 'I'll tell you. I am a 'Glototeli'. I transport heroin.'

Nargis gasped. Pouloud looked pleased. *He thinks I admire him.*

'I've come to see if you are interested in becoming a smuggler too. I can connect you with the right people. Help you get a good job.'

He failed to mention that there was a nice commission for every person he managed to recruit. Of the fifteen hundred dollar payment given to women, Jamshed had promised him five hundred dollars.

'It gets even better. The kids can also earn their way.'

'The...the kids?'

'Yes. Children carry it in their clothes or orifices and are hardly ever strip searched. Faisullo is too young, unfortunately. Even your moronic brother Said can get a slice of the pie.'

Nargis gazed at him, her eyes wide. Her face whitened. *The day I married this man was the worst day of my life.*

'I've already started designing a new house on scraps of paper and I'm looking around Dushanbe for a building plot.'

Jamshed had warned him that once his wife entered the trade there was no going back. Pouloud knew that Jamshed would easily blackmail Nargis into bringing in the whole family. Jamshed was a master at intimidation, a true inspiration.

'What do you have to do when you smuggle narcotics?' asked Nargis, stalling for time, trying to think.

'It is simple. The boss takes you to the heroin processing place, where you, as a woman, will swallow 25 vials of the stuff, about 600 grams. Of course I do more, 40 in total,' he said, puffing out his chest like a cockerel. 'Then you go to the airport and the boss gives you an air ticket. Once you get to Moscow you are picked up by an associate and asked to 'regurgitate the merchandise'. He paused. 'If I tell you any more I'll have to kill you,' he snarled, copying his new hero.

'You swallow heroin?' she said horrified. 'What if it leaks?'

'It doesn't. It's totally safe, nothing to worry about,' he lied smoothly.

Poulod got up from his stool and stared at Nargis, leaning forward and bringing his heavy fists down on the counter with a crash. Jars of sweets shook and one fell to the ground and smashed.

'I've already told you too much. You'll have to do it now, or the boss will not be happy. You know what that means.' He seemed to sense hesitation and decided to heighten the pressure. 'You need to come with me right now. We'll go see him. He's expecting us.'

Nargis baulked. Is he serious? Her mind whirled in panic.

'I-I am not going anywhere. I have to think about it,' she said. 'After all, while I'm grateful that you thought of me, this is a big decision to make. I have a job working as a nanny. My employers won't let me leave for days at a time. And… it's illegal.' Suddenly, she decided to face him down, no matter what the consequences. 'No, I won't do it. I don't want to.'

Poulod scowled.

'You stupid ewe, you've never been able to see when you have a good thing going.'

He stood still for a moment, a concentrated expression on his face. He was obviously trying to work out what to do with her next. Nargis clutched her knife with white knuckles. Poulod took a deep breath.

'Listen, if you'll just agree to come see the boss at the factory, all will be explained.'

Nargis followed his glance to the street. The evening had brought mashutka after mashutka to the mahalla, spewing workers out onto the road outside.

'We should meet again, at my place, to talk,' he said.

Nargis was silent. Poulod abruptly turned and made to leave the shop. Nargis timidly followed to close and bolt the door. Poulod hesitated, suddenly turned back and grabbed her by the neck, holding her under one arm like a vice, pulling her towards his car. Nargis screamed, struggling against him. Poulod slapped her hand and the knife fell to the ground. Then he hit her in the face.

'Let me go,' she screamed.

A pair of men from the mahalla nudged each other and started to come across the road to them. They were friends of Said.

'Hey you, what are you doing?' they shouted, starting to run.

Poulod cursed and ran for his car. He started the engine as the men reached them and wound down the window a crack.

'Nargis, I warn you, do not say a word to anyone. You should have agreed to my offer. Now you know too much. I will not be held responsible for what might happen to you, or to your little bastards.'

Nargis collapsed on the kerb, rubbing her neck. Her nose was bleeding. He drove off with a roar in the direction of her house, leaving clouds of dust in his wake, his music deafening passers-by. Slowly, shakily she crawled to the front stoop, legs trembling. One of the men asked her if she was alright and handed her a handkerchief for her nose. She nodded, panting. What if he sends his gang after us? She leapt to her feet and thrust the keys at the neighbour, asking him to lock up the shop for her and sprinted home. When she got there, she ran into the yard screaming.

'Hussein! Bunavsha!' They rushed out, looking frightened. 'Come here,' she said, half weeping, panting hard, holding them close. Gulya scuttled outside. Abdul was dozing on a quilted rope bed in the evening sunset. He woke up and looked at them anxiously.

'What's happening? Why did you wake me?'

'What's all the fuss about, girl? What happened to your face?' asked Gulya.

'Oh, Mother.'

Slowly she sank down onto a quilt set out near the cooking stove. She was still panting but tried to calm her beating heart. Gulya was cooking a stew with potatoes and onion for their evening meal and the flies were buzzing around the yard. The smoky ash from the fire blew into her nostrils making her cough as she sucked in deep breaths.

'Where's Said?' she gasped.

'He's at work. What happened?' said Gulya urgently. Abdul sat up, wiping his eyes. Nargis paused.

'Wait. Children, everything is okay now. Go into the house and play.'

'What about your nose, Mummy?' asked Bunavsha.

'It is nothing. I fell over, that's all.'

The children left, looking confused. Hussein looked at her suspiciously with big, watchful eyes but went indoors quietly with his sister. Once they were out of earshot Nargis whispered quickly to her parents.

'Mother, Father, listen. Poulod came to see me. He had a fancy new Mercedes and new clothes. He's joined the mafia and works as a drug smuggler. That's the reason he hasn't gone back to Russia for the year.'

'No.' Gulya stopped stirring the stew and stared at Nargis, appalled.

'Are you sure?' said Abdul quietly, stroking his small white beard.

'I'm afraid so. He tried to make me join their operation, swallowing narcotics and flying with them in my stomach to Moscow.'

'It's not possible.' Gulya gasped.

'I wish it wasn't true. I refused, of course. He said that now I know what he's doing, the mafia might come after me. Mother, I'm scared. I'm sure that if it weren't for the fact that there were so many people around, he would have succeeded in forcing me into his car. When he left he told me to watch out for myself and the children.'

Gulya started. 'Hodoiiman! The children? He threatened my grandchildren?'

'What shall I do, Father?'

'I don't know Nargis. You can't stay here.'

'Why? You think he will send someone to kill me?'

'I don't know. Anything is possible with him. He almost killed you himself once before, the donkey shit.' Abdul snarled. 'I know these people. Don't forget, I lost my beautiful house to those narcotics bastards. They would have killed my brother if I hadn't paid his debts.'

Gulya grunted. She was still not sure that had been worth it. His brother never managed to kick his heroin addiction, eventually dying a beggar's death on the streets of Dushanbe.

'Yes, but that time it was an accident. Poulod did not mean to stab me.'

'Why do you think we allowed you to leave him, Nargis? We thought he would end up murdering you,' said Abdul, frowning.

'He is stupid, but stupid men are sometimes the most dangerous,' said Gulya.

'I don't know where to go,' said Nargis. 'I have nowhere to live except here.'

'What about your Aunt Saodat in Ghissor, or a friend?' said Gulya.

'Poulod knows where Aunt Saodat lives and he'll go there if he doesn't find me here. I don't have any friends who can take me and the children. No one has space for all of us and no one wants a woman like me living with them,' said Nargis, tears brimming in her eyes.

'Actually, there might be somewhere, shireen. There's an old paper about it in the house,' said Gulya.

'Well?'

'It's a place where women can go with their children when they are being beaten by their husbands.'

Abdul snorted in derision.

'No doubt they deserve it,' he said, spitting into the fire.

Gulya ignored him. Nargis stood up.

'I know what you mean. Mrs. Emma, a friend of Mrs. Harriet gave that to me. Bring me the leaflet. I must go, right now.'

'I will accompany you,' said Abdul unexpectedly. 'When Said comes home to watch out for Gulya, we can go. Don't worry, shireen.'

Abdul put his arm around her protectively. Nargis's eyes overflowed. 'Thank you, Father.'

Ivan parked the car in a quiet side street.

'Please wait for me here. Call me if Mr Simenon needs the car.' A hot, dry breeze wrapped itself around Harriet as she got out. She leant against the door for a moment, slowing the merry-go-round in her head after the frozen air conditioning. Only half past eight in the morning, it was already stifling in Dushanbe. The sun had not yet emerged from the hazy clouds above but already she felt her clothing start to stick. She unscrewed a bottle of cold water and drank.

The address was in a neighbourhood that included Green Bazaar, the French Cultural Centre, the Russian Baptist Church, the Central Train Station and the 'Sadbarg' Rose department store for ladies, a chaotic indoor maze of small stalls where Harriet occasionally shopped for bolts of material and Turkish clothes.

She pressed an intercom and stepped through a grey metal door into a courtyard. She regretted her decision to dress in western clothes. Her nails were newly painted, her make-up in place, her blonde hair straight and glossy. She stood out like an orchid on a compost heap. Her kitten-heeled sandals clicked loudly on the uneven paved path, clamourous in the silence. She walked on tip-toe. The building, a one storey Russian house from the 1930's, was painted with white lime wash that had leached off the walls in the harsh winter weather.

Several women sat on a shaded bench with resigned, weary expressions. Their headscarves could not quite shroud their facial bruises. Harriet swallowed. Tears pricked her eyelids. She clutched her Armani handbag, trying to compose herself.

Nargis had slept fitfully, scared that Poulod and his new gang would return to the mahalla to threaten and hurt her family. She held Bunavsha's hand and Hussein sat near her, holding his school satchel like a talisman while they waited. She had not explained much, thinking that it would only give Hussein more nightmares. That evening on the bus, Bunavsha demanded to know where they were going.

'We have to go away for a while.' Abdul stowed her tatty suitcase and two raggedy quilts on a luggage rack. Bunavsha was petulant. She screwed up her face into a pout.

'But why, Mamma? I don't want to leave Bibi.' Gulya had insisted on walking to the bus stop, tying special charms for good luck onto the children's arms before she bent to hug them goodbye. Bunavsha started to cry.

'I forgot my dolly.'

'It won't be for long,' Nargis lied, cuddling her. Hussein stared at her with hooded eyes. He did not say anything at all. That almost worried her more. Nargis called the telephone hotline on the leaflet with a beating heart. A kind woman explained that for security reasons there were no identifying signs on the wall. It would look like any other residential edifice, with high white walls, a grey metal gate and a small white sign, number 182.

'We will be waiting. Please keep our location a secret, even from trusted relatives.'

Abdul had come with them as far as Green Bazaar, kissing them and turning away as though his heart were breaking as he left.

They sat in a lounge area waiting to be 'processed'. She had pictured the street beyond. A mashutka mini-bus whizzing past followed by a trundling, ancient green and white bus spewing out black acrid smoke. An old man working on a side street, filling the potholes in front of his haveli with old rubble from a wheelbarrow. Harassed, sweaty people hurrying to work past a young boy selling bananas set out on a cardboard box for two somoni each. A wrinkled babushka in black cotton with a prized antique pavlovo posad silk scarf on her head, stooped over small bottles of soda, cigarettes, packets of bubble gum and pay-as-you-go mobile phone cards. It was like any other residential street in Dushanbe. Poulod would not find them. She crossed and uncrossed perspiring limbs and stroked Bunavsha's plaits. All night she had tossed and turned. *What if they turn us out after only one night? After all, I don't have any evidence. What if he beats my parents, forces them to tell him where I am? Where will we go? How will I work? What will happen to us?* As soon as she thought Harriet would be awake, she called her.

Nargis glanced out of an open window to the inner courtyard. The refuge was guarded twenty-four hours a day and was calm and quiet. Green leafy shrubs, climbing white roses and apple trees provided welcome shade after the hot dusty street. Vibrant orange and yellow marigolds and calendula flowers grew in borders. An old stooping gardener with a leathery face and black velvet Tajik tubeteika cap soberly watered the little garden with a hose. The water threw up a fragrant scent of marigolds and soil. Two pale women sat nursing their injuries. They reminded her of the misery of her second marriage. *How many times had he given her bruises, blackened her eyes?* Her scar throbbed. She lifted her chin and squared her shoulders. *I will never go back to him, he'll have to kill me first.* Suddenly a familiar figure came through the gate and walked up to the entrance.

'It's Mrs. Harriet,' said Bunavsha, delighted. 'Is Alexandra here?'

Nargis stood up as she entered and Harriet took her by the shoulders. Harriet's eyes were dark.

'I'm so glad you called me.' Harriet glanced about. Children's toys lay in boxes around the room, and someone had painted it in bright colours, lemon yellow and orange and provided faded black velveteen quilts that lay along the walls. Young women sat in one corner in shabby kurtas with small children on their laps. A little boy with a shaved head squatted on the oriental carpet, playing with toy cars, pretending they were driving along tracks in the pattern. A woman nursed a baby, her breast discreetly covered by a shawl. They stared at Harriet and then ignored her. A plump middle-aged lady, sweating in a cotton kurta, appeared with a file.

'Assalom. I'm Fatima. I have been assigned your case. Please come to my office. The children should stay here and play.'

'Would you prefer to talk to her alone?' Harriet asked Nargis. 'I probably won't understand much anyway.'

'No, please stay with me,' said Nargis. Oddly, she felt more secure with Harriet there and knew she would vouch for her that she was telling the truth. Fatima started filling out a form.

Nargis weighed straight in. 'My husband and I are separated. He came to see me yesterday and told me that he's working with criminals. He wants me to smuggle narcotics to Russia, swallowing heroin.'

Harriet gasped. Fatima glanced up from her notes with wide eyes.

'Sorry, did you say he wants you to carry narcotics to Russia?' Harriet asked in English.

'Yes.'

Fatima tutted in disapproval.

'Are you sure?'

'Absolutely sure. He had a new car and fancy clothes and I'm sure that unless he'd found this new 'job' he would have had no choice but to return to Russia months ago. I refused and he became angry. As he left, he said I would have to be forcibly silenced by his mafia associates. He tried to pull me into his car, but luckily some neighbours were nearby and they intervened.' Nargis clenched her hands together. They had started to shake. Harriet touched her arm reassuringly. 'I'm terrified. He knows where we live and I've nowhere else to go. He's dangerous when he's angry and almost killed me once when we were married. Look, I'll show you.'

Nargis turned around and pulled down her kurta at the back to reveal the scar of a deep gash in her back. Harriet was horrified.

'Did he do that to you?'

'Yes.'

Fatima glanced up and then went on making notes. 'When did this attack take place?'

'Two years ago. He stabbed me with a pair of tailoring scissors. I was trying to leave him. The doctors said I could easily have been killed or paralysed.'

'And those purple bruises on your neck and face?'

'From yesterday, when he tried to force me into his car.'

'Have you tried to start divorce proceedings?' Fatima asked.

Nargis blushed.

'No. I always say that I'm divorced because that's what I want everyone to think. My parents are very against divorce. We're still officially married but I hate to admit it because it makes me feel like I'm still his property.'

Nargis turned to Harriet. 'I don't want people think I still married.'

'I can understand that,' muttered Harriet. She was ashen.

'As you are still married, I will need to take pictures for the file as evidence.'

'Alright.'

Fatima picked up a small camera and took two photographs, one of her bruises and one of her scar. Nargis turned to Harriet with a troubled expression. 'I promise, he don't know where I work. Even my parents don't know address of your house, only neighbourhood.'

'Perhaps you should tell your employers, so they understand why you're late today?' Fatima suggested. Nargis translated for Harriet who chuckled wryly.

'She is my employer,' Nargis said.

'I see. How much are you paid?'

'Two hundred and ten dollars a month.'

Fatima looked up in surprise. 'What do you do?'

'I look after the children and clean the house.'

'Well, on a wage like yours we'll definitely be able to find you a secure place to rent in Dushanbe where you can hide from your husband.'

Nargis sat still, the colour draining from her face. Tears came to her eyes.

'You make it sound so permanent. This is terrible.'

She started to weep. Fatima looked perplexed.

'What's terrible, shireen? I thought you wanted to hide from him?'

'No. I mean, yes. But he has our two-year old son. I'll never see my little Faisullo again.'

Harriet heard the word 'Faisullo' and understood her tears.

'Perhaps we can help you get him back,' said Harriet. 'If you divorce, the courts might give you custody.'

Fatima passed her a box of tissues. Nargis sighed.

'Mrs Harriet doesn't understand what it is like for us.' She turned to her. 'If I try to divorce he be more angry and want to find me,' she sobbed in her broken English. 'He now in mafia, don't forget.'

'Will you let her stay?' Harriet asked. 'Emma Brewster is a friend of ours. She will vouch for her.'

'Yes, we will. I'm sure she has nowhere else to go.'

Nargis turned to Harriet with blurry eyes.

'How will I work? I have no one to look after my children here.'

'Nargis, please don't worry about that.'

'I want to work. I need work.'

'Find somewhere to live first. Stay hopeful. Your job is secure, I will ask the cleaner to work more days while you are sorting yourself out. I'll visit you tomorrow with Leo, he'll be missing you.'

Harriet put her arm around her shoulder and gave her an awkward hug. Nargis laughed through her tears.

'Thank you Mrs Harriet. I don't know what I do without you.'

Harriet eyes reddened. 'It's the least I can do.'

She left. Nargis watched her children. Bunavsha had found a tea set and was busily giving a teddy bear a drink. Hussein played with metal cars, but watched her closely at the same time. She held her hands tightly, her smile as rigid and false as that painted on a puppet.

'I like the toys here,' said Bunavsha happily, all her anxiety of the morning gone.

Hussein was not as easily distracted. 'Mamma, why are we in this place? Is it a hospital? Are you ill? Why was Mrs Harriet here? When can we go home?'

'Mrs Harriet came to help. It isn't a hospital, it's a nice place where we might live for a while,' said Nargis.

'But why? I don't like it. I want to go home to Bobo, Bibi and Uncle Said,' said Hussein. 'What about school? My teacher will be angry if I don't come today.'

He was red-faced and on the verge of tears. Nargis felt miserable. He doesn't trust me, she thought. And why should he? A famous saying of the great poet Rukadi came mind. "Whoever doesn't learn from daily events, will learn nothing from an instructor".

She hugged his skinny, reluctant frame and looked into the ghost of Ahmed's eyes. 'Listen, it is not forever. We will have a happy time here and you will be completely safe and well looked after.'

'But why? Who is coming after us?' he asked anxiously.

'Is it a monster?' asked Bunavsha from her seat on the floor.

'No. There's no monster. No one's coming after us. We will find our own house, an even nicer, better place where Bibi and Bobo can visit us.'

Hussein nodded uncertainly. She could see he didn't like it, but at least he was not going to resist and cause a scene. Fatima appeared at the door.

'I've spoken to the director and she says you may stay for up to four weeks.'

Hodooiman, Thank God. 'Rahmat. I'm grateful.'

'In the meantime we'll try to help you to obtain a divorce, if that's what you want and, of course, it will be our priority to find you a new home. We serve basic meals here, at eight in the morning, at noon and at six in the evening, as well as tea at eleven. There are three other women staying here at present with their children. Feel free to come and ask questions if you need to.'

Nargis stood up. She felt light-headed. Could it only be yesterday afternoon that life was normal?

'Children, I am going to lie down,' she said.

There were twelve metal beds in the dormitory. Each bed had sliding curtains that could be pulled across for privacy and several china basins hung along one wall. It was brightly painted in light pink, with small screened windows that looked out across roses, shrubs and flower beds. Some cheap, red oriental-style rugs lay on the floor and someone had left bedding and faded pink towels on one of the beds. A toothless cleaning lady in a purple headscarf mopped the floor. Nargis sat down heavily on her bed and stared at her hands.

May 15th, 2008, Tajikistan Countdown: 2 Months

I told Henri about Nargis. I feel so guilty for not offering her a bed here. Of course it was out of the question. Henri would never allow that kind of intrusion. He was deadpan, almost blasé about it. Apparently Nick, that red-faced, jovial old boozer, left Tajikistan yesterday. He'd been receiving death threats because of his freedom of the press project. Henri didn't tell me because he thought I'd be frightened. He never tells me anything, I am always the last to know. Nick came home last week and his apartment had been ransacked. Glass everywhere. He went to the police and was detained for over forty-eight hours in a cell and interrogated like a criminal. The British Ambassador had to intervene. Two days ago his driver stopped at a traffic light on the junction between Rudaki Avenue and Somoni Street and a man dressed all in black threw a deadly viper into his lap. That was it, the last straw. He booked himself onto a flight and left a few hours later.

Henri says cotton and aluminium prices have fallen through the floor, so heroin is the main income earner. I could see he was worried for all his bravado. He's going to have a word with the guards to be extra vigilant. He didn't say it, but I think he plans to fire Nargis as soon as he gets her alone. I won't let him have his way this time.

29

Nargis had been at the refuge for five long days. It had started to feel like an open prison. Four weeks. Nargis fancied she would be mad after two. Hussein woke up screaming every night. Pale with dark circles under his eyes, he repeatedly begged to go home. He clung to her at night, refused to sleep alone and was jumpy and unhappy in the daytime. He didn't speak of Poulod, as though saying his name would summon him to them like a demon. Nargis gathered her courage and darted out to buy sweets at a kiosk nearby. Every car that passed made her jump. Ordinary sounds of the street, a car door slamming, a man hollering, a backfiring mashutka; they all had her running for cover. The evening before, Nargis crept to the back garden of the refuge and called Said. Gulya had snatched the phone from him.

'Nargis?'

'Yes, it's me. Have you seen him?'

'No. But your young girl working in the shop saw a silver Mercedes parked nearby yesterday afternoon. The driver didn't get out but sat there for at least two hours playing loud, Afghani wedding serenades. She doesn't know what Poulod looks like, so she wasn't sure if it was him.'

Nargis clenched the phone tighter. A pair of ezore trousers and a sequinned kurta hanging above her on the washing line glittered and flapped in the orange sunset.

'It was him. Oh, I wish he would leave us alone. I changed my SIM card, but I so long to hear Faisullo's voice.'

'We miss you.'

'The people here are kind. They are helping me to find a room to rent where we can hide. They said it will be about eighty dollars a month, which is a lot out of my salary but it can't be helped. They are going to take me to see a few places this week. The children have to start a new school but I don't know how I'll take care of Bunavsha and Hussein in the afternoons when I'm working.'

'I can come and help.'

'How? He will follow you straight to my door.'

The next morning the children met a new boy of six called Nurullo. He and his mother arrived in the night, two lonely figures tapping on the compound gate. Natasha had dark brown hair, high cheekbones and blue eyes. She wore a faded pink sweater and cotton trousers. A gold orthodox cross hung from her neck, yet she spoke perfect Tajik. She had endured a decade of violence and two secret abortions. Nargis guessed that she was probably half Tajik, half Russian, a true child of the Union of Soviet Socialist Republics.

'I did not want to bring another child into that world. My husband is evil, a monster. He's in the military.' Her face was scarred and she was missing several teeth. She caught Nargis staring at her scars. 'Usually I cover those with make-up, sorry.'

Nargis looked away, embarrassed. 'What will you do?'

The woman held her head in her hands and pulled her hair so that her skin was taut.

'I am not sure. I feel numb. Like I am in a dream and I can wake up at any moment. He will be crazy when he comes back from Uzbekistan and sees I have taken his only son. No one in the apartment building saw me go though and I told no one, not even my sisters. I have my jewellery, my ID card and passport, my school and university certificates, Nurullo's birth certificate, all the money I could find as well as cash I saved secretly. I threw my SIM card away and bought a new one. His father had been ill for a long time. He's quite rich now that his father passed away. I knew I had to leave while I still could. I saw the leaflet for this refuge at my local pharmacy. His mother is supposed to come from Bukhara to live with us. I would have been a prisoner in my own home with that witch monitoring my every move. How could I prevent another pregnancy? He has forbidden me to use contraception, but I have been taking pills in secret. This was my last chance. The refuge is going to relocate us to another city, change our names, try to find me a job and a room where we can live quietly. Maybe one day I can find a way to get my son out of Tajikistan. Then we can go to Russia.'

Nargis smiled at her. 'You are brave, I admire you.'

Natasha's eyes narrowed. 'I don't think so. If I was truly brave, I would have left him ten years ago.'

After lunch, the children had a nap. Even with all the windows open and the curtains closed, their dormitory felt hot and claustrophobic, a fine sheen of sweat oiling their faces. Nargis decided to go to Green Bazaar and buy meat and vegetable samosas for the children as a special treat. She felt trapped, stuck in the refuge all day. Only sixty dirams each, they were served from white kiosk windows dotted around the periphery of the market building. Natasha agreed to call her if the children woke. Wandering down the baking street, Nargis passed imperious local housewives with sweaty boys pulling blue trolleys laden with vegetables and fruit. The street kids are certainly earning their money today, she thought. Her legs tingled, ready to run if needed. She took care to walk on the inside of the pavement, constantly vigilant for a flash of silver.

The market was busy, crowded with jostling customers and traders. Nargis had disguised herself by covering her hair and lower face with a scarf, borrowed from the refuge. It was difficult to see and she kept her eyes down, careful not to fall into the rank drainage ditches criss-crossing her path. For once, she was thankful that Tajik women all wore the same style of clothing, made with the same synthetic, shiny rolls of material. She blended into the crowd but was unaccustomed to the extra material on her face. Even in disguise, she still couldn't stop herself scanning the crowds for Poulod. Startled by the loud noises and traders shouts, she felt jumpy. At a fruit stall, she haggled for a while and bought a kilo of black cherries for the children. They would be so happy, she could not resist. Walking quickly through the market, she stopped to order fresh samosas. A woman in a white coat dumped them down in front of her on a paper plate. Looking around cautiously, she pulled her headscarf down to uncover her face. Dipping little triangles into hot sweet chilli sauce, she relished their meaty softness. Suddenly she heard a man's voice.

'Nargis, it is you.'

Nargis swung round, pale with fear, choking on her mouthful. Her samosa fell to the ground. Before her she saw a thickset man, greying black hair, confused.

'Zavon. Hodoiiman!' she cried in relief. She leant against the wall and fanned herself with a napkin. He looked taken aback at her reaction.

'I'm sorry, Zavon. I thought you were someone else.'

'So did I. I have been looking at you in my taxi, you see the rank over there? I was wondering if it was you. You were difficult to recognise in that hijab.'

'Well, that was the point,' Nargis said, panting. 'You almost gave me a heart attack.' She pulled the material up again over her hairline so that her eyes were hooded.

'Are you in disguise?'

'You could say that,' said Nargis. She shook her head. What am I saying? She composed herself. 'Of course not. I have a sore throat and so I am wearing this scarf to keep me warm.'

Picking up her samosas she headed towards the market exit. Zavon followed her, stumbling a little to keep up. Nargis checked the time on her phone. I've only been away fifteen minutes. It felt like a lifetime.

'Where are you going in such a hurry? Won't you join me for a quick pot of tea?' he asked. His shoulders were slumped in disappointment and he wiped his brow, already sweating in the hot sun. She hesitated. *He has been so kind to me and now he must think I'm rude.*

'Well, okay, just a quick tea.'

They entered a dark, cool café. After the sunny brightness of the afternoon Nargis had to stand still for a minute to let her eyes adjust to the gloom. The walls were covered in ancient grime and the table tops looked sticky and crawled with flies. It was empty aside from three old men with long white beards playing backgammon in the corner over green tea and cigarettes. Thin streams of blue smoke rose to the ceiling from overflowing ashtrays.

'Woman, Green Tea,' called Zavon into the shadows.

A fat cook with dirty yellow fingernails to match her stained cooks coat flip-flopped to the table with a pot of steaming tea and two bowls. Zavon ordered a plate of steamed mantu meat dumplings as an afterthought. Nargis took the scarf off and rearranged her hair. Zavon glanced at her bruised neck before she could cover it with her plait.

'How have you been?'

'Fine. You know how it is. I drive my taxi, do some mechanics here and there for neighbours and take care of my old dad. See my daughter Dilya when I can. You?'

'I'm okay,' she said lightly, sipping her tea. She did not meet his gaze.

'Wouldn't you usually go to Varzob Bazaar to do your shopping?'

'No. Actually I've moved.'

Zavon looked surprised. She fiddled with a napkin.

'Really? Somewhere round here?'

'Yes. Just temporarily. I'm staying with a friend until I find a room to rent for me and my children. It's a little complicated.'

'Ah.'

Zavon slurped his tea and looked at her with sympathy. *He must think I have fallen out with my family and have to live alone,* she thought. She knew she was looking haggard, her face gaunt after a week of sleepless nights and poor appetite.

'I wish I could help, for old time's sake, of course.'

She smiled faintly. Two bowls of steaming mantu arrived at the table and Zavon tucked in.

'What about your other son? Will he be living with you too?'

'I don't see him at the moment.'

'Ah.'

'It's complicated.'

'Alright.'

Mention of Faisullo made her weak.

'I can't have anything to do with my ex-husband.'

'I understand.'

She glanced at him, embarrassed.

'No, I mean, he can't know where I live. Because of that, I can't see my little one.'

Zavon's brow knitted but he did not ask more. They finished their snack in companionable silence. It was time to go back to her children, they would wake up and be anxious if she wasn't there.

30

Two days later, Nargis left the refuge. She was glad to go. The flowers and colourful paint could not mask the underlying sadness of the place. She watched an endless stream of injured, miserable women arriving each day for medical treatment, the majority of whom returned home, bandaged, to face more violence. It was hard to be reminded daily of her own wretched past, of poor Savsang, rotting in the ground.

'He gets angry because I talk too much,' one woman said.

'He came home and there was no dinner, it was my own fault,' said another with two black eyes and a cut lip.

'He's only jealous because he loves me,' was another refrain.

Many had been dismissed by police officers who told them, 'Go home and be better wives.'

Hussein withdrew into himself, refusing to play with his sister or the other children, not speaking for hours at a time. Nargis did not know what to do. Earlier, Mrs Harriet had brought Bunavsha a doll, a gift from Alexandra. Leo came too, happy to toddle about with Bunavsha in the lounge. His blond curls and smiles cheered everyone. Even Hussein came out of his shell. For a few moments, Nargis and the children forgot the injured women, their tears and the cruelty of domestic fear.

Waving goodbye, they drove to the apartment building in an old Lada belonging to the refuge. Nargis kept her face hidden, crouching low in the back. Hussein saw her duck down at a traffic light and watched her, his face stiff and pale.

'I have an ear ache, that's all,' she said, touching her scarf to her ear.

Hussein frowned. 'Stop lying.'

The evening before, Fatima had come to tell Nargis about the room.

'The landlady, Saamana Nokrova, used to work with us as a cook. She lives with her son in one of the old Soviet apartments near Sultoni Kobir Market. She urgently needs to rent a room to pay school fees and doesn't mind a refuge client, provided they're responsible and employed, the type of person who'll pay the rent on time. Her husband died ten years ago and her other children are grown up, married. She stopped working when her diabetes became worse, so she's more or less confined to her apartment. We can go there tomorrow and if she likes you, you'll move in right away.'

Nargis called her mother.

'You can't live there,' she said. 'You don't know the family. What kind of people are they? Your father will never agree.'

'It isn't up to him.'

'Impertinence.'

'Anyway we're going to live with a respectable old widow.'

Gulya spat into a ditch.

'Who knows what she might turn out to be like. Seventy-five dollars a month for a room is a lot.'

'It's cheap for today's prices.'

As they slowed to a halt, Bunavsha and Hussein gazed out of the window at a shabby, grey high-rise. It had ten storeys with an assortment of different styles of window replacing the old originals on each floor. Balconies were strewn with washing, flapping wildly in the sunny breeze. Tall sycamores grew in between the blocks, shading a large, dusty clearing and some ancient playground equipment. Children played tag in the dust and a proud, glossy-haired newly-wed in a glittering kurta sat on a rickety bench with her beau.

'It looks great,' said Bunavsha, eager to get out of the hot car. Hussein looked at the children and his eyes narrowed.

'Who are they?' he said. 'Do they live here?'

The children ran over to the vehicle and the air filled with excited chatter.

'Salom,' said Bunavsha cordially. 'I'm going to live here too.'

As the driver hauled the suitcase and two rolled quilts from the trunk, Fatima led the way up a dingy, damp stairwell to the fourth floor.

'What if she doesn't like us?' Nargis murmured.

Fatima gave her a reassuring smile. 'Don't worry, she'll like you.'

'Children, I want your best behaviour,' Nargis hissed.

At number eight, she knocked on the door. A large, blustery woman in a cotton headscarf opened it. 'Hoosh Omaded, I'm Saamana, and this is my son, Shuhrat.'

Behind her, a shy, gangly looking youth with bad acne hovered, stepping from one foot to another.

'Assalom.'

Nargis introduced herself and the children. They came forward shyly to shake hands.

'What lovely children. You must be so proud.'

Bunavsha smiled.

'This is my dolly, Sitora. She is very naughty and talks too much.'

Saamana patted her on the head. The hallway was carpeted in a faded oriental runner and as she stood back they all entered, first removing their shoes. Saamana closed the door and removed her headscarf to display a greying bun and an impressive set of jowls. She had a large mole on her cheek from which several grey hairs protruded. She gingerly hung the scarf on a metal hook by the door and looked at Nargis, a shrewd, assessing stare.

'In case of gentlemen callers. Not that I expect you'll have any.'

Nargis gaped.

'No, of course not.'

She hung back and kept her eyes downcast. The balcony door was open and a cooling breeze blew into the living room. Old trinkets and medals sat in a glass cabinet. An ancient television set hummed in one corner, a Tajik film of traditional dancers swirling gracefully in Technicolor gardens. Saamana beckoned to a sofa covered in small lace-edged cloths. On a low table there were bowls of nuts and dried fruit and glasses of RC Cola prepared as a welcoming gesture. The walls were papered with orange roses and a Chinese picture of a waterfall hung on the wall. Fatima went to sit down. Her eyes flickered between Saamana and Nargis.

'This is lovely, Aunt Saamana,' Nargis said, perching on the edge of the sofa. She kept her hands clasped in front of her. The children studiously ignored the snacks in accordance with traditional manners. Saamana chuckled, her ample bosom wobbling.

'Thank you, dear. I hope that you will consider yourself my adopted kelline.'

Nargis's back stiffened and Hussein looked up at her, wide-eyed. So that's it, she thought. I shall be doing the cleaning and cooking. She sighed inwardly. It was to be expected. Fatima smiled thinly and studied her fingernails.

'You know it's very hard to rent a room. You never know who you will get,' Saamana said, sighing in exaggerated consternation. She helped herself to dried fruit and offered the bowl to the children. 'I shouldn't really eat sugary foods, my diabetes...' Saamana put plump arms around Bunavsha who gave her a gap-toothed grin. 'What sweetness. I hope you two kids will treat me as your Bibi while you live here.'

Nargis brightened. A new grandmother? Free babysitting would be useful. She allowed herself to relax a little.

'Of course they will, won't you children?'

'My husband fought in Afghanistan. He was a Captain in the Soviet Army infantry.'

Chatting all the while, Saamana showed them around the apartment. Nargis saw an gas cooker attached to city gas, a cracked sink with hot and cold water taps and a small melamine table covered in a plastic cloth. 'Most of the time we have water and electricity, but it cuts in the winter a lot. I cook on a woodstove in that case and we sleep in the kitchen.'

She showed Nargis a special hole in the wall for a chimney pipe. There was also a water closet with a standing toilet and a small shower. This is wonderful, Nargis thought happily. No more cold water, smoky wood fires or smelly, muddy latrine. Just like where I lived before. Their room was at the back of the flat. Painted long ago, the walls had darkened to the colour of rotten cream. Mottled brown stains bloomed below the window. A frayed pink tablecloth was pinned to the window frame with drawing pins as a makeshift curtain. Two quilts lay rolled up on the threadbare orange carpet and there were hooks on the wall.

'For hanging your clothes.'

It was clean and large enough for three. Nargis pictured Faisullo joining them, would he fit? Bunavsha smiled and leapt on the rolled quilts.

'I want to go to sleep right now, Mamma.'

Hussein did not smile. He edged towards the hall and stood poised, as if to run away.

'Mamma, this is just like Poulod's house,' he said.

'Yes, shireen. All the old Soviet apartments look like this.'

'Does he live near here?'

'No. He lives on the other side of town, far away.'

Hussein started to shake and turned red, on the verge of tears. Saamana looked shocked.

'Poulod is your husband, their father?'

Nargis met her eyes. 'He's my husband, yes, but not their father.'

'My real daddy died,' Hussein yelled.

Saamana's hands went to her mouth. 'Oh, poor boy.'

Nargis crouched down to cuddle him. 'Shireen, please don't be scared. You will never see Poulod again.'

He looked at her with doubt. 'Really? Never?'

Nargis swallowed. 'I promise.'

A few days later, Nargis and Saamana sat in the semi-darkness of the living room, enjoying the evening breeze. Nargis was tired, having returned to work that day to find chaos. That stupid cleaner did nothing while I was away, she thought. Her phone rang. It was Zavon. She hesitated. I can trust him.

'Yes, I have found a room at an apartment near Sultoni Kobir Market, off Abay Street.'

'What a coincidence. My garage is just opposite Sultoni Kobir Market on Karaboev Avenue, number two-three-one. You should stop by for tea.'

'I will.'

Everyone had windows and balcony doors open onto their apartments to let in cool air and banish the heat of the day. All around, one could hear the comforting sound of people moving about, televisions and radios blaring into the sunset. On the quiet street below, an occasional car went past. A lonely street lamp flickered orange, the rest having broken a long time ago. Nargis yawned and poured herself another bowl of tea. She was amazed by how easily they had moved in. Granted, they did not have many possessions and she did not think they would take up much space. But she felt comfortable, as though she had a new, readymade family. Hussein and Bunavsha had started school. Saamana picked them up, offering to feed them and watch them until Nargis returned.

'Why is your son so afraid?'

Nargis glanced at her. 'My second husband used to beat him all the time, especially when he was drunk. He is insanely jealous of any man coming near me, even Hussein.'

'These men. Was there a reason for it?'

'He reminded him of Ahmed, my first husband who died. They look alike.'

Saamana frowned and shifted uncomfortably in her seat. She reached for a bowl of nuts with a chubby hand. 'Well, I will look after that little boy now. What a bastard.'

Nargis smiled sadly.

'Yes.'

June 13th, 2008, Tajikistan Countdown: 1 month 15 days

Nargis is back. I was relieved to see her, not just because the children have been asking for her but because I have missed her easy company. She looks drawn, thin, with dark circles under her eyes. Unusually for her, she stopped for tea many times today, sitting down as though the weight of the earth was on her. She does not want to take the children out, but prefers to remain here in the garden. 'The less I go out, the better,' she said. She is really jumpy. I made her favourite chocolate cake and gave her half to take home for the children. The ordeal of the last few weeks has aged her. At least she has this new friend who is helping her, that taxi driver. He drives her back and forth to work now as apparently he has a garage near her new place and the less she walks the streets with that lunatic looking for her, the safer she will be. The guards don't know about it as he drops her off on a parallel street and she walks the last hundred metres. I can't help but wonder... but something in her eyes stops me from asking.

It is so terribly hot. I can barely believe it was minus twenty only four months ago. No matter what I wear I cannot bear to be outside until at least four o'clock. The sun gives me migraines and my eyes are blinded by the whiteness of the concrete pathways. Leo only wants to be naked, he has heat rash everywhere and has already peed twice on the carpet today. I covered him in calamine lotion so that he resembles a little phantom. Nargis laughed and said he looks like her brother Said, come back from a day working at the cement factory.

31

Relieved to have Nargis back, Harriet spent the afternoon at the Elite Beauty Salon, a Russian-run temple to beauty run by an ex-model with prices and piped music to match the luxurious products used. After an hour in the cool, bright surroundings of the salon, she felt relaxed and restored. As she left though, a wall of heat whacked her in the face. Her car was like a roaring fire pit. It was quarter to four and the air conditioner was going full blast, yet the air streaming into the car was like a desert wind. Ivan had spent the last hour sheltering on a bench under trees next to the car. It was against office policy to keep the engine running, wasting petrol. The thermometer read forty-four degrees Celsius. Ivan opened the windows and drove faster to get some breeze. They picked up a sweaty, complaining Alexandra from school and were turning off Rudaki Avenue to go up the bumpy, potholed side street to the house when Harriet's phone rang. It was Veronica. She sounded strange. Her voice was cautious, guarded.

'Harriet, can you come over? I need to see you urgently.'

'Can you talk about it on the phone Ron?'

'No, I must to see you in person.'

Harriet sighed, wiping her brow. 'Would five o'clock be alright? It's a little less warm then.'

'No. Can you come now? I have stuff to do at four thirty.'

Harriet frowned. The car swung into the driveway. The guard opened the gate to reveal a green oasis, the borders brimming with white Michelmas daisies and scarlet roses. It was at least three or four degrees cooler inside than on the glaringly hot, dusty street beyond the compound. Alexandra jumped out, running to plunge into the paddling pool with Leo. A fat chlorine tablet fizzed and bubbled in the water.

I want to spend the rest of the afternoon lying on the tapshan with good book and a jug of iced lemonade as the sun goes down, Harriet thought. A ten-minute drive to Veronica's concrete fortress did not entice. Her back yard consisted of a dusty, reeking square of brown grass surrounded by concrete, covered in little piles of dog muck and acid stains left by two pampered, pedigree mutts. Her children sat watching TV through the summer in an air-conditioned playroom under artificial lights, there being hardly any ground floor windows for reasons of security. It was a depressing house for a young family, but it came free from the German Embassy. Harriet sighed and gestured to Ivan to turn the car around. I suppose it's her husband again. I wonder what he's done now?

'I'll be there in five minutes.'

Ivan dropped her off and left for the office.

Veronica greeted her soberly, dressed in a shapeless black top and tracksuit bottoms that emphasised her enormous, sagging rear. Her hair was damp and hung in dirty blonde tendrils like seaweed. She smelled good, of chocolate buttercream and vanilla essence. Her children, six-year old twins, Brigitte and Suzanna, were ensconced in the playroom with the nanny, quietly working on a puzzle. Cookies lay on a wire rack, cooling for their afternoon snack. Veronica arranged some for the two of them on a saucer with large glasses of creamy milk. Harriet accepted it, feeling like an overgrown pre-schooler. She compared the icy cold, indoor, carpeted environment with her green lawns under fruit trees at home. This was certainly a different way to bring up children. Only last week, hosting toddler group, she had been shocked to meet a young American missionary with a two-year old too scared to step on the lawn.

'He's never seen such green grass before, only concrete and dust,' she said.

The women sat down in a conservatory, the only bright room in the house. The windows were streaked with dust and covered in netting, though no one could possibly peer in over the twelve-foot walls. Harriet wondered why Veronica didn't make more of her tiny courtyard, at least growing herbs and flowers in pots, watering the grass and banning her dogs to the garage. Sunlight streamed in and the air conditioner pumped out freezing blasts making Harriet dizzy after the hot car. She shivered in her cotton blouse and reached in her bag for a cardigan.

'Another cookie?'

'Sure.'

Veronica's face was set, eyes worried and narrow.

'So here we are. What did you need to talk about?'

Veronica drummed her fingernails on the table. Harriet waited patiently, giving her time. *I wonder if she's caught her husband fooling around again?*

'Harriet. I need to tell you something,' she started awkwardly.

'Go on.'

'It's difficult.' She blushed. Harriet put her hands on Veronica's.

'Is it Christian?'

Veronica looked blankly at her. She frowned angrily and pulled her hand away. 'No. Why would you say that?' she asked indignantly. 'Of course not, my husband is just fine. It's your husband I want to talk about.'

'Mine?' Harriet recoiled. 'Henri? What about him?' she asked, baffled.

Veronica looked mysterious. 'I saw him…' She paused dramatically. 'In a restaurant, having lunch with a strange woman.'

Harriet baulked and then smiled. She laughed in relief. 'He was probably on a work lunch,' she said with a chuckle. 'You brought me all the way over here to tell me that?' Harriet giggled again. 'Henri's always lunching with different colleagues. Believe it or not, some of them are female. You mustn't be so suspicious all the time.'

239

Veronica frowned, wrinkling her face in irritation. She spoke sharply. 'I thought this was different. I wouldn't tell you otherwise. I'm not stupid Harriet.'

'I'm sorry. So... What did you see?'

'Well, does Henri always fondle sexy female colleagues?'

'Fondle?'

'Yes, touch them under the table? Kiss them?'

'Kiss...?'

Harriet felt her face start to burn. 'You saw him... where?'

'At Kiev Restaurant. I was seated in a corner and he didn't notice me because I was behind the pot plant. This new embassy wife just arrived in Dushanbe and I needed to tell her where to buy meat and so on, you know, my community liaison work. It was definitely him. He had his back to us. He was with a very tanned, red-haired woman of about forty years old, big blue eyes, smoking a lot, pretentious with a very annoying voice and an accent, maybe Polish? I don't know. They were drinking chilled vodka and eating blini with red caviar.'

Harriet cleared her throat. She felt faint. Her heart had started to beat painfully against her ribcage. 'I know who she is. Please tell me again, what exactly did he do?'

Veronica listed with her fingers, almost as if she could see a list of accusations written in a notebook.

'*Ein*, he touched her arm; *Svei*, two, he held her hand across the table; *Drei*, I saw her stroke his face, and four; she did kiss him on the lips, a quick kiss. She also, five; took off her shoe and stroked him with her foot under the table.'

'So it was only a quick kiss. They aren't necessarily *together*. Maybe they're just good friends,' she whispered.

Veronica looked at Harriet with undisguised pity and took her hand.

'Harriet, your man is either having an affair already or thinking about it. I have accepted it as part of what all the men do. It will be over soon, don't worry. That woman looked like someone for the fling only, no strings attached.'

Harriet got up from the table on unsteady legs. She felt sick and faint. A cookie lay untouched on her plate. 'I have to go home,' she said weakly. 'Please don't tell anyone.'

Veronica's eyes were expressionless. 'Of course not. If it helps, I know exactly how you feel.'

I can't write this down.

32

Harriet sat before her dressing table in the cool darkness of her bedroom. Henri's business case lay open on her bed, detritus spilled out across the duvet. Her head throbbed and her face was puffy and sore. She had had to stop and wipe her eyes by the Chinese Embassy on Rudaki Avenue, her tears blinding her. Officious traffic police had glanced at her curiously. As she walked home, she wondered, is he with her now? Sunglasses clamped over her eyes, she had managed to pass Nargis and the children in the garden unnoticed, darting into the house. She took out a cotton facial pad and some cold cream, cleansing her face. I need to get a grip, Nargis will leave soon.

It had been about a month since Silvana arrived in Dushanbe. A month since she was at their house. Harriet remembered that he said he met her in Khazakstan at a five star hotel. She could visualise the expansive king-size bed he must have had in his room, porn on the television, the Jacuzzi hot tub and room service for champagne on ice. I know what he likes. And all the while, she had sat here miserable, lost, bored and waiting for him like a loyal mutt.

What if all Silvana's talk of looking for a new husband had been a veiled warning or a message of intent for Henri? She had been blind, too naïve to see it. It's been going on since the winter. Six months, perhaps more. How could he do this to me? The tears started again. With *her*? Silvana was surely as far removed from herself as it was possible to be. Inconsiderate, undomesticated, liberated, a user of men who broke hearts with impunity. But Harriet could see the attraction. Overtly sexy, Silvana had big blue eyes, plump kissable lips, shiny, dyed hair and wore short skirts revealing long, gorgeous legs. She was surely great in bed, oozing sexual confidence. She was obviously also an interesting woman with her witty tales of survival. It's such a fucking cliché, Harriet thought, thinking of her parent's marriage, her father's frequent affairs. The days her mother spent in the darkness of her bedroom with a headache, drinking herself into oblivion. She had heard it all from her seat on the stairs, an overweight eight-year old with no company except her faithful border terrier, Flash, who sat with her, licking her hands for biscuit crumbs as she listened. The arguments that woke her often raged into the early hours. Her father eventually left when she was twelve with a suitcase and a sad smile, never to return. Occasional weekend visits followed. Dispatched to a penthouse apartment in a fancy part of Bournemouth overlooking a sandy beach, the churning Solent, the white pinpricks of the Isle of Wight Needles, Harriet had to confront a new, leggy twenty-five-year old "model" each time she visited. Fury started to take over from sadness, choking her with rage. She stood up and ripped the heavy brocade curtains apart.

'Fucking bastard,' she shouted. 'He will not turn me into my mother.'

Henri came home late that evening to find the the house in darkness. The children were asleep and there was no sign of his wife. There was no dinner on the table, no welcome drink. He removed his Italian leather shoes in the hall. His business case stood against one wall for some reason, though this week, for once, he was not travelling.

'Harriet,' he called. 'What's for dinner?'

On entering the bedroom, he was surprised to find that the door to the en suite bathroom was locked. He knocked.

'Harriet, are you in there?'

A teary voice came from within.

'Dinner's in the kitchen. Eat on your own, I don't want any.'

'Harriet, are you alright?'

He leaned his hot forehead against the cool door. There was no response. He shrugged and took off his linen jacket. Sitting down at the kitchen table he turned on the air conditioning and the television and began to eat, watching a news channel. Tinned tomato soup, it was passable but bland, not as good as Harriet's cooking. He smothered it in black pepper and Russian sour cream and poured himself an ice-cold lager. When he was nearly finished, Harriet came into the kitchen wearing a bath robe, her hair damp. He reluctantly looked away from the television towards her. She was pale and her eyes were red-rimmed.

'Harriet, *ma cherie*, what is it?' he asked, worried. 'Have you had some bad news from home?'

She gazed at him. His face became guarded. He knows that I know, she thought.

He squared his shoulders and balled his fists.

Harriet drew a ragged breath. Then she picked up the remote and switched off the television, an advert for 'Incredible India'.

He waited.

'Veronica saw you in the Ukrainian restaurant with Silvana. You were all over each other apparently. She took the liberty of telling me about it this afternoon.' Her voice cracked on the last sentence. She put her hands over her face and started to weep.

Henri sat stock still. He pushed his plate away and looked at her. He had turned pale and a nervous tick jumped on his eyebrow.

'What exactly did she say?'

Harriet stopped crying and looked at him through her fingers. 'What does it matter what she said?' she cried. 'Who cares about the fucking facts? You're either having an affair or you aren't. Which is it?'

'I'm not having an affair.'

'Bull-shit.'

'I promise you, I haven't slept with her and I'm not going to.'

Harriet brought her hands down and slapped the table. Henri started. 'I don't believe you. You are a g-goddamn l-liar.'

The muscle in his face flickered more wildly. He ran his fingers through greasy hair. His eyes widened. 'Please. Harriet, I would tell you if I had slept with someone else.'

'No, Henri no, I don't think you would. How can I trust anything you say?'

Henri was silent.

Harriet blew her nose into a paper serviette.

He gazed at her pleadingly and reached out for her arm.

She shook him free. 'Don't touch me. I want you to leave.'

'Move back into the spare room?'

Harriet took a breath and screamed as loudly as she could. 'No. Leave.'

Henri jumped up from the table. 'Harriet, please. Stop. I admit that I nearly slept with her this afternoon. That much is true. But in the end I couldn't do it and she threw me out.'

'You went to her apartment after lunch?'

'Yes.'

He had already put it down to the vodka. Her place, a one bedroom apartment in a charming, burgundy-painted building was close to the restaurant and they walked there tipsily at her suggestion, for a not-so-innocent espresso. They started to kiss in the corridor entering her mahogany doorway in a messy tangle of lust, lips and tongues. She started to undress him in her living room, clawing at his tie, unbuttoning his shirt and pushing his hands under her blouse. He responded by unclipping her brassiere and felt her breasts fall into his hands, her nipples beneath his fingertips. She moaned and he was lost for a moment, hardly even able to see her, drowning in her exotic scent. Hard, he wanted her like he had in Kazakhstan. A one night stand, never to be repeated, he'd promised himself ,and yet he found himself there again and again, every business trip, back at her apartment.

When her hands reached for his trouser zipper, something happened. Suddenly he didn't want to. It was too fast, too ill-considered. He had lost control, yet he never, ever allowed himself to lose control. Besides, he had enough problems to deal with. Silvana felt him hesitate and watched in disbelief as he removed his hands from her body and stepped back in panic. Her face was covered in a sheen of perspiration, flushed from vodka and lust. Gradually he saw her expression change into something ugly and cheap. His thoughts went to Harriet and to the other issues he still had not managed to rectify. He was horrified. He looked at Silvana apologetically.

'I can't, I'm sorry. Not here, not in Dushanbe. I have too much to lose.' He was calm and collected, back in charge, back in control.

She threw him out, hurling insults.

Harriet's voice was choked.

'Why? Why would you risk all we have for a stupid fling?'

'I don't know. It was foolish.'

'Why her?'

'I honestly don't know. She tried to seduce me and I didn't see it coming.'

Harriet snorted. 'Oh come on, Henri, you two have been flirting for weeks. You must have slept with her in Kazakhstan. That was where it started wasn't it? All those fucking business trips all through the winter. Skiing. Weekends away in Kazakh mountain resorts. You were with her all along.'

Henri was silent. He had folded into his chair, cornered. He did not move. Harriet stood up, her hand on the door. She felt shaky, standing on the precipice of her marriage, deciding whether or not to push him off the cliff. She wavered. Maybe I should let him stay? What if he goes running back to her apartment? What if he leaves me for her?

Then Henri cleared his throat. 'You've disregarded my opinions a lot lately. You don't care about me like you once did. Perhaps that was why I ran into the arms of another woman.' He spoke in a monotone, rational in the face of her tears, her hysteria.

For the first time, he seemed pathetic. Old. If anyone is fooling around in this marriage, it should be me. I'm the catch, not him. Her tears dried up.

'Henri, do you really think that patronising me is going to make me change my mind?'

He ran his fingers through his hair. It was thinning on top. His fingernails needed cutting. He tried to look sincere, pouting. 'I've behaved like an idiot. All I can do is apologise to you.'

'That's not good enough.'

'I know.'

He tried to take her hand again. She moved it away.

'Henri, I'm not a young girl anymore.'

'What do you mean? I know that.'

She sighed. *I found the condoms in your business case, fool. We haven't used condoms in eight years.*

She turned to him. Her voice was quiet, controlled.

'Like you've always said, *Il vaut mieux être marteau qu'enclume*; it's better to be a hammer than a nail.'

Henri's head jerked up and his mouth fell open.

'Just go.'

June26th, 2008

Henri is staying at a hotel near his office. I haven't told anyone, he is so often away from home that the children won't notice. Tomorrow is a public holiday but I have given Nargis the day off and will stay here

247

alone with the children. Nargis doesn't know either, I am too humiliated to tell her. Maybe I will call Henri and ask him to take them to a park. I don't think he has ever done that before, been alone with the children outside the house for an afternoon. Let's see how he handles changing Leo's nappy in the boot of the car or on a peeling, rusty Tajik park bench while Alex runs off in the opposite direction.

In truth, I have no idea if I will cope in the UK on my own. Perhaps I will give in and go to Nairobi after all, everything is still arranged. Henri called me with the news, he will be transferred to Kenya in September. I received his news with something like dull resignation. I don't know if I can be alone. I am so accustomed to being told what to do and where to go by him. I hate myself as I write that sentence, the apathy of it. It is the truth though and I might as well face it. I could return alone to England but I no longer feel like it is home. I don't think I will ever feel at home anywhere, ever again. Henri's arms were my home, his unstinting confidence in himself; my anchor.

So I ask you, Journal, what life would I have in Britain as a single mother, struggling with two children under those grey skies, in the endless weeks of winter rain? When I am there I feel nearly as dislocated from normal people as I do in Tajikistan. I have seen too much to squeeze them back into the narrowness of the English middle class identity or single motherhood in some small English town. I don't fit in anymore. My mother writes to me about her village flower show, the spats in the Women's Institute and her boozy ladies lunches. Friends call and regale me with tales of office politics, rugby club quiz nights, school fairs and drunken girls' nights out down the Rising 'Scum' (Sun). I have no more a vision of myself leading their lives than if I tried to imagine living on the moon. The truth is, I am still adrift in expatriate limbo and Henri's cheating has not changed that. I inhabit an imaginary world where the only people I can relate to are as rootless as me. We belong to a stateless state, an international diaspora, cut off from our origins by the changes that have taken place in our absence as much as by the relentlessly dull sameness of it all when we return.

33

Nargis lay snoozing with her children in their new room. She had the day off, a Tajik public holiday for the Day of National Reconciliation. A small metal tanduk chest sat in a corner for their clothes. The warm summer breeze wafted in and the faded tablecloth hanging in the window fluttered and flapped, fanning the sleeping children. Nargis could smell the scent of frying onions from the apartment above. She could hear the shouts and laughter of happy children playing under the trees below. Saamana had left early, weighed down with a tin of syrupy halva, dragging a reluctant Shuhrat with her to visit her daughter. Nargis bought Saamana jasmine soap as a present after her namesake flower. She wished she could visit Gulya, Abdul and Said, but didn't dare. Maybe they would walk down to Zavon's garage and bring him a cold RC Cola, just to get out. Listening to the soft snores of her children in the semi-darkness, Nargis's thoughts went to Faisullo. She longed for him as much as ever. It's been over five weeks now, the longest time I have ever not seen my baby. He is probably forgetting all about me.

A few days later, Nargis gave in. She was at work, playing with Leo in the garden. Perhaps Poulod is back in Russia? He has to work after all. After sitting, staring at her phone for what seemed like hours, she held her breath and dialled. She prayed Poulod would not answer. If he answered, she decided, she would hang up immediately.

'Assalom,' came a shrewish, nervy voice. It was her old mother-in-law.

'Assalom Hoosh Donam,' said Nargis cautiously.

'Nargis? My dear kelline. It has been too long. Where have you been and why have you not come to see us?'

Clearly she had no idea about the new 'business' Poulod was involved in or what had gone on between them.

'I'm sorry, Firuza. I haven't been to visit because Poulod and I had a quarrel and I don't really want to see him at the moment. How is my baby?'

'Faisullo is fine. What quarrel? What are you talking about? Do you know where he is?'

'No. No I don't. He's not there?'

'No. We haven't seen him for six days.'

'Has he gone to Russia?'

'We don't know,' said Firuza. Her voice shook. 'He left all his things here, so we don't think he left for Russia permanently. Usually, these last few months, when he tells us he's going away for business, he's always back in Dushanbe within three days, but this time he's been away a week and we've had no word from him.'

'I'm sure you'll see him tomorrow, or later,' said Nargis cheerlessly.

'I hope so.'

If he were dead, I would wear my brightest red lipstick, Nargis thought, paint a mono-brow with usma herbs from Green Bazaar and go dancing to wedding music on his grave. She picked up some plastic toys from the lawn and flung them into a bright red toy box. Leo grinned and she kissed his chubby cheeks. A burden lifted a little. I can go to the shop this evening to pay wages, take stock and visit my parents with Hussein and Bunavsha if Poulod is safely in Russia.

'What's Faisullo doing? Is he asking about me?'

'Yes. He always does, you know that, kelline. I took him to a park today and he played with some other children. He's well.'

Nargis's heart ached. She took Leo's hand and led him inside to prepare lunch.

'Please…please may I speak to him?'

'No. He's asleep.'

Nargis could hear a child's voice in the background. She slammed the door hard and kicked off her flip flops, replacing them with slippers. She resisted the urge to smash her phone against the wall. There was a long pause.

'You know, Nargis, we're not stupid,' Firuza whispered. 'Suddenly Poulod brings home thousands of dollars each week, he buys a new car, talks about building a new house. He won't tell us where the money comes from, only that he has new business opportunities and we should be happy for him. His father tried talking to him, but he just got angry. We know he might be working with dangerous men.' Firuza's voice caught in despair.

'I can't say anything about that. I mean, I don't know anything.'

'What if he's lying somewhere injured, or dead?' she said. 'He's my son. I can't stop thinking the worst.'

'I haven't heard from him either, not for five or six weeks.'

'If you do hear from him, please let us know, won't you?'

Nargis grimaced. The chances of her speaking with Poulod would, she hoped, be non-existent.

'Yes. Alright, I will.' Nargis took a deep breath. 'Firuza, I would like to see Faisullo tomorrow after work, but I want to meet him in Kamzamulski Ozera Park so we can have a little walk and play on the rides. Is that possible?'

'You really don't want to see my son do you?' Firuza sounded indignant. She had never understood why Nargis couldn't love him, seeing as he was the centre of her world.

'No, I don't. Please don't tell him that I called.'

'Alright. I suppose I can come out, though it is very hot and not good for my blood pressure. I'll see you tomorrow at the entrance at five-thirty.'

The next evening, Nargis took a mashutka to the park. She asked Saamana to watch Hussein and Bunavsha, explaining she needed to see her youngest child. Saamana readily agreed, looking at Nargis with renewed sympathy. The park was on a lake, with fairground rides and a small zoo. It was a popular place for families to stroll in the summer evenings and buy a chewy, fatty shashlik lamb or beef kebab from small blue and white striped marquees to eat under the trees with naan and chopped, salty vegetable salad. Gypsy children ran around begging and young courting couples sat on the ground under the trees.

Hesitantly, she approached the entrance to the park, on the lookout for Poulod. She did not trust Firuza, but she was desperate. She arrived fifteen minutes early and darted in through the entrance, hiding behind a small toy train. She wore a black headscarf and could see the sloping approach to the park as well as the entrance gates. Twenty minutes later, she saw a silver-haired lady in a black kurta walking down the hill to the gate with a small boy skipping alongside her. There was no sign of a silver Mercedes or a thickset man. Nargis watched Faisullo wait anxiously with his grandmother for another ten minutes before she removed her headscarf and emerged from her hiding place. Running to her son, she picked him up and hugged his curly head, kissing him all over his little face.

'Hello, my baby, Mamma's missed you so much,' she cried, tears in her eyes. Finally she set him down on the ground and shook Firuza's hand. Firuza frowned, her eyes black and appraising.

'Assalom, Hoosh Doman,' she said formally. I hate this woman, Nargis thought savagely.

'Assalom, kelline,' said Firuza, equally formal.

Faisullo wanted to ride on a creaking blue toy train for toddlers, another remnant from Soviet times. Waving at him as he rushed by, she turned to Firuza.

'So, Poulod hasn't yet returned,' she said pointedly. It was a statement of fact. Nargis knew that if he had, he would be there.

'No.' She turned to Nargis, her eyes pleading. 'Please dear, I know you're angry with me but I am a mother who loves her son. He's my only son and my whole life, Nargis.

252

But he's very irresponsible making his old parents worry so. I can't understand why he doesn't just call to let me know he is alright. His phone is switched off, but he knows very well I'm worrying about him.'

Nargis squared her shoulders and raised her chin. I'm also a mother who loves her son, but what price my love? Tajik families thronged back and forth and children shrieked in excitement on the fairground rides. A small path eked its way through the rides to the artificial lake beyond. The smell of steaming chicken hotdogs, sausage patties and popcorn cooked in huge metal woks wafted towards them from stalls dotted along the path. Above the park, a major highway of Dushanbe, Somoni Avenue, hummed with rush-hour traffic. The air was hazy with car fumes, hotdog steam and dust, blocking out the mountain view.

Firuza looked bereft. Her face was ashen and her mouth turned down at the corners. Her grey bun was unravelling in the heat and she limped a little as they walked, her hip playing up. Her ringless, liver-spotted hands were twisted with arthritis. Faisullo ran along fearlessly, swerving in and out of the crowd, a handful of a child. Nargis felt a little sorry for her, despite herself.

'Poulod was never a very good husband but I suppose he's a good son.'

'He is. Despite what you say, kelline, he did love you. You know what they say: "Meat doesn't come without bones". You should give him another chance.'

Firuza started to cough noisily, wheezing into an old yellow handkerchief.

Nargis looked away, exasperated. She will never give up.

'Firuza, I promise you, I don't know where he is. I suspect he's probably gone to Russia, but that's all I can say.'

Soon they reached an artificial lake. It was brimming with beige snowmelt from the surrounding mountains and shimmered in the evening heat. Beyond the lake, construction workers were finishing for the day at a large building site designated for yet another new hotel. Orange rays bounced off the water, making them squint. A man stood by the water selling small plastic boats. Faisullo ran ahead to a shashlik kebab stall and turned back to grab Nargis's hand and propel her forward.

'Mamma, I'm hungry,' he whined. 'I want a shashlik.'

'He hasn't had his dinner yet,' murmured Firuza.

Nargis tended to spoil Faisullo more than her other two children, feeling their visits were too precious to deny him anything when they met so seldom. He did not have their good manners, nor their restraint when it came to asking for treats. They sat down at a plastic table under the trees and ate fresh lamb kebabs and a plate of oily osh pilov with naan. An old red and blue fairground wheel made a slow rotation in the distance. They ate in silence. Nargis and Firuza had never had much in common, even when they all lived together. Poulod kept his abuse of Hussein from Firuza as much as from Nargis, though as she never commented on their bruises and carried out Poulod's wish not to feed the children proper meals, Nargis considered her complicit. Thankfully, Firuza had never treated her like a traditional kelline, beating her or forcing her to be a domestic slave. They had kept a polite distance during the two-year marriage. This lasted until Firuza agreed to keep Faisullo, providing Poulod with the childcare that allowed him to return to Russia. For that, Nargis would never forgive her. Faisullo was two and a half years old. She had already missed so much. He stood on a chair chewing on his lamb kebab with vigour. Grease dripped onto his t-shirt and he grinned in pleasure, his face covered in meat fat. He looked a little like Poulod, his chest puffed out in pride. Watching him, Nargis felt a familiar anxiety. What if he turns out like his father one day? He might, brought up by this old ewe, if I don't get him back in time.

'This good, Mamma,' he said happily, delving with his hand into the pilov. Laughing, he fed her a chickpea. They finished their meal, washed their hands in a stream of water provided by the chef's purple plastic jug and it was time to go home. Street children appeared from nowhere to beg for scraps and a moody teenage waitress with red lipstick and a frilly French apron over her glittering blue kurta shooed them away. Nargis wrapped up the leftovers to take home. Firuza stood up painfully, pressing fingers deep into her hip socket. She turned to Nargis, suddenly angry.

'I want Poulod to take Faisullo to live in Russia,' she spat. 'I am getting too old for this. I told him last week, save your money, build a house in Leningrad. We will join you there, sell the apartment.'

Nargis gasped. She felt cold, despite the hot breeze.

'Has he said he's moving to Russia?'

Firuza glared at her. 'No dear, but he won't wait for you forever, you know. He should build a new life with his son, start again with a proper virgin bride, not some used up old widow with airs.'

'But what about me?'

'What about you, kelline? You have made it clear you will never return. You ruthlessly abandoned your own blood and now you expect my sympathy?'

Firuza limped off towards the exit, dragging Faisullo by the hand. Nargis was too shocked to think of a retort and hesitated a moment before following. Families were leaving the park, children balanced on their father's shoulders and mothers pushing plastic Chinese prams. There were queues at the bus stop. Nargis debated whether to snatch Faisullo and run. I can't. Firuza will cause a scene and I will get into trouble. She stopped at her minibus queue, her mind a fog of confusion.

'Where are you headed?' asked Firuza curiously. 'That's not the right direction for your mother's house.'

'I have to go and deliver some money I owe to a friend,' she lied. 'Faisullo, my little man, I will see you very soon,' she said, leaning down to give him a kiss. He moaned softly and clung to her legs. Nargis hated their partings, but now, wondering if she would ever see him again, she was beside herself. She knelt down on the pavement and started to cry, holding him to her. Firuza anticipated problems and yanked him roughly by the arm, darting into a minibus, knocking his head on the doorframe on the way in. She clasped him to her lap and slammed the door shut. His face screwed up and he started to scream.

'My head! My arm! Mamma! I want to go home with you, not Bibi,' he bellowed.

The mashutka veered off into the busy traffic, taking his cries with it. Nargis stood staring at the mini-van as it sped off up the hill, wiping her eyes with her finger tips.

'Bye-bye, my little love,' she whispered sadly.

34

The next day Nargis was preoccupied, her thoughts taken up with Faisullo, whether she would ever see him again. She had lain awake all night, debating whether to go Poulod and beg him to stay, in return for what? She didn't know. I can't go back to live with him and nor can I smuggle drugs, but perhaps I can be more friendly, delay him a little, she thought. She shivered. She dreaded the prospect of his foul lovemaking and hasty fists but it was better than losing Faisullo forever. I will wait until he returns from Russia, then go to see him, she decided. Her mind was tangled, her thoughts returning to Faisullo at every moment. Even so, she couldn't help but notice that Harriet had spent the past two days in a strange mood, slipping past her with her head lowered when she went to the kitchen, only to go into her room and stay there until it was time for Nargis to leave. She had stopped all her usual activities, sending Nargis with Ivan to do the school run, cancelling appointments, switching off her phone, her land line left off the hook. That evening, Nargis had knocked discreetly on her bedroom door.

'Mrs. Harriet, I shall go home now.'

'I'll be down in a minute.'

Harriet opened the door. She wore pyjamas and an old woollen cardigan. It was dark inside. The bed was ruffled, used tissues strewn across the floor.

'I can stay until Mr. Henri comes? Can I bring you tea?'

Harriet's eyes were puffy, her hair unruly and mussed. She struggled to keep her face still as new tears sprang to her eyes and she tried to smile. Nargis looked away, embarrassed for her.

'It's alright Nargis, I will be fine. You go home now.'

Maybe someone passed away in England? Nargis left the house with a sense of disquiet.

It was half past six and the heat of the day was just starting to die off. Peachy-red sunset rays streamed into the living room on the other side of the apartment and flies buzzed at the window. An ordinary evening. Shuhrat was at chess club. Bunavsha was curled up on the sofa like a cat while Hussein sat at Saamana's feet. All three were mesmerised by the latest twist in a Russian soap opera. Six round balls of naan dough sat covered with a cloth in the kitchen, waiting to rise. Hussein had covered the table with pencils, having completed a drawing for school.

'Hussein, come and clean up,' she called. She was satisfied to note that he had written an accompanying explanation for his drawing in perfect Russian cyrillic. Their new school is much better than the old one, she thought. She deftly sliced up a bag of potatoes and threw them in a skillet. They spat and sizzled in cotton oil. Her phone rang.

'Alo,'

'Assalom, kelline,' came a tearful voice. Nargis turned down the gas. Immediately the crackle and pop of the potatoes ceased. She was panicked at the sound of weeping.

'Firuza? Mother-in-law? Is it you? Why are you crying? Is it Faisullo?' The weeping continued while Nargis pictured all sorts of terrible scenarios. 'Please, Firuza. Tell me what's wrong,' she shouted.

Saamana and the children rushed to the kitchen.

'What's happened?'

'Wait.'

Firuza composed herself enough to talk.

'Faisullo is fine. But we've had some terrible news.'

Firuza started to sob again. Nargis's head started to spin. Poulod.

'W-what is it?' Nargis felt nothing at all, empty. 'Is he dead?'

The children stared at her wide-eyed. She smiled reassuringly.

'Faisullo is fine,' she mouthed. Saamana started rummaging in a cupboard, listening all the while.

'No. My Poulod... my baby. He's in prison in Moscow. He collapsed getting off a flight a few weeks ago and almost died. The stupid boy was smuggling heroin in his stomach. Can you believe it? All to support us, his old parents and his l-little boy.'

At this, Nargis almost laughed out loud. You delusional old ewe, he never did anything for anyone but himself, she thought contemptuously. She flipped a potato with a flick of her spatula and waved the kids back to the TV.

'They gave him an emergency operation and managed to pump his stomach out in time but he was arrested as soon as he was coherent. Now he is sitting on remand in Butyrka Prison, a miserable Russian hellhole, looking at a fifteen year sentence with no parole. He called us an hour ago, the first time he's been allowed. All his cellmates are waiting on remand but haven't been given trial dates. Some have been there two years or more. He's terrified he'll die in prison, that his employers will find a way to kill him in retribution. He says he knows too much to be allowed to live but he's too scared to make a plea bargain. He's already been beaten by the guards and is surviving on porridge and watery soup. They have to sleep in shifts, eighty men to a cell. Oh... it is too much.' Firuza dissolved into tears again.

Nargis could barely believe it. Poulod, safely locked up in prison. Sealed away in an impenetrable Moscovite fortress where he would not be able to hurt her or her children, ever again. It was like a dream. A burden of terror dissipated. Nargis stopped cooking and sat down on a chair. Tears of relief glistened in her eyes. Saamana flapped about in the kitchen like a startled pigeon, sending her anxious looks. Hussein grabbed by her by the hand and gave her a dark stare.

'My husband has been arrested in Russia,' she whispered, by way of explanation. Hussein whooped and fistballed the air. Another surge of joy went through her.

'I am coming to get Faisullo, right now,' she said into the phone. Saamana's face broke into a delighted smile and she clapped her hands..

'We thought you would do this,' Firuza said bitterly. 'He's all we have left. Please don't take him from us, I'm begging you.'

Nargis snorted. 'Poulod always said he could look after Faisullo better than me. Now he's in a Russian prison, a common criminal. I earn a good salary and I want my son.'

'We won't allow it.'

'He's my child, not yours. It's not your choice anymore.'

Nargis rang off, grabbed her bag and walked out of the apartment. She started to run, down the dingy stairs of the high rise tenement, jogged along the uneven pavement, taking care not to fall into a pothole. In her haste, she realised she still wore her apron and house slippers. Rushing into the garage on Karaboev Avenue, she found Zavon tinkering underneath an ancient Volga.

'Zavon,' She cried. 'Emergency. My ex-husband has been arrested in Moscow. We have to go to Poulod's parent's apartment and get my son before his grandparents try to take him away.'

Zavon slid out from under the car, his face smeared with engine oil.

'Arrested? Hodooiman? Do you really think they would try to take him?'

'I don't know, but I'm not willing to risk it.'

Driving to the apartment, Nargis clenched her hands together. She stared out onto the tall grey high-rises, the quiet, hot streets and the people hurrying home from work. They swung onto a busy highway by the State Circus, a modernist hulk from Soviet days, joining the stream of vehicles heading west towards Jabbor Rasulov Avenue.

They passed the chaos of the monthly sprawling four-day car market held in an unused wasteland area surrounded by the grey husks of industrial buildings looted during the civil war. Thousands of German and Russian cars brought in from Uzbekistan were lined up on muddy hillocks, their owners jostling for attention in their black leather caps. Zavon made some comment about the traffic being worse than usual but Nargis did not respond, she was too caught up. What if they have left, gone, without a forwarding address, kidnapped him? She clung to the door handle, silently willing Zavon to drive faster. She would not be able to stand losing Faisullo again. Anything seemed possible at that moment and child abduction to Russia was a common tale in Tajikistan, men marrying new wives abroad unbeknownst to the first wives at home. Of course, only fathers were able to abscond with Tajik children, never mothers.

It was already dark when they arrived. Nargis didn't wait for Zavon to park, opening the door while the car was still moving and jumping out.

'Nargis, wait,' shouted Zavon. She paid him no heed and rushed to the middle door of the block, climbing the stairs two at a time. Six storeys up, she banged hard on the peeling, royal blue door. After an age, the door opened. It was her father-in-law. A shrunken figure of the man he once was, he looked defeated and broken. Nargis took him in as they stood wordlessly on the landing. He had aged a decade since their last meeting.

'Is my son here?' she gasped, panting from her exertions.

He stood aside and she rushed in, closely followed by Zavon. Faisullo was sitting on the living room floor next to Firuza. She was crying in an armchair, a faded cotton handkerchief held to her eyes. At the sight of Nargis she cried harder. Faisullo wore his pyjamas and a brown puffy overcoat.

'Bibi cry,' he said, pointing.

His clothes and toys had been packed into large plastic bags that sat by his grandmother's feet. For the first time since she heard the news, Nargis felt a prick of sympathy for her in-laws. She sat down gingerly on the shabby, carpet-bag sofa and Faisullo came to sit on her lap.

'Mamma, I go in your house?'

'Yes.'

'Oh.'

Firuza stopped crying and lowered her handkerchief. She winced when she saw Zavon and her expression flashed with rage.

'You brought another man here?' Firuza spat. 'Your poor husband is rotting in jail and you've already taken up with a new one?'

Nargis stood up, flustered.

'Excuse me Firuza, I should explain. This is Zavon Ismailov. He's a friend of the family.'

Firuza snorted.

'I always said you were no good.'

Nargis caught Zavon's eye.

'I think we'll be going now.'

Faisullo looked uncertainly at his grandmother, then toddled to Nargis who picked him up and hugged him. Firuza continued to weep into her sleeve, not looking at them.

'I'm sorry about Poulod, for your sake,' said Nargis quietly.

'Don't be. He is as good as dead to us now, except we don't have a funeral to prepare,' said his father gruffly. 'We will never see him again. We have no son.'

Firuza sobbed harder at his words and left the room. They could hear her wailing in the bathroom. Zavon picked up the bags and they edged towards the hallway. Suddenly, the old man came forward with a brown paper envelope.

'This is what Poulod left here in the apartment,' he said. 'I am guessing it is savings he made from his dirty activities. I have decided to keep half of it aside for Faisullo's schooling.'

Nargis peeped inside and saw a large number of dollar bills. She felt chastened. Perhaps she had been wrong, after all. She looked up, shocked.

'Did Poulod...?'

'No.' He smiled sadly. 'It's our idea. We feel something good should come from all of this.' He took the money and pocketed it. 'I will keep it safe until the time comes.'

Zavon bowed his head in respect but Nargis shrivelled inwardly. I hope I never need to ask you for help, she thought.

'Please call me when you would like to see your grandson,' Nargis said stiffly. 'You are both welcome in my house.'

July 2nd, 2008, Tajikistan Countdown: 28 days

Something strange happened today. It wasn't planned. Ivan leaned over to place something in the glove compartment and brushed my knee with his hand. All of a sudden, he ceased to be Henri's employee and became a young, good looking man.

We sat still for a few moments and then I looked into his face. What I read there then gave me the courage to grab his hand and trace his fingertips up my leg, all the way up to my waist, then up to my breasts, slowly, deliberately. His hand burned through the cotton of my Tajik salwar khameez. I could see thoughts pass through his mind, his face a kaleidoscope of emotions; excitement, confusion, pride, shock, lust, even fear, I think, but I didn't care. There was a rushing sound in my ears, time was suspended. If we had carried on, I don't know what would have happened. I wanted to climb onto his lap and fuck him right there in the car, but the horn of an impatient, sweating Lada driver sounded behind us, slicing through the moment.

He drove me home in silence but as he pulled out of the driveway he caught my glance. We made an unspoken pact. I doubt Ivan knows what Henri did or why he is sleeping at the hotel. I suppose he wonders if I am lonely. I am, of course. How laughable. I've been lonely since I got here.

35

Two months had passed since Nargis left the refuge, yet her whole life was different. Like a woman trying not to drown in rapids, she had spent the years since Ahmed died clinging to every floating log, twig or leaf she could see, even when she knew they would not hold her from the raging torrent for long. It was wonderful to be free of fear and the burden of shame for leaving her husband. Now she could hold her head high. The people of the mahalla sent messages of sympathy and stopped Gulya in the street to talk about her lucky escape.

'I always knew she was right to leave him, he was a rogue.'

'Poor Nargis, she did well to escape, nothing but a common criminal.'

Gulya was only too happy to be able to retort; 'Of course, my daughter was too well brought up to stay with such a man.'

The restoration of her daughter's reputation went some way to assuaging Gulya's disappointment when she decided to stay on with Saamana. Nargis had no desire to return to live in her parent's overcrowded, wretched haveli, no wish to give up her newfound independence. Gulya agreed to take Faisullo a few days a week when Nargis was in the shop, in return for her help with bills. This arrangement pleased them both. Gulya set about teaching Faisullo some traditional manners and put an end to his petulant tantrums. Once a week, Firuza visited Saamana's apartment to take care of him. She had shown up the next day, full of apologies for her outburst.

'If you will let me, I'll take care of Faisullo for you while you are working.' A single tear rolled down her face, settling in the creases in her cheek. 'He is all I have left in the world now and I can't bear to live without him.'

'It's like I am new person with a completely new life,' Nargis told Harriet.

Zavon still sometimes picked her up after work at a designated spot on Rudaki Avenue a few blocks away from the road where Harriet lived. Nargis didn't want the guards to talk. They spent hours chatting on the forecourt of his garage, perched on ramshackle metal chairs with bowls of steaming tea. Zavon was the last person Nargis thought of at night, a man who came to her in disturbing, erotic dreams and the first person she wanted to speak with when she woke up.

On Bunavsha's birthday, they arranged a little trip to one of the kiosks at Green Bazaar. Nargis wore her prettiest kurta, a new, blue, shimmering dress that caught the sunlight like peacock feathers. She made an effort with her hair, leaving it long with side plaits and put kohl on her eyes, painting a little line cross her eyebrows. Then she caught sight of herself in her cracked cosmetic mirror and hastily rubbed it off, shaking her head at her own vanity. She was no bride, only an old, used up widow. Zavon had become her best friend, her closest advisor. She had grown to love everything about him, his easy going gait, his relaxed laugh, the creases around his friendly, brown eyes, his big, clever mechanic's hands stained with oil where it would not wash off. The manly, salty smell of his duffle coat when she sat behind him in the back seat of the taxi. Of course, she scolded herself, we are just friends.

One evening he called. Nargis was scrubbing clothes in the bath tub and asked Bunavsha to hold the phone to her temple.

'I need to see you. May we go for a drive?'

'What is it?'

'I can't speak about it on the phone.'

'Alright. I'll be free from work at six tomorrow. Pick me up.'

Nargis rang off. She hoped he had not decided to return to Russia. Perhaps his business was failing, the new garage he had set up might be leaking money or crippled by customers asking for work on credit. Perhaps he missed his wife and had decided to go back to her.

The following evening, Nargis waited for him on Rudaki Avenue. As soon as his car pulled up she hopped in the back, pretending for the sake of any nosy passers-by that she was simply taking a taxi to town. They drove across the river and up to a viewpoint above Varzob Bazaar that overlooked Northern Dushanbe. Nargis could clearly see the white smoke from the cement factory where her brother worked, her mahalla hidden by a bluff. Farther below lay the rocky riverbed. Zavon left the road and entered a farm track that led to a precipice facing Varzob Lake. The sun had nearly set and it was getting dark but she did not care. They sat in his black and yellow taxi, among old beehives and fields of barley. His arm lay along the back of the seat, close to her neck. When she touched him by accident it was as though they both had an electric shock. She could feel the heat coming off his skin. Her body ached in secret places.

'Nargis, I have contacted my wife in Moscow to ask her for a divorce. I want to marry you,' he said, holding her little, stubby hand tenderly in his big one. 'I love you.'

She realised with astonishment, that somehow this kind, wise man was giving her another chance at love. She had not thought such a thing possible.

'I... I think I love you too,' she said. Her heart felt as though it would explode. Then the reality of her situation hit her. She was a widow with three children and worse, still shackled by marriage to a criminal. It would be a scandal. I can't go through it all again, the stares, the whispers behind hands, the jeers in the street. She pulled her hand away.

'It's too soon. I have to think of my children. They have only known you a few months and they will always come first.'

She held her breath. The twinkling lights of the cityscape below were reflected in his big brown eyes but she could not read his expression.

'Nargis, if I marry you and become your husband, then it follows that I will also try to be a good father to them,' he said solemnly. 'That means, of course, that they will be as welcome in my house as you.'

Nargis frowned. She had heard those words less than three years before.

'Zavon. I need to think about it. I mean...three children...it's not easy, especially when they are not your own. You have a daughter I have never met. Your father...'

'My father has agreed. He knows that I love you and he feels that regardless of what people may think, I should marry again rather than spending the rest of my life as a bachelor. Of course, he prefers I marry a young, unmarried virgin bride, but as I told him, I don't care about Tajik traditions. I want you and no one else.'

Nargis looked at him. The mention of her virginity brought her up short. What business is it of theirs? She thought. She frowned. Where was the yearning? The anticipation? Does he think I will just acquiesce like a sacrificial sheep at Eid al-Adha? It quite suited her to be married now that Poulod was locked up in prison. For the first time in years, she was respectable, her reputation restored as the righteous victim of her marriage to a man gone sour. Old school friends had called since the news spread, asking her for tea and gossip with their mother-in-laws tut-tutting in sympathy under the shade of their tapshans. She had promised Hussein that she would not marry again.

'I cannot remarry as I won't be able to get a divorce. Poulod will never agree to grant me one from prison in Moscow, that much I know.'

'But, Nargis…'

He looked so disconsolate that Nargis slowly, deliberately put his hand on her heart.

'We don't need to get married just yet. We have all the time in the world if you will only wait. Besides, between us, I am already yours.'

The following evening when Nargis went to check her shop takings she called in to see her mother.

'An old friend of Ahmed asked me to marry him, but I refused.'

Gulya made a noise like a deflating balloon and hid her face in her hands.

'Nargis, haven't you had enough husbands for one lifetime?' she stuttered.

Nargis shook her head and backed away a few steps. 'Mother, of course, I said no. Anyway, Poulod will never grant me a divorce, you know that.'

'It is a scandal that this son-of-a-donkey even asked you. Who is he now? Someone else for me to worry about? I'm glad you said no. To be married three times. Three men in one lifetime. You might as well be working in the street. Sitora would have been overjoyed.'

July 3rd, 2008, Tajikistan Countdown: 27 days

After dropping Alexandra off at school, Ivan drove us to a quiet spot outside Dushanbe. We made love in a forest on an old blanket taken from the car. His muscular body felt so youthful after Henri's spongy belly, I could hardly take my eyes off him. It was urgent, blinding, he ripped the buttons on my shirt in his haste but I didn't mind. Later we made love again, more slowly. We didn't speak, either before or after, apart from once. 'Madam Harriet, you deserve happiness,' he said, cupping my chin with a hand. My eyes filled with tears. He was right, I do.

I know I can trust the taciturn Ivan not to tell. I feel so much better now. In fact, I feel more myself, more me, than at any time since I married Henri. It's ludicrous, but true. I lost myself trying to be his perfect version of womanhood. Ivan has helped me to exorcise the spirit of Silvana from my head and I can go to Nairobi with my head held high. That's if I go at all.

36

Some time passed before Nargis realised that Henri was no longer living at the house. He had always left before she arrived in the morning and returned after she departed so that there was little change until Saturday, when she noticed that his laptop was not in the study, his long fingers no longer tapping on the keys, no smells of aftershave and espresso lingering in the kitchen. Harriet no longer took much trouble over her appearance, content to be bare-faced, her hair tied back in a plait like a Tajik. She resembled a fragile, bent flower, yet she was calm and in control. She stopped drinking wine in the daytime, busying herself instead with the little details of their move, wrapping paintings and sorting through toys. That morning, Mr Henri called Nargis on her mobile phone. He sounded angry.

'Please ask Madame Harriet to speak to me, I have not been able to get through to her.'

He showed up half an hour later and left after angry words were exchanged, slamming the door with a blue linen suit on his arm and a bag of underwear. Harriet did not comment on his absence so Nargis did not either.

The next day, Harriet sought her out and invited her to come outside to the tapshan. Nargis was in the bedroom folding washing, Leo toddling at her feet.

'Nargis, leave those clothes and come have a cup of green tea with me.'

'Alright.'

They removed their shoes and climbed up onto the shady platform. The roses had long finished their flowering but their bushy branches growing up and around the frame onto the roof of the structure kept the sun off, like a green-leaved cave. The garden was warm, an Iranian style fountain sprinkled water in small dribbles and flowers of different types and colours waved gaily in the summer breeze. Pomegranates were ripening on the trees and plants covered in red cherry and yellow plum tomatoes leant against a south facing wall. The grapevines covering metal trellises above had started to produce the buds of green grapes. The grass was green and fragrant, watered twice daily, so that the garden was cool under the fruit trees. Nargis felt her hot body relax in the shade of the tapshan. She stretched her legs out onto the purple velvet quilt and wriggled her toes in pleasure. She was wistful. I will really miss this place. Harriet poured out green tea into little bowls from a blue and white Uzbek teapot. She passed her a bowl.

'Nargis, I know it is terribly sudden but I hate long drawn out goodbyes. I am leaving for England in two weeks to live with my mother for a while before joining Henri in Nairobi. She lives in south England in a place called Dorset, in a quiet village near the sea that could be described as the English equivalent of a Floridian retirement community.'

Nargis only heard 'two weeks', the rest rushed past her like a train whistling through a station. She was speechless. Two weeks? It was hard to take in. Harriet seemed impervious to her reaction. Nargis gazed at the roses, blinking hard. Harriet touched her arm. Nargis looked at her through a blur.

'Nargis, let's not be sad. This is not the end. We will stay in touch.'

Nargis wiped her eyes with a corner of her kurta.

'I suppose so. But, it is very fast. I wish…'

Harriet waved away her protests.

'It has to be this way. I need to get away from here to be able to think.'

Nargis sighed.

'I know.'

Harriet shifted on the cushions and poured another cup of tea from the pot.

'I would like you to supervise the packers when they come and make sure that our possessions are sent separately, all Henri's clothes, the kitchen-wear and the contents of the living and dining rooms to Kenya, the children's and my clothes and possessions to the U.K. I will make a list. I'm not sure I'm going to go to Kenya permanently. I think I need my own life. I need roots and friendships that last longer than twenty-four months. I need stability.'

Nargis eyes filled with tears again.

'But Harriet, two weeks... I thought we still had four week left. Why you leave us early? I will really miss you and the children.'

'We'll miss you too, but it can't be helped, it's life. It's the way it is for us expatriates, we have to live for today, not knowing where we will be sent tomorrow.'

She picked up her laptop, business-like and brisk.

'Now, on a more practical note, I know we really have to find you a new job while I am still here to recommend you in person.'

Nargis winced. Just like that, Harriet could move her on, shifting her elsewhere like an old taxi for hire. Harriet tapped on a few keys.

'Here's a woman who has just arrived to work for the World Bank. I emailed her, sang your praises and gave her a reference. She's divorced, American. She has a child, eighteen months old. I told her you'll call her today. She's desperate.'

Nargis tried not to feel hurt, after all, she was just trying to help. Most nannies were abruptly dumped to fend for themselves when their employers left. Harriet stared at her. Nargis could not speak.

'You'll get the job, try not to worry.'

The ramifications of unemployment would send her straight to the asylum. I have no choice, Nargis thought.

She bowed her head meekly in a traditional Tajik gesture of respect and mumbled her thanks.

Later, while washing up Leo's dinner things, Nargis overheard Harriet talking on the phone, her voice raised in irritation.

'No Patty, I don't feel like meeting him. Yes, he keeps calling. No. Veronica says that tart has already moved on and taken up with the German Ambassador, a pompous ass with an enormous beer gut and a penchant for smoking Cuban cigars, so I don't think they're together still. No. Henri claims that he ended it that same day.'

Nargis grimaced. So that's it.

July 7th, 2008, Tajikistan Countdown: 13 days

I told Nargis we were leaving. When I saw her face redden, the way she struggled to hold back her tears, I nearly crumbled. I cannot allow that, however. I CANNOT. If I let one tear fall, I will break and run back to Henri.

I have to stick to practicalities, keep my mind busy and focus on the tasks ahead. It is the only way to stem the emotion, keep myself busy, busy, busy. I absolutely must not allow myself to think beyond the next two weeks.

1. Sort, pack, organise and make everything as normal as possible for the children.
2. Secure new jobs for Nargis and the guards. Ivan will be fine, he will keep his post as an office driver.

Patty and Veronica want to host a leaving lunch at the French Restaurant. Just a few women from the International Women and Book Clubs. Of course, they know Henri cannot come because he is working, so it will be for ladies, a daytime event. I shall lie to everyone, pokerfaced, about looking forward to our new life in Nairobi.

July 12th, 2008, Tajikistan Countdown: 8 days

This morning Henri came over before work to pick up some files and clothes. He looked terrible, his hair lank and greasy and he smelt of stale booze. He had brought an enormous bouquet of flowers with him, as if that will undo the lies and erase the intimacies he had with Her. How clichéd he is, not an original thought in his head. He reminded me of my father. His lilies reeked, a putrid, cloying smell in the heat that made me nauseous. He begged me again to come back and tried to embrace me, tears in his eyes.

I broke the news to him about our departure to England in eight days. I wanted to see what he would do. I have to admit, I enjoyed it, tormenting him. He was shocked, his little fifille Harriet, buying air tickets without permission. I knew he was thinking, 'I have to move the money from our joint account.' Well, I've already moved it all online, to mine, an old one that he doesn't know about. I'll tell him once I'm in England of my decision to come to Nairobi, not before. I think he needs to suffer a little longer. He was furious, unleashing a torrent of insults. He threatened to cut me off and to fight me for custody of the children if I leave without him. He's cornered, the rat, he knows he has no chance against me in court but I have hidden our passports as a precaution.

He sent Ivan away, said he was going to walk back to the office to think. His way of making me feel guilty I suppose. Ivan kept his face expressionless, the perfect model of subservient discretion. I threw the foetid flowers away in the rubbish can outside and went back into the garden to lie in the tapshan. A car backfired somewhere, a loud bang that resonated through the neighbourhood. It set off all the dogs in the neighbourhood and woke Leo.

37

Harriet received the news from Henri's boss a few hours later. It was a bomb, he said, buried in the greenery of Kokhi Vahdat, 'Palace of Unity' Conference Hall, headquarters of the ruling People's Democratic Party on Rudaki Avenue. It was set off by an old gardener weeding the roses as Henri was walking past.

'Why would anyone want to blow up Kokhi Vadhat?' Harriet gasped. Prickles of fear goose-bumped her arms and she reached for a chair. Her pulse quickened, throbbing hard in her temple against the phone receiver. Nargis often took Leo and Alex for a walk there. She rushed to the vestibule. The pram stood in its usual place. The children were safe, playing in the garden.

'No one knows. It was probably planted by the Islamic Renaissance Party as revenge for the death of their leader in police custody last year. Didn't you know about the bombs in 2005 and 6, Harriet?'

'No. Henri never told me. Was it deliberate? Was Henri targeted because he's a Westerner?'

'No, we don't think so.'

Harriet grabbed her purse with shaking fingers.

'I have to go there, to the hospital. I have to go.' Harriet leaned out of the window and yelled. 'Nargis, Henri is in the hospital.'

Nargis glanced up from the picnic blanket where she was reading books to Alex.

'Harriet, stay calm. He's okay. Just a bit of shrapnel, nothing to worry about. They are sorting him out as we speak.'

Harriet sat in a gloomy corridor outside the operating theatre of the Russian Military Hospital and watched a black rimmed clock as it ticked past the minutes. The stench of the hospital latrines wormed its way along the corridors. Her mind was whirling, her heart numb. What was this place? Bombs. Islamists. Drug lords... Murdering husbands wielding sharp weapons to slice their wives open. She couldn't believe she had once thought Dushanbe safe, mundane, even. The bomb peeled back the tranquillity of the city surface.

She called Henri's colleague from the hospital.

'I am here now, outside the operating theatre. Have you booked the SOS air ambulance?'

'Yes, you're all on the three o'clock flight out.'

'And you say they bombed Dushanbe before? I can't believe I never knew.'

'Well, it was hushed up at the time, but I'm surprised you were unaware of it. It could have been the Hizb-ut-Tahrir.'

'Who?'

'One of the ten banned Islamic groups who want to unite central Asia as an Islamic Super-State. They killed several Kyrgz and Tajik border guards last year, you must have heard about it?'

'No.'

'It was not clear at the time whether it was the drug gangs or the Islamists. The Government has imprisoned as many of their senior leaders as they can find and is demolishing unregistered mosques here in Dushanbe, clamping down on all religious expression. The U.S Marines held two months of training in counter-terrorism last spring.'

Harriet bit her lip. She thought of the huge American fortress on the edge of the city, the glamour and the significance of the glittering Marine Ball they attended at the US Ambassador's residence last autumn. She had agonised over which cocktail dress to wear, whether she should get her roots done.

'Henri doesn't tell me anything. I feel like such an idiot,' she whispered.

'Well, he probably didn't want to worry you. Today, he was the unlucky victim of a message meant for the President. The Prime Minister was due to give a speech there about an hour after the bomb went off.'

Harriet heard a sigh.

'Look, Harriet it might not have been a religious-based act at all. It could have been drug lords, domestic political opponents or even the government itself, trying to frighten the population in order to strengthen their political grip. In Tajikistan, one never knows.'

After a few hours in theatre Henri was wheeled out, unconscious in a metal framed bed painted olive green, his face and torso hidden under bloody bandages, various pipes and wires attached to his body, wrists and head.

'The explosive device went off close to him and there was shrapnel in his chest but we think we got the majority of it out,' a faceless surgeon explained in rusty English. 'He is lucky, it did not hit his heart and they were fairly shallow wounds. He should be able to fly out of here in twelve hours or so.'

Harriet stayed by his bed in the recovery room, waiting for the anaesthetic to wear off. A harassed Russian nurse came to check his vitals and looked at her with disapproval, as though she were the one responsible. Ivan went to Novo Clinic to pick up morphine, new bandages and clean needles, as they were always in danger of running out.

Harriet's mind went back to how Henri had left, how angry he had been. How stupid I was to make him think I can live without him, she thought. She felt raw, exhausted. Her phone rang. Ivan was at the gate, he couldn't park, could she come down?

'I don't want to leave Henri, he's still unconscious,' she said. She could hear angry horns, furious patients yelling, demanding that Ivan move his car. On shaky legs, Harriet left her post, half running down flights of stairs and jostling behind slow queues of weary looking Tajiks pushing pallid patients in ancient Soviet wheelchairs. Not more than ten minutes later Harriet burst back into the room, panting.

A woman she had never seen before stood at the bed. About thirty years old, she had long blonde hair and eyes the colour of glacial ice. She wore a Russian Embassy identity card around her neck and tears had left furrows in her make up. Her abdomen was distended, a broad curve. Harriet halted, unsure if she was in the right room. Yes, it was Henri lying there. He had just come round. He had his eyes open and a strange expression on his face, as though unable to look away from a horrific car crash. Harriet cleared her throat from the doorway.

'Excuse me, Dotchka, may I help you?' she asked.

The woman started. She glanced at Harriet with a look of pure hatred. 'No, no you can't help me. Only he can, but he refuses to do so.'

Harriet's eyes swivelled from her belly to Henri, lying prone in the bed. He looked from one woman to the other. The woman turned and ran.

The doorbell rang several times and Nargis hurried to the great wooden door to find Harriet cowering on the steps. She looked haggard in her bright Tajik clothes, her hair hastily plaited. She smelled of hospital disinfectant and sweat. She glared at Nargis.

'You took your time,' she snapped. 'I forgot my keys.'

'We leave tonight, Nargis, to Istanbul on the three o'clock flight.'

Nargis stood aside as Harriet stormed into the vestibule and kicked off her sandals, throwing her handbag on a side table.

'What about the packing?'

'I will have to ask you, as a friend, to help me with the children tonight while I pack. I must take everything we need and go to the airport.'

Nargis swallowed. 'Yes, Harriet, of course.'

Suddenly, Harriet burst into tears. She collapsed onto the floor and sat with her head in her hands, wailing. Nargis bent down to pick her up and helped her to walk to the kitchen where she sat like a broken doll on a wooden chair, legs splayed, shoulders hunched.

'Harriet, please not cry. Mr Simenon will be alright, you will see. You say the doctors say you he doing well.'

Nargis put the kettle on and found the tea.

'Oh Nargis, you don't have any idea.'

Nargis frowned. Luckily, Leo and Alex were in the study watching a Loony Tunes DVD. How ill is he? Did he take a turn for the worse? Is he going to die? Is he already dead? Nargis awkwardly knelt down and embraced her.

'What happen? I thought the operation went well?'

Harriet wiped her face with her fingers and clutched the table. Her voice was strangled. 'He has done it again. Only this time, this time I can't forgive him. This is too much.'

Nargis frowned. Harriet took a few deep breaths and blew her nose on a tissue.

'What you mean? What he do?'

Harriet's voice lowered to a whisper. The sun was setting outside and cast pink rays onto her face, highlighting the dark shadows under her eyes, her pale skin.

'I saw her, Nargis. I saw her, this blonde woman. Standing in his room, staring at him. A Russian, I think. She certainly knew who I was. The way she looked at me, I know she was his lover. And she was pregnant with his baby.'

Nargis's mouth fell open. 'Are you sure?'

'Absolutely sure.'

Nargis pursed her lips. 'Then you should leave him. Get divorce. You can, you English. Start again, new life.'

Harriet winced. 'I can't.'

Nargis grinned. 'Mrs Harriet, if I can leave a husband, you can leave a husband.'

38

The Simenon family left, a quiet, quick departure to Istanbul on the air ambulance. No leaving parties, no fanfare or grandiose speeches. Just a quiet hug with a few sad well-wishers who came by in the evening with hastily bought Tajik souvenirs for the children. When Nargis came to work she found an eerie silence and a few boxes of children's clothes for Faisullo and Bunvasha with her name scrawled on them. Harriet's Tajik clothes hung forlornly in the wardrobe. An envelope sat on the kitchen table, stuffed with somoni, a packing list and a note:

Call Emma next week. Tel 53 68 27 361. I will email her and arrange everything. I will miss you xx Harriet.

Nargis couldn't believe it. No more cuddles with little Leo or reading to Alexandra in the playroom. No more calls of 'Gis-Gis, come Leo.' No more blini on Saturdays. She walked about the house woodenly. In the study she picked up each African statuette, noticing for the first time how sadly they stared. The house seemed bereaved, the walls bare, the parquet floors hollow underfoot. Children's doodles on the playroom walls were highlighted in a stream of sunlight. In one corner, Harriet had measured the children as they grew, writing their names in biro on a doorframe. Nargis traced them with a finger and her eyes stung.

For two more weeks, Nargis continued to come every day to clean, wash the carpets and sit brooding with bowls of green tea. She missed her afternoon tea companion on the tapshan, the rose stem in a delicate vase, legs stretched out on soft velveteen quilts, the scent of hairspray and chocolate cake; her foreign sister with golden eyes.

She did as asked when the packers came. A group of burly Tajiks carefully wrapped Harriet's crockery and glassware in paper, bubble wrap and cardboard for their long journey. It felt perverse; their grubby hands manhandling Harriet's personal things. She barked orders and scowled in disapproval, wrapping the most fragile items herself. She watched sullenly as they disassembled furniture, putting legs and table top and whole sofas into huge cardboard boxes. She missed the cheerful laughter of children. She fancied that Alexandra and Leo would have had great fun playing in the chaos of the move, using the boxes as makeshift houses, wrapping their body parts in paper and packing tape like mummies. The boxes were packed into two containers to cross Uzbekistan by train to Iran, pass on a boat to Dubai and sail on container ship to England. It would be a long journey covering thousands of miles, taking months. When the packers finished, a colleague of Henri's came from the office to sign the paperwork and the last of the boxes were loaded onto a huge truck and driven away.

Nargis locked the great wooden door for the last time and gave the key to Musso. The landlord would stop by later. She stepped out of the compound gate onto the dusty street. It was the end of another chapter in her life but Nargis was reconciled to the facts. As Harriet had said, this was how it was, working with expatriates. She felt a twinge of sadness as the gate closed on the lush oasis within, a moment of regret that things could not have turned out differently. Outside on the street, the sun stained red across the sky, casting beautiful scarlet and orange reflections onto high whitewashed walls. In a few months the weather would pivot to hover hesitantly in autumn for a few weeks, allowing leaves to turn and fall, the farmers to harvest. Nargis imagined God riding clouds in the sky, turning a navigator wheel to allow the northerly Siberian winds to rush in. The first fresh snowfall would appear on the mountain peaks above the city, yet Nargis felt none of the usual dread. Her new job was starting in a few days, thanks to Harriet.

A week before, Emma had come to see her.

'She wants to send you money for fees until your three children finish school, like a foreign sponsor,' she said. 'It's all arranged, I'm going to be your link. When I go, we will find someone else we can trust.'

Nargis was speechless for a moment. 'But I cannot…'

Emma laughed. 'I love being the bearer of good news. It's all settled then.'

High up in the evening sky the kestrels soared, coasting on waves of hot air rising from the parched earth below. Ahead, Nargis could see Zavon waiting for her in a side street. Life would be good, she felt it in her heart.

October 30th, 2008, England

Last night I dreamt again of the woman with his baby growing inside her. I woke up in a cold sweat, tears on my cheeks, an acrid, bitter smell on my body. I still find it hard to think of his Turkish confession, when the drugs had lowered his guard and we were alone in that stark, white room, Henri in a green nightgown, bandaged and stitched together, too feeble to deny his wrongdoings. Alex and Leo may, by now, have a half-sister or half-brother somewhere in Russia. I don't want to know the details, there'll be less to lie about.

In return for my silence Henri will leave me properly feathered in a new nest with gold in the bank. A thirty-three year old Russian Embassy secretary, 'just a fling'. How many were there? Unlike the other one, she wasn't interesting or even that pretty. Was she in love, did she think he would leave me? All that time, he lied and accepted my gratitude. Yet all along, he was never leaving Tajikistan for us, he was just running away from her.

I left him in the American Hospital in Istanbul and flew back here to an August of beach trips for cream teas, fish and chips, dressed crab and ice creams. Solitary, enraged, I took long walks in the rain and screamed at the grey sea, the wind drowning out my howls. Mum berates me for brooding and kicks me out every Friday night. Her kitchen smells reassuringly familiar; Yorkshire pudding and Earl Grey tea. Her embraces are warm and gin-scented as of old so that I feel like a child again around her.

I'll burn this journal in a few days on November 5th, Bonfire Night. A few guests, sparklers, fireworks and a sacrificial Guy Fawkes burning to loud cheers and the smell of tomato soup in mugs and sizzling sausages. My innermost thoughts can light up the night sky and dance in the flames as a symbolic cleansing of the past.

As the autumn draws in and the days get shorter I am more and more relieved to have a real reason to get up each day, brush my hair and put on smart clothes. It is part-time work and a wonderful return to normality. With each week that passes I feel myself rewire, the connections like tiny sparks as my old self comes back to life. The woman Henri wanted to disguise in beige twinsets and pearls bows and recedes, accepting her time is done. The children started school and pre-school back in September. I am still amazed how easily we have settled to the English modus operandi, as my father would say. I didn't think it possible.

Alex still asks for Daddy at bedtime. My ribs tighten around my heart in painful spasm when I hear his syrupy timbre on the phone. The yearning and the regret makes me feel sick. My face grows hot and I have to fight the urge to snatch the receiver. For all his faults, I miss him, especially at dawn, before I wake up properly and the world goes back to being crazy. I miss his masculine arrogance, the feeling of being looked after, of being lazily in love. He wrapped me in the certainty of a marriage I thought as enduring as steel when in fact we were weak as candy floss. It won't be long before he has someone new to keep house. I brace myself for the inevitable. He cannot be alone.

The children constantly spoke of Nargis when we left. Leo was the worst. 'Gis, where Gis?' he asked repeatedly. Alex was more forthright. After a few months, she seemed reconciled. 'We will never see Gissie again, will we, Mummy?' Her eyes were like great pools. I could give her no answer. I've sent the school fees for the year to Emma, a paltry amount I can easily afford. We have spoken a few

284

times since we left. As time passes, I feel more and more reluctant to call. I would rather forget the pain of it all, keep her as a fading memory. Her face is fuzzy, her voice breaks on the poor connection. 'My new job is okay, the boy is sweet but it not the same as when I was with you.' I'm secretly pleased, I must admit.

I have decided to study to be a lawyer. I start University next year. I'm still young and strong, only thirty, I have time to learn, to succeed. I'll do it in her name. Whenever I feel frightened of the future, uncertain of whether I can manage alone, I think of her. What would Nargis not be able to do in Britain? What could she not achieve without tradition and poverty holding her back? Her trials were so much worse than anything I have had to face, yet she prevails. She inspires me forward, into my new, uncertain life and gives me the determination to succeed. And so I will.

Glossary

Alo:	Hi (Russian)
Aksakal:	Elder
Amour:	Love (French)
Assalom/ Salom:	Hello
Assalom alai'kum:	I greet you with God
Babushka:	Grandmother/old woman (Russian)
Baba Ganoush:	A Middle Eastern dish of aubergine and sesame paste.
Baltika 7:	A Russian lager
Bénie soit-elle:	Bless her heart (French)
Blini:	A type of Russian pancake
Buzkashi:	Ancient Mongol precursor to polo where men on horseback compete to ride with a goat carcass around field markers. It is played in Mongolia, Afghanistan and other countries of Central Asia.
Choi (hona)/(kabood):	Tea (house)/(green)
Chusti:	A traditional embroidered black skullcap worn by men.
Deg:	A large wok used for cooking pilov
Dotchka:	Lady (Russian)
Eid al-Adha:	festival of the sacrifice, celebrated seventy days after the end of Ramadan
Ezore:	Trousers worn under the kurta
Farzandi Azizam:	The father advises his children
Fifille:	Old fashioned endearment for a girl (French)
Gul:	Flower
Haram:	Shameful/ scandalous
Haveli:	A traditional Tajik house
Hizb-ut-Tahrir:	A banned Islamic political party
Hodoii:	Prayers/God
Hodoiiman	My God
Hoosh Doman:	Mother-in-law

Jomas:	A traditional ankle-length, buttonless coat
Kelline:	Daughter-in-law
Kohki Vahadat:	Palace of Unity (conference centre and headquarters of the Democratic People's Party, the ruling political party)
Kurta:	A traditional Tajik ankle-length dress
Lola:	Tulip
Mahalla:	A hamlet
Mein schatz:	My sweetheart (German)
Ma mignonne/chou/cherie:	My darling (French)
Mullah:	An Islamic minister (officiates at weddings, funerals etc.)
Naan:	flatbread/staple food.
Nargis:	Daffodil (narcissus)
Osh berinj:	Special rice used for pilov (see below)
Picheen:	biscuit (Russian)
Pilov:	Traditional rice dish
Rien:	Nothing (French)
Roatan:	Chinese instant noodles
Saaman:	Jasmine
Sad bagh:	Rose
Sanduk:	A traditional metal/wooden chest used for storing clothes or bedding.
Savsang:	Iris
Sehnsucht:	(German) An individual's search for happiness while coping with the reality of unattainable wishes.
Shashlik:	A kebab of cubes of lamb or beef, served with peppers and onion
Shireen:	Sweetness (an endearment)
Shorba:	Soup
Tapshan:	A traditional Persian raised platform for drinking tea/relaxing outside
Usma:	Herbs pounded into a black paste to make cosmetics for a traditional Tajik monobrow

Exchange rate in 2007-08: 3.5 Somoni to $1 US Dollar

Rudaki (byname of Abū ʿAbdollāh Jaʿfar ibn Moḥammad), born *c.* 859, was a Persian writer and poet, honoured in Tajikistan today.

Somoni: Abu Ibrahim Ismail ibn Ahmad, a Persian, died November 907, better known as Isma'il ibn Ahmad, the Samanid amir of Transoxiana (892-907). His reign saw the emergence of the Samanids as a powerful force. He was a descendant of Saman Khuda, the founder of the Samanid dynasty who renounced Zoroastrianism and embraced Islam. The Tajik currency as well as a main avenue, hotel and restaurants in Dushanbe are named after him and it is often asserted that the President of Tajikistan is a modern-day Samanid hero.